The Tymorean Trust
Book Three

THE RETURN TO EARTH

by

MARGARET GREGORY

TAT Publishing

ISBN 978-1-925332-03-2

Publisher of record
TAT Publishing
www.tatpublishing.com

Prologue

Prophecy spoken by High King Governor Tymoros
to the Great Ones - Tymos, Kryslie and Llaimos

Final year of the Seventh Great Age – Tymorean calendar

"Children will come at the beginning of the New Age."

Chapter 1 - Great Ones

The three Great Ones were something more than human; they were a Living Force, capable of wielding the life energy of their world. In this bodiless form, they roamed above the land and water. They caused the air temperature to rise and the surface water to evaporate. Hurricanes formed from multiple individual whirlwinds, the power of the Living Force fed the winds, whirling them faster so that they drew in air, water, and the surface soil. Every molecule and particle that was above the glowing protective layer, and everything that was not attached to the ground, fed the vortices.

Day became night, and after some unmeasured time, darkness blanketed the whole planet. The clouds, heavy with moisture that would not fall, were full of trapped dust, poisons and radioactive particles spun up by the vortices. They began to glow.

No structures, except those of metal, stone, or protected by Tymorean power, survived. Anything still alive outside of the protected places – died. The hurricanes grew and grew – until there was no longer anything to sustain them. Near the planet surface, there was an almost perfect vacuum.

Needing no air to breathe, the Living Force moved over the planet's surface, seeking any remaining traces of poison.

The heavy black clouds reached up high into the stratosphere, all over the planet. They began to swirl and mix, but still did not dissolve into rain. Lightning flickered from point to point in the clouds. At the planet's surface, the temperature began dropping to well below freezing point.

The Living Force became part of the dark clouds — aware of the potential energy waiting to be directed. Lightning forked from the clouds – not in random surges, but in accurately directed strikes. Some hit the alien aircraft where they lay after being thrown around by the winds. The craft exploded; the remaining fuel igniting and burning until all the dreadful weapons remaining in the craft reached critical point. One of the horrifying weapons was Burnfire and once freed, the pyrophoric substance spattered in all directions. It became a creeping and insatiable red glow that moved in ever-expanding circles. The low temperature and scarcity of air controlled its virulence, but not its voracious hunger for organic fuel.

More lightning struck the myriad places where the Great Ones had cached canisters of Burnfire stolen from the alien ships and garrisons. These too exploded and began to burn in expanding circles. Fire burned the surface soil, cleansing it of poisons. It could not burn past the deeper soil layer protected by Tymorean power.

Occasionally there was a fiery flare as the Burnfire found fuel or pockets of poisons, but the slow onward creeping continued relentlessly over land and the frozen ocean surface. It took time - days, years, decades or centuries – there was no way to know and when the whole planet glowed with the redness that was Burnfire, it finally began to rain.

When the water/dirt/air falling as frozen drops landed on the glowing surface it flared into brilliance. The Living Force waited, slowly circling the planet. They sensed a protected place, rich with power, high above the rest of the land.

There they hovered, half way between energy and human flesh, needing neither food, nor water nor air — aware now of their separate parts. They merged with, and passed through, the protective shield of the high mountain forest and separated into their original selves.

They stood absorbing the sense of life around them. Here, protected under the shimmering mauve barrier, plant life thrived and the animals reproduced. How many generations had passed, there was no way of knowing.

The Great Ones - Tymos, Kryslie and Llaimos - felt no need to speak aloud. Their minds were fully open to each other.

In time, when the land outside was once again fit to support life, the plants and animals in the protected places would be able to spread far and wide.

The Return to Earth

For now, the Great Ones could rest and remember what it meant to be entities of mere flesh and blood.

They ate, they slept…time passed.

The forest was full of life, burgeoning like springtime in multicoloured shades of green, and smelling of the shy blossoms flowering on the low bushes. Tymos lay awake, relishing the sense of vibrant life until he realized that the shimmering barrier was no longer over the forest. He was looking up through a gap in the leafy canopy, at a pure azure sky, with no clouds. He leant over and shook his brother and sister awake. With the same thought in mind, they all stood and ran to the edge of the forest and looked out…over a completely barren landscape.

The barrier, placed around the forest to protect animals and plants within, was indeed gone. There was no further need for it, but all three remembered what the land had been like, poisoned and glowing with radioactivity from the deadly bombs the alien invaders had detonated.

Llaimos knelt at the edge of the green covered ground, lifted a handful of the black, ashy dirt and let it trickle through his fingers.

"The land is waiting to be reborn," he told his siblings, thoughtfully. The dirt felt dead, a stark contrast to the sense of life in the area behind him.

"The animals can leave the forest," Tymos noted. "The plants can start spreading."

Kryslie disagreed. "No! Not yet! There is no wind or weather cycle; nothing can live out there!"

"There must be a catalyst," Llaimos considered. "We drew power from the aura to preserve the seeds in the ground for the rebirth and to seal the cities. The power of all our Royal cousins was freed for us to use when the Temple of Dira was destroyed…"

"Then we must return there – to Dira – to bind the power again and find the catalyst for life to start," Tymos completed the thought.

The three Great Ones joined hands and merged their consciousness so as a single force they teleported into the Temple of Dira, materializing amongst the wreckage where the great meeting hall had once been.

They arrived on rubble and needed to adjust their balance, or fall onto the stones. The picture of the Temple as it had been was in their minds when they looked around them. The basic structure remained, though the balcony walls that had been along the upper level walkway, had collapsed and fallen down to the meeting area. Adding to the debris and overlying all the other rubble, was the shattered glass and tile shards from the Temple roof.

Instead of having the white tones of the marble stone or the clearness of glass, both walls and rubble were dusted with ashy black. The Burnfire had burnt through the Temple, finding fuel there too, but not as the terrible weapon it had been designed to be, instead it was the means to purify the place that was sacred to the Guardians of Peace.

The Great Ones walked carefully over the loose debris, moving apart to examine different sections. Llaimos explored the cubicles leading off from the walkway behind the arches around the lower level. Each one was empty, except for the metal stands for the lamps, and these were on the floor as the wooden tables where they had once stood were ash. His memory of the rooms as they had been, were from memories he had shared with his siblings. In his mind, each room had contained a simple wood frame bed, the small wooden bedside table, and a cloth curtain on a rod across the opening. Only the notches in the stone of the doorway showed where the rod had rested.

Kryslie examined the large open lower area that had been the main gathering space. The wooden benches were mere ash, half hidden by rubble. She found two places of thicker ash that contained a layer of molten metal. The bodies of two of the Aeronite Warlords had been there - for the metal would have been the remains of their armour. Carefully moving ash aside, she found that one area of metal was on one of the circular tile murals.

Tymos found the stone stairs at the front of the Temple, near the arched entryway, and explored the upper level, finding three more areas of molten metal. The six Aeronite Warlords had paid the ultimate price for believing in the promises of the Ciriot. He searched all the rooms opening off the upper walkways, including the large north and south meeting spaces and all the little rooms off them, but found no sign of the evil Ciriot.

They came together again, in the relatively rubble free front entranceway. Kryslie and Tymos had known every part of the Temple and shared their memories of it with Llaimos who had seen only the Altar Room. In their mind was the certainty that the answer to how to bind the free Tymorean power was within the Temple, perhaps hidden under the rubble.

Incredible power still obeyed them and they merged their minds and power, gathered all the shards of broken glass and tiles and formed them into their original shapes. Three merged minds lifted the solid matter back into place and sealed it in position. Next, they raised the stones from the balcony wall, back up along the upper walkway and set them firmly together. Now they could explore the Temple once more to see what other changes had occurred and seek the answers they needed.

Llaimos walked slowly around, seeing the details of the Temple for the first time with his own eyes. He was intrigued by the tile murals on the floor of the different sections of the Temple. He studied each of them, noting details that his sibling's memories had not given him.

"Have you really looked at these?" he asked Kryslie, who was crossing the lower meeting room, heading towards the entranceway. "They have amazing detail."

"Yes, the Elders spoke of them when we came here for the first time. They portray events from the distant past. The Elders all had a different interpretation of their meaning," she called over her shoulder.

"There are three of them, or four if you count the glass mural near the beam-in point upstairs," Llaimos called aloud. "Do you know why they are here? In each of the rooms of the Temple?"

"That was something the Elders did not mention," Tymos spoke down from the south balcony. "But they still thought of us as children then."

Kryslie stopped to look at a part of the stone floor of the gathering chamber. A number of the brown stone slabs forming the floor were speckled with silver and gold flecks. She crouched down to touch the surface and a vivid image came into her mind. She saw the final moments of their elder sister's life and sensed her brothers shared the vision.

"Vila died here," she stated. Her voice sounded odd in the still air. She had fought against Vila, but didn't really know her. The mind of her estranged sister had been poisoned - first by the Aeronite invaders who had abducted her as a child and later by the evil Ciriot.

"The Guardians freed her spirit," Tymos murmured as understanding came to them, in a whisper from the Guardians of Peace. "She chose death, to protect Pyr. Her true essence remained pure, in spite of the Ciriot and their control of her."

"This rock is sacred," Llaimos said with awe. It had been touched by the Guardians. "We should make it part of the Altar room."

Tymos glanced up towards that highest part of the Temple, realising that his earlier explorations had not taken him there. Kryslie stood up, still looking at the changed stone. Ideas flowed between three minds, as they realised that the Altar room had not been restored when they had cleared the other rubble. Knowledge came to them, of events they had not personally witnessed.

"The Altar was destroyed and the collective power of our kin was freed," Tymos spoke slowly. "It was the focus – the capstone - and Royal blood was spilt there."

They recognised the need to go up to the ruins of the Altar room and teleported without requiring the metallic devices needed by lesser Tymoreans.

The remains of the Altar, mostly hand sized pieces of marble, glowed with mauve light. They were rich with Tymorean power and were, like the stone slabs below, speckled with gold and silver. They had found where their estranged elder brother, Jordan, had died. Kryslie did not touch the rock this time. The truth of events was apparent to them.

"The Guardians used him," Kryslie acknowledged. "He was truly of Royal blood, and he had to die for our power to be freed."

An idea began to form in her mind, of a monument to recognise his sacrifice. Now Kryslie began moving the glowing speckled rubble into a pile. Her brothers came to help her, and they shared ideas between them. They would use this sacred rock to form the new capstone, a new Altar.

As they worked, the round tiled mosaic in front of the Altar was cleared. Tymos and Kryslie recalled the Elders speaking of the picture worked into the design. The artist had been greatly skilled, working in tiny tiles of a myriad of colours. It showed three figures with a mauve aura outlining them looking at a column of bright light as other figures knelt in homage.

Yet as they looked at the picture this time, the figures seemed to move – as the images did in the room of the Seven Ages, in the Royal Palace – but now the three tiny figures had red hair and might have been themselves. Those figures vanished, and others replaced them, as a picture emerged of what had happened here, but in reverse, from when the Great Ones arrived in the rubble-filled room, back through the time when the Ciriot became incandescent torches, the light erupting from the centre of the planet emerging through the Altar. They saw Jordan's death and then Jonko, Keleb and Pyr, their friends and younger brother, fighting to keep the Ciriot out of the Altar room. This was followed by the centuries of peace, seen as flashes of dark and colours of people passing, then again three distinct figures, two blonds and a redhead this time – building the Altar and creating the mosaic they studied.

Understanding came as a sudden revelation. Those they saw now were previous Great Ones who bound the world's power as they created the Altar. They had not created the mosaic, but restored it – for their power had been freed when that mosaic had been defiled.

The new Great Ones sent their awareness out into the other parts of the Temple – sought the other mosaics and felt the faded residue of death and blood on them.

"It makes sense," Tymos murmured. "The Aeronites would have had old legends of this world. The Ciriot would have learnt about us from them. No doubt they believed they could destroy us by destroying the Temple – and achieve that by defiling the mosaics."

"But our predecessors changed the power focus to the Altar," Kryslie mused. "Was it deliberate? Or did the Guardians plant the idea with them?"

"It is not important. That change confused our enemies for long enough for us to understand what we became," Llaimos concluded.

The image of the intact Altar came back to them, reminding them of the need to rebind the world's power. Yet it did not fit with the feeling they shared. Yes, they must rebuild the Altar, but…

Tymos stepped up to where the Altar had been and considered the picture memory of the bright light blasting through the stone. Now, the only light was from the repaired roof and the unglazed window behind the Altar. He stood on a circle of glassy, fused rock. He adjusted his eyes to see the energy patterns and saw a faint wash of mauve light over everything except that circle. At that point, he had the sense of a very deep hole. Curious, he went to study the mosaic, and realised that the tiles covered another circle of fused rock. Once, that area had been a power conduit too.

Kryslie interpreted the picture in Tymos's mind and spoke aloud. "The energy is now spread throughout the world – in the air, in the ground, in the protected areas and the protective shields. We cannot gather it to return it here. We must find another way to draw it back. Somewhere outside, since we can feel the aura more strongly by touching the ground."

"I would prefer to use these stones elsewhere," Llaimos admitted. "Our brother, Jordan, died here. While I know his sacrifice was necessary, if we were to build a new altar with them, changed though they are, it will seem like remembering his death, not his life."

"The marble is attuned to our power," Tymos pointed out. "It will attract it and ground it."

"Then we can use it to bind the power…but in a different place and a different form - something that would also embrace and celebrate life," Llaimos insisted.

"We still need an Altar to use to focus and attune the minds of our people to the Guardians' wisdom," Kryslie pointed out. "But I share your view. What if we use the stones from below? Vila died to give Pyr a chance to live on. Creating the new altar from the stones touched by her blood – will be a way of remembering her life and sacrifice."

"Yes, in that way she will be a part of our victory too. It feels right," Llaimos decided.

Piece by piece, the three Great Ones lifted six huge slabs of flecked slate from the floor of the meeting room and transmitted them to the Altar Room. Two roughly semicircular in shape and one nearly square were placed against the back wall. The others would form the base of the Altar.

Kryslie and Llaimos held the largest slab on the circle of fused rock. Tymos held his arms around the slab, felt his siblings join their power to his, and then felt the rock moulding itself to the picture in his mind of a four-foot high circular column, that melded itself with the fused rock. From the two other slabs, they created two more supporting pillars – not as wide – and placed these on each side of the first.

After that, Tymos, Llaimos and Kryslie each lifted one of the last three slabs and balanced them on the supports. They merged minds again and became semi-solid figures as they moulded the rock pieces into the shape of an elongated oval – by breaking and reforming the atomic bonds within the rock structure. When they separated again into their individual physical forms, they saw that the brown slate had been bleached to the colour of marble, but still sparkled with the gold and silver flecks.

Llaimos went to where two oil lamps lay on the floor – battered and broken. He returned, placing one at each end of the Altar. The oil reservoirs were empty, the glass reflectors broken, but when he set them on the Altar, a flame ignited in each.

The Great Ones bowed to the presences they sensed hovering above the Altar. They recognised that the essence of the Guardians of Peace had returned…watching, approving, not interfering, merely waiting for their Advocates to take the next step.

The vast power of the aura of the planet was a part of the three Great Ones, but now they needed to draw it back from ranging freely in the atmosphere – to infuse it into the soil, rock and water of the planet's surface.

Pictures, images, ideas flowed between the minds of the Great Ones.

"What can the other mosaics tell us?" Tymos suggested, and he could immediately recall the detail of each from when they had first visited the Temple.

Kryslie summarised their impressions from them, "All did, indeed, previously bind the power. Each tile as it was laid in place, bound more and more – like bricking up a doorway. The Altar too, was formed originally, stone by stone."

"We don't want to wall it away from us – we still need it to stimulate and nurture the new growth and create weather," Llaimos contended.

The idea had been there, and now it flowered. "We take the stones from the old Altar and use them to create the focus outside…. We can build a fountain, and bring water there to nourish a new garden…"

"And mix the static power protecting the planet's surface with the free power, get both circulating again…" Kryslie continued.

"What of the portal of Dirakee?" Llaimos considered. "I know we three are the portal – but should there not be a structure to symbolise that…for our kin?"

"Yes…" Tymos and Kryslie agreed.

Without further delay, they went outside. The black ashy soil puffed up and settled as the Great Ones scrambled up the terraced section of the dead Temple gardens. They paused where the ground flattened on the level of the Altar room. Instinctively, they kicked off their worn out footwear and felt the aura in the ground with their bare feet. The protective layer, existing some six inches below the surface, felt warm. Around them, the blackened and burnt soil stretched for miles – broken only by the light stone of the Temple and the mauve glow of the shields protecting the nearby city of Dira. Moving instinctively, they walked to a place between the Altar room and the south chamber. They had the sense of 'here'.

They looked around with the vision of their new structure in their minds. As they faced the south chamber, the arches and pillars along the outer walkway slowly, gently, collapsed.

The Guardians of Peace had shared their vision and approved – withdrawing their power from the protections on the Temple structure and giving them the means to create their vision.

Thinking and acting as one, the three Great Ones lifted the columns and arches, and erected them in a new position. When they had moved all the parts, they had created a roofless, hexagonal structure of pillars, topped by arches, surrounding an area of ashy ground twice the size of the Altar room.

With their vision still not complete, they returned into the Temple, carried out all the stones from the old altar, and arranged most of them into a roughly circular shape. Once again, they moulded stone as if it was potter's clay, forming at first a circular slab that was six inches thick and then separating the circle into six, elongated oval petals around a circular centre. Each part was then recessed into a bowl and they formed a hole in the very centre.

The Great Ones stood back and considered their creation, seeing the gold and silver flecks glinting in the sunlight. Then, standing to one side, they again became one bodiless consciousness as they dove down deep — past the central hole in the rock fountain, past the layer of ash, through the protective layer of static power – drawing on it, stirring it to life and taking it down through the layers of rock. Following cracks and fissures, the combined consciousness moved within the deep places of the planet until they found a trickle of water seeping down from one of the high mountain water-storage lakes. The water, placid under a layer of power, stirred and seeped faster, following the will of the consciousness as it retreated back and back to the central hole in a new rock structure. Pressure from the water in the high lake sent the trickle spurting six inches into the air. The drops fell to fill the central bowl, to overflow into the petals, and then to the ground around the new fountain.

The overflow soaked down into the soil, turning black ash into rich brown loam, until the nascent garden within the hexagon looked to be created of newly turned soil.

In the minds of the Great Ones was a vision of what the garden would become — lush and self supporting, full of evergreen plants and colourful flowers.

The last of the glowing metallic flecked stones became stepping-stones from each of the six arched openings, to the fountain. In time, the stones would be hidden, but the Great Ones would remember.

"This will become a garden of Peace," Llaimos predicted, as the faintest of breezes ruffled his hair and cooled his face.

His siblings felt the zephyr too, and as one, they adjusted their eyes to study the energy patterns around them. The aura was beginning to coalesce and swirl outwards from the garden. The final knowledge they needed came to them.

As they had done before the Cleansing, they did again. Each Great One faced a different direction and drew gently on the free energy, drawing it into themselves and grounding it so that an area of low pressure formed about them. The air began to move towards them, and then to swirl gently. The three Great Ones separated, pictured distant locations in their minds, moved themselves there and began the process again. Deserts, seaside, mountain and plain, the pattern of weather began to form.

As they travelled, they were again beings part flesh, part energy, and when they finally returned, they had formed breezes that were evaporating water from the oceans, and the vapour was rising to form clouds, and with the rotating of the planet, beginning to swirl.

Once again, the three merged their essences, and circled with the free energy, hovering unharmed amongst the moisture rich clouds as lightning and thunder grew in intensity.

A touch of power, and the clouds began to rain – not heavily as in a normal storm, but gently, to wash the ash from the soil, to soak it, to caress the sealed and hidden places like a mother caressing her child…Kryslie.

Power touched the land, waking up the sleeping soil creatures from the very tiniest, to the worms and insects, making it ready with the instinct of one who must provide…Tymos.

Dormant seeds roused, felt the warmth of the sun, the moisture, and the nutrients and obeyed the will of one who had experienced swift growth from youth to maturity…Llaimos.

Then, as the Great Ones circled the planet once more as beings of living energy, a filmy layer of greenness followed them. Black ash, turned to rich soil, grasses sprouted first – trees and food plants would follow as other dormant seeds roused and other seeds spread on the winds from the forests.

The Living Force paused over the City of Ecla, and felt the power of the Guardians at work there, doing miracles. The mutants now sleeping there, once unfortunates with unstable DNA, were being changed one last time. When they woke, the constant changes that caused their sometimes violent and unpleasant behaviour would have stopped. Many would still be unattractive to look at, but they would be serene. Most importantly, they would no longer be outcasts, and they would be able to recall with pride that they had helped save their world.

Finally, the Living Force was drawn to the tall mesa, where the sun glinted off the Royal Palaces, making them seem as if they were embossed with gold. The relief that their home was still intact drew the Living Force closer. They separated into three pillars of brilliant light, and then became entities of flesh as they collapsed onto the flagstones of the Royal Court. The power that had made them as light as air and as powerful as the strongest winds, diminished.

The Great Ones felt themselves become solid and for a brief moment, they each felt bereft. They had been, for a time, something more than human. Now they felt drained, as if something of themselves had been lost. Instinctively, they drew on the aura around them and felt it refresh them. It came from the stones of the palace and the flagstones under them. They realised that it would always be there for them to use. The power of generations of Royal Tymoreans had seeped into those stones.

When they stood up again, they saw that they were in front of the High King's palace and the doors were open – welcoming them. They glanced around at what had once been ornate gardens, and even here, the grass was sprouting. With fresh eagerness, they ran inside – only to pause on the threshold of the Great Hall as they realised the Palace was still deserted. They felt the touch of the Guardians of Peace, drawing them up two staircases to the Room of the Seven Ages.

Here weariness overcame them, and they sank to the floor – falling asleep within moments. In the last instants of consciousness, they knew that they had fulfilled the reason for their creation.

Time passed

Around them, unperceived, a new mural was being created. History was being recorded – heralding the Eighth Great Age. Those of Royal Tymorean blood would need to remember, to learn, clearly and in detail, what had happened. In that way, they would know to guard against such a war happening again.

Chapter 2 - A prophecy fulfilled

The crowd stared skyward at the cloudless blue sky. Mutters of unease began to spread as a soft murmur. Someone in the mixed crowd of city folk, villagers, farmers and herders spoke loudly.

"The barrier is gone!"

The voice held a touch of hysteria, and more people looked up and many began moving uneasily as if feeling the need to run and hide. It was not a completely irrational fear. The shimmering mauve barrier had been part of the city's skyscape for a long time. During the war, it had protected the inhabitants from the alien bombardment, and the poisons and mutagens liberated in the bombing. When the city had been cleansed of all alien artefacts, and the aliens themselves had gone, the Great One Kryslie had instigated the Great Sleep. It had been there still when they had all woken, weeks before.

A man in the well-patched working clothes of a farmer added loudly, "What are we to do? The Great One put it there to protect us – how will we survive without it? What if those alien creatures return again?"

"What about my sheep? There's nothing to stop them wandering out. I don't want them eating poisoned grass," a man dressed in leather breeches and a laced up poncho stated with equal volume.

The murmuring increased in pitch. A woman began to speak, "And our children…"

Without realising it, the crowd began to edge closer together, huddling nearer their neighbours as if for mutual protection. They all remembered how aliens had infiltrated the city, sabotaged the defences and tried to bring the shields down. If the people working with the Great One Kryslie not stopped them, they all would have died, for back then, the air outside the barrier had been unfit for life - poisoned, radioactive and lethal.

Into the fearful hush that fell over the crowd, one of the children, a boy of fifteen, muttered loudly. "The Great One killed all the aliens."

A man nearby instantly retorted, "The Great One isn't here now, neither are any of the Royals. What if more of them creatures come now?"

The nervous movements began again. The wide eyes of many people nearby suggested they were on the edge of panic, and only staying because of the protection of the crowd.

The boy, who had spoken before, did so again, more loudly. "The breeze smells like summer."

People nearby shoved him aside and told him to be quiet, for the Mayor had emerged from the council building. The boy's sister caught him before he fell under the feet of the people now pushing to get closer to the city's highest authority.

"They're idiots. All they need to do is go out and look," the boy told his sister. "If the grass was poisoned, it wouldn't look so green would it?"

"They're scared," the girl explained.

"That don't mean we oughta stay stuck here in the city now. There's no need."

"Come on then. Let's go tell the Mayor what we've seen." The girl grabbed her brother's hand and pulled him after her, as she pushed her way between huddled groups.

Finding the Mayor wasn't hard, getting to him was. He had managed to get to one of the wooden benches set around the edge of the town square, and was now standing on it. The crowd in front of him was two dozen deep, and five deep behind him.

"Come on," the girl urged again. "We can climb onto the baker's front roof."

"Tarri, we'll be in trouble!"

"Sim, we need to make these thick heads wake up. We will be close enough to the Mayor to shout at him."

Since they couldn't get to the roof from the front, they went behind the stout brick building to where the ovens were set into rear wall. They scrambled onto the oven, and continued quickly so that the heat did not get through the soles of their sandals. Within moments, they were up and over the tiled roof ridge, and easing themselves down onto the smaller roof over the front door.

Once there, Tarri urged her brother to do his whistle. He could whistle so loudly that once he had been heard from one end of their village to another. Now it silenced the nearby people and had heads turning their way.

Before the angry city folk began to berate them for interrupting their elders, or for being on the roof, Tarri called out, "The barrier is gone because we no longer need it. I have looked outside the city – all the damage has gone and the fields are full of growing things – just like the Great One promised."

The people, who had, until then been trying to tug on the Mayor's long robes, to get his attention, now glanced at the girl standing boldly on the baker's roof.

"Child, how could you know what the Great One was going to do?" the Mayor of Reva asked gently.

"Kryslie told me that we would sleep until the world was cleansed," Tarri stated, staring at the Mayor.

"It has only been a matter of weeks since we woke, and we can't have slept all that long. None of us look any older than when we went to sleep," the Mayor claimed, and his belief was reasonable.

Tarri shook her head. "We must have slept for a long time. My brother had a bad cut on his arm - before the sleep. It looks long healed now - and didn't you hear what I said? Outside the city - everywhere, things are growing wild. The air is sweet, and there are trees overloaded with fruit. And they taste wonderful."

The faces that turned to look at her wore expressions ranging from hope to censure. A man with a weathered face, and rough working clothes, and the build of a man used to physical labour, glanced at the girl and said, "Tarri, you are a very foolish child."

Tarri was unabashed. "Joshi, you yourself told us how the Great One had helped to mature your root crops in half a season, before we came here. Do you doubt that she could make the plants grow for us now?"

Simio added his support, "Yeah, now, when we need the food. We all know the stores we had are almost exhausted."

A new babble broke out as that statement penetrated the scared minds around them.

"We're out of food?" a high voice demanded.

The Mayor roared for silence, before the babble became a clamour.

"The young ones are right," he announced. "I thank them for proclaiming their faith in the Great Ones and for seeing the truth. Since the end of the sleep, the light has been bright blue beyond the barrier, when before the sleep it was dark and orange. We should go out and see for ourselves what these children have seen. If there is indeed no sign of the poison dust on the plants, then we can once again collect fresh food."

Now that the Mayor had spoken, the crowd began to relax and move apart. He continued to speak, "The Great One, Kryslie, spoke to me as well. She said that after the world was cleansed, those of Royal blood would return. We will need their help to rebuild the villages and the towns."

The murmur of agreement was unanimous.

"We need to send an envoy to Dira, where the Elders went, or to the Royal Estate," the Mayor went on, looking over the adults in the crowd, waiting for a volunteer, but finding no one willing to meet his gaze.

Not all of the fear had gone yet, and although the suggestion was important, the people seemed to draw together again in apprehension.

Simio nudged Tarri. "I want to go back to the Dales."

"Me too," Tarri agreed. Then she drew in a deep breath and called out again. "I'll go."

She had no doubts at all. Yes, she still remembered the war, but her faith in the Great One was absolute. "I know the way from here to the Dales of Arrawen and from there to the Great Road. Once there I could go to either place. My friends will come with me. And there is not much else we can do until we are allowed to go back to the Dales to rebuild."

Doubtful looks passed amongst the nearby adults, but no one was quite ready to protest the offer. They saw a cocky girl, not much more than a child, who was surely not old enough to look after herself outside of the city.

An old looking woman spoke from next to the Mayor. He had helped her up onto the bench. "My daughter is too modest," the woman spoke in a quiet voice that nevertheless gained instant attention. "Last winter, when I was ill, she provided for my whole family. She knows how to hunt, and forage for food. I have no doubt that she can, and will, do as she has offered."

The doubtful looks turned to smiles of relief, and the Mayor turned to Tarri and gave her a faint bow of respect. "It seems that I have underestimated the determination and enthusiasm of our young people. You have the blessing of the town, and we will provide you with what you will need for your journey. Bring your group to see me when you are ready."

Simio elbowed his sister in elation. "Let's go now!"

Tarri's grin matched his as they swung down from the roof into a group of their friends who had pushed their way closer.

"I am going too," Tarri's next younger brother insisted. Toby was only a year younger than Simio, and a mere three years younger than Tarri who was seventeen years old.

"Me too," Jaime, Tarri's younger sister insisted. She was only ten.

Tarri saw Simio scowl, and inwardly agreed with his preference to leave her at home.

"What would Mama do without you?" Tarri suggested. "You have such a talent for keeping Anima out of trouble."

Jaime began to pout, and Tarri spoke quickly to forestall an argument. "This trip won't be easy. We will have to travel long hours for days to get to the palaces. I don't think our shoes will last, and we will be sleeping on open ground each night."

Jaime's expression changed, "Might there be spiders, or whizzers that bite?"

Simio nodded, but kept his expression serious. "There use to be. I expect there still will be."

With a shiver, Jaime decided, "Can I help Mama with the cooking when you're gone?"

Tarri paused to make it seem like she was granting a reluctant favour. "So long as you don't get so good at it that Mama won't let me cook when I get back."

She hid a smile at her sister's determined expression, but only until her sister ran off to find their mother.

"She's too young anyway," another girl said.

Tarri spun around and saw two of her friends. "Do you want to come too?"

"Try going without us," the two girls spoke together.

"We want to see what is left in the Dales too," one admitted.

The other added, "And I am tired of being called a child. After we do this, they'll know we are grown up and maybe Baern will notice me."

From the rise overlooking the Dales, the familiar view of gullies, tinkling streams and rolling hills looked unchanged. The five adolescents ran eagerly down the hill to the village and almost ran right through it. All the wooden houses had gone and only the stone chimneys remained. Plants were growing thickly where the houses had been. The children looked at each other.

"We will have a lot to do here," Simio, commented to his sister. "I will rebuild our house myself."

"That can be our next piece of grown up business," Evie, one of Tarri's friends, spoke to remind them of their current errand.

At the Great Road, they stopped and decided to go to the Royal Estate. They had recalled that commoners could not enter the Sacred Temple at Dira, where the Royals had gone.

Nothing on their travels resembled the blasted landscape that the adults had described. Apart from themselves, they saw no other people or animals. However, fruit and grain plants were growing wild and the leaves of common root vegetables were often visible. They had no worry about making their food supply last.

After two days of travel along the Great Road, with trees, bushes and plants of all kinds growing lushly on either side, they came to a rise and caught their first sight of the Royal Palaces, high up on the top of a huge mesa, and glowing golden in the evening sun.

"Wow!" Simio expressed his relief that the palaces had survived.

They walked more eagerly the next day, but even so, they had to camp in the open for another night before they reached the base of the steep road leading to the top of the mesa. Once there, they decided they would not wait another night before climbing.

They found the steep zigzag path tiring, but their excitement kept them going all the way to the top. Once there, they saw the decorative iron gates were standing open with no guards in sight.

"What if they aren't here?" Toby expressed the first doubt.

"Let's look," Tarri suggested, undaunted. She led the way into the wild and untamed garden, following a track paved with some kind of stone.

The stone area was wide enough so that the bushes and shrubs had not succeeded in blocking it. The greenery ended abruptly as the children emerged onto a huge paved courtyard.

"Ahh!" they all sighed together.

Close up, the three palaces were the most magnificent structures they had ever seen. The two four-storey buildings on the left and right looked to be closed up and shuttered. Right in front of them, the tallest of the buildings had its huge ornamented doors standing open – as if welcoming them. The children slowly drew closer, taking in the contrast of the still shuttered windows with the open door.

"Someone must be here," Simio said, wanting it to be true.

"Should we go in?" Evie asked with trepidation. They did not belong in the palace. They were commoners.

"We need to find someone," Tarri argued, and they all looked at each other and wordlessly agreed.

As a group, they entered the large entrance hall. It had curtained off archways all around it.

"Each of us look in a different room," Tarri suggested. "If we meet someone, we apologise for intruding but ask to speak to someone in charge."

Tarri went to the furthest curtained off alcove and looked in, moving the curtain quietly. The room seemed untouched, neat, but like the usual occupant would be back at any time. She went to another, and another. All the rooms were empty.

The grand staircase caught her attention. She called softly to the others and they ran up it with cautious enthusiasm. They marvelled at the smooth polished wood railing and the deep soft carpet on the stairs. The palace was like no building any of them had ever seen or even imagined.

All the doors on the second level were closed and locked. A smaller, but no less splendid staircase ascended further. They continued up and found many open doors, which all proved to be empty offices.

A final staircase rose to yet another level, with only three doors, all open. They had no way of knowing that there were more rooms behind the walls that they, being commoners, could not enter.

The door directly in front of them drew their attention. Light from a window or somewhere, lit the far wall, framed as it was by the doorway. It looked like a section of a painting – a really large painting – the like of which the village bred youngsters had never imagined.

With mouths gaping in awe, they moved into the room and saw that the picture spanned the walls. It was one continuous series of images that extended almost all the way around the room. With their eyes captured by the clear detail, they remained unaware that this room was not deserted, and one of three sleepers was rousing.

Great One Tymos recognised three of the children and enjoyed the amazement on the five faces. A movement at one end of the mural caught the attention of Tarri, who went to examine it more closely.

"Hey! There are pictures of us here!"

The others went to see what she meant. They stared in amazement, and were a little afraid.

"What does it mean?" Jodith, Tarri's friend, asked.

Tymos was half sitting now, and he chose to answer in a soft voice that still caused the children to jump guiltily and turn around. "History is being recorded."

He grinned to reassure them, but they all bowed to him in an automatic gesture of respect. He spoke again when it seemed apparent that none of the children knew what to say. "We were told to expect children."

Kryslie and Llaimos were stirring now. The children seemed to move closer to each other, until Tarri recognised Kryslie.

"Is there something in particular that we can help you with? You have come a long way for some reason," Tymos went on, inviting the children to speak. He chose not to stand, to keep himself as unthreatening as possible.

Tarri wasn't afraid of Prince Tymos, who she belatedly recognised. His face now had the beginnings of a beard. Nor was she afraid of Princess Kryslie. She had met both of them before. The third figure, although very like Tymos, was a stranger to her.

"The barrier above the City is gone, Prince Tymos," she said quickly. "I told the Elders it was because it was no longer needed, but they seemed to be afraid."

"You were correct, Tarri, and your elders may need time to feel safe again – many suffered quite deeply during the war. You may assure them that all aliens are gone and the land has renewed itself. You could let them know that the Royal Governors, the Elders and our cousins, the missionaries and scholars will be returning shortly. After we have spoken to them, those that once lived in your city will return to provide you with whatever help we are able to give you."

"Our village doesn't even exist anymore!" Simio grumbled, earning him a sharp look from his sister.

"There will be a lot of rebuilding needed everywhere," Tymos admitted. "Even here, the lesser buildings are rubble. It will take time and the energy of everyone, even young ones like yourselves. Our primary concern was for the living."

Tarri only noticed then that Kryslie and Llaimos were now sitting up and quietly studying them.

"Did we wake you?" Jodith asked, looking at Kryslie. "We didn't mean to."

Kryslie grinned. "It was time we were awake. I suppose I ought to offer you refreshments, but I have no idea if I can find anything edible. Water might be all I find."

She stood up, and paused a moment for circulation to return to her legs, before trying to move.

"The rest of this place is deserted," Evie commented. "Have you just got here?"

"No," Kryslie told her, "But we were sleeping for a while."

She leant over and helped Llaimos to his feet before reaching into her pocket for her personal transmitter. Tymos was getting up unassisted. She moved away from her brothers and used her transmitter to get to the kitchens, instead of walking down to the lower levels of the palace. She had never had a previous need to visit the palace kitchens, and so only had a vague idea of where things might be kept. It took her a while to find plates and glasses and a jug for water. In the process, she found some well-preserved biscuits. She tasted one to be sure they were still edible. With everything balanced on a tray in one hand, she transmitted back to the room referred to as the Room of the Seven Ages.

On her return, she found her brothers explaining some of the history of their world as depicted in the murals. They took a break and helped hand the water and biscuits around.

"Go and get freshened up and change," Kryslie suggested to her brothers, once they had all eaten. "I will stay here for now."

"I have nothing else to change into," Llaimos commented quietly.

Tymos punched him gently. "Come to my suite, you can probably fit into some of my clothes for now."

They transmitted away and Kryslie took over the history lesson until they returned. She was more than glad to have a chance to wash and freshen up. She had slept in the drab brown travelling clothes she was wearing. Before that, she had fought in them and been travelling from town to town. As she dressed in fresh garments taken from her wardrobe, it occurred to her that their guests might wish to freshen up too.

On her return, she invited the three girls to her suite and showed them how to use the hygiene facilities. She then withdrew to her sitting room to wait. Tarri was the first to re-emerge.

"Prince Tymos told us you were born on another world," she said with a faraway look. "What was it like?"

"A lot like here," Kryslie said, not willing to admit that she remembered nothing of her early life.

"How did you come here?"

"This may sound strange, but I can't remember," Kryslie finally admitted. "I expect that Tymorean missionaries recognized our power. I know we had to come here to be trained — because of what we were destined to be."

"I am destined to go back to the Dales and marry, have children and watch them grow up," Tarri complained.

"Many people only want that sort of life," Kryslie suggested, but she felt a stirring of a premonition.

"I want to learn more than just how to cook and hunt and keep house!"

"You could stay in the city. When the Elders and scholars return, you can ask them to teach you."

"I would like that but my mother still needs help," Tarri said despondently. "Why did all the scholars and Elders go to Dira anyway?"

"They went there so that their power would be available for us to use," Kryslie explained.

Tarri accepted the statement and asked, "So when will they return?"

"Soon, now that we are awake. My brothers and I will leave with you, and head to Dira after you turn off to the Dales. When we are at the Sacred Temple, the Guardians of Peace will tell us when to call everyone back."

Tarri didn't understand. "Can't you just tell them it's time?"

"No."

Tarri decided to stop quizzing Kryslie when her friends emerged, full of amazement at the sonic shower they had used to get clean.

The Great Ones walked with the children until they took the smaller road leading to the Dales and Reva. Llaimos watched until they were out of sight, and then trotted to catch up with his siblings.

"Tarri is an intelligent girl," Tymos remarked to his brother, having noticed that he had monopolised her company for most of the way from the palaces. He gave his sister a wink.

"Yes," Llaimos agreed, thinking nothing of it.

"I think she liked you," Tymos teased.

"So. Why shouldn't she?"

"Never mind," Tymos desisted. "Shall we pick up the pace? I feel like a good run."

The three Great Ones covered the remaining distance in ground devouring strides using their power to maintain what felt like an easy pace. They could have transmitted to Dira, but it was a balm for their souls to see the land growing pure and green and to feel the vibrant new life.

Chapter 3 - The portal to Dirakee reopens

Tymos, Kryslie and Llaimos found themselves drawn to the place they called the Garden of Peace.

Even though they had built the six-sided open structure from a part of the original temple, they now looked at it with the eyes of strangers.

They entered the garden through one of the five open archways, and stopped to appreciate the almost tropical abundance of lush plants that now grew within. Some of the plants had even grown up through the open roof.

When they had left the garden after building it, the place had been barren, but now it was as they had envisioned it and only a narrow clear path remained around the outer edge of the garden, just inside the arched pillars. Elsewhere, huge fern fronds and tangles of vines and other plants, obscured the ground and the central fountain, although in the quiet stillness of the garden, faint splashing sounds were audible.

The Great Ones knew exactly where the stepping-stones were placed between the archways and the fountain, and walked on them, gently pushing the vegetation aside, to reach the relatively clear central space and the six petals of the fountain's stone basin. There, they each sat on one of the petals, staying quiet and still, thinking back to the time of the war against the alien Ciriot, and the Aeronites whose distant ancestors had been Tymorean.

The Guardians of Peace had created them, having seen the inevitability of the conflict now past. They recalled how, for a time, they had been more than simply human and had wielded the power of the entire planet. Now, the world's power was again bound into all the living things, into the soil and the rocks and the water. Bound by the fountain where they sat, where the sunlight from above glinted on the sparkling gold and silver flecks of the stone that had been touched by Royal blood.

In the peace of the garden, the Great Ones each raised an arm, high into the air as a gesture of thanks to the Guardians of Peace. Thanks for the reality of the garden, for their survival, and as a promise of future service.

Even though the sky was a cloudless blue, a rumble of thunder was audible. The Great Ones heard and understood the message. "It is time!"

As one, they stood and faced the opening looking away from the Temple. They each raised both arms high and a light more brilliant than the sun shone through the arch – the portal of Dirakee opened.

Only the Great Ones, now bathed in the light, could open the way to the legendary fortress of the Tymorean Royalty. It was why they, themselves, could not enter.

The three Tymorean Governors were the first to emerge from the portal. They were followed in order of rank by their consorts and children, the Elders, the missionaries, the scholars and by the palace staff. Except for an elite few, everyone else had some degree of Tymorean Power.

The people kept moving around the edge of the garden towards the archway into the Temple. They all showed surprise, for the Garden had not existed when they had come to the Temple, and they had entered Dirakee when the portal had been in the Altar Room. In spite of that anomaly, most were keen to return to the palaces to see what changes had been wrought there. The line of people, moved steadily through the Temple, and down the front steps and along the path through the revitalised Temple gardens to the road that would take them to the City of Dira. In that newly awakened city, was the means for them to transmit back to the Royal Estate.

The three Tymorean Governors and a small group of people waited in the Altar Room to greet the Great Ones.

When the exodus was complete, the portal of Dirakee faded into ordinary daylight, and the archway once more showed the landscape outside the temple. The Great Ones needed a while to settle back into themselves after being in the presence of the Guardians. Only then, did they follow their kin into the Temple.

A no longer small figure raced at them with a yell, leaping into Llaimos's arms and reaching out for Tymos and Kryslie.

"Pyr! You've grown!" Kryslie said with surprise. She embraced the boy who had grown inches since they had last seen him. It told her that some years must have passed in Dirakee, but not as many as must have passed on Tymorea, while the planet slept and recovered.

Tymos and Kryslie, unencumbered, ran to embrace their foster father, the High King Governor. A few paces back, was another person they recognised.

"Daniel!" they both said at once, as a flood of once repressed memories became clear in their minds. Now they were able to remember their natural father and the fifteen years they had lived on the world called Earth. They broke free of the High King to run and embrace him too. Daniel was full of emotion. He couldn't help but feel pride at what his children had become.

After a time, two others came forward to greet them. Jonko and Keleb had been born on Earth too, but they had played an important role in protecting Tymorea. Jonko had the knowledge of plants and skill in manipulating them to mature faster, and Keleb had empathy with animals.

High King Governor Tymoros was talking quietly to Llaimos who hadn't been able to greet his father with the same enthusiasm as his elder siblings. The reverse was not the case, Tymoros had no qualms about hugging this son of his, and speaking whispered words to relax him.

Governor Xyron and President Governor Reslic greeted the Great Ones with the bows of equals and smiled at the flush of embarrassment on the three faces. Tymos, Kryslie and Llaimos, despite what they had become, had never once thought of themselves as equal to or superior to the three Governors.

This last group followed all the other people down the hill from the Temple to Dira and finally transmitted back to the Royal Estate.

Chapter 4 - A new direction

There was a great deal of work to be done to return the Royal Estate to its normal working efficiency. The Governors and their administrative staff worked from dawn to dusk with just the routine tasks.

The Elders, scholars and missionaries were meeting daily to attend to matters involving the cities and towns of Tymorea, but no one had invited the Great Ones to participate.

Tymos, Kryslie and Llaimos bored and feeling they were no longer useful. They kept together, as an instinctive gesture of solidarity, and spent most of their time in the High King's sanctum. Their restlessness was noticed by Tymoros, when he returned to spend the evening with, Tanya, his consort. Speaking with the utmost courtesy, he asked what was bothering them.

"Father, is there anything we can do?" Kryslie asked. She sprang up from the armchair and began to pace. "I know that your administrative team are quite able to handle matters around here, but the Elders haven't invited us to their meetings. All of the elder children of Governor Xyron and Governor Reslic are involved. It is as if we no longer have a purpose. The servants see us and just gape at us and our Royal cousins are acting as if they haven't seen us before."

"Great One, may I speak frankly?" Tymoros asked. He betrayed no sign of the incongruity of a Governor asking permission of one much younger.

"You don't have to ask us for permission to speak," Kryslie insisted, stopping her restless pacing and staring at him with surprise.

Tymoros merely nodded in acknowledgement. "No matter how the three of you feel, you each have the title of Great One – for what you have done in saving our world and because the Guardians of Peace have touched you. Everyone with even a trace of power can sense the difference in you."

"So...why does that mean we have to feel like outcasts?" Tymos asked, from the chair where he still sat.

"Hardly that. However, you are no longer simply my heirs," Tymoros told them, and then realised they had no idea what he was referring to. He gestured Kryslie back to the chair she'd vacated and sat himself in another. "Normally those of us that are Governors are the highest level of authority on our world. You three, as Great Ones, are no longer part of the normal power structure. We cannot give you orders, but if you were to give orders to anyone – they would be obeyed."

"But...that means we could give orders to you or the President," Kryslie swallowed that idea with difficulty. Her eyes were wide with the enormity of the implication.

"Yes," Tymoros agreed calmly. "And that is why the Elders did not ask you to attend their meetings. They will not presume to influence your actions."

Not one of the three Great Ones could find a response to that explanation. Tymoros continued, making a suggestion.

"There is no reason why you can't invite yourselves to the meetings. The Elders would welcome you all, and I think you do need to talk to them. My fellow Governors and I would welcome a chance to have private discussions with you some evening."

"We expected you to ask us things," Tymos admitted. "And I agree, I think we do need to talk to the Elders. I think there is still much we can learn from them."

"So, we will take your advice, Father, and invite ourselves," Kryslie announced. She stood up again, and looked at her brothers to see their agreement.

Llaimos was a silent listener to the conversation. He had no personal memories of what were once the normal activities of a Prince of Tymorea. He had simply shared the feeling of needing something to do.

The overwhelming sense of reverence from all those meeting with the Elders, embarrassed the Great Ones. It was this very phenomenon that had kept them together and away from others. Tymos and Kryslie had been instilled with a solid respect for their Elders, and Llaimos who had learnt all he knew from them in a moment of mind melding, shared that sense of respect. Everyone in the room was older in years than the Great Ones, who still had a lot to learn about themselves.

It was as their father had explained. The Elders, who had foreseen the rise of the Great Ones, knew the three of them were, in every way, worthy of respect. The aura of controlled power about them was obvious, as was the touch of the Guardians.

However, to Tymos, Kryslie and Llaimos, their own power did not feel extraordinary. They could not see each other as the Elders saw them.

"We didn't come to disrupt your meeting," Kryslie apologised softly. The meeting room had fallen silent as soon as they had entered.

"That is of no great concern, Great One. The routine matters we were discussing can wait," Elder Josep assured them. "Is there a matter we can assist you with?"

"We do need to tell you about events that we experienced while you were all in Dirakee," Tymos told them.

Those present who were not Elders, rose quietly and left the room. Kryslie sighed, deciding not to protest. What they were going to say was traditionally meant only for the Elders and Governors to hear.

"Before we start, could we say that we would be more comfortable if you would call us by our former titles? And, we haven't suddenly become too afraid or too important to get involved in work, so if you have anything we can help you with, please let us."

"If that is what you wish, Prince Tymos," Elder Josep agreed on behalf of all the Elders.

Tymos felt his teeth clench, and forced himself to relax. He went to a seat that had been vacated and when his siblings had seated themselves, began to relate the events that had occurred after the Elders had entered Dirakee. He started with the factual account of the state of affairs when the missionaries had been recalled, and proceeded to outline his own actions from that time. Llaimos and Kryslie continued in turn, relating their own actions and experiences.

They left out only one detail. It was an absolute command of the Guardians of Peace, that this knowledge remain secret. In no way did they suggest or imply that it had been the spilling of Royal blood on the Altar that had destroyed the Temple and freed their powers.

For several hours afterwards, the Elders discussed their revelations and asked questions to clarify points they found unclear.

Finally, the Great Ones tired of the questions and Kryslie spoke up. "There are certain things that we need to have done."

She had the instant and respectful attention of all the Elders. "It must be a priority to locate the Ciriot home world and to discover the fate of

Aerdna," she began. "And I would like an official delegation to go to the City of Ecla to examine the new inhabitants and to ratify the charter I wrote for them. The surviving mutants went there, but all helped us and deserved to be saved."

Tymos had his own perceived needs. "Representatives of the Governors need to go to every town and village, not just the cities, as soon as possible. The people need to have us available to listen to their concerns and organise essential supplies. Trade between regions needs to be re-established with some urgency so that all may have what they need to rebuild."

Llaimos added thoughtfully, "There will be a lot of people with buried traumas. Not everyone has forgotten the war. When the towns have been rebuilt, or sooner, our physicians need to be available to help them."

The Elders remembered everything the Great Ones said. Most of the suggestions would need to be attended to by the normal administrative processes, and this would reassure the people of the return of peace.

Later that evening, the Great Ones requested to speak with the Governors. They chose the private sanctum of the High King for their talk and had the servants bring in additional comfortable chairs. Here they repeated what they had told the Elders, and added some details that were only for the Governors to hear.

"Father, Jordan and Vila are dead. They were killed by a Ciriot-Aeronite hybrid. They gave up the chance to return to Aerdna and chose to be our allies and both fought bravely," Kryslie said gently.

Tymoros bowed his head, but did not betray his grief. It had been a severe shock for him to learn that two of his children, that he had long thought to be dead, had been raised to hate all Tymoreans.

"They died defending the Temple," Tymos added. "They bought us the time we needed to be ready."

He thought of, but did not mention, the silver and gold-flecked stone in the temple where Royal Blood had been spilled.

"The Temple has changed," Governor Xyron remarked, providing a distracting subject.

"The Temple had to fall," Llaimos said softly, shyly. "To free the world's power. To free our power and allow us to act. The Ciriot were the agency chosen to achieve it. In the moment they thought would be their triumph, they ensured their downfall."

"No Ciriot on this world survived," Kryslie stated bluntly. "Their colony ships would have been outside of our planetary system. We do not know where they are now. They lost six of their Princes, and countless lesser males. I believe they will be weakened for a time."

"As for the Aeronites, we returned all that we could to their base ships, and allowed them to leave. In the case of the Warlords, the Guardians judged them and only Xezir returned to help Xan. Both were given the title of Peace Lord," Tymos added.

The Great Ones sat back and relaxed as the Governors meditated on the information given to them.

Finally, Xyron spoke. "I was aware of the extra data you added to the files on the Ciriot. It is much more than we knew before. I agree that we need to find their homeworld and when we send out the missionaries again, I will instruct them to seek any information that may be available on other worlds."

"We have a duty to the Aeronites too," Tymoros admitted. "Even though we gave them what they needed to survive the cataclysm we know will occur to that world, they are still our kin."

Reslic had listened intently to all that the Great Ones had revealed. "When we re-activate the fleet, we will send scout ships to look for Aerdna."

The Great Ones retreated to the highest level of the High King's palace, to the room with the murals. It was now being called the Room of the Eight Ages.

In the newest section of the mural, the picture had already progressed beyond the arrival of the children and was showing the rebuilding. It was a montage of scenes from all over the populated continent. It was beginning to show the Elders returning to the cities, and Tymorean scholars travelling to the smaller towns and villages.

"The Elders told us we would have a mission on Earth," Tymos commented, as they followed their recent life in the murals. "That was before they even knew what we were to be here. I wonder if that was why we were born on Earth. Or if it was only so we would be safe until we were old enough to protect ourselves."

"We draw our power from this world," Kryslie followed the thought. "Perhaps we needed a link with the planet Earth, so we could do the same there."

"Then perhaps we should concentrate our energies on helping to prepare for the Earth mission," Tymos mused. "Certainly there is nothing here that needs doing that others couldn't do as well."

"I have noticed a strange quirk in my mind," Kryslie commented, suddenly. "We have a great deal of knowledge, gained from the Governor's memories when we mind-melded with them. So I can look at a problem and know the answer, but if I had to start something from the beginning – there are gaps. Do you realise, that we never finished our education here, and if they were to evaluate us, they would not put us back into study. I feel that I would like to learn consciously, the science and technology that will be needed for the Earth Mission. I want to learn from the basics to the advanced principles."

"I know what you mean, Krys," Tymos admitted. "I asked myself what would be needed by our missionaries. My mind produced an overview – no details – just factors to be considered. I thought about shields and a mass of information flooded my mind. I think it must have been on every type of shield Xyron knows about. I specified visible distortion shields, and all those details came into my mind. I can't always ask the right question – and like you said, I can see gaps."

"What you say is true for me, also," Llaimos said slowly. "I was never in lessons, but I do not need the technical knowledge – I won't be going to Earth."

"No," Tymos agreed thoughtfully. "You will be High King after our Father, and with his memories in your mind already, you will probably be an excellent statesman. At least, you will have years yet before you need to take that role."

Kryslie finally deduced the cause of the restlessness in her younger brother. "You are unsettled because you don't have a past – especially a past as a child. We have finally recalled our childhood on Earth. You don't even have that. You missed it all by being matured from toddler to man by the Guardians and I don't think they will make you revert back."

Llaimos shrugged. "I don't think I would want to revert back."

"I think," Kryslie said, and then paused. "That you need to spend time with Father, getting to know him as well as we do and I think you need to spend time with Tanya. She is your mother, and she missed out on having you grow up. I know she has Pyr to mother now, but it isn't the same. And there is another reason to talk to her. She may have been born a commoner, but those chosen to be Royal Consorts have a knack for bringing serenity."

Tymos thought of another suggestion.

"Another problem you have is that you missed out on the routine of being a child. And truly, you may decide that you are glad you did!" He laughed ruefully. "The point is – our teachers were often the Governors themselves or their brothers. If you were to offer to assist the teachers, you will absorb the lessons and the sense of being there. If you assisted with the physical training – you could demonstrate the exercises to the youngsters and experience them for yourself. I think that might have been why they had us doing the nursery inspection. We could start that again – with you."

"Then Tymos can set those cheeky children onto you, instead of me," Kryslie interrupted. Then she smiled, "At least the little ones don't treat us as unapproachable."

Llaimos grinned at the memory he saw in his sister's mind. "And when I have proved to myself that I deserve to be out of the nursery and school – what then?"

"Then you might challenge the President to duel with whatever weapon or technique you'd like to try," Tymos suggested. He kept his mind purposefully blank.

"Something Tymos should do," Kryslie grinned suggestively. She knew what he was meaning. "It is probably guaranteed to shrink his Great One sized ego back to a suitable size."

"We should all spend time with Pyr," Llaimos said. "I feel complete when I am with you both, but he doesn't have that."

"He must be feeling as strange as we did when we first came here," Kryslie agreed.

Llaimos took his siblings' advice and began to spend more time with his father during the mornings, alternating that with assisting some of the teachers, often when they were instructing Pyr's level.

Tymos and Kryslie spent most of their time on the purposeful preparations for the Earth Mission. In the evenings, they didn't neglect their family or their former classmates and close friends. At first, their friends were totally in awe of them and it took time to get them to accept them as easily as before.

Only then did they decide to ask about something that had teased their minds. They were curious to know what those of Royal Blood had experienced in Dirakee – the fabled fortress of Tymorean Royalty.

They sought out their friend Stenn Reslic one afternoon while he rested between training drills.

"It was strange," Stenn commented in answer to their question. He sat hugging one knee, on the grass, and watched his classmates taking turns throwing spear like weapons. "Being there seems dreamlike now – but otherwise it was a lot like being here. There were dome like buildings for us to live in. We had to forage and hunt for our food, instead of getting tithes from the common people. The weather never varied from what felt like early summer and we had actual water to swim in, not the pseudo aqua we use here. We still had lessons and were not allowed to idle around – but if you were to ask me how long we were there – I honestly couldn't answer. I would guess several years because most of us have gone up two levels. I am in level beta now."

"We couldn't tell you how long you had been away either," Tymos admitted. "Krys noticed, as she went from city to city, that time seemed to be going very slowly. She spent only a day or two in each one – but multiply that by almost a hundred cities and that is almost a year. Yet where ever she went, the cities looked only recently damaged."

"I didn't worry about it," Krys added. "It was enough to know I was arriving in each city in a timely manner. Right when I was needed most."

Jonko and Keleb wandered up during the conversation and Stenn asked. "Has my father decided where to place you yet?"

"Not quite," Keleb answered, amused. "He has Jonko helping him to train the lower levels in weapons work and he has asked me to teach defensive tactics. We are to take morning lessons with level alpha for a while at least."

Tymos glanced at his sister and spoke mind to mind. "Jon and Kel should be part of the Earth Mission. Perhaps we should suggest to his Excellency that they help Daniel."

Krys nodded her agreement and he stood up to put his idea into action.

Tymos waited and watched while Reslic completed an evaluation of a level alpha student.

"Great One," Reslic greeted neutrally, aware of the silent watcher behind him. He turned, and waited for Tymos to speak.

"Do you think Daniel could make use of our two fellow Terrans?" Tymos posed his suggestion as a question.

A slight smile softened the lines of Reslic's face. "Daniel has co-opted over half of Xyron's staff already. I am sure he will be happy to have two more," he commented softly. "I will suggest it. Is there something else I can do for you, Prince Tymos?"

"Yes, Sir, there is," Tymos said, diffidently. "I wanted to evaluate my skills. Sometime when you have finished with the students."

"Certainly, Prince Tymos," Reslic accepted the request. Instead of refraining from questioning a Great One, he decided to ask Tymos what concerned him.

Tymos took a while to answer. "I think I would like to know if being a Great One has limits. I really don't feel any different. But Krys suggested that we challenge you. I know how good I was before, but I want to know if I have become better."

"Perhaps, an hour after dinner – in my fitness room?" Reslic suggested. "Your sister and brother would be welcome too." The invitation was non-committal.

Kryslie did decide to accompany her brother that evening, but Llaimos declined. He had already made other plans for the evening.

After the ritual courtesies for a challenge between friends, Tymos and Jono Reslic began a battle with swords that were not merely practice blades. All the other equipment normally in the room had been moved out.

Kryslie moved about the otherwise empty room as she watched the duelling pair from different angles. She used senses other than just her eyes. Almost an hour later, at an appropriate moment, Tymos drew back and signalled a halt. Neither combatant was noticeably sweating or out of breath.

"How did it look, Krys?" Tymos asked.

"Faultless," she said at once. "I could see nothing between you. At no time did either of you seem to be in a superior position. In terms of power flow, you were identical to his Excellency."

"I feel like I could keep going for hours," Tymos remarked thoughtfully. "Krys..."

Tymos tossed the sword he had used to his sister. She caught it, in spite of the spin that moved it through the air, with a perfect grip on the hilt.

"This is still not my preferred technique," she commented as she in turn bowed to Reslic and allowed him to commence.

Kryslie recalled, perfectly, the lessons she had received in blade-work, but the skill had never come so easily. It seemed as if Reslic was taking it easy for her. Yet her sense of the flow of power revealed that this battle was as intense as it had been with her twin.

After twenty minutes, Kryslie disengaged, stepped back, tossed the sword back to Tymos and switched to unarmed defensive tactics. Within five minutes, she executed a move that would have disarmed any opponent less skilled than Reslic. He acknowledged her skill with a slight bow and passed his sword to Tymos.

Reslic suggested a form of martial art and he and Kryslie fought for ten minutes, both going full out. Kryslie switched to a second martial form and continued to battle. Ten minutes later, Reslic switched to a third discipline.

Suddenly, five figures clad in dark body suits with slits for eyes and mouth transmitted into the small gymnasium. From the faint smile on Reslic's face Kryslie knew that this was prearranged.

Tymos also smiled as he watched his sister facing six to one odds. He didn't move to help her because he knew she was intuitively aware where each opponent was placed. She moved instinctively as each attacked.

There was no lack of coordination between the six opponents, which enabled Tymos to deduce that four of them were probably the President's brothers. The fifth was likely to be Gann, who had recently graduated from level alpha.

From his vantage point, Tymos identified the weakest opponent. The difference was slight. Kryslie was concentrating her attack on that one whilst defending against the others. She disabled first one and then a second opponent, temporarily, but when they rejoined the battle, Tymos decided to join in. He sent a mental invitation to Llaimos who agreed to come and arrived moments later.

Smoothly, the two brothers joined in and Kryslie accommodated them as easily as she had the extra assailants.

The teamwork of the Great Ones was flawless. In a very short time, with only two to one odds, only Reslic remained fighting and with an unexpected smile, he said, "I yield."

At Reslic's surrender, the other five assailants removed their face covering. Tymos saw his deduction had been correct.

"Your assessment, Princess Kryslie?" Reslic asked neutrally.

"Something has changed," Kryslie admitted. "I have never been that good at sword-work. And, when you increased the odds in the unarmed combat, it seemed like I could see in my mind where everyone was and what they were going to do – like I have seen Jonko and Tymos do."

"Why did you target Gann first?"

"I sensed he was slightly weaker than the rest," Kryslie explained. "His defence, rather than his attack."

"I have to agree," Reslic stated. "Prince Tymos, I noticed that your defence has strengthened too. It was as noticeable as your sister's improved blade work. An effect of the Guardian's touch."

"How do you mean, Sir," Llaimos asked Reslic.

It was Perrin Reslic, the President's brother, who answered.

"Before Jono became President, he and I were equally matched. I could defeat him half the time. When he accepted the Sword of Judgement, the Guardians touched him too. It was as if he became a different person. I don't know if the difference is so noticeable when a person ascends to the Professorship or Kingship."

"The changes are there," Reslic admitted. "They are more subtle though. The President Governor is by tradition the Absolute defender – except of course when Great Ones turn up."

Reslic smiled again and wondered how long it would be before these Great Ones accepted their importance and place in the Guardians' scheme of things, without blushing.

"Prince Llaimos." Reslic turned to the youngest Great One. "Perhaps you would like to run through the basic sword movements you have been studying."

Llaimos nodded after a moment and accepted a sword. Reslic worked him through several of the practice routines his siblings had once learnt. He was flawless but that was not surprising for Tymos had bestowed on him the mastery of his power in the moments after the Guardians had matured him from a child.

"I can see glimpses of both Prince Tymos and Princess Kryslie in your technique," Reslic commented. "That was perfectly executed."

Llaimos was pleased, but determined to develop his own style.

"Thank you for your time, Sir," Llaimos bowed to the President and transmitted away.

Tymos and Kryslie offered to practice with Gann if he had time to spare from his other duties. He agreed after glancing at his father. Reslic maintained a neutral face.

Later that evening, in the main room of the High King's suite, Kryslie relaxed playing a lap harp, accompanying Tanya, as her foster mother played the great harp. Unlike her sudden grasp of many subjects since the mind meld with the Governor's, Kryslie had discovered she didn't know everything about playing music. None of them played an instrument. She had only Tanya's early teaching, but now her mind was so much more retentive and she could learn new music by hearing it once. Using the smaller harp, she delighted in creating a duet with Tanya. Her father and brothers enjoyed listening.

At the end of the third piece, Kryslie ceded her harp to Pyr who was learning music as an anodyne to his memories of terror and death.

Chapter 5 - Earth Mission prelude

The former system of long distance travel on Tymorea had not been completely restored, so the Tymorean space fleet's atmospheric wing were transporting scholars and Elders to the more distant cities.

These aircraft had been stored in a vast underground hangar within the base of the mesa, and had been sealed against dust and damage. Several of these ships were also capable of space flight and were recommissioned to take crews into space to where the huge fleet ships were moored around an asteroid. Nothing there had been disturbed in the time since they were left.

The primary destinations were three large transport ships, and one of the returning smaller craft docked to each of the larger vessels. The skeleton crews entered from the docked ships and began to reactivate the systems and prepare them for flight. When they were ready, the three ships were flown back to Tymorea, and settled into a stable orbit around the planet. Once there, each ship became a hive of activity, supplies were transported up from the surface, and each vessel was carefully serviced. The first of these great ships would begin to return missionaries to far-flung planets. This ship had room for a fleet of the small one or two person flitters used by missionaries who went to worlds where there was a high level of technology. These flitters were stocked, ready for their deployment in space near the missionaries' destinations.

Missionaries on less technological worlds would be flown closer. The transport ship would settle into a cloaked orbit and the people would transmit via a long-range beam to the surface.

Another three of the smaller air and space going craft were commissioned and presented to the Great Ones. The unexpected gift was accepted with great enthusiasm, as it gave them the means for independent travel. They had not wished to use their new rank to monopolise transport that was already being over taxed for vital tasks. They each took time from their other activities to familiarise themselves with their new craft.

Llaimos contented himself with short air and space hops to learn the peculiarities of his ship. Of the three, he had most actual hands on flying experience. He chose to take over the role of pilot for his father. It gave him a reason to be with his father and act as the High King's assistant. However, the common folk did not look on him as a mere aide. They knew who and what he was, and the mere fact that he had come with the High King Governor, gave the common folk reassurance and fresh enthusiasm.

Kryslie flew to visit some new villages that had sprung up by the distant ocean. The need for fresh protein, when the herds of cattle and sheep were just beginning to increase again, had caused many people to consider the previously untouched bounty of the sea. A new industry - fishing - had been created. She went to each new settlement and taught the fisher folk which 'fish' were to be left alone - the ones that were the juveniles of the ancient ocean consciousness.

When she had finished there, she began a systematic round of visits to the newly awakened cities, offering advice and promising contact from the Royal Estate. In Ecla, she was greeted with absolute reverence. She knew many of the citizens there, both commoners and former mutants, and many of the latter came to her to tell of the marvellous miracles that had occurred while they slept. It gladdened her heart to hear how the mutants had been stabilised, and their new serenity was as clear to her senses as if she had been a medical scanner. Now, an outsider could not tell the difference in the origin of any citizen.

One who greeted her without the sense of awe prevalent in everyone else was Morin, the young son of Ecla's newly elected Mayor, the former mutant Mithas. He raced up to Kryslie and flung himself at her.

He was babbling his thanks and gratitude for doing as she had promised, when his father hurried out to greet her on behalf of the town.

"I see my young scamp has usurped my speech," Mithas said with an indulgent smile. "The Elder who came to ratify the Charter, offered him a scholarship, for when the Elders had time to teach again. This one almost refused, he says he wants to serve you and your brother."

Morin spoke quickly, "The Elder said I would be more useful if I could read and write."

Kryslie could not stifle a grin. "You won't be able to escape learning that much and everyone has the right to learn as much as they wish. As for helping us, I would be honoured, but my brother and I will be leaving for another world, in a few months."

Morin's face became ecstatic. "Could I come too?"

His father looked startled, "I don't think…" He glanced at Kryslie, not sure what to say, then settled on, "Commoners do not leave Tymorea."

Kryslie found a great deal of information flooding her mind, and needed time to sort through it. Her moments of silence, turned the hopeful expression on Morin's face, into one of dejection.

"It is true that few ever wish to," Kryslie said slowly. "As far as I know there is no law to prevent you. Commoners don't become missionaries, and there is a reason for that, but I cannot see why intelligent commoners could not join the spacefleet. They are allowed to join the Peace Corps."

Morin looked at her with pleading eyes, like the trusting look of a young animal. Kryslie was not immune.

"You are still very young," she said, looking at Morin, and he was about to make a retort, but Kryslie's look silenced him. "Which will only be a passing inconvenience. I cannot promise you a place in the Earth Mission, but I will recommend that you be considered for the Peace Corps. To be accepted, you must study hard with the Elders, and the other teachers. Learn everything you can. If, after a year with the Peace Corps, you still wish to try for the spacefleet, talk to your superiors and ask them to recommend you."

Kryslie could hear the boy's thoughts, for he was a telepath like his father.

He was thinking at her, though looking down at his feet. "I want to work with you - help you with the important things you must do."

She spoke the same way, ensuring only he heard her. "Tymos and I do not know what the future will hold for us. I cannot promise anything yet. I appreciate your offer, truly, but even if you cannot help me now, make the most of every learning opportunity. You have a great deal of potential - you should have every possible chance, now, before anyone tries to tie you down into a boring career. I will tell Governor Xyron of your aspirations."

Morin's face stretched in a huge grin.

Tymos went to the space coordinates of the planet Aerdna, to investigate the system now the planet had broken out of its orbit there. He did not land on the three over crowded colony worlds, just approached into a cloaked orbit and studied the level of technology and general life. On his return to Tymorean space, he docked with one of the transport ships. The captain immediately offered him a tour, and took him to observe all the preparations. There was no secret about the vessel's destination. It was being prepared to go to Earth. All the crew knew that they would have the honour of transporting two of the Great Ones to that world. Those of the crew who saw and recognised Tymos, bowed with deep respect until he passed, and then went back to work with greater fervour.

Once again, Tymos realised that there were things happening that no one had seen fit to tell him. He had not realised that the plans for the Earth Mission had taken priority over seeing that the Tymorean commoners had all they needed to rebuild the towns and villages destroyed in the war. Yet, the Captain had taken it for granted that the plans of the Great Ones were of such importance that they had precedence over everything else.

When he would have begun to contradict the captain, a faint shiver of premonition caused him to refrain. Such feelings were subtle hints from the Guardians of Peace. He began to wonder why the Earth Mission was so important. He had thought, at first, that the fuss and plans for a proper base were because everyone assumed the Great Ones must be pampered. Now he began to realise that there was more to it than that. No great vision came to him from the Guardians of Peace, but then, they would reveal their wisdom in their own time.

Thoughtful, Tymos decided it was time to return to Tymorea, and discuss this feeling with his sister.

"The missionaries from Earth have sent some preliminary reports," Tymoros remarked late on the evening of Tymos's return and after Tanya and Pyr had retired for the night. He had the attention of all three Great Ones.

"Anything of urgency to note?" Tymos asked, his attention focussing on the subject. He had not expected any reports yet as the missionaries had only been gone a matter of weeks. However, he had not forgotten the shiver of awareness he had felt earlier in the day. He sat in one of the spare chairs in the High King's Sanctum. Kryslie was already occupying another.

"The humans there are recovering from a global war. It ended about three decades ago. The twenty new missionaries that have gone there have accumulated a great deal of historical information and have suggested several sites for our base."

"Fast work," Kryslie approved. "Sounds like they don't need us yet." Yet just then, she felt a shiver of disquiet.

"Have there been wars on other worlds as well?" Tymos asked. He had shared his sister's uneasiness and her eye's with an unvoiced question. It was not yet a thought - but more of an emotion through their twin bond. What must we do there if peace was already returning to the peoples of Earth?

He was thinking of the Tymorean saying, 'When there was peace on Tymorea there would be peace in the universe.'

"Troubles of varying degrees of magnitude on many worlds," Tymoros admitted. "Most of those worlds have begun to settle again."

"Have the missionaries estimated how much time has elapsed on Earth since our earlier missionaries were recalled?" Kryslie asked, curious. She too was wondering at the sense of urgency moments earlier.

"About a century," Tymoros told her.

Kryslie looked thoughtful and decided, "I think I should look over the reports." Tymos nodded agreement, but Llaimos excused himself for the night.

"Any thoughts you have would be worth hearing," Tymoros suggested as he decided to retire as well.

The information indicated no immediate problems. It was clear though that the missionaries had wasted no time in assessing the new situation on Earth. The most detailed report was a summary of significant events since the recall of the missionaries. It had accompanying details of some events, including contributing factors to the noted events as seen from each side of the situation. Most of these reports were signed 'Rhyn' and that was a name they didn't recognise.

Tymos and Kryslie went back to spending much of their time with their natural father Daniel, who was co-ordinating the preparations for the Earth Mission. Even though he knew they were now considered important people, his lack of awareness of how the Tymoreans truly saw them, made him assume the extreme respect was simply because they were the adopted children of one of the Governors. However, they were also his children who had turned into intelligent adults, and he saw no sense in wasting time bowing, or phrasing his questions with long-winded formality.

His attitude was refreshing, and his single-minded determination to finish organising the Earth Mission made him a comfortable person to be around.

Llaimos had met Daniel, but only briefly, but he remarked to his elder sibs one morning after their exercise session, that some of the scientists were scandalised by his casual attitude to Great Ones.

Tymos grinned and said, "It is a relief to be able to act like myself around him, and not feel like some supernatural and strange being."

Llaimos admitted that he agreed with that sentiment. Kryslie added, "At least by helping Daniel, we are doing something useful and I think we should get back to him. Keleb sent me a message saying that he is muttering at the computer."

"When considering that the computers he knew about on Earth are nothing like the ones here, he isn't doing too badly. At least we can help him extract data from the archives," Tymos explained.

With a grin at their brother, who was on his way to help Tymoros, Tymos and Kryslie transmitted to the science labs.

A great deal of the preliminary planning for the base had already been done by Tymorean scientists, who had worked from a standard floor plan. Dan Ward, as a native of Earth, was able to add local knowledge to the plans, and this advantage had been recognised by most of the scientists who were helping him. Now, only the details had to be finalised. Within months, those who would be building the base would be leaving for Earth.

"Do you know where I can find information about atmospheric interference with long-range transmitter beams?" Daniel asked as soon as he was aware of their presence. He was staring at a computer screen full of a list of file names, and jabbed his finger on a button to select the next. In a room, a short distance away, a group of people were huddled, discussing a different problem.

Kryslie told him where to look in the Compedia for the data, and then added, "A rough summary is that you don't try transmitting through a storm and you can't shield the beam."

"It's why they excavated underground tunnels between here and the nearest cities," Tymos told him. "There is an extensive network so we have the option of transmitting underground."

Daniel looked interested in the information. "I have got so much to learn," he muttered to himself. Then he demanded, "What about technical manuals? Young Keleb can't find any."

"He was probably looking in the wrong place. He will need to access Xyron's technical archives," Tymos said, the information suddenly in his mind.

"And is that where I would find the schematics and specifications for shields and shield generators?" Daniel asked.

"Exactly," Kryslie confirmed.

"Could you please help Keleb to find all that?" Daniel asked, dismissing that matter as soon as Tymos agreed. His mind was already on the next problem, and he cleared his computer screen and started another search.

The Great Ones expected no trouble and indeed, as soon as they began to search, using yet another computer, the technical manuals were easy to find. They sent the data to Daniel's data pad. However, there were gaps in the data folders where the shield data and the shield specifications were stored. Files had been created to store information on some new types of shields and generators, but they were empty.

Kryslie stared at her twin, at a loss to explain the fact when all the information coming into their minds from the memories of the Governor's indicated that the data they needed was there.

They made lists of the full and empty files and downloaded what was available onto a portable data pad.

"I am convinced that stuff should be there," Kryslie told her brother.

"So am I," Tymos agree, thinking hard. "And since neither of us has studied the subject, we must be remembering something from Xyron's mind. I wonder who should have stored the data."

"There should be an index of the researcher's names," Kryslie said aloud. She began checking.

"Tamir Janzoet," Tymos read over her shoulder.

Kryslie typed a search command on the name.

"Status unknown," Kryslie read first, and then recalled how to enter a command for personal details. When asked for a pass sequence, the correct one came instantly to mind. She began to read the information. "Earth! He was on Earth as a missionary, but he didn't come back."

"Read down further," Tymos told her. "It says what he was developing and why. Look at those screen configurations – they are the exact ones we were looking for."

The purpose of the shields was stated clearly and the first thought Tymos had was one of incredulity that such shields were needed on Earth.

Kryslie nudged his mind, and pointed to a later paragraph. "No wonder though, if the Earth scientists were beginning to experiment along those lines – and that was a century ago," was her mental comment. She went on, "We need to find out what they are capable of now."

Tymos considered that complication. "Yes. The advance missionaries might be able to find out, but initially, we need to be able to counter the kinds of things Janzoet mentions here. We can probably duplicate some of the data from other sources, but for the rest...we are going to have to find him, or his research, once we get there."

"And find it fast," Kryslie stressed.

They gave all the information they had found to Daniel and then went to find Vincent, Xyron's brother. He had been a missionary on Earth before the recall.

Vincent was in the infirmary collating information from the latest batch of staff evaluations.

Tymos interrupted him quietly.

"Prince Tymos, I am at your service," Vincent gave them his full attention.

"I realise you are busy, but Kryslie and I are trying to track down some data for Daniel that appears to be missing."

"Tamir Janzoet was working on Earth, researching some new screen configurations. What happened to him?" Kryslie asked bluntly.

"I don't know," Vincent said immediately. "He acknowledged the message I sent, warning him we were being recalled and when. He did not come to the rendezvous point. I am sure he would have, if he could have. I was unable to contact him and we could not delay our departure any longer. Once here, we had no way to continue trying to reach him."

"How many other missionaries didn't return?" Kryslie asked.

"All missionaries on all worlds were told to return," Vincent stated. "You and Tymos gave the order."

"What if they had families?" Kryslie asked. It was a point she had not considered back then.

"All our missionaries know that they can be recalled at any time. They are taught to make provision for their families if they marry non-Tymoreans."

"What if two missionaries married?" Tymos asked.

"In those cases, the children came with them so that they could be evaluated and trained if they had inherited our power," Vincent explained. "That is the normal practice."

Something still niggled at Kryslie's mind, but she couldn't focus on it. She thanked Vincent and returned with her brother to where Daniel was scanning the data on shields they had provided for him.

"Where is Tonos?" she asked.

"He was here a moment ago," Daniel replied absently.

Tonos had once been the Principal at the Earth school that Kryslie and Tymos had attended.

"Never mind," Kryslie decided aloud. "I hoped he might have been able to tell me something."

Tymos sat down next to Daniel. "We can't find all the screen configurations. There are some empty files. Some of the work was being done on Earth and the researcher didn't return here."

Daniel looked away from the computer, with concern on his face. He tapped some keys on a pocket computer.

"These are the screens recommended for that radiation site you suggested. Are any of them amongst the missing ones?"

"The last four," Kryslie knew as soon as she looked at the list.

Daniel scratched his head and frowned. He began to pace, taking jerking steps.

"I can probably find alternatives for two of them," Tymos said quickly. "At least I think there might be something amongst that mass of information we downloaded from the Ciriot ships. Krys and I had better look through that. It might not have been cross referenced yet."

"As for the other two," Kryslie thought aloud. "We should be safe enough in that radiation zone for a time. If we can't find traces of Tamir's research, we will be able to study the problem there and find a solution."

Some of the worry left Daniel, until Kryslie asked an unrelated question.

"Do you have a plan of the base?"

Daniel brought it up on his screen.

"What sort of personnel quarters have been planned?" Kryslie asked then.

The appropriate areas were highlighted.

"Not bad. What about furnishings?"

Daniel tried to avoid the question. "Everything we need has to fit into two transport ships," he reminded her. "And budgeted for!"

"Cost won't be a problem," Kryslie said dismissively. "I will arrange for a means to make the quarters less Spartan and more personalised. Do you have any objections? I will tell you what space allowance I need."

"Great One," Daniel placed a slight emphasis on the title. "Who am I to question you? However, as my daughter who has suddenly taken on a look I never trusted in my wife..." He left the sentence dangling.

"Thanks, Dad!" Kryslie told him cheekily, walking a few steps away to transmit to Tanya's solar to talk to her foster mother. Tymos was left to find the Ciriot data and to wonder what had just got into his sister. He figured it out when he realised that Daniel was no longer tightly rigid with worry.

Chapter 6 - Sudden Urgency

Llaimos knew no one would question him if he chose to leave his self-appointed place at his father's side, but doing so made him feel strange. Since the return, he had assimilated the discipline and expectations that all the Royal children lived with. He liked the feeling of doing something worthwhile to help the common people get their lives back in order. However, it increasingly reminded him that he had no past to remember. He had been a mere toddler, when the Guardians of Peace had matured him, so that he could become one of their Advocates. His siblings had made worthwhile suggestions, and for a time, they had helped.

Sitting in on the lessons of the younger students, did little more than teach him that the Royal children were trained to serve the common people, and to consider others before themselves. The subject lessons, taught him nothing that he didn't already know. He considered how his siblings were teaching themselves the basics of the sciences, to fill in the gaps in the knowledge bequeathed to them with Xyron's memories. Unlike his sibs, he had no need of the advanced sciences. He didn't know what he wanted to learn more about.

With his mind in a chaotic state, he decided to go to the one place where he could find peace - the garden at the Temple of Dira.

His request to have his ship readied was obeyed immediately. He had right of way to take off when he was ready, all other air traffic would be cleared from his path. His stated intent to land in the Temple Gardens met with no resistance. Traditionally, everyone walked up from the base of the hill - but he was a Great One, and outside the normal authority structure.

He had the memory of a memory from his siblings, of the forbidden fun of being disobedient. He felt nothing like that, and doubted that either

Tymos or Kryslie would feel like that now. It just felt right and steadying to be at the Temple.

Sitting on one of the petals of the stone fountain, amongst the lush greenery, he let the peace of the garden wash over him, and the inner tenseness that had been building within him, eased. With his mind cleared of all the uncertainties, he relaxed into meditation, losing all track of time.

He became aware of himself, and realised that he had sensed the arrival of his brother and sister. Glancing at the angle of the sun, he realised it was now late afternoon, and he had been there since morning. Instinctively, he turned his head to the direction from which Tymos and Kryslie were approaching. He felt the bond between them merge to include him, and the image of a very odd and colourful creature came into his mind. With it was a strong impression of mirth; he recognised the feel of his sister.

"You look like a garden gnome, sitting there, with only your head sticking out of the greenery," she sent mentally, providing proof that she could see him as well as he could see her from the distance.

"A what?" he asked with amusement, and then laughed as Kryslie enlightened him.

"An Earth myth. One that I just remembered - seeing you with your red hair against the green."

"Did you come here just to make fun of me?" Llaimos asked. Should he be surprised that they knew where he was? He hadn't made it a secret, but when he had left they had both been deeply engrossed in deciphering the Ciriot archive.

Kryslie's mental tone turned serious. "No, we found the program the Ciriot used in their translator boxes and after that anyone that wanted to could access the data. Daniel had half his staff of helpers looking for references to shields. We were, once again, superfluous. So, since we knew you had come here, we decided to join you."

"I was feeling much the same, superfluous," Llaimos admitted, knowing that his siblings were aware of that. "Why don't you sit with me?"

Effortlessly, Tymos and Kryslie moved along the stepping-stones, easing the branches of the plants out of the way and sat on the stone petals either side of him. Just being together, with them, gave Llaimos a feeling of completion. He was one part, and together they were a whole. His siblings were a calming presence; they brought with them the sense of knowing what they had to do next. Perhaps, sitting here, the Guardians of Peace would enlighten him to his own role.

Or not, he told himself, as the three of them sat in a comfortable silence, alone with their individual thoughts, and with no prophetic visions disturbing them.

"The Guardians do not tell us everything," Tymos said gently, when several hours had passed. "If it is within our knowledge and skills to solve a problem, they let us work to a solution. Can we help you with yours? Krys and I know you have been unsettled."

Llaimos didn't answer immediately, but eventually he spoke aloud. "I will miss you both, when you leave to return to Earth. But I know it will be good for me to be out of your shadows."

What he didn't say, or even try to make into a coherent thought, was still understood by his brother and sister.

To Tymos, it was as if he was seeing a small child looking up to him.

"You are wrong to think that you are any less than Krys and I," Tymos protested. "Not now, not any more. You are no longer that little child."

"You worked as hard as we did, to save this world. You are our equal in every way," Kryslie insisted.

Llaimos shook his head, and admitted, "I sense you both as solid presences, but I feel so insubstantial."

Tymos moved his arm and pushed his unsuspecting brother backwards. "You feel pretty substantial to me."

Now Llaimos grinned ruefully. He could feel the rock around the centre of the fountain digging into his back, as the spray from the fountain splashed onto his face.

"That rock is, at least," he said, pulling himself back up.

"What I meant, is that assisting the teachers and working with the youngsters, helped for a while but it isn't enough anymore."

"Give yourself time, bro," Kryslie advised. "I know we are considered Great Ones and we may know a lot, but it is by no means everything. There may be a fountain of instinctive wisdom in us but I think even Tym and I still need to grow into it."

"Even with a sixteen year head start on you – I still don't really feel like an adult yet," Tymos said thoughtfully. "At times like this, when we have no important task to do, I don't feel much different to how we were before the war. I look in the mirror, and see that I look older, for the Guardians of Peace matured us too, but that is only on the outside."

"So, that might be your problem too," Kryslie agreed with perfect seriousness, and her thoughts were shielded from her brothers. "Your mind is telling you that you are less than two years old. Life can be very frustrating to a two year old!"

Llaimos felt a laugh wanting to erupt from him, and he allowed it. "I know I am not still an infant," he stated. Then he added, "I know so many things, but I don't know who I am."

"Great One? Prince of Tymorea? Father's Heir?" Tymos suggested helpfully.

"All meaningless titles, and perceptions of me through the eyes of other people," Llaimos argued. "I found, when I was travelling with Father, that I was ignored at first. I was merely one of Father's children, learning to be like him. They listened to what he said, because he, as a Governor, had the authority to order what they needed."

Neither Kryslie nor Tymos commented, for they both sensed that their brother was trying to think through the way he felt.

"Eventually, before we left each place, the word spread that I am a Great One. Not Great One Llaimos, just a Great One. Then, if they were not trying to touch me to see if I were real, they turn mute and look at me as if I, alone, should fix all their concerns in an instant."

He didn't need to look at his siblings to know he had their complete support. "It isn't as if I don't want to help them."

"But you are only one person, and every commoner probably thinks that their problem is the one needing an immediate solution," Tymos summarised.

Llaimos gave a sour laugh. "And not when the less knowledgeable are saying that during the war, Great One Kryslie single-handedly did this or that." He glanced at Kryslie in time to see her blush.

"I didn't work alone," she said, though she didn't need to say it. "But you make your point. I was the one they all looked to. And now, everyone from commoners up, expect Great Ones to be miracle workers and serious all the time. Even our friends were in awe of us."

"Until we taught them differently," Tymos finished. "I have no interest in being put on a pedestal and told I have to stay there and be adored. There are things we can do, because we are the best ones to do it, but we do not need to be worrying about things that others can deal with. Maybe that means we should deal with a particular person's problem, but more likely it will be something that affects a wider group of people. And it certainly shouldn't mean that we are not entitled to have some fun."

"What possible use is there for us to be outside the structure of Tymorean society if we cannot be ourselves," Kryslie proposed. "Surely there is a time to be serious, and a role model, and whatever else, and a time to be relatively anonymous."

"How can I be that, when one look at me betrays my lineage?" Llaimos asked.

The simple, logical answer was, "Have Tanya dye your hair brown, like that of the commoners." Kryslie added nothing more, for that idea had unleashed a flood of possibilities in Llaimos's mind. Exciting ideas, until they were tempered by the knowledge of what was expected of Royal children.

So that he didn't dismiss the idea, out of a sense of propriety, Kryslie added, "Bro, you have no need to be in a hurry to grow old and serious. Heavens, look at Stenn Reslic. He's almost an adult and he still likes playing juvenile tricks. The thing is, if you don't look like a Royal, no one will expect you to act like one."

"But, what would people say?"

Kryslie knew Llaimos still didn't have the point she was trying to make. "Try this paradox for size. Is Pyr your younger brother or your older brother?"

Llaimos pondered, contrasting logic with emotion. Logic said Pyr was older, having been born ten years before him. Emotion said Pyr looked younger than himself.

"Pyr is my brother who is smaller and less knowledgeable than me," Llaimos summarised.

"A well balanced answer," Kryslie commended. "Now, consider this. People will judge you on what their eyes first see of you. They will accept that you are the age that you look to be."

"But they will hear my name…"

"Use a different one, bro," Tymos told him. "Take yourself away from the palaces, travel where the whim takes you, fend for yourself, help when you can, get blind drunk if you want to - but experience for yourself how the commoners live."

Kryslie added, "Use the knowledge that you have, to make your own decisions. They may not be the right ones every time, but learn from the mistakes. Try your hand at whatever appeals to you, deal with what you stumble into. Be you!"

Sensing that Llaimos was both calm and thoughtfully considering their advice, Kryslie rose. "I'm all for getting something to eat. We should all keep the vigil tonight. And spurning any pre-conceived notions of a woman's role, you men can get your own suppers."

She left through the arched way that led into the Temple.

The darkness of the night was lightened by the two candles on the altar and the two battered lamps that were now placed reverently on small shelves on the wall behind the altar. The mystical flames stilled burned brightly, with no physical fuel to sustain them.

Llaimos had offered to stay awake first and as his siblings slept on the benches placed around the Altar room, he pondered their words and their certainty that he would be the one chosen to succeed their father. He hoped that there would be a great many years yet before he needed to. Still unable to settle, he spent most of the time wandering idly about the room.

Kryslie relieved him part way through the night. She knew that the vigil was a means of coming closer to the Guardians and becoming more receptive to their wisdom. She knelt in front of the altar, heedless of the hard stone under her knees. She remembered the first time she had kept the vigil and felt the Guardians' presence. Now, as she watched the candle flames flicker in the faint breeze, she let her mind wander where it would and the thoughts that came were of the time when she was still on Earth.

Since she was soon to return, such thoughts and memories were not surprising. What made her thoughtful was the increasing sense of urgency she felt.

"It won't be the same. So why do I feel I must go there? That time and place existed a long time ago. How can I?"

There was no sudden leap of intuition – just the feeling of needing to do something and being late.

Tymos in his turn paced around the Altar Room, aware in part of his mind that Kryslie had not returned to sleep. His mind was also filled with vivid incidents from his years on Earth and a sense of something important he had not done.

"We have to go back to the Estate! The Earth Mission will have to leave tomorrow."

Kryslie sat up, fully awake.

"Yes. I sensed the urgency, but not the reason why."

"Why must you leave," Llaimos asked, having been woken by their voices. "The base won't be ready yet."

"The Guardians know," Tymos said. "That is enough. We must go now."

The Great Ones trotted to Llaimos's ship and he flew it back to the Royal Estate. He landed on a cleared area of the mesa at the rear of the Royal Estate. They had radioed ahead to have a crew ready to prepare the craft given to Tymos and Kryslie for transport to Earth and for Llaimos's to be taken to the storage cavern beneath the estate.

Their return caused more than a stir, for they used their authority as Great Ones to have the Governors summoned from their beds. Within moments of them arriving in the Conference Room, Tymos had imparted to them the sense of urgency he felt. The Governors acted without questioning them, leaving to issue the orders to speed up the loading of the first transport ship and to rouse the extra missionaries assigned to Earth as well as servants to pack the gear all would need.

Several of the Elders who lived on the Estate came to wait with the Great Ones and as they sat in some of the chairs around the table, Tymos and Kryslie related the thoughts that had come to them during the vigil. While the Elders pondered, Llaimos considered his own thoughts.

"With memories that vivid, there is the danger of arriving in the wrong place," Elder Gracien warned after a while. She was a wizened, elderly woman of nearly ninety years.

"We will be going with the builders and additional missionaries," Kryslie told her. "We will not be directing the beam."

Gracien nodded. "That is as well."

Elder Timenon spoke then. "We agree with your sense of urgency. There is something that must be done quickly. Something related to the Earth Mission. Great One, do you have any idea what that might be?"

"Yes," Tymos said at once. He explained about Tamir Janzoet and his missing work.

"Certainly that will need to be found," Timenon agreed. "However, I feel it is more than that. We will consider what you have told us until the hour before noon. If we have any thoughts to add to yours, we will speak them at the briefing."

Chapter 7 - Arrival

The final briefing for the extra missionaries, who would now be going with the builders, was being held in the Conference Room. Although it was not yet dawn, the room was crowded.

Professor Governor Xyron had briefed the builders first. They would be returning to Tymorea as soon as the base was erected. Then he turned his attention to the thirty extra missionaries assigned to supplement the twenty Tymoreans who had already settled on Earth. He recapped the information they had already studied of the social, cultural, political and economic situation on the distant planet.

Tymos found his mind wandering from the briefing. Too many phrases were evoking floods of images and information from when he and his sister had shared and assimilated the memories and experiences of the Triumvirate Governors of Tymorea.

All the missionaries standing around him were going to Earth, to them an unfamiliar planet, but he was going home. He knew that he had been born there, and that Dan Ward, the man standing near him was his biological father. However, he couldn't remember leaving Earth.

The mental touch of his twin's mind proved that she was also distracted.

"We were at school," she thought at him. "Dan taught there and Tonos was the Principal."

More memories surfaced.

"Yes, and Vincent brought us to Tymorea. They must have sedated us because we were being difficult, barely controllable." Tymos knew they were not his memories that he saw now, for he saw two children on stretchers.

Regardless of his abstraction, Tymos heard Xyron telling the assembly, "Before the war, when we recalled our missionaries from Earth, Tamir

Janzoet, one of our scientists, chose to remain. He was working on a new kind of protective shield, and our base on Earth will need it to be fully protected. Finding his work is a priority."

Xyron paused, bowed slightly towards Tymos and Kryslie, and asked, "Great Ones, is there anything you wish to add?"

Instantly, his mind filled with the details he had learnt of Janzoet, and he explained to the assembly exactly why the research was vital. "It is as Governor Xyron has said. He was concerned with the trend of human research, and aware of dangerous scientific explorations. If he is dead, he will have ensured its safety of his scientific notes until our return. The Guardians have told us that we must leave at once to begin the search for them."

He stepped back when he had finished speaking, returning the control of the briefing to Xyron with a slight bow. His face remained composed as he let his mind and memories merge with those of his sister.

"All we have to do is ask the right question," Kryslie thought at him, returning to the matter that consumed their attention. She shared vivid mind images with him. Images that evoked the physical sensations of walking to school, of being at a school that was half way across intra-galactic space and a century back in time. If they closed their eyes, it was as real as if they were there.

Xyron continued speaking, "You have all been issued with a kit. It includes a communicator capable of contacting Vincent from any place on Earth. He and Daniel will share the duties of Mission Controllers. Initially, Daniel will be concentrating on getting the base built and operational. Olassa, my daughter, is currently coordinating the advance missionaries. She knows to expect your imminent arrival."

Reslic took over and added, "Departure is scheduled for three hours from now. You should ensure that your personal items conform to Earth restrictions and you should keep your bags with you. The ship will be transported into Earth's orbit and cloaked at all times. All equipment and supplies will be transported to the surface, after the personnel. Due to the nature of the site chosen, you will all need to activate personal force shields before you arrive there. Those who will be staying at the base will need to wear the protective suits. Any questions?"

Reslic dealt with the queries and then asked, "Would you like to add anything, Prince Tymos? Princess Kryslie?"

They both shook heads, indicating a negative, and forced their minds to consider the present.

The meeting ended, but Vincent stayed behind to speak to Tymos and Kryslie. Llaimos departed with Tymoros.

"The Elders mentioned a matter to me that they wish you to be prepared for," Vincent told them.

"Go ahead," Tymos invited.

"Simply put, they feel that you who were born on Earth may require a period of transition. It may take you longer than the usual moments to complete the journey from ship to surface."

"Transition?" Tymos mused. A vague feeling of premonition ran like a shiver down his back. "We will take that into account. Was there more?"

"Yes. They also asked me to suggest that you, as well as Jonko and Keleb, should be prepared for a degree of culture shock."

"I do see that," Kryslie admitted. "When we return we will, effectively have travelled in time."

"So, we should make ourselves aware of the subtle cultural differences in the structure and behaviour of Earth society," Tymos nodded. "We will warn Jon and Kel."

Vincent withdrew. Kryslie and Tymos went to find their friends.

"What exactly did he mean?" Keleb asked. "Culture shock?"

"It means, in our case, that in our childhood on Earth we were trained or conditioned to react to certain stimuli in various ways. Or if you prefer, our body language is based on the Earth of a century ago," Tymos warned them.

Kryslie emphasised the point. "If we don't keep alert, we may rouse suspicion in people's minds. It's like the changes in fashion, hairstyles and so forth over time. We should quickly assimilate the changes and use them to blend into the population."

"My memory of Earth is quite hazy," Keleb admitted.

"So is mine," Jonko agreed. "I do remember thinking I was already grown up. How old do you think I will be there? Twenty three or one hundred and twenty three?"

"Age is arbitrary," Kryslie told him. "You, physically, haven't aged that much."

"So I am as old as I feel, then?" Jonko decided.

"Do you really think we will need a period of transition?" Keleb asked. "I didn't understand that point."

"I don't think you will," Tymos said thoughtfully. "Krys and I have vivid memories of before we came here. The Elders seem to think we may end up arriving where we used to live. We might have to trek across the world to get to the base."

"So don't be perturbed if we don't arrive with you. We will still be coming," Kryslie assured her friends.

The mission crew and builders assembled again in the Great Hall with their personal packs.

Tymos and Kryslie stood with Daniel, the only person in the group who was sufficiently distracted to be oblivious to their own abstraction. They felt that there was more to be deduced from the thoughts they'd had in the Temple the previous night. It was fortunate that their servants had packed bags for them with necessary clothing and hygiene requirements.

After the building materials and supplies were transmitted up to the transport ship, the confirmation came for the personnel to come up. The mixed group stood together in a tight group in the hall. Each person had a locator tag on them, and a second one on their packs. When the transmitter beam was activated, the people and bags arrived together in an equally large space on the transport ship.

For Tymos and Kryslie, the process did not seem strange, for they had many second-hand impressions of being moved by the bulk transporters, and it felt like the ordinary transmissions by long-range beams. The crew on the transporter assigned quarters to all the personnel, most as barracks style accommodation. The Great Ones decided not to make a fuss about being given use of the captain's cabin, since they would not need it for more than half a day. They kept to themselves during the brief journey to the terminus of the long-range beam that would begin to take them to Earth's solar system.

Tymos and Kryslie returned their attention to the present, as the great transport ship began to slow. They were approaching Earth, but were still more than 40,000 km away. In half a day, they had travelled countless light years across space, pausing only at each new relay point for the long-range beam to be reset to the next point. Now they only had to wait until the ship attained a cloaked geosynchronous orbit about Earth before the powerful bulk matter transporters would move both people and supplies from within the ship, to the place chosen for the Tymorean base.

Vincent clad in one of the protective suits, addressed all descending personnel in the large central chamber of the transport ship.

"Activate your personal shields now," he reminded them. "Keep them on all the time you are on the site of the base. You will need them to protect you from the radiation until the permanent force shields are operational. When we arrive on the ground, we need to move outwards in an expanding circle until we have a cleared area the size of this chamber. The supplies and equipment will be sent down then and each batch will need to be cleared before the subsequent ones arrive. We will be erecting a geodesic dome for protection and generating a visual distortion field over that."

The excitement of the moment affected all the missionaries. Most of them were young and this was their first posting. They all moved into a tight group around the Great Ones as the warning was given.

Tymos and Kryslie obeyed the command to activate their personal shields, and thought of the description of the base. They had the oddest feeling that they had been there before, but that was impossible. A glow began to surround them, and then new sensations drove all memories out of their minds. Instead of the familiar tingle and brightness of the long-range transporter, they felt like they were being thrown around in some twisting, image blurring, dimension of time and space.

Even in the darkness of the moonless Earth night, Daniel was aware that Tymos and Kryslie were no longer with them. He had been warned of the possibility and he pushed his concern aside so that he could deal with the delivery of the non-living cargo. When the first pile materialised, the ring of personnel moved in and hefted boxes and crates away from the landing zone. When the all clear was given, the next load arrived. The process was repeated and then the third and last load arrived and Daniel began issuing orders.

The technical specialists began to prepare the distortion field generator and to assemble the communicators that should enable them to contact the advance missionaries and Home base. Missionaries and builders alike were sorting out the pieces of the dome and the initial ring was being assembled with the precision of a well-drilled team.

When Earth's sun rose over the blackened landscape, the black dome was complete and it covered an area three times the diameter of the initial landing zone. The visual distortion fields were operational, making the dome undetectable. That and the signal transmitter were working off batteries and by the following night, solar chargers would have charged up the spares. A backup system that would draw energy from the ambient radioactive emissions would be constructed in the future.

During the first day, signals went out to the advance missionaries, and each sent coordinates so that one or two newcomers could transmit away. Until the base was built, there were only facilities for the builders and a handful of others.

By the evening, only Daniel, Vincent, Jonko and Keleb, remained with the builders. All wore the protective suits that were similar to Tymorean space suits. The administrative staff would arrive when the base was more advanced. Four small huts made from prefabricated building slabs had been erected for the builders to use in shifts for sleeping. A fifth hut, slightly larger, was an eating and rest area. All food was of a liquid consistency and like the drinks, were sealed in radiation proof containers. To consume them was awkward, but achieved through a connection in the protective suits.

Late in the evening, a visitor arrived, unannounced. She did not have a suit on, but the faint mauve glow about her skin revealed the presence of a personal force screen.

"Hello," Keleb said in surprise, looking at the short blond haired woman who had transmitted into the kitchen hut, right where he happened to be looking.

"Olassa!" Vincent turned and greeted the woman warmly.

"Hello Uncle Vin," she smiled back at him, recognising his voice even though it came through a speaker in his suit. "I have a report to give you and Daniel that I was instructed to bring personally."

"I am intrigued," Vincent admitted. "Keleb, fetch Daniel please."

Dan Ward, moving awkwardly, entered the hut with Keleb following. Olassa wasted no time.

"Uncle, your earlier message asked us to look out for Prince Tymos and Princess Kryslie. The fact is - they helped us when we first arrived. From what they told me then, they had been here on Earth for five years or more already. Most of the reports I sent home were provided by them."

"How is that possible?" Keleb demanded, amazement overcoming politeness.

Olassa shrugged. "They asked me specifically not to mention them in my reports home and to come here in person to tell you when you arrived."

"Five years?" Dan said, totally bewildered. "Where are they now?"

"I do not know, Daniel. I think it is their intention to contact you when they are ready. I have had the opportunity to read that report and it is fascinating. You need to read it, but basically it seems like they have been travelling through time."

"How can they travel through time?" Jonko asked. The notion seemed impossible.

"I don't think time is a barrier to the Guardians," Keleb suggested. "Remember the Great Ones are their Advocates. Surely you recall how time seemed odd when we were visiting the cities before they were sealed."

"Yes," Vincent mused. "That's what we didn't see. The Elders felt that there was a time effect to prepare for – they saw that Tymos and Kryslie would arrive here later than the rest of us. We interpreted it to mean that they might have arrived back where their memories were vivid. In that place, but in this time, so that they had to travel by local means to get here."

"Why didn't it happen to us," Keleb asked. "We were born here too, although I don't recall it that vividly."

"You said it before, Keleb," Vincent reminded him. "The Great Ones are the tools of the Guardians. If they arrived back in time, it was because there was a need for them to do so. I will give the report close attention. Thank you for bringing it, Olassa."

"A pleasure Uncle. Oh, I also have to tell you that there is a vast underground chamber beneath us. Prince Tymos mentioned it to me. You need to go down there, something about a generator."

Daniel's attention was caught. "Did he say how to get down there?"

"No, he didn't."

Daniel trotted out of the hut to talk to the builders.

"Uncle Vin, let me know when you are operational here and I will hand over my coordinator's role to you and Daniel."

"I'll do that. Meanwhile, if you get to hear where Tymos and Kryslie are, let me know. We will set out tomorrow to look for them. I will stay in touch, but you should leave. Those force screens can only handle this radiation for a short time."

Vincent spent a lot of the night studying the reports Tymos had given Olassa to send on to Tymorea. They were mostly computerised text reports, but some were voice and he recognised Tymos as the speaker. Using his data pad, he rapidly scan read or listened to each of them, but he also had the reports analysed by a special program. The program ignored the message, but detected certain properties of the signal. The initial result showed that the data had come from Olassa's base. Using more advanced techniques, earlier signal data was recovered. Vincent considered these results thoughtfully.

A secondary signal showed they were sent from a location he estimated to be in the same country as he was currently in. Beneath that signal was often a third signal and these varied widely, indicating they had been sent from places all over the world. This third signal also revealed the names of the initiating missionaries and they were, for the most part, unfamiliar.

Some of the very earliest reports were dated just after the missionaries had left Earth and the names teased at his mind. Later reports were signed by someone called Rhyn, and the most recent ones had no underlying signal data beyond the other American location and were unsigned.

"Rhyn," Vincent mused. He thought on the electronic signature on the majority of reports from prior to two years ago. The name meant nothing to him but he took the originating coordinates and plotted them onto a large-scale map of Earth. He zoomed in and noted the position was within America and he memorised the address.

Vincent sat back and let his mind wander back to his previous time on Earth – before the war on Tymorea. The names of his fellow missionaries flicked through his mind. It was like reviewing index cards. The answer came as suddenly as sun from behind a dark cloud.

"The children! Of course!" he said aloud, recalling now the anguish of four of the missionary couples who had left behind their grown children and grandchildren.

The children had been told nothing of their parent's origin – or had they? Vincent could contact Homebase later and question those couples, but the benefits of their actions were more valuable than raising the issue of disregarding rules.

The children of mixed human-Tymorean couples were not involved, just the children with two Tymorean parents. These children must have been told of their parent's origin and purpose and decided to continue with the work – reporting to a coordinator and trusting that one day their work would be recognised. It must be the grandchildren of those, or great-grandchildren, who were now carrying on the tradition. The notion excited him. He suddenly knew where the Great Ones would be.

Chapter 8 - Homecoming

Two red heads stood on the footpath along the road that led down to the high school. Neither could recall how they had come to be there, when the sun indicated noon and classes had been in progress for three hours.

They heard the muted roar as students emerged from the last of the morning classes to begin the lunch break. Their eyes instinctively looked that way and confusion showed in the look they then shared with each other. They realised then that they were not even wearing their uniforms, and the one-piece coveralls they did have on, were unfamiliar.

Wordlessly, they shared the belief that they had left home that morning, as usual, in plenty of time to get to their first class.

Home was only two kilometres back along the road, and they had walked that distance often enough in the past three years, to know exactly how long it took. They had walked that day, because their father, the school's deputy Principal, had needed to leave earlier than normal, to prepare for a seminar he was to attend that afternoon. Both the boy and the girl looked back towards their home and tried to recall what they had seen on the way.

Cars passed, travelling both ways along the road, but they couldn't even remember crossing the road at the traffic lights.

"Tim, Cindy," a voice called, making them turn back towards the school, and at two approaching boys.

The red haired boy, Tim, recognised the speaker and grinned with undisguised relief.

"Paul, Ed, are you skipping classes again?"

"Yeah, it's science next and after yesterday, we didn't want to be there. When Rogers returned after throwing you two out of class, he began picking on us," Paul explained. He then asked, "What did they do to you? Expel you?"

"No…" Tim answered as some memories began to stir sluggishly. "A two week suspension…"

"They brought in some kind of doctor to talk to us," Cindy added, slowly.

Paul studied her as he commented, "Yeah, they had some guy come in and talk to the class. Then Howard gave us a warning." He shrugged at Ed to indicate he meant both of them. "Uncanny he is. It was almost as if he knew that I would have liked to have punched Rogers myself."

"It's not as if that arrogant sot doesn't deserve it," Ed added quickly. "But I never expected you…"

Ed's face suddenly turned white and he said urgently, "Its Howard, he's coming this way."

Paul and Ed dragged the two red heads into a nearby garden and pulled them down behind a privet hedge.

None of the four made a sound, but somehow their school's principal, Howard, knew exactly where to stop.

"Mr Avery and Mr Jacobs," Howard said quietly, his voice carrying no further than the listeners.

Neither of the named students dared to pretend they didn't hear him. They knew that when the Principal used that very quiet tone, he was at his angriest.

Paul Avery and Ed Jacobs stood up and didn't even glance at the two who were still hiding. If Howard didn't know they were there…they wouldn't enlighten him.

"Come back to school with me, boys," Howard instructed.

If an observer had noted the red heads just then, they would have seen ashen white faces, and two crouched figures that were shaking.

They would not have known that Tim was recalling the sudden urge that had made him walk up to the science teacher and punch him in the face - and how incredibly satisfying it had felt, then. Now, it appalled him.

Cindy re-experienced the rage that had erupted within her mind when her brother had been bodily forced from the class. She could not understand what had caused it.

Neither wanted to go home, or closer to school - for surely their father, the deputy principal would be justifiably livid with them, for putting him in a thoroughly awful position.

"What did Dad say?" Cindy asked aloud, finding no trace of a memory in her mind. "I remember that doctor…"

Tim shook his head, as if trying to wake up. "I don't remember. I only recall Howard talking about suspension…"

There seemed to be something wrong with his memory.

"We should apologise to Mr Rogers," Tim stated abruptly. He stood and began to walk off.

"Yes," Cindy agreed. She felt the shakes ease as the need to act manifested. Rising, she began to follow her brother towards the school.

To the drivers of the passing cars, they seemed to be running.

Rogers pointed to an empty classroom after coming out of the staff room to talk to them. He carried a steaming mug of coffee in his other hand and followed the two students as he sipped it. Remembering the behaviour of the two red heads the previous day, he left the door open and leant against the doorframe.

He listened as Tim apologised, and read the sincerity in the flushed face. He saw how pale Cindy was, but she insisted on meeting his eyes as she added her own apology.

"I didn't expect to see you today," Rogers commented. "Your father said he was taking you out of school until the end of term. I am impressed that you felt so strongly that you had to come here."

Hoping to learn more, the teacher asked, "Have they given you some kind of medication?"

When he saw their identical shrugs, he decided that someone else needed to take charge of them.

"I accept your apology, but I think you should go and wait in your father's office and let him take you back home."

Tim nodded, agreeing. His memory was full of blank places. "We will," he said, glancing at his twin and moving to leave the room. Rogers stepped aside to let them past.

Once away from the teacher, he shared with his twin his relief that they had completed the difficult interview and the awareness that the teacher was still watching them. The feeling of being watched ceased when they had entered the deputy principal's office.

Dan Ward's office was unoccupied, and in fact, it did not look as if he had been at work that day.

"He was going to work today, wasn't he?" Cindy asked as she collapsed into the chair in front of the desk.

Tim moved the spare chair beside her. "Yes, that's why we had to walk today…"

All the days they had walked to school were blurring into one. However, the memories of attacking their teacher were so fresh as to have just happened.

In the process of sitting down, Tim heard the office door open, and the Principal's voice speaking from out in the passage. They both stood up and quickly moved to stand close to the bookcase, near the door.

"We can talk in here, Tamir," Howard said to someone following him. He entered the room, and a tall, lean man followed. The stranger was wearing an odd looking, but very elegant grey suit.

Howard closed the door and gestured the stranger to a seat. He sat himself behind Dan Ward's desk and the tall stranger sat on the seat Cindy had hastily vacated. Neither noticed the twins standing like statues by the door.

"What is so urgent as to bring you here, Tamir?"

"I need to speak to Vincent," the man said in a voice as soft as Howard's. "I tried to call him but got no answer. That science group in the centre are starting on a dangerous line of investigation. We need to get someone in to watch them. I can't do it."

"Vincent had to go home," Howard explained. "I will send one of our other missionaries to investigate. Is there something else bothering you?"

"When will he be back? I want him to look at my wife. She's sick and the human doctors can't find anything wrong," the tall man sounded desperate. "I think she might be pregnant as well."

"I cannot say when he will," Howard admitted with sympathy. "He needed to go home with two of the students from the school here. They were in a dangerous stage of transition. I will have him get in touch as soon as he gets back. Is there anything I can do?"

The man shook his head.

Cindy watched as the man rubbed his face with long elegant hands as if trying to scrub away his concern. His face was narrow, his hair dark but showing streaks of grey. He would be handsome without the worry pinching his features.

She glanced at her brother and mouthed, "They can't see us. It's as if we're ghosts."

"Paul and Ed saw us. So did Rogers," Tim whispered faintly.

Cindy shrugged them away. This time she spoke aloud to prove her point. "Howard didn't know we were with Paul and Ed, and he can't see or hear us now." She was watching the Principal and he didn't even twitch. She went on, "He said that Vincent had taken two children somewhere. That was us."

They both stopped talking when Howard escorted his visitor from the room.

"I remember," Tim said, shaking off his confusion. "They took us to Tymorea. We don't belong in this time. We are not meant to be here now. That is why Howard couldn't see us."

Suddenly, they recalled who they were - Great Ones, no longer ignorant of their heritage - not the naive children they had been then.

"This is not reality. I am Kryslie, you are Tymos…"

It was as if that realisation was the key to a powerful force. They suddenly felt themselves plucked from the office of a century before and dragged into a whirlwind of blurred images. This time, they did not forget who they were as their bodies endured the buffeting of travelling to another time and place - to another tomorrow.

Chapter 9 - Suspicious strangers

Kryslie rolled as she felt solid ground under her. Tymos lay sprawled out where he had landed. They were both in the centre of a recently harvested field, where the stubble had not yet been removed. Looking around, there was nothing that Kryslie recognised, nor did she sense any other people close by. Feeling safe, she pushed herself into a sitting position, and found that her clothes were covered in black soil. She tried to brush it off, but it simply smeared on the clothes and dirtied her hands.

"Any idea where we might be, Tym?" Kryslie asked her brother once he began to look functional rather than stunned.

Tymos looked around and shrugged. "We're not still at school, that's for sure!"

"Obviously! But that was so real. Were we really there?" Kryslie asked.

"It sure felt like we were, at least at first," Tymos considered. "We were almost at school, at a place we often stopped, even if we didn't remember getting there. It was like how we came to be here. Paul and Ed were always skipping classes. And we wanted to apologise to Rogers..."

"So, was it an illusion or delusion based on unfinished business?" Kryslie persisted.

"Perhaps in part," Tymos decided. "But there were moments when I felt what I was seeing was wrong. What settled it was Tonos not seeing us. If we had been there in reality and were unconsciously shielding ourselves with our power – I am sure he would have known we were there anyway."

"I didn't feel any different to what I had been like then," Kryslie admitted. "Now, I know I am not that child self anymore."

"So do I," Tymos agreed. "It could be like the Elders reasoned – we had vivid memories of that time and that influenced where the transporter took us."

"We certainly weren't thinking of this place - wherever it is. But..." Kryslie paused to catch an elusive thought. "Last time we didn't go where we were meant to – it wasn't our doing. In this case, I think the Guardians sent us back to that time. The beam we were using was set to take all of us and our packs. There was no need for us to think of our destination. We could have been a crate of supplies for all the effect we would have had. We already know time isn't a barrier to the Guardians...so perhaps they were letting us finish things..."

"No!" Tymos shook his head. "It wasn't for that. Remember the man with Tonos? His name was Tamir. And there was something about watching a science group somewhere and a sick wife."

"Tamir Janzoet!" Kryslie exclaimed. She was thinking of a lost opportunity to talk to the man.

"I think, for some reason, they wanted us to witness that conversation," Tymos stated with confidence. "I can't think why, yet."

"I am sure this is not where our base is going to be," Kryslie said with equal confidence. She gave her surroundings another sweeping inspection. "So this time will be real until..."

"We've seen something..." Tymos added.

"Or done something," Kryslie finished.

"Well, we can't stay here," Tymos noted. "We need to clean ourselves up and find something to eat."

"My brother is ruled by his stomach," Kryslie teased as she stood up. A loud grumble in her own belly betrayed her agreement. "I would like to change clothes, but what ever brought us from the transport ship, didn't think to bring our packs."

A group of twelve men, several armed with shotguns, approached the riverbank. They were forming a loose semi-circle about two strangers who were asleep in a patch of sun and wearing dark brown jumpsuits that looked nothing like current fashion and were reminiscent of prison garb. Only the difference between the two people was the length of their red hair, which suggested that one was male and the other female.

Kryslie woke, suddenly aware of the so far silent men closing in. She touched her brother and spoke to his mind. "We are being surrounded, Tym."

By the angle of the sun, they hadn't been sleeping very long, maybe an hour, but she was not as tired as she had been.

She rolled off her back so she could face the men. Tymos followed her movement but neither started to stand up. The weapons of the few that were armed were pointed at them and the wielders looked ready to shoot.

Kryslie glanced at each man in turn and then met the implacable gaze of the only one who was wearing a uniform.

"Who are you?" the policeman snapped.

"My name is Tym," Tymos said quietly.

"Krys," Kryslie said in turn.

"What are you doing here? It is private property."

"We needed a drink and to get clean," Kryslie told him without making a move to sit up. "And we were tired."

The angle of the weapons lowered a fraction.

"Where have you come from?" the policeman asked in a less hostile tone.

"We've been travelling around," Tymos claimed. "We used to live in North Box Hill – if that means anything to you."

"How long have you been here?"

"Long enough for you to gang up on us," Kryslie said, sounding annoyed. "We haven't done anything wrong, so why the guns?"

"I'll have no smart cracks from you, young woman!" the policeman insisted. "Do you have any identification?"

Since their packs, which had contained simulated Earth style identification, had not travelled with them, the short answer was, "No."

"Well, then, you can come with us and talk at the house."

Tymos and Kryslie stood up, knowing all the eyes were on them. They made pretence of brushing dirt and leaves from their clothes to give themselves time to think.

"I don't like this, Krys," Tymos communicated silently. "These men are suspicious of shadows. They have a lot of questions in their minds and until we know when and where we are – we won't be able to answer them. I think a retreat is called for."

"I agree," Kryslie told him. "Even though it will increase their suspicions of us."

"Let's go," the policeman insisted.

Just as two of the unarmed men reached out to take an arm of each of the strangers, they ducked and ran off. The group of men were left gaping at their speed. In moments, even though they gave chase, the strangers were lost to sight in the pear orchard that extended almost to the river.

Once within the trees, Tymos and Kryslie slowed. They hadn't gone far, just enough to be out of casual sight. Instead of running further, they stood next to one of the trees and remained very still, cloaking themselves with power drawn from the energy aura of the living things around them. The men were still in range and Tymos and Kryslie were sensing their thoughts. The minds of the men seemed to be shouting their disbelief at how fast the strangers had run.

"That was a mistake!" Tymos confessed. "I had forgotten that we would be a noticeably faster now than we used to be."

"So had I," Kryslie admitted in turn. "And it seems we have frightened the men even more than they were already. Did you pick up that series of pictures in the policeman's mind? The people he had encountered that had acted violently?"

"Yes, and something about animals," Tymos mused. "When we allow ourselves to be found, we could say we were frightened because we had been chased into that field and lost our belongings somewhere."

"I dislike lying, but I think there is a mystery here we need to solve. We won't be able to do that if we cannot move about freely," Kryslie told her brother.

"True. We will have to convince the locals we mean no harm...Krys! Behind you!"

Kryslie turned quickly, hearing a savage snarl. She saw a huge dog leaping directly at her. Its mass should have knocked her down, but she stood firm, one arm raised to protect her face from its slavering jaws. Her free arm knocked the beast aside, so that its leap was diverted and it fell against one of the pear trees.

Kryslie trembled with reaction. "That dog's mind was tampered with. Whatever or whoever did it felt alien to this place. I felt like I had a jolt of electricity when I touched it."

Tymos leant down and touched the dog. As it started to rouse, it whined softly in pain, but licked his hand.

"There is nothing abnormal about it now," Tymos told her. "But if this is an example of how people are affected..."

"Then we have the power to help them. Maybe we are the ones who must find the cause and neutralise it," Kryslie proposed. "I feel really weak right now and I can't seem to draw power from around me."

"Why don't you sit down then?" Tymos suggested. "Those men are not far away and searching for us. They will probably find us about dusk. I'll hang onto the dog, and look concerned for you. I think they will believe we have had an awful fright...even though this fellow is no more vicious now than I am. He's hurting from landing against the tree, but I can heal him. Do you want me to do the same for you?"

Kryslie shook her head. "Save your energy, in case we need to act later. I will feel better soon enough, even without drawing on the energy aura. Heal the dog. I didn't intend to injure him."

When the men appeared, they saw Tymos restraining the dog and trying to check his sister. The dog was growling softly at the approaching men.

Tymos obeyed the command to stand up, but he did not release the dog.

"My sister can't," he told them. It was nearly the truth. "The dog jumped at her and knocked her down. It was growling and slavering before, but now it seems like a normal dog. I don't understand it."

"Looks like Fred's dog," one of the men commented. "It's been missing a week or so. Kip! Here boy."

The dog stopped growling and gave a happy bark. Tymos released it and it ran to the man who looked it over, not missing the dried saliva around the dog's mouth and below on its chest.

"Are you going to come with us, quietly, or do you intend to run off again?" the policeman demanded.

He glanced down at the red haired woman, lying on the ground with her eyes closed.

"I can't go anywhere without Krys," Tymos pretended to be both worried and resigned. "Where would you be taking us?"

"To the local police station," was the implacable answer.

"Could you have a doctor look at my sister? She was knocked out for a bit," Tymos asked.

"We'll do that," the policeman agreed. He gestured to one of the men to carry the woman, and took a firm grip on Tymos's arm and urged him to move.

"Look, I'm sorry for running off. We thought you were another lot of gun happy vigilantes," Tymos told the policeman, but his escort did not comment.

Tymos didn't try to break free, but did twist to see his sister being carried in a fireman's hold and knew she was still pretending to be unconscious.

The men walked through the pear orchard to a dirt road. Across the road was a field of yellow flowers that stretched quite a way. They followed the dirt road to the main road where Tymos knew the men had vehicles parked. The grip on his arm remained firm. The policeman still had suspicions of him.

Back at the cars, Tymos was told to hop into the back of a Nissan four-wheel drive police vehicle. Moments later, Kryslie was gently helped in beside him. She had decided to become conscious, and thus make it easier for the man to lift her in. Tymos supported her as she sat next to him.

The policeman climbed into the driver's seat and one of the men was in the front passenger seat, and in a position to watch the two in the back seat. At least the guns were no longer in evidence.

Tymos used the short trip to feed power to his sister, and comment mentally, "I can draw energy from around me."

Krys thought back, "I'll try again later. It is probably a temporary problem, and possibly from that zap from the dog. And I do have a headache."

Tymos stayed quiet during the ride. He wasn't surprised when the car was driven into a driveway next to a building with a lit Police sign. When he was told to get out, he did not expect to be directed to the house beside the station building.

Kryslie was being carried again, as they approached the house. The policeman wasn't holding him anymore, and he had gone ahead to open the door and turn on a light. He ushered Tymos inside, and kept the door open for the man carrying Kryslie.

Tym glanced around, as a smartly dressed middle-aged woman with neatly permed hair came to meet them.

"Who do we have here, Melvin?" she asked, scrutinising Tymos and seeing Kryslie being carried.

"Tym Ward, Mam," Tymos answered for himself. "And my sister is Krys."

"Come through to the front room," the woman suggested. She had made her own assessment of the unexpected visitors.

Kryslie sank gratefully into a grey leather armchair. She thanked the man for carrying her.

Melvin turned to the man who had travelled with him. "Stan, tell Harry to take the dog and have the vet check it out before he returns it to Fred. Then go and tell Doc Drake to drop by here."

The man simply nodded, but gave the 'prisoners' one last glance before he left.

Tymos went and perched on the end of a leather couch, at the end nearest his sister.

Melvin watched them. The woman walked out through another door as the rest of the men they had seen near the river entered the room and took positions against the walls. They all stood with arms crossed and eyes on the strangers.

Tym glanced around at them, they all seemed like farmers, but all were equally determined to find out about the strangers.

Krys had closed her eyes again, but Tym knew her mind was searching for clues to help them.

"The newspaper is dated July 2015," she mentally told her brother. "We are still in Australia."

The policeman pulled up a chair for himself and faced his 'guests'. He crossed his arms across his chest.

"I am Senior Sergeant Holborn," he formally introduced himself. "I need to ask you some questions and as long as you co-operate, I will keep this on an informal basis. I will have a man taking notes."

Tymos nodded, not daunted by the silent watchers, but not taking the implied threat lightly. Lies and evasions would not be tolerated, because these men were worried. They hoped the strangers could throw some light on some of the strange happenings they had been fighting blind for far too long.

"I want honest answers and I will be checking what you tell me. If I find out you are lying, I will have to detain you pending further enquiries."

The Sergeant's wife re-entered the room with a tray of hot drinks and a fleeting look of distaste on her face at the mention of being detained. It was accompanied by a fleeting thought of how prisoners were treated at the regional detention centre. She handed everyone a cup of coffee. Tymos put his on the table, and Krys made no move to take the one placed beside her.

"I don't know that we can help you much," Tymos said politely, deciding to take control of the questioning. "Like I said, we've been travelling around a lot since we left school."

"Convenient," one of the men challenged.

"Is there anyone who can vouch for you?" Holborn asked. Tym shook his head.

"We used to live with our grandfather, but he's dead. And I can't show you any ID because I have no idea where our stuff is. I feel like I have been running for two days."

"So what happened to you?" Holborn asked. He gave no sign of whether he believed Tymos or not.

"We were walking along the main road when a group of people, not much older than ourselves, surrounded us. Some of them had guns. They started pushing us around; some of them grabbed our backpacks and dragged them off us while others held us. They dumped all our stuff onto the ground and looked through it. I don't know what they were looking for but when they tried to drag us into the trees, we decided cowardice was called for and we struggled free and ran off. We hid in a field for the afternoon and then went down to the river."

Kryslie surprised everyone by speaking. "You frightened us, earlier, surrounding us with guns drawn. What did you think we would do?"

"We were not taking chances," Holborn admitted. "We have had strangers through before and when approached they have been violent."

"So what has been going on around here?" Kryslie demanded.

One of the men in the silent ring spoke up. His thoughts were in turmoil.

"Our children have been turning violent at the slightest provocation. The younger ones have been wandering off and later returning with no memory of where they have been."

"I see," Tym said softly, and he did have a better picture of the strange happenings from the minds of the men in the room. "Have there been other incidents involving animals, like the one that jumped at Krys? Have adults been affected?"

"Adults...no," Holborn said looking thoughtfully at Tymos. "Some other animals have had to be destroyed."

"Seems to me that the cause of this is selective," Tym suggested. "Have you tried to find any patterns in the events?"

"We can only say for certain that different age groups have shown certain behaviour changes," Holborn admitted, deciding to see what Tym was getting at. "What sort of patterns are you thinking about?"

"Variations on the obvious," Tym said thoughtfully. "Something like – if the children affected come from town families or farming families. Do they come more from the say the west of town or the north, south or east. Are incidents confined to certain groups or random? In a group is one affected or all of them. Can you find out from friends or relatives where the affected ones have been, were going, or normally spend their time. Are changes are gradual or sudden and when and where the people were when it happened. Are some children affected more frequently than others?”

Most of the audience was astounded at the logic of what Tymos had just proposed.

“If you put all those details together, a pattern might emerge and you might be able to locate the source of the problem,” Kryslie added. Her soft voice sounded loud in the silence of the room. “You might also, for our information, find out how widespread the problem is and tell us how many strangers or visitors to the district have been affected. Do you know when the events began happening?”

“Mel, are you going to let these kids take over?” one of the older farmer types growled.

Tymos stood and faced that man that had spoken. “We are not kids!”

There was no mistaking the aura of self-confidence in his stance.

“Steady down,” Holborn urged. He was looking at his two ‘guests’ and saw something in their manner that reminded him of some of his superiors. He promptly forgot the rest of the questions he had intended asking. The opportunity to solve the problem that was breaking the town apart was foremost in his mind.

“They have offered constructive suggestions,” Holborn pointed out. “We would be foolish not to act on them. All of you go home and get some rest. Tomorrow, we will start visiting everyone in town and work out to the farms. John, will you contact the other squad leaders and tell them to assemble their teams here in the morning. I will have a plan of action worked out by eight.”

The men dispersed, but Holborn continued to scrutinise his visitors closely.

“I don’t know who or what you are,” he said carefully. “And you have told me very little that I can use to check your identity. What you have told me has the feel of a quickly fabricated tale. It implies you have something to hide.”

Neither Tymos nor Kryslie reacted.

“So perhaps you would like to tell me more about yourselves?”

Holborn had the strangest feeling that the two young adults were communicating with each other. He’d caught the faintest hint of movement, as if they had started to glance at each other and stopped.

Kryslie spoke softly.

"Grandfather's name was Daniel Ward. He lived in North Box Hill, Victoria. Out Father's name was Tim Ward, and he was still at school when we were born. I doubt that our mother was much older. Grandfather used to teach at the high school, until he got left holding the babies – literally. We were born about 1996."

"That's much better," Holborn told them. He still sensed they were hiding something.

"I hope I can find something to corroborate your story, because if I can't I will be constrained to hand you over to the federal authorities and they will find out what you are hiding."

"Why?" Tymos demanded, challenging his gaze.

"This area is under investigation by more than the police," Holborn told them. "National security is involved."

Kryslie nodded. That made sense. "You have evidence against us."

Holborn glanced pointedly at their clothes. "Ever been in trouble with the police?" he asked sharply.

"No!" Kryslie said immediately, her gaze never leaving his face. "And we have no intention of starting now. We are here, because we chose to be here. If you try to take us where we don't want to be – we won't stay there!"

Holborn was not intimidated by her threat.

"You are not used to authority," Holborn commented. "In this town, young people respect their elders."

"We don't disrespect authority, Sergeant," Kryslie told him bluntly. "We do have a problem with people who see that we are young and expect us to know nothing. We don't intend to antagonise anyone but if people can't accept us as we are, it's their problem. If you could use our help, we would be pleased to offer it."

"Well, now that we have that in the open, let's call a truce. You can stay here with my wife and I until this business is over or your story checks out. It is a civil way of requesting that you don't choose to disappear. Do we have a deal?"

Kryslie shrugged, not committing herself to an answer, but at that moment Mrs Holborn, the woman with he permed hair, returned to the room escorting a tall man carrying a black bag.

"Drake," Holborn greeted civilly. "Thanks for coming. This young woman was knocked out for a short time earlier this evening. Fred Evan's dog leapt at her. I want to be sure there are no hidden problems."

"What about the dog?" Drake asked.

He placed his bag on the chair Holborn had just vacated.

"Apparently back to normal. Harry Coles is to take it to the vet to be checked."

Drake nodded and turned to Kryslie, who agreed to be examined.

Holborn, his wife and Tymos left the room.

"Have you had anything to eat?" Mrs Holborn asked Tymos.

"No, Mam," Tymos admitted. "Except some windfall pears this afternoon." The mention of food made his stomach growl.

"I will fix you something then," Mrs Holborn promised. "Would you prefer something other than coffee to drink?" She had noticed that his drink hadn't been touched.

"Water, thank you," Tymos muttered, following Holborn through to another room. This one looked like an office.

The doctor checked Kryslie's pulse and breathing, and then her ears and eyes. She had admitted to a headache and tiredness. He put antiseptic on the scratches on her hand that had been made by the dog's claws.

"How do you feel now?" he asked her.

"The headache is going, but I feel shaky. Not as bad as earlier."

"When did you last eat?" the doctor asked her. Krys mentioned the pears, but the doctor wasn't put off by that. "And before that?"

"Yesterday," Krys admitted quietly.

"I see," the doctor commented thoughtfully. "Well, I can't find anything wrong that a decent feed and a night's sleep won't fix. Stay off coffee tonight, and drink some water."

Holborn left Tymos in his study, eating away at a pile of sandwiches, to go and talk to the doctor. He went out into the passage and closed the door.

"What did you find?"

"She is in excellent physical shape, basically clean, except where the clothes don't cover. I think all she needs is a good night's rest and a decent meal."

"That's what I thought too," Holborn said. "Thanks Doc." He saw the doctor out and returned to where Kryslie was resting.

"Come join your brother before he finishes all my wife's sandwiches."

Late that night, after Tymos and Kryslie had eaten and gratefully gone to sleep on the two camp stretchers in Holborn's spare room, Grace Holborn joined her husband in his study.

The Sergeant was creating the promised action plan for the morning. He was happy enough to stop a while to get his wife's impression of his guests.

"I can't say I have met anyone like them," Grace Holborn admitted. "I heard them talking to you, forceful and strong willed, but they were polite to me. They made me feel special."

"Have you seen anything like their clothes?" Holborn asked.

"No, but they would be very hard wearing and utilitarian," Grace decided. "I said I'd wash them, but the water just rolls of the fabric. I haven't seen anything like it. What are you doing about checking on them?"

Holborn sensed his wife was not in agreement with his intentions.

"I've rung Sydney and asked them to talk to Melbourne. By rights, I should have contacted the Federal Authorities. They have no ID and no one to vouch for them. I'm supposed to report all strangers."

"Why haven't you?" Grace asked.

Holborn shrugged. It wasn't a rational reason, but the boy had proposed some workable options to help solve the puzzle that he hadn't managed to solve.

"I don't see those two as terrorists or whatever they think they are looking for," Grace persisted.

"I don't want to think so," her husband admitted. "That boy had some excellent ideas, but I spoke to all the regional officers in the surrounding districts. I asked about hikers and backpackers – none of them have heard of, or seen, our guests. They have orders to look out for strangers too and they get reports from all the hostels and camping grounds. It is almost as if those two young folk arrived on Tom's property from nowhere."

"Perhaps they did," Grace suggested, causing her husband to stare at her.

"That is preposterous! Ridiculous! It is more likely they sneaked into town."

"Maybe, maybe not," Grace countered. "Strange things happen. You have an excellent record for apprehending human offenders – but in three years, you are no closer to solving the cause of the evil things happening around here."

"Are you actually implying that the cause is not human?"

Grace merely shrugged. "I am simply saying that Tim and Chris are unusually intelligent and have offered to help you. That may be why they are here. So what if they are hiding things about themselves. They may not be at liberty to tell you everything, but that does not mean what they are hiding is criminal."

"If they are government agents, why don't they say so?" Holborn settled on a logical explanation and shied away from implications that his guests were aliens or something. Drake had noticed nothing odd about the girl. He tried not to think about how fast they could run.

"Alright, I will accept them for what they appear to be unless I hear back from Melbourne with information I can't ignore. Any hint of criminal activity or associates and I will have to notify the federal authorities."

His wife accepted that decision, certain in her own mind that her guests were not bad people. She left her husband assembling a list of questions for the townsfolk to answer.

Tymos and Kryslie were awake early, but they didn't appear for breakfast until after the last of the squads had departed and Holborn himself had gone.

They thanked their hostess for the spare clothes she had found for them, chatted politely on general topics, steering away from current news events as they had no idea of them. After they had thanked her for breakfast, they told her they were going to try to find their packs and belongings.

Grace Holborn had no instructions to stop them, or report their movements.

Tymos had been noting the route they had travelled to the police station, and now he led the way back to where Holborn had found them. From there, they retraced their movements on foot, being careful to keep their pace to a normal running speed. Back at the orchard, they looked for tracks of the dog and followed them. The soft ground of the orchard showed the marks clearly. The dog had come from the direction of the river. The ground along the riverbank was more solid and the tracks were harder to see. Still, their keen eyes saw other evidence of its passage – fur on brambles, the discolouration of dog urine on trees and broken bits of bushes.

At first, they followed the river, then when farmland gave way to forest, the tracks entered the trees. Thinking they were out of sight, and with their concentration on the task, they had set themselves, they did not realise that they were trotting faster than most people could run.

They were seen by some locals who were already frightened, and were suspicious of anything not quite normal.

Tymos mentally plotted the route they were following, and used the position of the sun to estimate time and distance. The dog's tracks emerged from the thicket of trees and then vanished suddenly in the middle area of clear ground.

Kryslie looked around, memorising landmarks, so they could recognise the place again. Her attention was caught by a group of horsemen, heading towards them at a fast trot. The open area was on a hill that overlooked the town.

"Company," Krys thought at her brother. She passed the image of the riders.

They took off at a trot towards the cover of the forest. Once there they zigzagged through the trees until they came to the edge of town. As soon as they reached that point, they slowed their pace to a purposeful walk and returned to the Sergeant's house. They had been gone only three hours.

Holborn returned mid-afternoon and found his guests working in the police station back yard, removing grass and weeds from between the stones of the driveway. He grunted a greeting and went into the police station.

Reports from some of the squad leaders had come in and Holborn began to glance through them. He was pleased by the degree of detail but was soon overwhelmed.

He read a report of two people who were running incredibly fast along the riverbank - red heads wearing brown clothes. He had no doubt who they were. With a faint smile, he put that report aside – he would challenge his guests later. They had told his wife they were looking for their belongings along the road on the opposite side of town from where they were seen and nowhere near the hill where they were the horse patrol and lost them.

When Holborn crossed to the house for his dinner, he had the reports with him. He placed them on the table next to him, and told his guests, "I have a couple of reports that neither of you will wish to ignore."

He turned his attention to his dinner of roast meat and vegetables, but was aware of the looks of puzzlement on the two faces opposite him.

"What's his game?" Kryslie thought at her brother while chewing on a roast potato. "He is blocking me, by not thinking about what is in those reports. I wonder how long he can keep it up."

"Long enough," Tymos thought back, as he too concentrated on eating. "Have you found any patterns yet?" he asked aloud.

"Yes, I have. I began sticking pins in a map to mark the position of reported incidents. So far, they fall in a roughly circular area, roughly twelve kilometres in diameter. There is a central area in a hilly section of state forest that is clear and a ring around that where most of the incidents occur, an outer ring with fewer incidents. The area covers two towns and numerous small farms."

"And those reports you mentioned?" Tymos asked casually.

"Read them at your leisure," Holborn invited, nodding at the folder that was just out of their reach.

Tymos and Kryslie continued to eat their meals, and hid their interest in what was in the reports. They kept their conversation to a minimum after that and spoke mainly to Grace Holborn. Both sensed that Holborn knew they were pretending disinterest and were ignoring his subtle provocation.

Finally, Kryslie stood and collected the folder. She scan read the reports of the two suspicious acting red heads, and passed the folder to her brother. Holborn was watching them closely and saw their expressions harden. In no other way did they betray their thoughts.

"You were correct, Sergeant," Tymos remarked neutrally. "Thank you for bringing this to our attention."

Kryslie thought to her brother, "We will have to be more careful."

Tymos thought back, "Why don't you offer to help the Sergeant? His wife has asked me to help her move some heavy things."

"Would you like some help analysing your data, Sergeant?" Kryslie said with a pleasant smile on her face.

Holborn would have liked to quiz his guests about the reports, but decided to wait a while.

"Yes. You had some good ideas last night. I'll see what you come up with now. Come on then."

Kryslie followed him when he stood up to return to his office in the station building.

Holborn's desk was stacked with neat piles of reports. There didn't seem to be much of the wood top showing. Krys glanced around and saw a computer on a side bench.

"Why don't you use the computer?" she asked.

"I am a policeman, not a computer genius," he growled. "I have requested a police programmer, but he won't be here until tomorrow. I can't do anything until he has devised a program."

Kryslie smiled, liking how Holborn felt to her empathic sense. He was honest, just, and determined to solve his current problem.

"If you have no objections, I'll give that a go," Krys offered. She enjoyed the look of narrow eyed scrutiny Holborn gave her. "Do you have one of your blank incident sheets and your list of questions?"

Holborn sorted through a filing drawer beside his desk and handed her the requested sheets with a look of appraisal. He didn't ask if she was sure she could do it. He was going to wait and see.

Krys thanked him and went to sit at the computer. He went to his desk and began to read reports at random, but he was watching his guest. He noticed that she seemed to know how to get onto the system, after only a brief glance at the folder of manuals and the programs available.

Kryslie already had an idea of what she wanted her program to do, based on the data being asked for. It helped that the basic spreadsheet was standard – and that it had advanced data sorting capabilities. It also helped that it could be linked to a variety of other programs including a plotting program she could use in conjunction with a map of the area.

Soon, her fingers were rapidly typing on the keyboard and occasionally clicking the mouse. Holborn stared at her in disbelief.

"Have you finished your work, Sergeant?" Kryslie asked without turning around.

It drew an involuntary, "No," from him, and he went back to reading reports and adding pins to his map. But he kept glancing her way, more than a little curious about what she was doing.

During the late evening, his squad leaders dropped in with more reports. Strangely, none of them seemed be aware of Kryslie working at the computer, even though they all stayed for at least five minutes. He made no mention of her, but he was still amazed at her concentration and stamina.

About five hours after she had begun, Kryslie announced, "That should do it."

She rose and turned to Holborn. "All your programmer needs to do is feed the data in. The program explains how. I have written a series of macros to help you sort data in various ways."

"Why don't you show me?" Holborn asked.

"Would you let me look at some of those reports the men brought in?" Krys asked.

Holborn handed her two from the top of the newest pile. Krys sat back down and explained how the information was to be entered and showed him how it could be plotted and otherwise sorted.

"Impressive," he was forced to admit. "Where did you learn advanced programming in your left school and travelled life?"

"Never mind!" Krys dismissed the question. "You are convinced we are odd balls. I'm just proving it. Though I would rather you didn't mention that I had anything to do with it or you might have the townsfolk hunting witches to your door." She turned to leave.

"Krys?" Holborn halted her with the gentle implied question. "What do you expect of me?"

Kryslie turned back. "Nothing. You should do your job. We will help where we can, but don't stand in the way of what we have to do."

At that moment, Tymos entered the office. "It's true," he said quietly. "What you are thinking. We don't belong here and we don't know how we came here. And we are strangers, suspicious strangers. We plan to maintain a low profile from now on, but there are still things we are discovering about ourselves that we haven't learnt to control or hide."

"What are you?" Holborn asked.

Tymos shrugged rather than admit the truth. "I think we can help sort your problem."

"Very well, I will accept that for now. Why were you up the hill?"

"Today, before the riders spotted us, we had tracked the dog from where you found us back to there." Tym pointed to a place on the map.

"The paw prints just suddenly appeared. We need to return there and look around. I think you will find that the place is on your inner circle," Kryslie added.

"We have a vague idea of what is behind all this," Tymos admitted. "Not enough to speak of yet."

"Could you share that much with me?" Holborn demanded.

"Not until we know more. It would be best if human agencies workout the cause," Tymos told him.

"Human agencies?" Holborn queried. "Are you implying you aren't?"

"Oh, we were born on Earth," Kryslie said carefully. "But we know things most people don't."

Holborn shook his head. It was too late at night to try to understand these two enigmas. They were plainly avoiding direct answers.

"I am calling it quits for the night and I suggest you both do the same," Holborn announced. "I also suggest you do any looking around in daylight.

We have an unofficial curfew around here. People out at night need to have a good reason for it."

He assumed his guests agreed, because they followed him back to the house without comment.

Holborn dropped off to sleep, but his sleep was disturbed by dreams in which he was hunting his guests. The reason in his dream was so perfectly logical. If he killed them all the rest of the district's problems would stop. Everyone in the town believed it. He woke in a sweat and felt immediately chilled as he recalled the dream.

"No!" he said to himself. "They are not evil! I don't care what the people think..." But he couldn't shake the dream.

He would have been more concerned if he learnt that his guests were not in their beds.

Chapter 10 - Alien Child

The police programmer only had to make minor modifications to the program. He was impressed by its intrinsic efficiency and the easily followed instructions.

He set to work entering the mountain of data already obtained, even as more was being delivered.

Tymos and Kryslie were not around when the programmer was working, but when he had returned to his motel at night, they visited Holborn and manipulated the data in different ways.

"It is so obvious!" Holborn berated himself. "I should have seen it years ago."

"Not really, Sergeant," Tymos told him. "You probably only heard of a fraction of this in your official capacity. And if you look at your map, the centre circle is in state forest. No major tracks cut through it and the fire trails are closed to four-wheel drive traffic, except in emergencies. Adults have no reason to be up there on most days due to their day jobs, and the off roaders will usually keep to the open tracks."

Kryslie commented on the other finding. "The not quite adults and the teenagers – if they are not at school or working, tend to wander all over. It is the ones that don't tend to stay near home that are affected most. They leave in the morning, say, as their normal selves, return later, argumentative or violent - the effects wearing off by the following day. Most of the incidents would be put down to adolescent touchiness, a bad mood or a fight with friends. The timing fits in with the victim's normal free hours."

Holborn had to agree.

To him, the most unexpected trend concerned the younger victims – the children that were not old enough to go far from home on their own. There were fewer incidents, but in each case, the children apparently wandered off, couldn't be found for some hours and returned with no memory of where they had been.

"The really odd thing," Holborn told his guests, "is that all the incidents with the younger children centre in a circle around the Grainger farm – or at least the children live near there or are known to play with Tammy Grainger. In quite a few instances, were last seen with him or were seen returning with him."

Grace Holborn walked in to talk to her husband. She heard the comment and asked, "Are you suggesting that ten year old Tammy Grainger is behind this?"

"No," Krys assured her. "He is most affected and as yet we don't know why. What do you know of him?"

"He is a right smart lad," Grace recalled. "A class ahead of others his age. He is looked after by a housekeeper. Not sure what became of his dad."

"Well, it may be he wanders more because he is less supervised," Krys suggested.

Tymos continued to point out other possible correlations for discussion until after Grace Holborn had retired for the night.

"This is all very interesting, and there are some clear avenues for investigation, but what is actually causing the behaviour changes?" Holborn finally asked.

"My guess," Kryslie told him. "Would be that the people are being affected by some kind of sub-audible or ultrasonic emanation."

"Really?" Holborn commented to hide his ignorance of such things. He promised himself to run the idea by Doc Drake in the morning.

"So what do you both think should be done now?" Holborn asked - just to see what they would say.

"Whatever your well trained police instincts suggest," Tymos shrugged. He was not going to tell Holborn how to do his job.

"Very well – what are you two planning to do?" Holborn looked and sounded every inch the no-nonsense policeman.

Kryslie grinned disarmingly. "We have already done some investigating on our own. Most of the past few days, we have been tramping around the line of that circle on your map. I mean that quite literally. There is meant to be a trig point on that hill and a fire track leading to it. You can see the trig point, but you can't get to it. Our eyes tell us we are walking toward it, but in fact we walked in a circle. There is nothing visible causing it."

Holborn didn't change his expression. "Go on."

"Later in the day, coming on dusk, we were heading back here when we saw some teenagers climbing the hill. While they were still uphill of us, they suddenly stopped as if paralysed and collapsed on the ground. After a few moments, they began to get up, clutching their heads. They began stumbling down the hill, but as one touched another, they began fighting." Kryslie reported.

Tymos added more. "On another occasion, when it was late evening, we saw a younger group approach that general area – they suddenly turned pale and fled. We approached that spot and were subjected to severe hallucinatory visions – dredged up from our own minds. We realised that they were being induced and ignored them, but still had to counter a strong irrational urge to flee. We kept pushing forward until we reached a point where we simply couldn't move forward any further. It seemed as if we had encountered a wall of solid air. It grabbed us and threw us away. We were okay, but decided to go back down the hill. We looked back up there and saw a shimmering wall."

"I think... I need to observe this for myself," Holborn decided. "I think – now would be an appropriate time. You'll come with me."

Neither Tymos nor Kryslie objected.

Holborn drove his police vehicle as close as possible to the top of the hill. That proved to be a kilometre from where he had thought to reach, because at that point the car suddenly lost power and stalled.

Refusing to be concerned, he left the car in the middle of the track and he continued on foot. He allowed Tymos to lead the way and didn't need to use the torch he carried for the moon was bright that night.

Tymos and Kryslie had not come to this point before, but it was on the same circle line that they had mentioned to the policeman.

It was not hard to tell when Holborn began to experience the hallucinations. He swore inventively.

Kryslie touched his arm gently. "It isn't real," she told him. "It isn't happening."

Holborn forced himself to continue and felt the need to run and fought a real battle to stay. Tymos went ahead and stopped when he sensed the final barrier. He broke a slender branch off the nearest tree and poked it.

"I hope you believe me that the last barrier is here," Tymos told Holborn. "I don't think you should try to touch it."

Holborn, however, insisted. He felt something grab him and hold him immobile. He felt an incredible pain shoot through his head before he was thrown backwards. He came to his senses with Kryslie massaging his neck.

"Oh my head!" he groaned. "Don't stop the massage. It's helping."

"Where is the pain worst?" Kryslie asked quietly.

"Across the front of my face, above the eyes," he told her, and she moved the massage there.

In a few moments, the pain had receded.

"Let's get out of here," Holborn directed, pushing himself to his feet.

Tymos led the way back to the car and was sufficiently far ahead to push it a few feet backwards and not be noticed.

When Holborn caught up and climbed into the car, it started with no trouble. They returned to the police station at a slower than normal speed. By then, it was well past midnight.

Kryslie put her hand on Holborn's arm, subtly distracting him from getting out of the car.

"We also watched Tammy Grainger. He had two friends with him who seemed to be in a trance, and he took them as far as that last barrier. They stayed there while Tammy kept going."

Holborn simply nodded, unhappy about that report.

"What do you think you will do?" Tymos asked.

"I'll have to call in the army," he decided. "They have more chance of dealing with this than I have."

"You are right," Tymos confirmed. "Now, you need to listen carefully…"

Holborn nodded again, not aware that these young strangers were about to give him instructions that he would later think were his own ideas.

"Tomorrow night, you will take a squad with you to patrol that area. You will see movement and follow. There will be no difficulty in identifying us; no doubt that we are acting suspiciously. Your men will be able to follow us to that last barrier if you warn them of what to expect. When they report on the shimmering barrier, you will call out the army. If they act promptly, they will be able to have their assault team here within two hours. By then we will have gone through the barrier."

"What must the assault force be prepared for?" Holborn managed to ask.

"To completely destroy the region at the centre of that inner circle on your map," Tymos told him without emotion.

"But – you will be killed!"

"We are not suicidal," Kryslie said with perfect calm. "But everybody in your squad must be convinced that we are part of this odd business already and will believe the same of anyone that can cross that barrier. They need to see tangible proof of the destruction or they won't believe that the evil is gone."

"Do you know the mastermind behind this?" Holborn asked to delay thinking about the implications of what had just been proposed.

"That is not important," Tymos said quietly. "If this is some secret government business, the army high ups will know and will not issue orders to destroy it. I do not believe that is the truth. We will deal with what we find behind the barrier."

Kryslie removed her hand from Holborn's arm and allowed him to leave the car. He seemed to have forgotten the conversation he had just been part of. She and Tymos slipped quietly away to the Holborn's spare bedroom and waited until all was quiet before walking to Holborn's study. There they composed a letter for the Sergeant that they would leave with his wife for after they were gone.

Tymos and Kryslie were not around the next day when Holborn prepared for his intended night patrol. Before he went ahead, he spoke to his police superiors and voiced his conclusions of what needed to be done. They were going to contact the army and national security team and have them out there that night.

The mounted patrol was at its furthest point when movement was spotted in the bright moon light. In the open area, two figures were easily identified by the gleam of their red hair.

"What the devil are they up to?" Holborn muttered quietly, have completely forgotten the previous night's conversation.

"Thought those two were a bit shifty," one of the squad commented, as he patted his horse's neck. "I still can't get over how fast they can run."

"I haven't learnt anything about them to suggest criminal activity," Holborn cautioned. He did not mention that no one could find anything at all about them. He kept quiet about his belief that they were decent, law abiding citizens because right then they were acting very suspiciously. The two national security men voiced their own agreement - the two suspects were disobeying the curfew.

When the red heads began to run, he urged his squad to follow and the horses began to trot across the open area. Even then, the horses were not keeping up and they slowed even more when they reached the trees.

"There is a fork up ahead," Holborn told the national security agents. "It comes out just down the hill a bit. I will take half the squad there."

"We'll keep following the trail," one security agent decided.

The trail was wide enough for two horses side by side, but the leading horses stopped suddenly.

The rider of one used his handheld radio to report to Holborn. "They have stopped up ahead, crouching behind some bushes to watch something."

"Go closer on foot and watch what they do," Holborn instructed.

The two security agents dismounted, handing their reins to the next nearest riders. These two crept forward with the stealth of hunters. The two fugitives seemed oblivious to their nearness and that from the rear they were visible.

The watchers found a position where they could observe their quarry and see down the hill where the others were watching. They saw, and Holborn identified, the small figure coming up the hill. It was Tammy Grainger. The policeman had the child in sight and watched him climbing up the hill to a point past his watchers. He had been alerted to a group of people following the child.

This group did not attempt to hide their movements. They were identified as the Grainger's housekeeper and her neighbour's two teenage boys.

At a point not far from the police watchers, the boys suddenly jumped back as if they had seen something frightening.

"We're outta here," one said, loudly enough to be heard. He turned to run back down the hill, followed by his brother. The woman watched them with obvious unease, but turned and continued determinedly up the hill. She went a further four steps before she suddenly froze and then fainted.

Tymos and Kryslie walked towards the woman. Kryslie squatted down and seemed to be checking the woman for a pulse, Tymos was glancing around, as if watching for anyone else that might see them.

When the woman began to stir, both of them went up hill after Tammy Grainger.

Holborn went to check the woman, as he followed the movements of the child and the redheads. Suddenly, a shimmering wall appeared in front of the child, briefly silhouetting him, before he disappeared into it.

The red headed pair ran quickly to that point and appeared to be trying to feel the barrier. Holborn sent two of his squad after the red heads, warning them of what to expect. They lost time as the effects were manifest, and when they had managed to overcome them, the red heads had disappeared through the barrier too.

The squad members didn't try to follow, but returned down to speak to Holborn.

"Exactly as you reported, Sergeant," the national security agents agreed.

"That's it then," Holborn said to himself.

"Those red heads must be part of it, to be able to pass that barrier," the agent went on.

"How else indeed," Holborn seemed to agree.

Inwardly, he didn't, and he had mixed feelings hearing the national security agent give the order that would mean killing Tym and Krys and Tammy Grainger.

"Help Mrs Hatfield down to her place," Holborn directed two of his squad. He watched them assist the woman, who was still a little dazed and unsteady. He had no doubt that Krys had eased the effect of the barrier for the woman as she'd done for him.

"John, call the other squads and have them move in around the hill. Tell them to stay below the safe line and apprehend anyone trying to come down the hill and detain anyone going up," Holborn directed. "Tell them to maintain radio watch – they will have ten minutes warning to evacuate when the army is about to bomb the hill."

He prepared himself for a long wait.

Tymos and Kryslie had not known what to expect when they walked through the shimmering barrier.

Nothing happened.

Tammy Grainger heard them behind him but although surprised, accepted their presence without question.

He went ahead to a tunnel that led into the hill. The far end of the tunnel opened into a huge chamber with equipment consoles around the rock walls. Several monitor screens showed the activity of the police. The lighting in this chamber was initially dim, but sufficient for the three that had just arrived to see clearly.

Tymos and Kryslie followed Tammy Grainger until he stopped moving and turned to stare at them. looking down, they saw that they stood within a circle etched into the stone at the centre of the cavern.

"Stop!" a powerful voice, challenged them. "Do not move or your life will be forfeit."

They could see no one else in the room, so obviously they were being observed from elsewhere.

A wall of a pale mauve light had sprung into existence around them. The energy powering it set up a resonance in them as if their blood was circulating much faster.

Tym looked at his sister and nodded. The sensation and colour of this screen had confirmed the thought that they had not mentioned to Holborn.

It was not a harmless force screen, and it would indeed kill a normal human – but it would not kill them. They both still wore their Tymorean personal force screens and their power would have protected them anyway. To demonstrate this they both walked through the wall of force and waited for the owner of the voice to notice. Tammy Grainger was no longer on sight.

"I see you are not ordinary human people," the broadcast voice noted after a moment.

Tymos sensed the closing of some door by the faint movement of air. The owner of the voice did not want them to escape.

"What do you want with me?" the voice asked calmly.

"We came to warn you that the people of this district will no longer tolerate the effects your force fields are having on them," Tymos thought as well as spoke. "At the moment they are preparing to level this hill."

The voice was silent for a time. "You caused that!" the voice accused. "So why come to warn me? Do you want to steal my research?"

Kryslie spoke up. "The decision would have been made soon anyway. We are warning you because we recognise the nature of the force fields, and that they are of Tymorean origin."

The lights in the chamber suddenly brightened and a man in a motorised chair wheeled himself in, with the child at his side.

"Who are you to say what I can and cannot do!" the man demanded.

"Tamir Janzoe – who do you think we are?" Tymos challenged.

The man in the chair paled, hearing his true name spoken by the intruders.

"How can you be here? No one remained and I haven't been able to call home for years..." He studied the two red heads. "You have the look of His Majesty, High King Tymoros..."

Understanding suddenly flooded into the scientist's mind. His eyes betrayed excitement.

"You are the two Vincent told me about! Is the trouble over? Can I go home?"

Kryslie went and crouched near the chair and spoke gently. "We are those ones. We were born here on Earth. I am Kryslie; my brother is Tymos. But no, it is not yet the time to return home. We were brought here to find you and we recognised the cause of what was happening outside here. There are flaws in some of the force shields – they are adversely affecting the humans who contact them." She described their observations and went on, "We could not permit you to continue your testing."

"No, indeed. I never intended such effects. However, since my accident, I have not been able to get out and see for myself, and Tammy is still very young. But you say the humans are planning to destroy here?"

"Yes," Tymos confirmed. "You will just have time to gather your work records together and any irreplaceable equipment and transmit away. Our future work on Earth depends on it. You must keep it safe for us."

"Prince Tymos... I am yours to command."

Tamir Janzoet would have knelt if he had been able.

"Then let us help you collect what you need," Kryslie told him.

"What of what I leave behind?" Tamir asked. "I can always rebuild the generators, but what if the people here find the machines?"

"Tell us how to disable them," Kryslie asked, and she listened intently.

Tammy Grainger was listening just as intently.

"But if this is all for you," the boy said, "You must take it when you go."

"Ah!" Krys said enlightened. "Tammy is your son!"

Janzoet nodded. "Yes, he is my one surviving child. But you haven't answered his question."

"We cannot take it with us. We are in transit ... out of our proper time... at the whim of the Guardians."

The scientist's eyes widened. He realised what that meant. "Great One..."

Kryslie halted his need to abase himself. "Yes, but we are not here to punish you, but to help you. Please, we need to leave here..."

"Yes, of course," he wheeled his chair abruptly around and began to issue orders to his son and his visitors.

Kryslie helped him collect all of his records into one container, whilst Tymos ensured that if any of the equipment was later excavated; it would not work, or its use be easily understood.

As Kryslie worked, she explained to Janzoet more of their circumstances.

"You probably know that we were born on Earth twenty local years ago," she began, "and we were taken to Tymorea when they realised we had Royal power. We are as you recognised, Great Ones. On Tymorea, the dreadful war is long past. The people are slowly recovering and rebuilding. We came to this world to begin the Earth Mission, but instead of arriving with the builders and missionaries, we found ourselves here. The Mission of which we are to be a part will not be arriving for another eighty or so years and contact between here and Home will not resume until then. In this time, back there, they are still in Dirakee."

Tamir nodded, realising that it would be unlikely that he could ever see Tymorea again. "What should I do now, Great One?"

"Just Kryslie," she told him. "Or Princess Kryslie. You need to get far from here if you want to continue your work."

Tymos passed through. "I'm done." He had heard the last comment and had what felt like a premonition.

"When you transmit away from here – you must become a gypsy. Move with them, be one of them and forget you are Tymorean for all but one day in a hundred. That is the only way you will be safe."

"There are no gypsies on this continent," Tamir told him.

"Look in other lands," Kryslie suggested. "Do you have a long-range beam generator?"

Tamir nodded. "I will do as you command, Great One. I still know the coordinates where the other missionaries had safe places."

Tymos wasn't finished. "Keep clear of the Mont De Ray tribe – they are doomed."

"Thank you, Great One, I will remember that. I will leave now. Tammy, are you ready?"

"Yes, Father."

Then the child spoke to the visitors. "I can understand your thoughts. You are not expecting to stay in this time reality much longer. When will you be back?"

"We don't know, Tammy. It could be many years. It is possible we are linked to you and your father, but even if not, we will contact you in the future," Tymos promised.

"I will wait to see you again and I will know you when I do," Tammy claimed.

"That is all we ask, apart from you keeping the work safe," Kryslie told him. "We will not have changed much."

"Are you leaving now? You seem to be fading."

Tymos had started to feel the pull of time rushing, but drew power from around him, dimming the lights, as he focussed his mind to stay. Kryslie with a similar effort remained beside him.

"Go now!" she commanded of the scientist.

"Can you help me move the trunk to the circle over there. I will activate a long-range beam."

Tymos obeyed at once, and Tamir moved his chair to be next to the trunk and his son stood close.

Tamir took out his personal transmitter and when the terminus of the long-range beam appeared, pressed the transmitter and the circle was empty.

Tymos and Kryslie felt a sense of urgency. They ran back along the tunnel, transmitted through the solid wall that Tamir had closed on it, ran downhill to the shimmering barrier, and stepped back through it. The hiss of incoming missiles alerted them, and they drew more power from around them.

The army had arrived within half an hour. Specially trained troops moved in and activated cellular surveillance cameras in a ring around the hill. Then all personnel, army, police and civilian retreated downwards. They did a sweep to ensure no living thing was near the designated ground zero area.

As this was being done, launchers were being assembled at strategic points to aim and fire the short-range missiles. The target zone was that area surrounded by the shimmering barrier.

Just prior to the attack, the local area was alerted via the emergency notification system. All people were advised to remain within their homes.

The police had reassembled at a point near the Grainger farm. Holborn had his wife come and be with the housekeeper who would be in a state of shock after she learnt of the events. He, himself, was observing the area where Tymos and Kryslie had disappeared, through night glasses borrowed from the army.

He could not share the eagerness of his men and colleagues, or the squads of locals, for the hill to be destroyed. They seemed to have forgotten that there was a child up there who, until yesterday was one of the townsfolk.

They did not care that the two red heads strangers would die. However, he knew that whatever they were, it wasn't evil. It was no comfort to see how right they had been. This was the only way the people around the town would believe the evil was gone. He certainly couldn't match Tym and Krys for courage.

In the moment just before the missiles landed, he saw two figures silhouetted against the barrier. When the glare of the explosion died down, the barrier was gone, and the top of the hill was no longer there.

As soon as the area was declared safe, Holborn hurried up to where the barrier had been. He was the first to reach what seemed like two bodies. The military doctor came up at his request.

"Dead all right," the doctor confirmed. "Killed instantly, I'd say. Funny thing though, there is no signs of injury on either body."

"Thank you doctor," Holborn forced himself to say. "I'll take it from here. I have orders to send the bodies to Sydney for proper identification. If any other bodies are found, I will need to be informed."

The doctor agreed with a wave as he walked off in the darkness. Holborn used his portable radio to summon a constable to drive his car up to him and to bring two body bags.

As he waited, he took a closer look at the bodies. He would swear they were now smiling. Irrationally, he touched Tymos and felt for a pulse — nothing of course. He was already feeling cold, but was not yet stiff.

Holborn wondered what to do. He had lied about having instructions to send the bodies to Sydney. He straightened and moved away to where he could watch for the constable. His mind kept returning to all the things Tym and Krys had said and done. He did wonder who they were, and regretted that they had died. They had been so sure they would not.

When he spotted his car coming up the track, he glanced back at the bodies and went cold all over. They were gone!

"Where do you want them, Sarge?" his temporary constable asked, referring to the body bags.

Holborn improvised quickly. "The army bods offered to take care of remains and send them on to Sydney. Who am I to argue? I've finished here. The officer in charge of the attack group will give us a report on what they find. Let's get back to town."

Grace Holborn woke in the early hours of the morning and found her husband was not in bed. She put on pink slippers and white dressing gown and walked to her kitchen. The milk and cake she had left in the fridge for her husband had been consumed and the glass and plate washed. Her husband may have been called out again, but she doubted it. The phone would have woken her.

She went to her husband's study and finding it empty, glanced into the front room, but it was deserted too. There had been no light in the bathroom, so she tried the only other room – the guest room. She found him there, still dressed, sitting on one of the camp stretchers. Both had been neatly stripped of bedding and everything had been folded and piled neatly on the end of the bed. The spare clothes she had found for her temporary guests were there too, clean and neatly folded.

Grace studied her husband; he was staring into space, or might have been asleep with his eyes open.

"Melvin?" she spoke softly.

Holborn looked at her. "I couldn't sleep."

"What happened tonight? I was allowed home before all the explosions."

"I called in the army. They flattened the top of Walters's Hill. There is nothing left of whatever was there."

"Did Tym and Krys go there? They said they were leaving but would be seeing you there."

"They were there." The flat tone was all the clue Grace needed.

"Where are they?" she asked urgently.

Holborn looked at his wife and said in a dead sounding voice, "They went up the hill following Tammy Grainger and they walked through that barrier after him. That kind of force field I told you about. They had just come back out when the missiles landed."

Grace sank onto the other stretcher bed looking pale and shocked.

"The military doctor said they died instantly."

"They are not dead!" Grace said suddenly.

It was her husband's turn to look shocked. "Grace, I was there."

She dug a letter from her dressing gown pocket, not remembering picking it up from the kitchen table.

"They left this for you but I read it." She pushed the envelope into his hand and stood up to turn on the light.

Holborn's fingers trembled as he took the two sheets of neat writing from the envelope and began to read.

"This is an apology, Sergeant," the letter began with no preliminaries. "We are sorry for making such an impression on you. It would have been easier if we had been horrible, but that is not our nature.

By now, everything in that centre circle of your map will have been destroyed. Everyone will be thinking that we were involved and no one but you and your wife will be regretting our demise. Please remember what we said. Everyone must believe that humans were behind the weird events and humans destroyed the cause.

It matters not, if we are remembered as villains. You may be assured that there will be no further incidents in this area or any other. That is what is important.

Now we must rely on conjecture and a very hazy vision of the future. We foresaw that you would be the one to dispose of our remains. If this is true, you will know that they didn't stay around to be disposed of.

We are placing our trust in a power much greater than either of us. By the time you read this, we will be in a time and place we can't predict. I hope that you can believe what we are saying and be relieved to know we are not dead because of an action of yours.

Thank you for your kindness to two strangers adrift in time."

"You were right, Grace," Holborn finally said. "They came from nowhere and they have moved on. The bodies did just disappear – but before then, they were smiling. They knew what would happen, and they went into it believing they wouldn't die. I have to believe they are alive somewhere."

Tymos and Kryslie had used their power to appear dead and the military doctor, being merely human, had not been able to see the betraying mauve glow of their hands. When he had gone, they relaxed, sensing only the friendly presence of Holborn. Immediately, they had felt the sensation of rushing time. The sergeant and the blasted hilltop faded from their perception.

The new scene had blasted buildings and there was an urgent awareness of danger.

Transition was not yet complete.

Chapter 11 - Psychic Captives

The sky was dark with thick clouds obscuring moon and stars. No artificial light illuminated the streets or revealed the stark horror of the bombed buildings.

Despite the intense darkness, Tymos and Kryslie walked silently along the streets of the ruined town, nimbly avoiding strewn rubble as if it were clearly visible.

Silence was as deep as the darkness. They walked, sensing danger coming closer to them. Without knowing what they were trying to hide from, they moved to opposite sides of the road and crouched down, using the rubble for cover. They each had a clear view along the road, perceiving their surroundings in differing shades of red and orange as individual objects re-radiated the day's heat.

The sense of danger had started when Tymos had thought at his sister, "I wish I knew what happened here."

Two bright orange humanoid forms came into Kryslie's view. Without even thinking the thought to her brother, he was aware of it and looked in the same direction. The figures came closer and stopped near to where they were hiding.

Very faintly, they heard a voice but it was too quiet to understand. The two orange figures looked around and separated. It seemed apparent that they too, could see well enough in the dark.

One stopped and raised a weapon, looking closely at the rubble where Tymos was crouched. Kryslie reached into her pocket and touched a metallic device - her personal transmitter. She teleported away as two weapons fired - one aimed at her from behind.

Tymos had not thought the weapon would work through the rubble, and when he heard the soft hum, he realised his mistake. "Run, Krys! Paralysis weapon."

"Gone!"

Tym, although paralysed, was still conscious. He saw the two men looking around and felt the thought, "There's another", pass between them.

Krys felt the thought too and switched to thinking in a different language. "Need help?"

"Not yet. Stay free," Tym thought at her, also in Tymorean. He was being lifted and carried to the edge of town and into the back of a van.

A thought, a rather odd thought, reached Kryslie's mind. She knew it was not from her brother, and it had a different quality from the terse thoughts of the two mysterious men. It was not in words. It was a picture of an undamaged church. No such building existed in this town now. All structures had been razed to piles of rubble.

Kryslie drew power from around her, now that she was well away from the men. The ambient energy tingled unpleasantly, but she could, and did, use it to create a field of distortion around her. Now, as long as she stayed still, she would remain undetected. This gave her time to recall the details of the town, things that she had noticed during her visual scan of the area during the afternoon.

When she and Tym had materialised on the outer edges of the town, strongly sensing danger, they had transmitted away to higher ground – the hills several miles away.

They had no trouble observing the town from there, for their visual range was equal to human using powerful binoculars. During their watch, they had seen nothing and no one moving anywhere.

Nor had they been able to identify the town. Earlier, when they were close, they had seen no signs of any kind. All they had been sure of was that the Guardians of Peace, for some unknown reason, were moving them around in time, wanted them there. To see something, or to do something. The unknown danger they had sensed gave them a focus for their attention.

Only when it had become dark, had they ventured down to explore the town ruins on foot and try to find out what had happened there.

The street plan of the town had not been completely obliterated. Kryslie knew not only where she was now, but where the church must once have stood. She had sensed, along with the image, the idea that she must go there for safety. That made her wonder who sent the thought at her and why. Of greater interest, was why the unidentified men had not sensed that particular thought.

Kryslie realised that it was the silent communication that she had shared with her brother that had betrayed them to these men. If these men could sense thoughts, she would not give them any more clues to her location. She refrained from thinking at her brother as he was transported along a road to the west. Instead, she considered fleetingly, that those who had captured him and were searching for her, could not detect her instinctive awareness of her twin. The deep twin bond would be their secret advantage.

As she stood unmoving, more of the orange humanoid figures seemed to be attracted to her position. One of them walked right past her where she pressed against the highest corner of a ruined building. That one was stopping every few metres to scan either side of the street. She was their target, and had some means of knowing that she was close by. Only her Tymorean power, controlling the distortion field, was hiding her.

Kryslie waited until that figure had turned a corner, and raced across the street and into a narrow alley. The walls abutting this path only came up to her waist. Keeping bent low, Kryslie scuttled along it. At the end, she crouched down behind more rubble and used her power to hide her again. She scanned this new area.

"Sector A3," came the terse and unemotional thought. Almost right away Krys saw two orange figures heading towards her. They were carrying weapons, long thin rodlike objects, raised to chest height, ready to be fired at any hint of movement. They, like the others, were scanning the sides of the road. They passed close enough to Krys for her to see they were wearing some kind of goggles. Once again, their sight passed over her hiding place and they moved on. They saw the narrow lane way and went into it, not needing to crouch down.

Kryslie waited for them to be well along it, before racing diagonally across the street and into another cross road.

"Sector A4, road 6."

Somehow, her movements were being observed. She decided to keep running in the direction of the ruined church, but stopped suddenly upon seeing one of the orange humanoid figures waiting near her destination. She had been seen, the figure saw her and raced towards her. Rather than transmitting away, which would be dangerous with all the orange figures suddenly appearing, Krys held herself still, fading into a semblance of invisibility. The figure slowed as he neared her position and began scanning the area. Whilst she stood there, two figures appeared behind her. She only knew of their presence from the hand signals given by the one she faced.

Moving very slowly, Kryslie looked around, judging distances and possible cover. She saw the outline of a doorway, inexplicably still erect, and serving no purpose. She did not have to be walking to transmit, and if she stayed still when she rematerialised she should not be noticed. It would be better than being in the middle of an open area. However, before she moved, she saw a child sized figure across the road where part of a building still stood. It may have once been part of the church, but the image in her head was only of the front door and the spire.

"Sector B4."

Three orange figures raced towards the small figure. The figure vanished suddenly as if it had entered an invisible door and closed it after.

Kryslie waited, immobile, while the attention was on that section of the ruins. It was more than five minutes before she heard in her mind, another of the terse directions.

"Sector C4."

The orange figures moved off away from her. She was amused at the game being played on them, even if it was a dangerous diversion. Krys transmitted to where the child-sized figure had seemed to disappear. She risked moving slightly to examine the structure.

"Come, follow, and think of nothing."

The unexpected thought startled Krys, but warned her so that the hand that gripped her arm did not make her react instinctively in defence. She was pulled gently through a door next to where she stood, and of which she had seen no sign. When the door closed behind her, Krys could only see a vague outline in faint red, of a person slightly shorter than herself. The grip never weakened on her arm as she was led slowly along a dark passage and down some stone steps. Reaching out her arm, she felt that the walls too were of stone. She felt the slight movement of air as another door was opened and later closed behind them. There had been no sound from the hinges.

Kryslie became aware of a very faint light. It gradually became brighter as they traversed a maze of subterranean passages. Finally, they reached a large open area. The lighting here was still subdued, but was enough to make out five figures seated on old chairs. They all stood up, warily, as Kryslie and her guide appeared.

"It is safe to talk and think here, but we keep our voices low anyway," Kryslie was told. "For some reason, possibly because we are underground, they cannot detect us here. I am Jeniss."

"I'm Krys. Thank you for bringing me here. I think those men would have soon found me. Is the small one who distracted the guards alright?"

"He's fine," Jeniss assured her. She gestured to a seat. "You got further than most people that wander into the town usually do."

"How is that?" Krys asked.

"Most of the strangers that don't see, or choose to ignore, the keep out signs are usually spotted right away. We became aware of you when the guards did," Jeniss went on.

"They have taken my brother," Krys told them. "Somewhere to the west."

"That's not good news," Jeniss said soberly. "But why were you here? What are you?"

Kryslie shrugged. "We are here because this is where we happened to be when dusk fell. I don't understand what you mean by what are you?"

"Are you gypsies?" another of the group challenged.

"No," Kryslie said truthfully.

"You understood our mental images," Jeniss stated. "And knew where to come. How is that?"

"We saw the town from up the hill a bit," Kryslie admitted. "We wanted somewhere to stay for the night. The place seemed deserted. We thought it would be safe enough since we hadn't seen any movement."

"If only you knew," came a mutter.

"I had a picture in my mind of the layout and when I saw the image in my mind I guessed where the church might have been," Kryslie told Jeniss. "When I sensed that picture, just after my brother was caught, I decided it did not come from those men and hoped whoever sent it could help me."

"So, you heard the thoughts of the men?" Jeniss asked her to confirm.

"Yes, that was the only way we knew they were around," Kryslie admitted. She guessed that the idea of telepathy was accepted by these strangers. "Who are they?"

Jeniss paused before answering as if she were deciding if she could trust the red headed woman. "They work for the government. This area, the town and a bit of the country around it, is monitored somehow. Anyone who ignores the keep out signs is arrested and taken off for questioning. They patrol the town on foot at night and must use some kind of infrared glasses to see, probably movement sensors too."

"They are creepy," a younger voice said. "You can't hear them or sense them coming or see them without IR glasses. And they want us real bad."

"Why did you project your thought to me? I mean, I'm glad you did, but it might have been a trick," Kryslie asked.

"No, they were hunting you," another of the so far silent group spoke softly. "The only time we hear their thoughts is when they are hunting someone or when they are trying to trick us – but then, we know the difference."

"We learnt to think in pictures and symbols, and so far they haven't sensed us sending. If you hadn't been able to understand our pictures, we couldn't have helped you. But there was a chance that you were someone we knew," Jeniss told Kryslie. "And anyway, their thoughts feel...different."

Kryslie agreed with that comment. Either the men had well trained minds, or the thoughts were somehow mechanically created.

"So, all of you are hiding from those men too?" Kryslie asked, looking around at everyone in the group. She was not reading their minds, because they all had effective mental shields. It told her something of what they feared. "How did you get here if the town is so well monitored?"

"That has only been recently," Jeniss explained. "They use the town as an experimental area. That's why they want to keep people out. It is owned by the Science Council and they made everyone move out. My family used to live here."

"So, what do they use it for?" Krys asked.

"My father told me they were testing various top secret projects – weapons mainly. We often hear explosions. But I think they test other things too – stuff that is not visible – wave and radiation and force effects. My father knows about such things."

Kryslie had an idea now why she and her brother had been brought to that time and place. "This doesn't seem to be a healthy place to be."

Jeniss shrugged. "We can't leave now, even if we wanted to. They know we are here somewhere, but they can't find us. Still, this is better than being back at the compound..."

"May I ask why you don't want to leave?" Krys glanced around.

"We have friends there. In the compound, that is," one of the others admitted. "We promised to try and help them..."

"Tell me about the compound – I assume that is where they will have taken my brother. I intend to help him and I might be able to help your friends too," Kryslie promised.

"You don't really have a hope," Jeniss told her. "The Science Council Compound is heavily protected. Our friends are in the high security section – some are prisoners and some are...well, they are experimental subjects."

Kryslie shared a shudder with all of the others. In her mind, the words evoked many unpleasant ideas.

Jeniss kept on, "Rachael, my brother Alistair, and I used to go to school in the compound, as our parents work there. There were twelve of us in all. One day, a dangerous radiation leaked. We were told an infiltrator had done it, but I think it was deliberate. Whichever it was, we were all sick for weeks and as we recovered we realised we could understand each other's thoughts. All but Jack and Heinz – they hadn't been at school that day."

Kryslie realised that Jeniss wasn't answering her question, but she didn't interrupt.

"We didn't let on to anyone else about it – if we had, we would never have gotten away. We would have been locked up with the others."

"What others?" Krys asked.

"Others that were locked up in the security section. We realised early on that we were hearing thoughts from people in there. Eight or nine of them, we couldn't be sure. They were research subjects, and had paranormal abilities, so they were being studied. Some of the tests being done on them were painful and we felt that too. It got so bad one night that I was screaming and Alistair was almost catatonic. My father wanted to know what the problem was and we told him then. He was horrified. That was when we started planning to help the others escape."

Kryslie sensed the story was not going to be all good.

"Father organised everything. There was an empty truck on the base, and he set up a hologram at the back to make it look empty. He took six of us to the truck and we hid behind the hologram, and he went to try for those in the high sec area. My mother got four more out from the school. I don't know how father did it, but he got five of the ones out of high sec. He was at the truck when the alarms sounded. Mother and father hopped in the truck and drove out of the compound before the orders came to stop anyone leaving. Mother told us where to hide in town and warned us of the guards."

Jeniss seemed reluctant to go on.

"And?" Krys prompted gently.

"We were followed and there were guards in the town waiting for us. We had to split up and not everyone made it here. Only six from the school and three from High sec."

"What happened to the others, and your parents?" Krys prompted.

"They were taken back."

"Do you know what happened to them?" Krys asked gently.

Jeniss nodded. "Our school friends were questioned by Schlech, the security chief, and given a beating and are in the detention cells. Glen and

Dimi were taken back to their individual secure rooms, but even if they were not beaten, the testing they had to endure got more painful. We could still sense them sometimes. My mother was punished and is in a detention cell. My father is still working, but under guard all the time. Dimi had a glimpse of him once."

Kryslie was shocked to her very soul. She controlled her rising anger and managed to keep her voice calm as she commented, "There are only five or six of you here..."

"Peter, Deon and Andrea were caught by the guards at different times. We have to go out occasionally and they didn't make it back. We know they were taken back to the compound, but after that, we could not receive anything from them. But we knew when they died."

One of the six that had not yet spoken said, "My name is Cleonie. Sven, Andrew and I were from the high sec area. We dare not even venture out of here. They would kill us on sight. We know what the Science Council are doing there, and they dare not let it be known."

"I guess not," Kryslie agreed grimly. "They are denying all kinds of human rights for a start. But you haven't explained how you have remained unfound here."

"The guards keep searching," Jeniss said. "But none of their detectors has managed to locate these tunnels — even when they tramp through the ruins of the church. I don't understand why, but my mother said we would be safe here and we are."

"I know why!" a very strong mental voice claimed. Krys turned to face the youngest of the six, and probably the one she had seen outside.

"I'm Alistair. I have been reading your mind. It is like that other one."

"What are you talking about, Alistair?" Jeniss demanded mentally and verbally. "What other one?"

"The one I told you about — the day Glen died," Alistair retorted mentally. His tone was smug. "I think that one told our parents where to go."

"Imagination, bro," Jeniss claimed.

"I didn't..." Alistair began to broadcast.

"Stop it!" Cleonie spoke suddenly. "Don't think so strongly. The guards will hear if you do."

Alistair was instantly contrite. "Sorry," he thought quietly.

"My brother is deaf and mute," Jeniss explained. "He reckons he hears more mental voices than the rest of us do."

"It may be possible," Krys confirmed and Jeniss stared back in disbelief.

"Who projected that thought to me?" Krys asked.

"I did." The last member of the group finally spoke. "I'm Rachael. Why did you want to know?"

"That thought illustrates my point," Krys explained. "You projected that picture at such a low, almost vague, level. The guards didn't receive it, but I did. So you can have different levels of perception."

"Makes sense, I guess," Jeniss decided. "But why him?"

"If he is not distracted by normal hearing...why not?" Krys suggested. She turned back to the youngster. "Tell me about that other mind, Alistair."

"When we first began sensing the thoughts of those in high sec, Glen and the others would tell us what they were doing to them. Glen would have to stop talking when the pain was bad. Those were times when I would sense that other mind. It seemed older than us, and it was distressed because he couldn't do more to help Glen and the others. However, he did help, somehow. I think he somehow helped deaden some of the pain."

Even in the dim light, Krys could see Alistair was crying. "On the day Glen died, it had been the worst; we were all sharing his pain. He didn't even know us anymore, and his thoughts were violent. That mind I sensed was projecting a feeling of calm and it soothed Glen so the doctors could sedate him. He never awoke from that sleep."

"Yes! Alistair is right," Cleonie said suddenly. "I have felt that too – many times. Something easing the pain in my head."

"Alistair, you claimed to know why you were safe here," Krys reminded the boy of his original statement.

"When we were here and running from the guards, we seemed to be being forced in this direction. Finding the tunnels seemed like a lucky accident, but we all felt we would be safe down here. But I felt the idea came from that same mind. I think whoever it is, is trying to protect us."

"That's interesting," Kryslie commented neutrally. "I will be alert for such a mind when I go to help my brother." Kryslie strengthened her own mental shields; she did not want the precocious youngster to read what she was planning. She went on, "He is in a kind of hospital room. Those that took him paralysed him first. He thinks they will question him when that wears off."

"How can you know that?" Rachael demanded. She seemed suspicious.

"I can receive my brother's thoughts," Krys admitted. Glancing at the others, she saw they didn't believe her, for most were frowning and edging away from her.

"Could you hear our thoughts earlier?" Krys asked, and they all nodded.

"Tym and I are twins," Kryslie stated, letting that stand as an explanation. She did not want to admit that her own telepathy was much stronger than theirs. "We have always had a strong bond."

The group relaxed. Jeniss asked, "Can you receive anyone else? At the compound?"

Kryslie closed her eyes and concentrated, ignoring the minds close by and extending her awareness outwards.

"I can receive a jumble of thoughts, but only my brother's are clear. It is late though." Krys felt that she could, if she knew the minds of the friends of her hosts, possibly hear them too if they were broadcasting.

Tymos woke from the second bout of paralysis and the drugged sleep that had resulted from his frantic attempt to escape. The initial paralysis had worn off much sooner than his captors had expected. He had twisted his body and slipped free of the guards carrying him. He ran off and vanished into the dark shadows in the open areas inside the Science Council Compound. He had decided that it would be better to escape then, and return to the facility at a time of his own choosing. Then he could scout around when no one was out hunting him.

He was confident that he could escape and so had used his natural and enhanced abilities to the fullest. The speed he knew he was capable of had allowed him to streak from place to place of concealment. The use of his power enabled him to mask his location when he stayed still. Those moments of total stillness enabled him to look ahead and plan his next move.

When the guards were still searching around the open space where he had broken free, Tymos had already reached the furthest wall of the compound – a brick structure topped by barbed wire.

As he observed that obstacle, Tymos extrapolated the height and knew he could get the speed to leap over it. The guards would have no idea of his Tymorean enhanced abilities. Without further pause, Tymos sprinted at the wall and then leapt high into the air. He automatically twisted his body so that he would land and roll in one fluid movement to regain his feet and continue his flight.

He cleared the wall easily, and took off at a rapid trot. A minute later, he came to an abrupt halt. Before him, he saw a shimmering wall, rising up to a height of five metres. He knew at once that it was some kind of force wall and as he could both see it and hear a humming noise emanating from it, he knew it was extremely powerful. The shimmer and hum told him that the wall was radiating on at least two wavelengths, but there was no time for him to do any further analysis. Since he didn't know all its properties, decided that it would be safer to leap over it than try to transmit through it.

Guards were approaching his location from three directions. Ordinary guards this time not like the freaks in the bombed town. He wasted no more time and began to sprint, putting all his concentration into gaining enough momentum to clear this higher obstacle.

A slight movement to his left as he leapt was the only warning he had of the other guard, before that one fired at him. The beam caught him mid leap and once again paralysed his body. His mind had only the briefest time to realise that the guard had not radiated a single thought as he approached, well ahead of his comrades.

With his body no longer obeying his mind, Tymos did not clear the shimmering wall, but slammed into it. As his body touched the wall of force, he lost consciousness, and a shower of sparks began as his body seemed slide down the wall of light - slowly as if slowed by friction.

Schlech, the Chief of Security, approached what he expected to be a very dead escapee, and pulled the body from the wall. He wore insulated gauntlets to do this. It was not until the body had arrived, under guard at the hospital section, that he was told the man was still alive. Accepting the amazing fact with no outward sign of surprise, Schlech ordered the man to be placed in a security cell, under constant surveillance.

Tymos became conscious, but his body was still unresponsive. At first, the whispering in his mind made no sense, but finally he recognised his sister's mind voice calling him.

"I'm...awake," he thought slowly, unable to project his thoughts far yet. A flood of warmth, concern, love and reassurance emanated through the twin bond. Then he concentrated as Kryslie slowly explained what she had learnt. He in turn, recalled what had happened to him. The fogginess in his mind was gradually receding and he began to be able to sense his surroundings.

"I am in a small room with white walls," he thought at his sister. "I am clamped to the bed, and the walls, floor and probably the roof are saturated with the same kind of force as that wall I hit. I am starting to tingle all over, so the neural disrupting effect is probably wearing off. Except for my power, I think that wall would have killed me."

He heard back. "I know where the compound is. Can you tell me anything more about your surroundings?"

Tymos continued to keep his eyes closed, as his mind scanned the room and beyond. He knew that Kryslie would see what he saw while using his odd talent for depth perception.

The bed was the only object in the room. Even the monitors were well concealed, but Tymos was aware of the video monitor in the roof above him. Beyond the room, corridors led in three directions but were full of sensors. Other rooms contained equipment for some unknown use. Guards were patrolling, but Tymos could not yet judge their schedule. They were paying particular attention to the closed rooms that, like his, contained a prisoner.

Tymos didn't attempt to touch the minds of the people that he sensed, not wishing to be betrayed by one of the guards. At that time of night, he could not sense the minds Krys told him about.

All in all, it was quickly obvious that he was in the high security area and escaping would be difficult. It would not be wise to try until he found out where they had taken his clothes and his transmitter.

Kryslie fingered her transmitter and wondered how she could get away unseen to use it. She had learnt all that her new acquaintances could tell her about the Science Council Compound and it was obvious that she would have to help Tym escape.

One by one, her new friends had gone off to their rough beds to sleep. They apologised for not having a spare bed for her. They invited her to make use of one of the chairs.

Alistair was too excited to sleep. He alone was revelling in being able to communicate mind to mind with someone who had a much greater degree of perception than any of his friends. Sharing his thoughts with her was not frustrating like it was with his sister.

"Alistair, I have to leave this place – my brother needs help."

"You mustn't. You will betray our location," Alistair protested.

"You went out. Your sister went out," Kryslie pointed out.

"We never go far, but if you try to go to the compound you will be captured."

"How do you get food?" Kryslie asked, curious.

"The gypsies bring it. They leave food in the church."

"Aren't the gypsies caught?" Kryslie asked thoughtfully.

"Sometimes, but they act really dumb. The guards threaten them and force them out of the town."

"Are the gypsies able to hear thoughts?"
"No. They are just very quick and nearly invisible."
"I really must go! Can you get Jeniss to lead me out?"
Alistair trotted off, but when he returned with his sister, Kryslie had gone.

Chapter 12 - Rescue of the Telepaths

Kryslie had no trouble retracing her steps to the door where she had entered the tunnels. At that point, having a clear picture of what was outside, she used her transmitter to get there. Once on the other side of the door, she stayed perfectly still. She estimated distance to a point just out of the town, and transmitted again to a place she remembered. This time she checked the way to the west, sensed no one and transmitted closer to the compound. She transmitted in stages until she was looking at the force wall that was the outer barrier around the compound.

She could sense no guards, but was still mindful of the freakish type that had roamed the town. Keeping herself ready for instant action, Kryslie probed the force wall with her mind. She determined it would be safe to transmit through, and this time her destination was the deserted schoolroom that had been very clear in Alistair's mind.

Once again, she did not move when she arrived. Her mental probe of the room and surrounding area, revealed no guards, but there were heat and motion sensors in the room. There was no need to move as she looked for her next coordinate, and recalled what her brother had 'seen'.

The room that looked like a library seemed to be the best option. When she had sensed the location for herself, she chose a secluded corner where her arrival was unlikely to be observed. From there she reached out for her brother's mind and touched it lightly. He was about to be moved for questioning, and she would need to be where no one would find her. If they gave Tym truth drugs, she would need to link to his mind to ensure he did not reveal anything about the two of them.

A small janitor's room just down from the library seemed ideal. She transmitted to the door, opened it and walked in. She had not been able to see into it, as the room was very dark. Once actually inside, she found a clear area and sat down.

Tymos realised, when black clad security men had come for him, that his own dark brown coveralls had been stripped from him. Now he was dressed in a grey one-piece suit of an odd design. It had many flaps held shut by some sticky fabric. One was where, if his hands were free to open the flap, he could relieve himself from. He had some not very pleasant ideas for the placement of the other flaps.

The paralysis was just wearing off for the second time, but these security men were taking no chances. His arms and legs were secured with restraints of some ultra strong metal reinforced material.

To move him from the hospital, they slid him into a cage, so he had no room to move or squirm. It was apparent to him that his earlier escape attempt had been witnessed, and they had deduced his strength and speed.

He was lying down in the cage, which was being wheeled on a trolley along white painted corridors and into a brightly lit laboratory. He had to blink a few times to adjust his eyes for the bright light.

The Compound Controller introduced himself as Paul Stryker and he advised the 'spy' that it would be wiser to answer all questions. The other man present was Marcus Schlech. Tym had already discovered his name and that he was feared by everyone in the compound. He had no mercy on anyone that disobeyed his stringent security restrictions. He was going to be conducting the interrogation.

The two guards that had pushed the trolley were told to set the cage upright and fix it to the wall and then they were dismissed. Both left the room promptly.

Schlech walked over to the prisoner and stared into the stranger's face.

"I am going to find out who you are and what you were doing in the town," Schlech promised. "You are a spy. I am going to find out who you work for."

Tym said nothing and did not even betray any trace of fear. Schlech observed this and considered it a challenge. He also wanted to know how this spy had survived contact with the deadly force wall.

He turned away and walked to where Stryker had prepared a syringe.

"This is a powerful truth serum. No one has been able to resist it. You will be talking very soon."

Schlech wondered why the prisoner was still not betraying fear. Could it be he had nothing to hide? But he did – he had to have. He jabbed the needle through the grey fabric, into Tym's thigh and forcefully pushed on the plunger.

Tymos closed his eyes and began to concentrate in a way that increased his metabolism. He wanted his body to filter the drug out of his system as soon as possible. He also willed his mind to resist the effects until then. He knew he would be vulnerable for a time, but the reason for his calm was that he knew Kryslie was linked to his mind. While his mind had no control, she would tell him what to say in answer to Schlech's questions.

Schlech was a master of interrogation and enjoyed applying various techniques to gain the information he wanted. In the short period of time needed for the truth serum to flood the prisoner's bloodstream, he attached three different sorts of electrodes to various parts of the prisoner's body. Tym learnt that his ideas about the flaps in the suit were accurate. He had electrodes attached to his head and chest, his wrists and ankles, his genitals and thighs. They would act as a lie detector system as well as a means to inflict electric shocks.

"What is your name," Schlech began.

"Tym Ward," Tym said, prompted by Kryslie.

"Where did you come from?"

"Melbourne."

"Why are you here?" Schlech demanded.

"You brought me here."

"Why were you in the town?"

"To find somewhere to sleep."

"Why did you ignore the keep out signs?"

"I didn't see them."

"Who was with you?"

"My girl friend."

"Where is she now?"

"She ran off."

"What is her name?"

"Cindy."

"Her last name?"

"Daniels."

"Who do you work for?"

"No one."

"Why are you so strong?"

"I just am."

"How can you run so fast?"

Kryslie felt her brother's mind resisting her, and thought more forcefully.

"I just can," Tymos repeated what Kryslie was telling his mind.

The answers he was getting didn't please Schlech. His instinct told him that there was more to this prisoner than what he had heard. The man had to be a highly trained agent to be so resistant to his serum.

It was time to increase the pressure. The truth serum did not stop the prisoner from feeling pain and it also made him more gullible. Often the threat of intense pain was enough to break any natural resistance to the serum. After having a sample of pain, they usually didn't need to have it applied often. However, he was hoping this prisoner didn't talk too quickly.

Schlech proceeded with his normal procedure, but the young red headed man didn't scream. Even the threats of more intense pain if he did not tell the truth, had no effect. The man had promised to tell the truth, but his replies were no more informative than before.

Schlech changed his questions to what and who the prisoner had seen in the town. He did not like hearing that the prisoner and seen and heard nothing.

Paul Stryker watched with no trace of pity. His aide brought him a message and wanted to retreat quickly. Stryker let him go, read the message and beckoned Schlech over.

"That prisoner is a very strong telepath. He is sending out thoughts that are making all my special patients react. All have needed to be sedated further and they all claim they know what you are doing to him and that they know everything he has thought and felt."

"Maybe I should question your patients to see what he is hiding," Schlech proposed.

Stryker agreed. "They won't be resistant to the serum, but you will need to wait until morning."

Schlech growled softly in frustration, but he thought to ask, "Are you a telepath?" He watched the lie detector screen intently.

"No."

"He has to be lying, but the signal hasn't changed." Schlech strode away from the prisoner, his face angry.

"How can it be possible?" Stryker asked.

"I don't know! However he is doing it – I will find out. Everyone can be broken – and I do not intend to give up until I know what he is. He is dangerous."

"If you intend to keep him here, I would like to test him," Stryker smiled unpleasantly. "When you have finished of course."

"If he is still alive – I have no objections. So long as he is kept in high sec conditions." Schlech gestured at the prisoner's current state. "I think he needs another example of pain."

Kryslie was listening to the conversation between Stryker and Schlech through her brother's mind. She did not like the idea of the other imprisoned captives being questioned. She needed to end this questioning, and soon.

"Tym, test the restraints on your hands," Kryslie told him when Schlech moved away from him.

"Solid, but I should be able to break them. I'm getting movement back – thanks to his little shocks."

Kryslie didn't waste time disagreeing with his definition of 'little'. "Do nothing yet – I will tell you when."

She was intending to get into that room and show those torturers that they were not invincible.

Part of her mind was searching for a place to hide when she got Tym free, but most of her attention had to be centred on controlling her brother's involuntary responses. Her fingers were almost digging into her temples and her hands were glowing bright mauve.

Some other sense suddenly warned her that she was no longer alone, just as Schlech used his shock treatment on the lower electrodes on her brother.

"Don't move."

Kryslie heard the voice, and in a quick glance saw only a humanoid shape in the doorway. She couldn't move at that moment, because she needed to numb her brother's agony and because she was wide open to him, she felt his pain in her own body.

Once the pain eased, Krys spared a fraction of her mind to sense who the intruder was. He hadn't grabbed her, but he wasn't radiating thought either. The man closed the door and turned on the light. He didn't look like a guard, he was too scruffy but it was obvious that he recognised her. His eyebrows had lifted into his shaggy fringe.

"Don't stop what you are doing," the man said quickly. "I know who you are. I am Tamir Janzoet's son."

"What are you doing here, Tammy Grainger?" Krys thought at him.

"Much as you are, but with less effect. You must not let Stryker begin his experiments on your brother or let Schlech near the others."

"Those creatures are on borrowed time," Kryslie promised, she did not hide all of her anger. "I was about to go and show them what I can do to them."

"I have a weapon. Use me as a hostage. I am believed to be a gypsy idiot, fit only for menial work and I am due to start cleaning the rooms on this floor. May I suggest that you cover your hands? The glow is so bright they won't fail to see it."

Krys nodded, and thought to her brother, "Tym, pretend to be unconscious. I am coming now."

Tammy Grainger found a pair of work gloves for her and helped her put them on, and handed her the weapon. "I was going to try and help the prisoner, and have fixed the security monitors between here and the lab. Then I sensed you."

They left the closet, and walked quickly to the door of the 'lab' where Schlech and Stryker were trying to rouse their prisoner. Only then did Grainger let his shoulders sag and put a dull expression onto his face. He opened the lab door and shuffled in, stopping just inside to stare stupidly at the scene.

"Not now, Tammy!" Schlech told him. When the gypsy didn't move he strode over with the intention of forcing him from the room.

"Actually, now is a very good time," Kryslie announced in a soft but menacing voice. She had slipped into the room behind Grainger and had her weapon aimed at the Security Chief.

"I have come for my brother," she announced.

Grainger moved aside at a silent command.

Kryslie had sensed the intention of both men, but did not move. Neither the paralysis weapon fired by Schlech, nor he laser pulse weapon of Stryker, had any effect on her.

"Get out of there, bro," Kryslie ordered mentally, and she grinned at the amazed interrogators.

Tym obeyed, first parting the hand restraints like a hot knife through butter. Then he forced the bars of the cage apart enough to sit up and be able to removed the electrodes and foot restraints.

Schlech moved his weapon in a rapid motion to aim it at Tym again, Kryslie was faster. Schlech was forced to drop his weapon as a beam of destructive energy touched his hand. He snarled, and thought her aim had been off. Stryker was more cautious, and contemptuous of the woman, who seemed to be unaware that he had a weapon.

"They deserve to die," Grainger thought at Kryslie. "You must know what they are."

"I do!" she thought back. "Leave them to me. You and Tym get out of here and help the ones that need help."

Sensing a slight drop in her attention, Schlech walked towards Kryslie. He seemed completely unafraid of the weapon in her hand.

Kryslie had changed the focus of her attention. She wanted both of the sadistic men to keep their attention on her. It was working. They were oblivious of the way Grainger was edging around the room. Nor did they notice when he handed something to Tym and they both disappeared.

"That weapon won't harm me!" Schlech sneered at the woman. He reached out to grab it, but found it held too tightly. Stryker moved to a console and Krys heard the door slam shut. "Nor can you get out of here."

Kryslie shook her head. "You have it wrong. I can get out of here, but the two of you will not."

Schlech casually moved to one side. Kryslie moved a hand to deflect the beam of energy from Stryker's weapon, back towards him.

"What!" Stryker exclaimed. "How did you do that?"

"As if I am likely to tell you that," Kryslie smiled at them. "And it is not because I have a skin tight force shield on. I'd like to see how brave you are without it."

Schlech grabbed Kryslie by the throat and tried to squeeze. He thought he was squeezing it hard. "How could you know about such things? They are a highly classified secret."

"Really?" Kryslie said calmly.

Schlech moved his other hand over her body trying to feel if she was wearing the same kind of shield.

"What are you?" Schlech demanded, only now realising that his grip was not affecting his captive. He tried to lift her off her feet, but found he couldn't.

"That question won't bother you for much longer," Kryslie assured him, her voice calm. She was aware that Grainger had already gathered the people in the high sec area that needed help to escape. He and Tym were transmitting them to an area suggested by Grainger. No one was, as yet, aware of anything untoward going on.

Kryslie intended to keep these sadists occupied until the vulnerable people had been placed out of reach. Then, Grainger was going to set off the fire alarms, so all people remaining in the high sec building would evacuate it. When they had, Grainger planned to seal the high sec building and set off the explosives he had set in there some time ago.

Schlech suddenly sensed that he was not in control of the situation; he glanced around, looking for the gypsy and the other prisoner.

"Where is that other prisoner," Schlech demanded of Stryker.

"Gone," Kryslie assured him. Schlech slapped her face. "I am going to enjoy breaking you!" he snarled.

Stryker went to check the door. It was locked. He looked around the lab, but there was nowhere the other prisoner could be hiding.

"Go after him!" Schlech ordered.

Stryker went to the console to override the lock, and then ran to the door.

Kryslie laughed. "Oh, no. I told you that you won't be leaving."

Schlech forcefully threw Kryslie to one side. She hit the side wall, but did not lose her footing. He went to the door and threw his weight against it. That was when the evacuation alarms began to ring. He tried several times more but the door had been built to prevent people escaping. He was beginning to realise that something was seriously wrong.

Kryslie was unconcerned as Schlech launched himself at her. She moved towards him and used his momentum to throw him over her shoulder. He roared an obscenity at her and sprung from the floor. He would not underestimate this woman again.

Stryker was moving behind Krys to get a shot at her, whilst Schlech was moving forward with extreme malice. They believed they were well coordinated, and Kryslie was aware of their supposedly subtle communication. But when Schlech grabbed her again and began to swing her into Stryker's line of fire, he found himself moved instead and he screamed when Stryker's weapon struck him.

"I think your shield malfunctioned," Kryslie muttered to him, before tossing him on to the floor and springing at the stunned Stryker.

In moments, both men were on the floor, unable to move. Before they had the wind to fight back again, Kryslie used the broken restraints and bars from the security cage to truss them up. The eyes of both men grew wide in disbelief as she casually bent the solid metal bars and twisted them into tight manacles. Soon after, the men began to try to struggle free and swear at her.

"What kind of abomination are you?" Schlech demanded.

"I work for peace," Kryslie said calmly. "Unfortunately for you, I have judged you both guilty of gross crimes against the civil rights of those you had imprisoned here. Those people are now free and will be telling their story to the human rights commission. However, I do not intend for them to try you and imprison you. My judgement on you is that you deserve death. I would like to make it slow and intensely agonising – but I am constrained by time. You may say your prayers now, for this building will be levelled in a few minutes."

"How will you get out?" Stryker asked her.

"The same way as my brother did," she told them. "You'll see – and it won't matter if you find out. It will be the last thing you think of except that you were overcome by a mere woman."

Kryslie waited until Tym assured her that the building was clear. Then she calmly removed her gloves and activated her transmitter. It did not worry her that they saw her disappear – they only had moments to live.

Kryslie arrived at the door of the hidden tunnel as a massive explosion lit the sky to the west. She felt the ground shake. Moments later, Tym arrived with a group of six people. He departed immediately and returned with six more. He repeated his actions five more times.

Forty-one men and women, some very young, looked around with bewilderment.

One asked, "How did we get here?"

"It isn't important. What matters is that you are alive and no longer in the high sec prison," Kryslie told the man.

"You blew up the building!" another realised with shock. "Why?"

Grainger spoke up as Kryslie advised in a quick mental exchange.

"It was necessary," he said in a firm voice. "Too many atrocities were being perpetrated there."

Everyone of the rescued party was amazed by the transformation of the man they thought was a dull-brained gypsy. "We should hurry inside. The guards that prowl here will not be distracted for much longer."

On cue, the door to the tunnels opened. Jeniss stared in shock at the crowd, but she recognised Kryslie and several of the younger people, and then saw her mother and father. She sprang at her parents.

"Everyone inside. Quickly," Grainger urged.

Tym and Kryslie watched for guards until everyone was in the door, and then they followed.

It was crowded in the chamber but no one minded. Grainger let the new arrivals be greeted by those they knew. It reassured them. Then he took charge of the group.

"We won't be staying here for long," he told them. "It will only be until my friends here take control of the compound."

There were questions, but Grainger gestured for silence.

"Many of you will be truly unaware of the weapons research that was being done back at the compound. The weapons being developed are deadly and terrifying. They were justifying the work by the state of uneasy peace in the world today. Rumours of weapons being produced on one side, lead to worse on the other. If this continues, a devastating global conflict is inevitable. It is time to turn the trend of science towards peaceful projects – defence not attack. Peace in preference to war. It will take time and much effort – more than any one man can do alone. You here, are the top people in your respective fields. Yet you have been treated like drudges. I intend to change that and train you to take over strategic positions in your various specialities so in the end we can unite all countries on Earth and expand knowledge in peace."

There was a murmur of agreement.

"Is this really possible?" one man asked.

"I have no doubts about anyone in this chamber," Grainger said firmly. "You all have the knowledge needed and you have perseverance and courage. I believe, and you must believe, that we can succeed."

"What about the rest of us still at the base?" a woman asked thoughtfully.

"I am aware that not everyone that worked there shares my views," Grainger admitted. "It is possible that many will be convinced to join our crusade. You can do that best by setting an example. Leave the doubters and adherents of the old ways, to me. For now, all you will need to do is act as instructed by the new base controllers."

"And who will that be?" a tired voice asked, fearfully.

Tymos walked forward. "I have no doubt that the base personnel are currently disorganised. My sister and I will take over in the morning." He was no longer in the grey prisoner coveralls, but a cleaner's uniform that Grainger had found for him.

Tymos arrived at the base openly, soon after sunrise. He had lightened his hair to gingery blond, borrowed some glasses from one of the refugees, and a suit from another. In no way did he resemble the prisoner brought in the previous night. The shocked perimeter guards, who had been on duty all night without relief, accepted his identification and immediately took him to the Controller's office.

As he was escorted from the gate, Tymos saw the thoroughness of the destruction of the high sec building. Crews were still dousing the fires with water, and people were staring at the collapsed rubble.

In the absence of Paul Stryker, the Deputy Controller was trying to deal with the chaos, and to summon assistance from the nearest army base. From his pleadings on the phone, it was obvious that he was getting nowhere.

John Fallon was nothing like Stryker. He was a scientist, not an administrator. When Tymos presented his carefully forged references and credentials (prepared in that very office the night before), he was relieved to pass the mess over to the newcomer to deal with. He never even thought to ask how the Science Council had known to send someone when he himself had been unable to confirm the death of Stryker.

"A report must go to the Science Council," Fallon suggested, reluctantly.

"Yes," Tymos agreed, briskly. "That is my first task. I will need to find out what everyone here knows. You could start, but there are other priorities. Have you accounted for everybody?"

Fallon paused for a moment too long, and then admitted, "No. We have been unable to find Controller Stryker and Chief of Security, Schlech."

"Are they the only ones missing?" Tymos asked, though he knew the answer.

Fallon's face betrayed him. He looked away from Tymos as he said, "No, another forty-one people are missing. They all worked or had quarters in the high sec building."

Tymos kept a straight face, and gave no hint that he knew the man had just told a huge lie. "Unfortunate. I will need the list of names for the official report."

It was a perfect way to let the rescued ones disappear, though that was not his intention. Officially, they would be dead, and the Science Council would not be setting hunters onto their trail. Meanwhile, Tymos had his own agenda.

Tymos was more than capable of running the base. With Kryslie acting as his administrative assistant, he dealt with the rescue effort, handled the Science Council investigators, audited the scientists' work, and instigated some necessary and overdue changes.

His right to be in charge was never questioned, for he had inserted himself in the Science Council computer system as an impartial auditor. His supposed purpose had been to investigated Stryker and Schlech. Their "disappearance" was being treated as suspicious – his contention that they had fled due to the investigation and had set the explosion in the high sec building to hide some fraudulent actions of their own.

His skill at diplomacy won over even those who had staunchly supported Stryker and his objectives.

Grainger was an unobtrusive addition to the staff, providing his insight to Tymos and between them, they began to build the nucleus of an organisation for peace.

Tymos knew that he would not be able to stay in the position of base controller, and from the beginning, he began to train several of Grainger's protégés to take over the guidance of the base. The most promising was a scientist named Wallis.

They had made their goodbyes, telling everyone that they had been reassigned. Now they walked through the forest that was no more than five miles from the Science Council base. It was quiet amongst the trees. Down near the river, a group of gypsies had come to camp. They were a colourful group, chatting happily and going about their normal business. However, none of them seemed to notice the two red headed strangers that walked through their camp to one particular caravan.

They knocked to alert the occupant, and received a call to come in.

Tamir Janzoet greeted them warmly, although he was scarcely able to rise from his bed. A young woman slipped out to give them privacy.

"I have waited a long time to see you again, Great Ones. You honour me by your visit. My son has told me of your recent work. I am relieved that those evil creatures are no more, and I have often been grateful for your wisdom. I might have been forced to work there and that would have destroyed me. Those people have long been a concern of mine. I warned home base of them many years ago."

"We are honoured by your service to Tymorea," Kryslie said softly. "We will tell of your great work when we can contact our world again. Like before, we will be leaving this time soon, but we wished this opportunity to speak to you. Your son should be joining us shortly."

Tymos asked then, "Was the girl that was here your child too?"

Janzoet smiled. "Yes, one of three girls. I found love again amongst these people. They do not reject me because I cannot walk. Another thing I will be grateful to you for."

"I think the Guardians were rewarding you," Kryslie told him. "The advice came from them."

"Why must you go again?" Janzoet asked then.

"We have not yet returned to our proper time. We estimate that another sixty years must pass before those that left with us will arrive. We are still 'in transit' and moving at the whim of the Guardians," Tymos explained.

Even though they had been working closely with him, Tamir Grainger still treated them with the awe his father had instilled in him. They had not discussed the promise he had made some twenty-one years before. Now he knew the subject needed to be raised. He entered the caravan quietly and bowed a greeting.

"I have the records of my father's work to give you," he told them. He carried a large box with ease.

Tymos shook his head. "We cannot take it yet. As I have explained to your father, we are still 'in transit' and likely to be so for another sixty local years. You must continue to keep it safe until then."

"Ah, I see," Grainger acknowledged. "Do you know when you might come again?"

"When something needs to be done," Kryslie shrugged at him. "At that time, or times, we will need to have a background prepared for us - something that explains our intelligence. When we finally arrive, and we cannot say exactly when that will be, we will need to be able to act without questions being asked."

"I will, of course, do as you ask," Grainger promised. "I look forward to our next meeting."

The Great Ones smiled warmly at the two men as they felt the rushing of time once again.

"Until then..." he heard in his mind.

Chapter 13 - Coming to War

The rushing images became a series of eye-blinding flashes, just before Kryslie felt the hard ground under her and instinctively curled and rolled to transmute the downward momentum. Unable to see where she was going, she slammed into something hard, jarring her whole body.

Now, her ears were assaulted by deafening explosions and the ground bucked and heaved under her. When the shaking finally eased, Kryslie uncurled and looked cautiously around.

Where she was, had been a park. Miraculously unscathed bushes and grass were interposed with blackened holes. Not far away, trees were burning, adding more smoke to an already particle laden sky - reddish in hue, not blue, as the sun tried to shine through the smoke.

"Tym?" she thought with her mind, for she could see no sign of him anywhere near her. She adjusted her eyes to see better in the murky atmosphere. Her brother didn't answer, but he may still need time to recover from the passage through time.

Kryslie studied the scene of destruction around her, looking for her brother, and tyring to understand what had happened. She had arrived in the middle of a war, but where was she? Her eyes showed her a kaleidoscope of orange heat images, and even if Tym had been standing close by, trying to discern his image would have been impossible.

There seemed to be an ominous silence, now that the wave of bombers and their deadly missiles had gone. She sensed no people, and wondered if everyone was dead, if they had been warned soon enough to evacuate, or if everyone was still sheltering somewhere.

She began to hear sirens from some distance away, and the revving of trucks, sounding like they were stuck in a hole and trying hard to get out.

A new sound registered, and she recognised the sound of jet bombers and looked for the source. A flight of twenty craft was approaching low, coming in from the west. They roared overhead. She heard, not saw, the screeching of the incoming missiles, and quickly curled back into a ball, and pushed herself against the base of the stone wall she had earlier hit. It was psychological comfort, not any real protection. Her eyes were shaded from the intense blinding flashes of burning magnesium. Had she looked directly at them, she would have been blinded.

Had she been merely human, or even merely Tymorean instead of a Great One, she would have died when the force a nearby impact detonation, plucked her from her position and threw her into the air. This time, she couldn't roll to lose momentum. She landed awkwardly, on what felt like miscellaneous rubble. More rubble, rained down onto her, but none were big enough to bury her.

Although her body throbbed with pain, her sense of self-preservation was fully active. She freed an arm and pushed the debris off her - bricks, plaster, metal pieces - and crawled to a slightly clearer area, and tried to pull energy from the world's aura. Almost immediately, she stopped. The feel of it sickened her. It was more than merely unpleasant - it was vile. All she had left to draw on were her inner reserves and that was little enough. Most of her energy must have gone into merely keeping her alive.

The roar of jets had vanished into the distance, no more bombs were falling, but delayed explosions continued and fires were lighting the smoke filled sky.

Kryslie did an inner inventory of damage, before trying to stand. Nothing broken - her Tymorean personal force screen had protected her that much, though she would have plenty of bruises. She felt her head, where it both stung and ached. Her hand came away with blood on it. She rubbed a hand along her arms and found more blood.

A quick glance at her force screen generator revealed the small metallic device had been smashed to scrap. At least the field had protected her from that last explosion before it had died.

She tried reaching her brother again, mentally and then by calling aloud. Still no answer. If he had been knocked out on arrival, he should be rousing. The sooner the better. They needed to find out the reason for this warlike attack and leave this place. They needed to go somewhere the energy aura was less contaminated; where they could draw on it to heal and restore their personal energy.

Kryslie felt every muscle protest as she forced herself to move, walking slowly and scanning the ground for signs of her brother amongst the rubble. Only the dregs of her energy and her innate stubbornness kept her moving.

Bodies she did see. The first was that of an elderly woman, eyes still wide with terror. Not Tym, she thought with relief as she checked for herself that the woman was dead, and then closed the eyes, very gently. Two more bodies, men this time, but both older than her brother. They had died under a falling wall. Looking up, the damaged building seemed to have once held apartments, but they were all exposed now, like sardines in an opened can. She had to pick her way through the debris, checking further, sensing in the twin bond that her brother wasn't far away. She saw the remains of children's toys, household goods, clothes - torn, broken, battered, useless. More bodies - two women and a child. Nameless now, beyond help. Kryslie wondered why they had been left where they had fallen.

Her mind tried to encompass the destruction. Who was doing this? And why? Was this still Australia? Where were all the other people? Extending her extra senses, she found flickers of life that were people, but very few.

One of the sirens was slowly coming closer, but she didn't try to find it. She had to find her brother. She guessed that the only people still here were the foolishly valorous rescue people. Did that mean that most of the town's population had escaped? Gone but without the time to bring the dead?

Her initial sense of disorientation was easing, but vital knowledge was still eluding her. She had to learn what had caused all this destruction, and how far it was spreading. She had to find Tym.

Kryslie was moving without conscious direction, reacting to the instinctive awareness of that came through the deep twin bond. Her path was through, or rather a scramble over, the debris of the building. Only steely strong concentration was keeping her aware of the dangerous shifting masonry, plaster, brick and twisted metal, and ensuring she did not trap feet or ankles in it. A distant part of her mind suggested that the ferocious headache she felt, was due to a concussion. It was dismissed as useless trivia. Too many other concerns filled her mind.

She only sensed the man when he abruptly grabbed her arm.

"Come on lady, come out of here. This way." He tried to pull her from her intended direction, and she resisted.

"Lady, the road is this way and more planes are coming."

"No. My brother - I must find him."

The extra energy needed to resist the man was too much. Her head began to spin and her vision cloud over. She collapsed, but didn't quite lose consciousness. She felt the man trying to help her stand, and then heard another person scrambling over the debris.

"Can't you see she is injured, Penjan?" a woman berated him. "Look at her hands – radiation burns."

"You tend her, Carla. There's another over there."

The man scrambled away, further into the rubble.

Carla took a tube of salve from a satchel, and smeared some lotion on Kryslie's hands and quickly swathed them in bandages. Then, as Kryslie seemed too weak to walk, she lifted her gently into a fireman's hold and began to stride towards a road, where she hailed a passing ambulance truck. Once her patient was aboard, she waved it on and began searching for more victims. Any more they found, would have to travel with them - that was the last of the ambulances.

A beep made Carla stop to check her phone for a message. It was the 'get out' warning she had been expecting.

"Penjan," Carla called to her brother. "We have to go."

Her brother appeared, carrying an injured man.

"We'll have to bring this one with us. We can't leave him."

Carla nodded.

A new wave of aircraft could be heard approaching the battered town. Penjan and Carla wasted no time activating devices on their belts. They disappeared from the town moments before pyrotic missiles began impacting and turning the rubble to smouldering slag. The enemy - the Eastern Alliance, were doing a very thorough job of destruction and evoking terror in the American population.

No one remained alive in the bombed town to witness their disappearance and in the next town in the path of the invaders; none of the fleeing people took notice of their sudden re-materialisation.

Here the evacuation was in its final stages. People were heading north or south out of the path of the destruction. The progression was still orderly. Panic would come later.

The young man on Penjan's shoulder became conscious, so he was lowered gently to the ground.

"What happened?" Tym asked. He was dazed and disoriented, but pushing himself up to look around.

"They bombed the town where you were," Carla told him. She was not sure herself what town it had been.

"You would be dead now if we hadn't found you. You left it a bit late to leave!" Penjan added, then asked, "What's your name, bud?"

"Tym," Tymos answered, starting to remember who he was. "Where's Krys? She was with me."

"Safe enough," Carla assured him. "I put her on one of the ambulances heading south. Like you, she had bad radiation burns on her hands. Can you remember how you got them?"

Tymos shook his head, but the significance of his bandaged hands became clear to him.

His hands must have been glowing, brilliantly purple, and these good Samaritans had assumed it was from radiation. They wouldn't have any way of knowing that his hands glowed purple when he was handling Tymorean Power. He could not remember drawing energy from the energy aura of the planet, so it seemed obvious to his mind that the Guardians of Peace had acted to protect him and Kryslie. Something must have happened in the instant of their arrival that should have killed them.

"What town is this?" Tymos asked, needing to get his bearings and find his sister. They were on the side of a major road, with cars crawling slowly towards the edges of the town. The cars often had piles of belongings strapped to the roof, and filling every cranny inside the car.

"Melville, I think," Carla said thoughtfully. There had been so many towns. "I've lost track. We are keeping just ahead of the bombers."

"Would Krys be here?" Tymos asked, his mind still felt dazed, and he couldn't seem to think.

"No, the ambulance was heading for Big River."

"How can I get there?" Tymos persisted.

"You can't, man!" Penjan warned sharply. "Even if you were fit to travel, which you're not, the only roads leading from here to Big River go through areas that have been bombed. The radiation levels there will be at least twice safe levels for weeks."

"Bombed? But why?" Tymos wanted to know. He needed to understand the situation.

"The Eastern Alliance, damn their terrorist hearts, is blazing a path of destruction to the Capital. They are zigzagging to the major cities, destroying all towns in their path. First with bombs, them with radioactive missiles, and then with pyrotic missiles."

There was no mistaking the horror in Penjan's voice. "The US Air force and reinforcements from all their allies have been trying to stop them but they keep coming and they have a way to disable the defending aircraft. It is all we can do to try to help the survivors."

"Do you have a trade or skill?" Carla asked. "If you do we can send you to join others of the same trade. With millions of displaced people, the sooner we start rebuilding, the less effect these bastards will have."

Tymos shook his head. "I know my name, and that Krys was with me, but little else," he claimed. There was no way he was going to reveal that his most recent memories were of a time in the past.

"There's a medical centre near here. We'll take you there. You're probably concussed. They will be evacuating to the north in an hour. You will go with the other injured ones," Penjan told him.

"What will you be doing?" Tymos asked.

"We have work to do, helping the injured that have no one to help them, since everyone is trying to leave as fast as they can," Carla told him. "Then we skip ahead to the next town in the path."

"How do you stay ahead of the bombers?" Tymos asked, wondering if it was a way he could use to travel to Krys.

"We have a helicopter," Penjan claimed, and Tymos sensed a lie. "The air force is managing to slow the planes a little, but that is about all. The bombers will be here soon. There's an ambulance, you'd best go with them."

"I'm okay. I'll find my own way. There will be others worse than me who will need the ambulance space," Tymos refused their suggestion.

"They are not busy yet," Penjan pointed out. "You will be safer with them."

He gripped Tymos's arm to stop him walking off. "In your condition, not knowing anything about yourself, you would end up in a military evaluation centre and be in uniform before you know it and probably dead soon after."

"It's true," Carla tried to convince him. "If your memory is shot, you won't recall any common sense strategy, you won't know where to go for safety or where to avoid..."

"Thank you for your help," Tymos said politely, and pulled his arm free. "But I must find Krys."

He had turned away from his rescuers, and was about to walk away when he heard them talking, about him. He looked back, they were staring at him, but their mouths were not moving. With a start of surprise, Tymos realised they were telepaths. He knew that telepathy was not common on Earth, but it was not unknown, but in that instant glance, something in the structure of the bones in their faces, revealed a startling truth.

Penjan was thinking, "He has a strong mind and I can't read it. He may have no memory, but he certainly has many questions. I think he is normally intelligent. We can't let him wander on his own. Hey!"

Tymos had suddenly moved close to Carla and yanked her gloves off. Her hands were glowing faintly mauve, confirming his realisation that Carla and her brother were Tymoreans. It was incredible, but just as indisputably true, but he dared not create a time paradox and identify himself to them.

Penjan sensed his recognition of their heritage and reacted by firing a stunner at him. He did not realise that Tymos was Tymorean, only that normal Earth humans had no knowledge of Tymoreans and anyone that did, was dangerous.

The beam paralysed Tymos, and while he collapsed back to the ground, he didn't lose consciousness. He was able to draw on the energy aura here to make the effect wear off quickly. Carla and her brother summoned reinforcements to help.

Six men arrived abruptly, materialising in front of Tymos. Who they were, Tymos had no idea, but they had transmitted from somewhere, they all had palm sized metal devices and only Tymoreans could use them. As Carla quickly explained that they should take him to the base, Tymos sprang up and grabbed a transmitter and vanished.

He had not transmitted far for he could still hear Carla and Penjan talking to the newcomers. He had only gone as far as the petrol station across the road, which was deserted and out of fuel. There was a screening pile of tyres between him and these enigmatic Tymoreans. If the eight strangers had not been so amazed by his use of a transmitter, they would have seen him diving for cover.

Tymos was astounded to find Tymoreans on Earth. As far as he knew, only one Tymorean had not returned to Tymorea, and that one would be dead now. However, he did not want to reveal his proper identity. It was not because he doubted the allegiance of these missionaries. They were proving to be worthy of their calling, but when communications were resumed between Tymorea and Earth, in some future time, he did not want any mention made of his presence in this time.

They could think what they liked about his ability to use a transmitter. Maybe they did not know that only Tymoreans could use them - the possibility had not occurred to them.

"Go back to your positions, but keep a watch out for that man. If he is able to use our transmitters, and none of us know him, he has to be considered dangerous. I'll report this to base, but we don't have time to hunt him – too many other people need our help," Carla directed.

Tymos crept further away. He still didn't know where he was and he felt an urgent need to find Krys. Somehow, he had to get his bearings.

Kryslie awoke from a deep sleep. She was instantly aware of the atmosphere of fear, despair, pain, and hopelessness around her. Without moving, she used all her senses to explore her surroundings.

The room she was in seemed to be like a hospital ward, even though it looked like it was once a room in a private house. It fit with the feeling of bandages on her hands and temple.

She tried to reach her brother, mentally. The reply was faint, so he was not close by. She moved slightly, and opened her eyes. On a stretcher bed next to her, there was a man with his head almost completely bandaged.

Her movement brought a woman striding down the aisle to her. She was wearing white and had small red crosses on her dress collar.

"Awake, my dear. How do you feel?" the woman asked Kryslie.

"My head hurts," Kryslie admitted. "But what happened? Why are my hands bandaged? And where am I?"

"This is the county refugee centre. You were brought in with severe radiation burns, concussion and shock."

"Am I a refugee? What happened?"

"You were picked up after the bombing of Denver," the nurse explained. "Don't you remember?"

"No," Kryslie answered slowly. "I don't have a clue why I was in Denver. I can't even remember the bombs."

"Can you tell me who you are?" the nurse asked.

"I think my name is Krys," Kryslie decided to admit no more than that. It was obvious that she had arrived in this time in the middle of a war. She needed to learn what was going on.

"Krys who?" the nurse prompted gently.

Krys shook her head. "I can't seem to remember."

"Don't worry just yet. We have seen so many here that have memory problems. Our doctors have helped a lot of them recall their past. Even if they can't, we will help relocate you and train you so you can help rebuild America."

"It wasn't just Denver?" Krys asked.

"No," the nurse admitted reluctantly, but she didn't explain. Kryslie saw in her mind the swathe of destruction that even now was continuing. "Try to sleep some more. The doctor will check you again in the morning."

Kryslie nodded, and settled down again, but she only pretended to obey. Contrary to her comments to the nurse, she did recall where she had been the previous day. It had been on a completely different continent. Now she was wondering why she had come to a war zone and what she needed to do.

When she sensed that the nurse left the room, Kryslie rose from the stretcher bed allocated to her and went in search a door leading outside, hoping that fresh air and being on natural earth and able to draw on the aura would help her headache. Her route was not a conscious choice, and as she wandered, she realised that the refugee centre must be a very large country house. In time, she found herself outside in a small, enclosed garden. A breeze cooled her face and her feet had grass beneath them. As she moved away from the door, a light came on but this did not alarm her.

The garden was a small area of lawn surrounded by walls that were hidden by a dense screen of old trees. Over to one side was a small bungalow, but she had no desire to investigate it. The short walk from the ward had tired her out and she wanted only to lie down and rest. She did this on the lawn, finding her muscles relaxing and her headache receding. She fell asleep without realising that she had been spotted from the bungalow.

"Professor! There is someone lying on the lawn between here and the house," one of the men imprisoned in the bungalow called softly. "It doesn't look like any of them."

Professor Grainger trotted over to the barred window and stared at the figure. If this was someone other than the guards, perhaps they might take a message out. He only had time for a brief glimpse before the security movement sensing lights turned off again.

"Kryslie?" he breathed softly. The light had revealed the bright colour of the stranger's hair. One of his aides pushed him aside and stared intently out into the moon lit darkness.

Alistair was deaf and mute, but he was a strong telepath and had caught his master's sense of recognition. He knew who it was that Grainger thought he had seen. He tried to send a mental message to the figure in the garden.

"I think she is asleep, Professor," Alistair thought at Grainger. "She isn't hearing me."

"Keep thinking at her, Alistair," Grainger thought each word carefully. He knew his young protégé would sense them. "She may remember when she wakes. Stress the importance of our need to escape – of our need to attend the politico-science conference. I don't know why she is out there, but it can't be co-incidence."

His thoughts became more private. Surely, this was some divine answer to his prayers. Kryslie and her brother had appeared twenty years before, out of nowhere, and helped him rescue the people at Rapid Creek. Surely this time, was as important a point in history - a chance to work for peace...

Alistair continued to stare out into the darkness. He had met Kryslie years ago and never forgotten her. She had been the first person he had been able to think at, who had not considered him a mere child. Her mind had been so crystal clear to him. He kept trying to reach her mind for two hours. When the guards discovered the intruder in the garden and roughly dragged her away, he stopped for he had seen the faint glow of the weapon they used on her, and knew she would be unconscious for some time. He would rest, and keep trying to send a mental message to her.

Kryslie had needed time to recover from her injuries and the sleep on the lawn gave her body time to restore itself using the energy from the Earth. She was in a very deep sleep when the guards spotted her. They had not approached closely enough to wake her or for her instincts to warn her to rouse. Instead, they had stunned her from a distance and then moved close and drugged her. She was carried back to her stretcher bed, but a discrete watch was initiated. She may have been sleep walking, as the security tape of her movements had showed no obvious sense of purpose to her movements. However, they would act to prevent a repeat of her intrusion into the garden. The only way into the garden was closely guarded but somehow, no one had seen her go past. The first they had known was when she had been spotted on a security monitor.

Carla continued to look for people needing help when Penjan transmitted to the Tymorean base. There were too few of them as it was, to do all that had to be done. The bombers were within fifteen minutes of the town.

The base being used by co-ordinator Rhyn was an abandoned house that should be just outside of the enemy's corridor of attack. The owners had locked it up and prudently moved away.

His equipment was portable and he too kept moving forward, from one empty house to another, as the enemy advanced. Rhyn was in his sixties, having been born after his missionary grandparents had been recalled to Tymorea, but he had been trained to co-ordinate the Tymorean missionary descendents by his parents.

"What is so important as to bring you here?" Rhyn asked, startled by Penjan's sudden appearance, and the lack of any prior radio contact.

Penjan reported the incident that had just occurred. "This was too important to broadcast. It might have been intercepted. This man knows what we are - I didn't want to risk him finding all of us."

"Describe the man!" Rhyn insisted, sharing the sense of alarm. "Details are important. I will pass the word to everyone to look out for him."

Penjan paused as he pictured the man's appearance and described him in concise detail.

"My height, dark auburn hair, not long, not short. Wavy. Medium build, well proportioned. He had his own kind of arrogance and insisted he was fine, but his eyes seemed a bit unfocussed. He claimed to have forgotten his past, but he had a well-shielded mind. Neither Carla nor I could touch it, so we couldn't tell if he was lying or not. When we found him his hands were glowing reddish-purple, pulsing more brightly than mine do when I am using power. I assumed from the symptoms that he must have handled or touched something contaminated with that damned Curithian radiation. He grabbed Carla's gloves off her and I swear he understood what he saw. He isn't one of us or we would have known, and I could only think that if he wasn't, but knew us, he was dangerous. I stunned him, or thought I did, because he fell down. That's when I called for backup, but he grabbed Hondo's transmitter and disappeared with it - transmitted away. Could he be one of our people?"

Penjan's question was one that worried Rhyn considerably. He chewed his lip, considering all that he had been told, and trying to find a clue amongst the knowledge his parents had given him. Then he went to his portable computer and began to scan records, from before he took over as coordinator. He felt sure there was some tiny insignificant fact that was on the outer fringe of his memory.

"He must be – if he could recognise and use a transmitter," Rhyn thought aloud, but he was muttering to himself. "And powerful, if he could use one not attuned to him. But if he is one of us, who are his parents and why did they hide him away?"

"There were two of them," Penjan suddenly thought to add. "We found a woman, another red head, just before him. Carla put her on the ambulance to Big River."

Rhyn was suddenly typing on his touchpad, abruptly sure of who the man and woman were, although unable to understand how it was possible. He found the holographic video record he wanted.

"Tell me if the two people looked like this."

Penjan stooped to peer closely at the screen.

"That's him! And the woman too." Penjan exclaimed. "Who are they?"

Rhyn just shook his head, trying to decide how much to say.

"This was taken at an important function on Tymorea. The night the youngest Prince was born. Those two, that you recognise, were born here," Rhyn said. "Some months before my grandparents left, they were found to have Tymorean power. They were taken to Tymorea to be trained. My records say they were fostered by the High King. But that was over sixty years ago, and from what you said…they are not much older now than they would have been then, but the names you mentioned…It has to be them. I don't understand how they have come to be here now. However, their condition worries me. Finding them must be considered as important as our other work. You can trust them, implicitly."

Rhyn felt no doubt about his statement.

"Has home base contacted you?" Penjan asked hopefully.

"No," Rhyn dashed his hopes. "There is still no answer, but I will try again to contact them. Perhaps, these two were sent here as missionaries."

Penjan nodded. "I'll be off then and tell the others what you said."

Kryslie woke again, and instantly recalled where she was. A quick glance at the ceiling above her was enough to tell her she was back in the same bed as before. The ventilation grill had the identical pattern of unnatural holes. She also recalled the scene where she had Tymos had been flung out of the time stream.

They had arrived in the midst of destruction, but the Guardians had protected them. Kryslie recalled the aches and bruises, the headache and weakness. All those had gone, and her mind was clear again.

By moving every muscle in turn, very slightly, she evaluated her condition. Then, she turned her concentration inward, to assess the mental responses. All these techniques had become instinctive when she had still been a student on Tymorea.

While sleeping, her body had healed itself of the damage she had experienced on arrival, but other oddities intruded on her awareness. Her mind was clear, but her reactions were slower than normal. The nerve pathways were tingling faintly, as if recovering from hyper stimulation. She had felt that sensation before, though under controlled conditions. It was the effect of a stun, wearing off. The slowness was from some sedative drug. When had they stunned and drugged her? And why?

Rather than make it clear she was awake again, Kryslie began a series of meditation chants - quietly, in her mind. Then, she thought back over every moment since arriving in this still unknown time and place.

Her memories, and the things noticed when her mind was still dazed, did not tell her enough. She was no longer in Australia, but in America. Had they come there to do something about the war?

"Tym?" she sent the thought to her twin.

His reply was stronger than when she had tried it before - or was that because she had needed to heal that time.

"How are you?"

"Better. Where are you?"

"I am not sure. But I am heading there to you. They said they sent you to Big River."

"They? You mean those two Samaritans?"

"Yes!"

Tym's mind betrayed what he had discovered.

"Tymoreans!" Kryslie thought back with excitement. "But how? The others can't be here, now. The war had been over for decades when we were to arrive. The only Tymorean to stay was Tamir Janzoet."

"Descendents - they have to be," Tymos thought back. "I have probably spooked them, but I had to get away from them. No one at home knew we were here, now. And these people must have been the source of all the data we received before we left."

"So why are we here?" Kryslie sensed that her twin was wondering the same thing.

"The Guardians picked this time," Tymos said, musing. "They wanted us here - for a reason."

They both considered the three previous time-landings, and the one linking connection.

"Tamir Grainger," Kryslie formalised the thought.

"And this war..." Tymos added. He was going to add more, but he sensed his twin's mind switch to some other concern. He waited.

Kryslie sensed movement near her, and recognised the nurse. She made her body return to a limp state feigning unconsciousness, and kept her eyes tightly closed. She felt a hand gently lifting her left wrist, and a finger placed on the pulse spot. The other hand brushed the part of her forehead without bandages. Throughout, she kept limply still, even when the nurse shook her gently and spoke her name.

A second presence moved to her side, but spoke in low tones to the nurse. "How is she?" It was a man's deeper toned voice.

"Still under. The last dose probably won't wear off until near morning."

"We will keep her under observation. We still don't know how she got outside. I'd say she was a spy, but if she was, why go out there and simply fall asleep?"

"She had a head wound, it might just have been that."

Kryslie had a sudden odd vision, of a door with a security keypad, vanishing into a dark garden.

"Krys, where was that?" Tym asked. He felt his twin trying to recall the elusive memory. He also shared her awareness if the nurse and man moving away.

"Outside, here," Krys began. "I wanted to feel the aura, to recover...I transmitted through the door - without my transmitter. I saw the garden, and found a spot to stretch out..."

While his sister concentrated on her movements, Tymos had spotted an image of a cottage in her mental scan of the garden. "What was in there?"

She didn't know. She had not given the cottage a thought. Now she did. Why was the entrance to the garden so well protected? Was she stunned and drugged because she had gone there? What was being hidden there? "Grainger..." her thought came like a leap of logic, or the voice of the Guardians.

Now she recalled the dreams she had experienced when she was sleeping on the lawn and those dreams made sense. She had subconsciously moved towards the people imprisoned in the cottage. People that urgently needed to be somewhere else, who had recognised her and expected her to be able to help them.

"How soon will you be here?" Kryslie asked her brother.

"I have a transmitter, but it isn't very powerful. I can't go far with it, and it takes ages to recharge - but as fast as I can."

"I will try and send a mind message to the people in the cottage. If it is Grainger, he will recognise my mind. And the nurse thinks I will be unconscious until near morning."

"Can you get back there?" Tym meant into the garden.

"They are watching me now," Kryslie admitted. "Better to try from a distance first."

At intervals during the remaining hours of the night, Kryslie tried to reach Tamir Grainger's mind. She had no success, but guessed he was asleep. Just as the other patients in her ward began to rouse, she felt another mind impinge on hers. It wasn't her brother, but it was clear and strong.

The touch was familiar, and it was the association of Grainger and their last meeting that completed the identification.

"Alistair?" she sent back with relief. He was a stronger sender and receiver than Grainger.

"Kryslie! I so hoped it was you that I saw, but why did you not come to us?"

"I was injured, and needed to recover. I could not have helped you then, and now I know the dangers I need to avoid," she explained. "Tell me what your situation is."

Alistair began to explain. "We are here with President-Elect Wallis. We were captured on the way to the swearing in. Someone wants to stop the President taking charge. And the Professor, they are afraid of what he can do. We have to get to Washington ..."

At that time, Kryslie became aware of the nurse walking towards her. She decided to sit up as if she had just woken. She quickly thought at Alistair, "Later. I will hear more in a short while."

Knowing that she was still under suspicion, Kryslie gave no indication of having recalled any nocturnal wanderings. The nurse asked how she felt, checked her pulse and temperature, asked if she felt up to going to join the other mobile patients for breakfast, and advised her that the doctor would be checking her over sometime in the morning. Sensing that her answers roused no further suspicion in the nurse's mind, Kryslie reinforced her 'weakness' by teetering a little when she began to walk. Had she been merely human, it probably wouldn't have been an act.

By the time she had walked from the ward to the end of the passage, Kryslie realised she was being followed. The man wore a nurse's coverall, and might have been ensuring that the stubborn female patient didn't overdo her recovering strength, but his mind was trying to picture her as some sort of spy.

The directions the nurse had given her took Kryslie in the opposite direction to that which she had taken in the night. Breakfast was being served in the extensive back garden of the house that had been taken over as the refugee centre. The reason quickly became obvious. Hundreds of people milled about the garden. Most of the people were wearing the haunted look of people who have lost everything. Some had slack faces and minds still in shock from what they had experienced.

Kryslie joined the food queue and waited patiently to be served. Her mind was assailed by fear and sadness. The thoughts of the people around her told her the story of lost loved ones, of being alone, of having nothing to live for, except the hope that the evaluations would find something worthwhile for them to do in the rebuilding of America.

Once she had her allotted portion, Kryslie took her food to a quiet corner of the garden and pretended to be concentrating on her food. In fact, her mind was taking note of her surroundings. She finally identified her new guard. This one was a plainly dressed man, sitting not far from her. What set him apart was the purposeful stride he had used when approaching, and the lack of the haunted look. His unguarded thoughts were informative.

"She doesn't look dangerous," the man was thinking. "But how did she get into the little garden? The door to that passage was locked. She had to be a spy. Sleepwalkers can't go through locked doors. But would a spy be stupid enough to go to sleep on the grass? If she wanted to release the prisoners – why didn't she? Well, the psychs will find out the truth."

Kryslie was in no hurry to finish her meal and while her watcher was vaguely distracted, she resumed her mental conversation with Alistair. The reason why the Guardians had placed her and Tym in that town seemed obvious now. It was a pivotal point in Earth's history, and she had the chance to nudge the precarious balance towards peace. She had time to promise help, but stressed they must wait until her brother was closer. Alistair was impatient, for they had been captives for over a week. However,

Kryslie knew she was under too much scrutiny to make another try on her own. She would be more effective as a distraction.

When Kryslie finished her breakfast, which was mainly cereal and toast with reconstituted fruit juice, she stood up and glanced around as if uncertain what to do next. Her watcher stood too, and approached, offering advice on where to take her tray and empty food containers.

Another man, the nurse from earlier, interrupted, "Excuse me, miss, I was told to tell you to go to the clinic as soon as you finished breakfast – for evaluation."

"Thank you," Kryslie said. "Ah – how do I get there?"

"I'll show you," her watcher offered. He led the way into the house and up onto the second storey. Here, if the sign was correct, her appointment was with Dr Deveraux who was both a medical doctor and a psychologist.

Kryslie followed as her guide went in the office without knocking. She kept her senses alert, but nothing seemed out of the ordinary. The only occupant of the room rose from behind a desk. He was wearing a doctor's white coat and his smile was friendly, his face full of laughter lines. Despite that, a shiver ran down Kryslie's spine. Her extra senses were telling her to be careful.

"It's Chris, isn't it?" Deveraux smiled as he held his hand out to shake hers.

Krys nodded, watching him warily.

"I'm Doctor Deveraux. I've just been going over the x-rays that we took when you arrived. There doesn't seem to be any skull fracture. Have you recalled anything more about yourself?"

Krys shook her head.

"We won't worry about that yet," he said gently. "I will need to give you a full medical examination – to see if I find any problems. John, would you ask Nurse Holt to assist me?"

Krys's guide nodded and left the room.

Deveraux guided his patient through to an examination room.

"Just hop up onto the bench there. I will look at those hands first."

Krys obeyed, using her bandaged hands to push herself up, and the doctor tutted her.

"We were told you had radiation burns," he commented as he carefully unwrapped her left hand.

"They don't hurt," Krys commented in turn, and it was truthful enough. She sensed he was a little surprised.

She was relieved to see that her hands were no longer glowing, but only faintly mauve. It looked now like the common sign of having touched something that had been irradiated with the Curithian devices.

"You were lucky. They are healing well. The initial treatment must have been instigated very quickly," he told her. He washed off the salve that Carla had administered using alcohol swabs and applied fresh salve and bandages. "How did you avoid the full irradiation?"

Kryslie found her mind full of information about the particular form of emission. It was lethal to living things, but left buildings unaffected - for the radiation didn't linger for longer than a few weeks.

The nurse arrived at that point and began removing the bandage from Krys's head.

"I was under some rubble," Kryslie murmured. "I had to push it off me."

The doctor merely agreed, "You were very lucky." He looked at the wound that had been under the bandage. "The wound has healed well. We will just put a light bandage on it this time."

He was thinking that she had recovered very quickly, and must be a very healthy specimen.

When the nurse had finished bandaging Krys's head, the doctor asked the nurse to show his patient where she could change into an examination gown.

Krys returned in a shapeless white outfit and allowed Deveraux to complete his examination and do a series of scans. His mind noted that she was in excellent physical condition. When he had finished drawing blood for further tests he began asking her questions and doing a psychological test.

She was careful to give answers that would tell him nothing about her and would respond to general questions, but in a thoughtful way. Finally, she was told to rest for a while and Nurse Holt kept her company.

Deveraux went through to a room beyond the examination room and closed the door behind him. This room was designed to be intrusion proof and completely free of bugging devices. He had no way of knowing that his patient was mentally following him and could hear, not his speech, but his thoughts.

"Well, what have you found?" he was greeted by another man who looked as if he should be in uniform.

This man had short-cropped hair, tall and solid frame and a stern face.

"She definitely had a concussion when she arrived," Deveraux reported. "But there is no sign of it now. She recovered from it very quickly. In addition, she is in excellent physical shape apart from that. She will answer questions on general things but seems unable to recall anything specific about herself. I think the amnesia is genuine, but the way she looks at me — makes me uneasy. I think we should question her again under hypnosis."

"Sound idea," the soldier type agreed. "If she is acting, Denis will soon find out. He'll be here later today. Have Marylyn start her on the IQ and aptitude tests."

Tymos used his awareness of his sister, to give him the direction for the town of Big River. He transmitted in stages and once out of the corridor of the bomb damage, the travelling had been easier. At each brief rest, he had tried to reach his sister and received a weak but strengthening response. He was limited to transmitting line of sight, so the trip took two days.

He already knew where Krys was and what treatment had been given to her. He was now feeling an urgency to get closer. His sister had seemed dazed for the first day or two, but now it was clear again. He knew about Grainger and the other captives and now he was almost there, he needed his sister to help him.

"Krys?" he sent. "What's happening?"

"I am being questioned. They think I am hypnotised and are convinced I have no idea of my past. I can handle their questions, so don't worry about that. Tamir Grainger and his associates need to be present when the world Science and Political councils meet and that is less than a week away. Those that are behind the bombing are also trying to prevent the meeting. I have been closely watched since I stumbled into the garden on the first night, so I can't get to them. Where are you?"

"At the edge of town. I'll see what I can do."

Krys spared no further time for contact with her brother or wondering where he had found a transmitter. She was fully occupied, controlling the mind of the interrogator and forcing her body to metabolise the powerful truth drug he had given her. They had told her it was a mild sedative.

It was just as well that her hands had been re-bandaged for they would have been glowing brightly.

Tym's mind call had come as the man, Denis Walker, had paused in his questioning to give the drug time to act. He didn't realise that his body and mind had been frozen for a brief moment.

Walker returned to the apparently drowsing patient and estimated that it was time to resume questioning her.

He was cautiously pleased that the answers were identical to what had been given before. He was fully convinced that she had no recollection of walking out into the garden, or seeing the building there. His excitement rose. This woman was a real find – physically fit, highly intelligent and without a clue as to who she really was.

Walker was unaware that his own mind had been controlled during the questioning and influenced to think of his patient as being exactly what he wanted her to be. He had no idea that his patient was resistant to hypnosis, and strong willed enough to have resisted the truth serum - even though the blood sample he took would show the right level of it in her blood.

Krys knew that he planned to implant false memories into her mind and prepare her to be an unwitting agent of the enemies attacking America. After he finished, she would seem to be a perfectly loyal citizen until a key-phrase was spoken, and then she would become a traitor.

When Walker returned, he had a file of papers. He placed this on a nearby table, and began to induce a trance on his still compliant patient. He watched her response to his suggestions to relax, as a way to determine when she was in the hypnotic trance. Using information in the file, Walker gave Krys a detailed background of experiences that would be the basis of her subconscious reasoning to obey the future commands. He repeated each part three times. Then he told her what she would have to do when a certain key-phrase was uttered.

All of this was instantly memorised by Krys, but at the same time, she was learning from Walkers mind, the aims of the organisation he worked for. She learnt the name of his immediate superior, and the hierarchy of enemy agents. He, along with Deveraux, the nurse in the infirmary and a man named Brady were in the local cell. His superior was a Major Grant. She probed for a list of other people he had treated this way, and what their key-phrases were. She also learnt where the group hid their records and the safety precautions on them.

Even after leaving the psychologist, Krys knew she was still being closely watched, so she did nothing to arouse further suspicions. It meant that she dared not go near the entrance to the hidden garden. Tymos was in hiding, not far away, but he had not yet succeeded in contacting the prisoners in the cottage. He did not know Alistair as well as Kryslie did, so he needed his sister's help and she had to find somewhere where her shadow could not observe her too closely.

She felt the increasing urgency to act, knowing that each day, groups of refugees were being sent off to placement centres to make room for more war-affected people. Krys knew she was well enough to be moved and would be as soon as the people running the centre could place her to suit their subversive purposes.

Therefore, she chose to wander aimlessly in the garden during the afternoon. When she found a suitably awkward corner, she sat, back to a tree and facing away from the house. To make her action seem innocent, she took on a pose of meditation. Her watcher, found a position not far away. With her back to him, the man could not see the blankness on her face as she sent her perceptions in the direction of Tamir Grainger.

She did not try to reach him immediately. Instead, she investigated the hidden garden and sought for the security devices around the cottage prison. She found, as Tymos had, that the only way they could get into the cottage was by transmitter. She no longer had one.

"Tamir Grainger?" she thought finally, channelling her query to where she perceived the scientist to be.

"Kryslie!" he recognised her thought immediately. "I had almost given up hope of help."

"My brother will be coming to get you," Kryslie thought quickly. "Get everyone together in one room and wait for him."

"Where are you?" Grainger thought

"Close," she told him, "But I am being watched, so I can't help you directly. Can you send me a picture where you will be?"

"I will get Alistair to do that."

Moments later a very vivid picture formed in her mind and she sent it to Tymos.

"Why did you not contact the Tymoreans here for help?" Kryslie asked casually. She had learnt of them from her twin.

"I was unaware that any remained on Earth. My father certainly didn't know," Grainger told her.

"To be honest, neither did we. However, we will ensure that you meet them later. They will be highly valuable allies to your cause."

Grainger did not make a return comment on that option, instead he said, "We are all together."

In the shadows near Kryslie, a figure dressed in dark clothes materialised from a vaporous cloud. It was there for only a brief instant, long enough to get coordinates from Kryslie's mind before transmitting away again. Tymos appeared again, this time in front of the eight men he had come to help. All but two were staring in amazement at his sudden appearance.

"I can take two of you at a time," Tymos said quietly, looking at Grainger. "I have found a secluded spot, not far away. Once you are all there, I can take you in stages to your destination, wherever that is."

"Tymos, take Governor Wallis and his aid, Steven Morris, first," Grainger decided. "Wallis is the elected President of the Political Council, but we were abducted before he could be sworn into office. His deputy is filling in and he's pro war, not pro peace."

Tymos nodded, instructing the two men to stand close to him. When he pressed the button on a small alloy device, the trio disappeared.

"Professor, you should have gone first. You are as important as Governor Wallis." Alistair argued.

"Perhaps, but Tymos did not say he was taking us to a safe place, therefore it is wiser for us to go separately. I will go last, that way you and the rest of you can protect Wallis and if we are interrupted here, I know they will not kill me because they want me to work for them. However, given half a reason, they will kill Governor Wallis because it will be a blow to our war effort."

When Tymos returned moments later, Grainger had already grouped the next two to leave.

"Bri Lambert and Paul Conway, my chief scientists," Grainger introduced. The men huddled close to Tymos, more than anxious to be away from the cottage. Again, the three disappeared abruptly.

Grainger felt Kryslie's mind touch once more.

"There may be trouble, Tamir," she reported calmly. "The men that guard you have become suspicious and are arming themselves. I should be able to delay them unless I am interrupted here."

Tymos appeared for the third time. He was already aware of the approaching men.

"Grainger, you next," Tymos directed. Grainger didn't argue, but motioned to Alistair to come with him.

The man watching Kryslie felt a vibration and reached for his communicator. He listened for a moment through his earpiece and then reported in a very quiet voice. "She is on the east side of the garden, sitting under one of the trees – meditating or something."

Kryslie heard the muttering and spared a part of her attention to determine what was about to happen.

"Bring her to my office!" the voice through the communicator ordered. "There is something odd happening at the cottage. My gut instinct tells me she is involved."

Kryslie knew the man was approaching, but she remained outwardly oblivious. For as long as possible, she would continue to control the minds of six men in a room at the far end of the house, and to jam the surveillance frequencies used to monitor the prisoners. The task required intense concentration.

The man reached over and tried to shake her and found he couldn't. She was relying on him not using his stun pistol unless she resisted. She was stalling, but finally, Tymos sent her an 'all clear' message.

"Can you get away?" Tymos asked.

"Not yet," Kryslie reported calmly. "Some people here are enemy agents. There is still a great deal I want to find out. I especially want to know who ordered Grainger and Wallis abducted. You get them away; I will deal with things here."

"Be careful, Krys," Tymos sent.

"You too, Tym," Krys sent back.

The guard watched the woman a moment longer. Shaking her had no effect, so he slapped her with the flat of his hand, once on each side of her face.

Kryslie fell over, and looked up as if dazed. She put her hands to her stinging face.

"I could almost remember," she said morosely. "What did you have to do that for?"

To the guard she seemed to look very young and vulnerable.

"Mr Brady, the placement officer, has asked to see you. I am to take you to his office."

Krys stood up carefully and followed obediently.

As they approached the office, a loud noise like a phone buzz startled her. The guard became suddenly more alert, but he continued to the office, pressed a call button and waited.

The nurse from the infirmary opened the door and allowed them to enter. Krys sensed her agitation and guessed that the escape from the cottage had been discovered.

Moments later, Brady summoned the woman into his office and noting that Krys was there added, "I will be with you shortly. Please wait here."

It sounded like a request, but the guard seemed to treat it like an order.

Krys went and sat on a couch and pretended to doze. In fact, she was 'listening in' to a conversation in the next room, hearing the agitated thoughts of two men and a woman. Brady was reviewing recent security video that showed her.

"There!" he said, stopping a playback. "A figure dressed in black, just beyond her."

"She doesn't seem to be aware of the person," Marilyn Holt commented. "Have you looked at the other records?"

There was no sign of an intruder in the secluded garden. Nor did any of the surveillance equipment used to monitor the prisoners show any indication of an extra person in the cottage.

Krys sensed that the other man in the adjoining room was Deveraux. They discussed the escape and tried to tie her to it. They couldn't, but Brady didn't trust her, and felt she could be have been planted by American Intelligence to try to trap them. Deveraux still wanted to use her and had ideas for ways to test his control. Brady also had ideas, but he kept them to himself. He would be making enquiries, he said.

Brady invited her into his office; he was now alone in there. Deveraux and the nurse had left by the room's other door. Kryslie was invited to sit in the chair in front of the desk, and observed Brady as he sat himself behind it. "Have you remembered anything more about your past?" he asked, after introducing himself and confirming that he was the placement officer.

Kryslie shook her head. No one would believe that her immediate past was twenty years ago, and she wasn't supposed to recall the false background just yet.

"Well, I've sent your description and fingerprints off – we might get some sort of reply. I've been told you should stay a few more days, and Deveraux wants to try hypnosis to see if he can help your memory. Either way, your evaluation tests were remarkable, I am sure someone will know you. Though if not, you would be an asset where ever you chose to go."

"Thank you, Sir," Krys said earnestly. "I appreciate your help. When will the doctor want me?"

"I will see if he is free now," Brady offered.

Krys spent the next hour convincing Deveraux that his hypnotic control of her was complete. He had used the purposing word, and she had immediately become still and blank faced. She maintained that composed facade whilst he had her obeying various commands. What he had her do was extremely unethical, but she obeyed without hesitation or reaction.

Brady was watching from behind a one-way window with leering appreciation. That session convinced him, that even if the woman was a very clever agent, they had control of her and he knew where he wanted to place her.

At the end of the session, Krys was released and she went to have a sleep. She was not expecting trouble from either Brady or Deveraux for a while. Brady had left the centre and Deveraux was busy with a new intake of refugees.

Chapter 14 - Confounding the enemy

Kryslie had only been asleep for an hour when she woke abruptly, feeling a tight grip on her arm. She was instantly alert, and ready to fight free, but the sight of a military weapon aimed at her, kept her wary. The man had a uniform with an armband stencilled with MP.

"On your feet, Private Trent," the man in front of her ordered.

It seemed prudent to obey, even though she knew they had made a mistaken identity. She could protest, and perhaps they might listen to her, but she could not prove who she was. She had no identification - of any kind - and was pretending amnesia. It would not do to admit that before arriving in the bombed town, her last memory was of a time twenty years before.

"I don't think that is my name...." She made a token protest.

Who ever was behind her lifted her roughly to her feet. His rough treatment, dragging her arms behind her and securing them, brought a yelp of protest. Yet as she thought and looked around, deliberating between escape and compliance, she saw the people in the nearest beds draw deeper under their blankets. Tymos had mentioned that many people were being drafted into the army, but this was different.

"You will be quiet!" the man in front of her ordered, as he lowered his weapon. He was still wary though.

"Private Christine Trent," he went on, "You are to be taken to Washington Military Prison for court martial on charges of desertion, fraternising with the enemy and seven counts of misconduct."

Krys didn't try to control her expression. It was suddenly clear that Brady had organised this. The only thing was, she had no idea why.

They hustled her out of the ward, giving her no option to collect any belongings, not that she had any - just the donated clothes that she had slept in. The clothes she had been wearing when she had been found had been taken away and destroyed.

In the short march from the ward to the front door, any of the other refugees that saw her drew back and tried to hide.

What followed was a half hour drive to a military airfield and a long flight in a military plane. During the flight, her hands were secured to the seat, except for the few minutes when she had needed to use the plane's basic facilities. Her guards not give her a chance to cause trouble. Or rather, any trouble a mere human could have tried. She could have freed herself, but several things stopped her.

Kryslie had soon determined that her destination was indeed Washington, and that her two determined escorts were loyal Americans, obeying orders and with no reason to think them false. The second was that her brother was in the process of trying to bring Grainger and President - elect Wallis to the American capital.

The flight was uncomfortable, but it gave her time to consider what the enemy agents were intending. They believed she had been brain washed to obey some future subversive commands. It made no sense that she was to be put in a military prison, unless they planned for her to be exonerated later. She would have to wait and see how things played out.

When the plane landed at the air force base nearest the Capitol, a truck and six more guards were waiting. Her original escorts held her arms, again secured behind her, and forced her down the steps. The new escorts, with weapons ready, took charge of her and shoved her towards the truck. There followed an uncomfortable ride in the truck which terminated at the military prison. Once there, she was unloaded within a secure compound and dragged to the Prison Commander's office.

The Commander had a process to follow, and when she claimed she could not confirm who she was, his face hardened. He took a piece of paper from a file and showed it to her. The sheet had an Id photo of her in the uniform of a marine private, and other identifying details. There was a page with fingerprints, and a blood group, but that was all she had a chance to see before it was flicked away again, and the Commander sent her off to be processed.

Kryslie endured being stripped, showered, having her haircut quite short, photographed and the rest. The supplied overalls were clean and fit better than the donated clothes, as well as being made of tougher fabric. However, it was clear that the charges against her were deemed serious, and that they considered her both dangerous and an escape risk. She was taken to a solitary cell in the women's section of prison.

In the solitary section, the treatment of the prisoners was designed to be demoralising. The more stoic the prisoners were, the worse they were treated.

She bore the routine, ignored the vocal insults and other humiliations, and used the long periods of aloneness in the six-foot square cell, to let her senses roam to learn what she could of her surroundings. She spent a lot of it seeming to be asleep, but she was learning about the other prisoners - most charged with violent assaults, the ones in charge - all seeming to be loyal, and keeping in contact with her brother who was still half a continent away.

Her court martial was set for the eighth day.

Tymos was exhausted when he finally had all of the men away from the cottage and into the safe place he had scouted earlier. However, he knew that 'safety' was only a relative term. It was in the open, but away from the cottage. They were only a few miles from the refugee centre, and needed to move again before roving patrols caught sight of them. All that this small cul-de-sac had in its favour was that it was merely a standing space behind a huge pile of uncollected rubbish. The faint breeze blowing across the pile made it necessary to breathe through several folds of cloth, but even so, the air smelt of freedom.

Grainger spoke the obvious. "We cannot stay here. Do you have another place in mind?"

Tymos hadn't - he was trying to locate an empty building, but so far, every place he probed was full of refugees. "No, I am unfamiliar with this area."

Grainger of course knew that, as did Wallis and Alistair. The others of the group had not met Tymos before. "I have a contact in Bankstown, a suburb on the east side of the city," Grainger proposed. "I know I can trust her."

"Tell me how to contact her," Tymos insisted immediately. "I will go, as no one knows my face. I can be quick."

Two of Grainger's group began to move uneasily, as if afraid of being left unprotected, in the open.

Grainger gave him an address and a phone number in a quiet voice, but he also thought hard on a visual image. Alistair picked it up and reinforced it. Tymos nodded and walked with caution, out of the small hiding place. He didn't go far. He needed to draw on the ambient energy before he tried to transmit to the visual reference. He felt it filling him and was surprised how much energy was available from the rotting garbage. As his tired mind cleared, he realised that he should not have been surprised.

He knew roughly how far, and in what direction he had to go, and with the picture in mind, he transmitted.

The house, or rather shop and house combined, was very distinctive. At first glance, it reminded him of a gypsy caravan, since it was made of wood and painted in bright colours. He glanced around to see if anyone had noticed his abrupt appearance. He sensed no amazed or agitated thoughts as he walked quickly to the door of the shop. A bell tinkled as he went in and he sensed movement in the dim interior. He adjusted his eyes and saw the willowy shape of a woman approaching. The heat image gave no indication of her age.

She stopped a short distance away and greeted him, "How may I help you, stranger?"

"I am Tymos. I have come from Tamir."

He sensed, rather than saw, the woman become very still and heard her intake of breath. Then, the light became a little brighter and the woman came close enough to examine him. Now Tymos could see her too and the recognition was mutual. "My father knew you! But how can you still be so young?"

"I need to be," Tymos said, cryptically. "Your brother needs help."

"Where is he?"

"Not far. Can I bring six people here?"

"Yes. Do you need help?"

"No, but I don't want to arrive in the street - do you have a back yard?"

The woman took his arm and pulled him through the front room and into another that was a sparsely furnished living room. A man sat there and the woman merely said, "Watch the shop." He rose at once and asked no questions. "Can you bring them here?"

Tymos experienced a moment of surprise. The woman laughed softly. "My father was remarkable. I don't know how he did some of the things he did, but hey, gypsies have all sorts of strange tricks."

"Thank you, I will be back soon."

Wasting no time, Tymos transmitted back to the cul-de-sac. He took Grainger and Wallis first, ignoring Grainger's protests. He made two more trips back and forward to complete the transfer. He did not mention how narrow an escape it had been. Alistair, however, had heard the sirens and sent a mental, "Phew!"

Tymos sank into the nearest chair. "I need to rest."

He scarcely heard the woman say she would bring food and drink for them. He did hear Alistair speaking to his mind. "Are we safe here?"

He sent a groggy, "For now. We won't stay long."

They were only twenty miles from the refugee centre.

Tymos woke to the smell of fragrant herbs and soft voices talking. He realised that his hand was resting on a large, odd shaped crystal. He felt refreshed, but before he moved on, he needed to find out what had happened.

Using a personal transmitter didn't usually drain him, not even when he had to anchor the far end with his mind and take others with him. It made him wonder what had happened just as they had materialised in this time.

Rather than move immediately, he enhanced his hearing and listened to the talk. The man he had seen before, was reporting on the hunt for Grainger's group. They were being called dangerous subversives.

"…have roadblocks at the edges of town. Doing a house-to-house search. Be some hours before they reach here."

Tymos sat up and everyone looked his way, but only Grainger stood and approached.

"So, what exactly have I got myself into this time, Tamir?" Tymos asked softly.

"A horrible, terrifying war," Grainger said with a sigh. "How and why it came about is a story too long to tell now. However, we must get to Washington, as soon as possible. Here is why…"

Tymos heard Grainger out, and as he listened, he felt the shiver of a premonition. He knew, without any doubt, that Earth was at a pivotal point in its history. Grainger and Wallis, working together, had the best chance to end the war and bring about a lasting peace. Nevertheless, without help, even they might fail.

"Tell me about the enemy."

Grainger sighed. "The Eastern Alliance is made up from all the little countries and power states that refused to join the United Nations. The countries that never liked the way America did things. They declared war, and I really think they only want to destroy everything that is good about western democracy."

"Who is their leader?" Tymos asked.

"Sorellen calls himself the leader of the Alliance but I am sure he is only a figure head and the real power broker is staying hidden."

That information was stored for future consideration.

Grainger dared to ask, "Where is Kryslie?"

"Still at that refugee centre, for now…" Tymos broke off, as he felt a surge of alarm from his twin.

He stopped speaking for a while and then continued. "She was watching the enemy agents there. They think they have brainwashed her. However, they have just begun some trumped up reason to send her to Washington. If they intend to use her as a spy or some kind of sleeper agent there…well, two can play that game."

Grainger asked, "Then you are likely to be here for a while. Are you here to stay?"

It was a strange question, but Tymos knew what he meant.

"Not yet, old friend," Tymos gave a wry grin as he stated the 'old'. "We were meant to arrive after the war."

"So you tell me that now," Grainger chuckled. "Do you know exactly?"

Tymos shrugged.

"No! I mean, yes, I know when the others will arrive. I didn't expect to meet you as a child, or a young man, or again now. It is at the whim of the Guardians."

"I see," Grainger appeared thoughtful. "I know you shouldn't betray the future, but can you give me a clue to what I must do?"

"Continue as you are," Tymos suggested. "If we get the Governor to Washington, and sworn in as President that deputy of his will have less pull with the war makers. If we get you to the Science Council meeting, the two of you will win out and when you do, what are your plans?"

Grainger outlined his ideals and for a half Tymorean with little trace of that heritage, he was a wise man indeed.

"A university," Tymos mused. "We will have to go there, but we will have no background, no references."

Grainger smiled. "I'll be ready for you. I will leave my father's work there.

"Where only we can get it?" Tymos suggested.

"Naturally," Grainger spoke neutrally. He returned his talk to the present. "I can't contact anyone who can get us to Washington. Have you the means?"

"I have been giving that some thought. None of my people know that I am here in this time. Yet I know that the two people who found me are Tymorean. That is where I got the transmitter. They did not know me, but as I have no resources of my own, my only option is to find them and convince them to help me. Do you know where the enemy are bombing now?"

"My sister has said they have reached the Kansas border. I don't even know how to get there."

Tymos simply smiled faintly. "Keep a low profile and don't let any of your group leave here. I will be as quick as I can."

Tymos walked out into the small back garden of the house and stood leaning against an old fig tree. He made his mind a blank, and drew on the life energy stored in the old tree. He sought for Tymorean minds. To him, the minds of Tymoreans were like bell chimes compared to static, and although very few of them were telepathic, he and his sister could talk to other Tymorean minds. He could read them and they would hear when he projected to them. He hoped that he might reach the minds of the two Tymoreans who had helped him. He sent his mental senses out, and felt his sister's mind. She knew what he was trying to do, and added her own efforts, even as she was being strapped into the plane that was to take her to Washington.

From the little he had learnt from the two good Samaritans, Tymos knew they reported to another. He needed to reach the coordinator and he hoped that person had not yet moved too far away.

With Kryslie acting briefly like the other end of a detection net, they sensed the mind they wanted, and Tymos was able to get an idea of distance and direction. He vanished from the little back garden as mysteriously as he had arrived.

He materialised back near where he had last seen the Tymorean group, and after moving into the shadow of a deserted building, he projected a thought to the co-ordinator.

"Rhyn?"

Tymos sensed a rapid mental shuffling, amazement that he heard what he thought was a voice, but having no one around, then comprehension.

"Prince Tymos?" The thought was not projected, but was followed by a sense of relief.

"Yes, and I need your help and absolute discretion," Tymos broadcast.

"I am at your service, Prince Tymos."

"I am not far from where Penjan lost me a few days ago. Can you come here and bring Carla and Penjan with you and please don't mention me to them yet. Let me know when you get there and I will join you."

He received the message about five minutes later. Using Rhyn's mind as his anchor, he transmitted closer, but made sure the area was otherwise deserted before arriving in their sight.

"You!" Penjan exclaimed.

Carla curtsied in a brief movement. "Prince Tymos, our parents and grandparents spoke of you."

"Please, I would rather we forgot the royal rigmarole – it means little here," Tymos said quietly. "I want to thank you both for helping my sister and myself – and to ask that you do not mention, even in your reports home, that you have seen us."

"But why?" Carla asked.

"This will sound strange, but I did not expect to come to this time. We knew nothing of the fact that we did, so I do not want to create a time paradox. However, I need help to transport eight people from Big River to Washington safely and quickly."

"We have a beaming point there," Rhyn began. "But we cannot take the local people that way."

Tymos didn't mention that the people had already experienced his transmitting them.

Rhyn thought for a long moment. "I know a couple of air force transport pilots that owe me favours. They are descended from some Tymoreans who married locals. I will arrange something. Big River you say. Do you know if there is an airport there?"

"There is an army base there, with an airstrip," Tymos was able to tell him.

Rhyn's face brightened. "I will contact the pilots and send Carla and Penjan with details. Where can we find you?"

"About twenty miles north of east of Big River. The house of a relative of one of those needing help. I can give you an image…"

"We need distance and direction," Penjan stated, as if he expected Tymos to know that.

"Bankstown," Tymos said, deciding he did not have the time to explain how to use a visual image as a focus point. Not all Tymoreans could do that.

"Carla can bring the details. I think I should help Prince Tymos protect these people," Penjan declared.

Tymos nodded agreement and watched the other two de-materialise.

"My apologies, Prince Tymos. I did not recognise you when we first met. I thought I could recognise a Tymorean anywhere."

"You were born here," Tymos concluded.

Penjan nodded and related the names of his parents and grandparents. It was the eldest generation that had been born on Tymorea.

"They trained you well, and I did not expect to find kin still here. However, you may have sensed that my sister and I were humans, which we are. We were born here, and only went to Tymorea as adolescents. But that does not matter right now. The Guardians sent us back in time to pivotal points in Earth's history – such as this."

"Is your sister well?" Penjan asked.

"Well enough. She is dealing with a bunch of enemy infiltrators who think they control her. We need to get back to those that need my help."

Penjan stood beside Tymos and together they transmitted to the house. The rescued men eyed the newcomer warily, but Grainger accepted his presence immediately.

"This is Penjan," Tymos introduced. "Some extra protection while I find another place to go if we need to leave here."

The young Tymorean did not ask for the names of the men he protected, but he had already identified one of them. Governor Wallis, the missing President-elect. The one man who had a hope of ending the destructive war.

Hours later, the need to move came true. A dozen police cars formed a ring around the house, but the men in the cars were not police. This time the moving of the people went quicker with two of them doing it.

Carla found them after the third move. The pilots had agreed to help them and would be landing a plane at an airport fifty miles away. She admitted to Tymos that they were uncomfortable with the idea of acting without orders.

Any reluctance in the minds of the pilots evaporated as soon as they recognised one of the passengers.

The cars, borrowed from owners who had left their cars in locked garages before evacuating, passed the gate to the military base without trouble. Tymos had impressed the minds of the guards to believe they had a legitimate reason to be there. However, he could not reach the minds of the viewers of the security cameras. As they reached the transport plane, a jeep was speeding towards them and others were following.

"Get on board," Tymos insisted. "Hurry! We will hold them. Tell the pilots to take off."

Tymos and Penjan fought a rearguard action, using weapons provided by the pilots. They gave the plane time to taxi and take off. As soon as the plane passed the boundary of the base, Tymos and Penjan transmitted on board and walked forward to the cockpit.

"How the..." the co-pilot began to ask how Tymos had boarded the plane and then decided he didn't need to know.

"You will need every bit of skill you have," Tymos advised. "You have just become America's most wanted and nothing will be spared to stop you."

"Since there are already four jets on our tail, I had started to reach that conclusion," the senior pilot said lightly, but his mind was full of doubts.

"You have recognised your passengers?" Tymos asked.

"Governor Wallis and the scientist fellow? Aye."

"They have been held prisoner by agents of the Alliance," Tymos summarised. "And from the strength of our departure committee, someone high up doesn't want him found and able to show up in Washington. Who do you think has benefited most from his absence?"

The co-pilot answered. "That slimy weasel, Jacksmith, the VP and acting President. I wouldn't trust him with dog droppings."

"Well, you need to proceed like this is a mission in enemy territory. Any plane you see is likely to want to shoot you down. Americans and Alliance."

Tymos left Penjan watching the radar and went to sit near the passengers. He ignored their questions because he needed to use all his senses to detect threats.

The four jets were merely following them at the moment. That could change at any time. The transport plane was no match for the jets as far as speed went and if the jets received orders to fire, there would be very little time to react.

The orders came in a very short time. Tymos sensed Penjan's identification of the missile, felt the plane bank to try to move out of the way. With his hands covered to hide their glow, he waited until the two missiles were close before mentally 'nudging' them into each other. Their pilots thanked their luck and hoped it would stay with them.

The pilots of the pursuing jets had no inkling of who was on board the transport. They would simply be obeying orders to fire on an enemy operated aircraft.

The times of maximum danger were the refuelling stops – when the plane was grounded. Tymos had instructed Rhyn to have only Tymoreans staffing the airstrips and his pilots never realised that the ground crew were the same at each stop. The Tymoreans skipped ahead using the long-range beam.

So far, their only advantage was that the transport ship had a longer range fuel tank than the fighter jets, and if they stayed under the radar, they had a chance to lose their pursuers when one group retreated, and before another group found them. However, the enemy surely guessed that they were heading to Washington.

Kryslie kept in mind touch with her brother as they neared the Capitol. She kept him advised of important information she had discovered. In her mind, the indignities she was suffering were minor compared to the dangers he was fending off.

She rejoiced when he reported that the President-elect Wallis was safe in Washington and waited to hear that Tymos had sent the plane on ahead, the pilot and himself safely ejected, and the auto-pilot taking it on a course away from inhabited areas. Its tanks were nearly empty.

Kryslie had overheard talking between her military guards. It had been announced that in the absence of President-elect Wallis, the acting President, Jacksmith, would be sworn in as the next president. There was no time for a new election - a leader was needed immediately.

Kryslie woke early on the day after Tymos arrived in Washington and when her breakfast tray was delivered, so was a message. Her court martial had been brought forward. She was to be ready right after breakfast. They gave her no reason why the time had changed, but she guessed that it had to do with the timing of the swearing in ceremony, scheduled for that day.

When she was escorted into the courtroom, she saw that the disciplinary panel consisted of eight military personnel, all senior ranks, seated at a long bench that had seats for ten.

A naval lieutenant greeted her when she had been led to a table on the left of the courtroom. He introduced himself as Jason Grey and told her he was to be her defence lawyer. He had just arrived and carried a folder of papers. While Kryslie sat on a chair, he quickly read over the evidence against her and the charges and his mouth looked as if the words he was speaking had a nasty taste. However, he seemed to be an honest and well-intentioned man.

Krys waited for him to finish reading before asking, "Is your expression of distaste for me, or from that load of rubbish they claim I did."

He was too honest to lie. "What I read here, paints a very bad picture of you."

"No doubt," Kryslie agreed. "However, I don't think it particularly fair that you only have a few minutes to read that before being expected to defend me properly. I think you are being set up to fail."

Grey's mind and face betrayed that he had been a last minute replacement.

"Hadn't Captain Marsden spoken to you before this? He made notes here."

"No, I haven't seen anyone," Kryslie said, meeting his eyes. "And, I can't really state that I did not do what it is claimed of me, because I have no memory beyond a week ago. I might be guilty, but I really don't know."

"That is a valid point," Grey admitted. "But even reading this through quickly, it seems that the evidence they have against you is so full of holes, you probably don't need me to defend you. Read this and tell me what you think."

Krys scanned documents quickly, considering them as if she were not the subject of the trial.

"Who are the empty seats for?" Kryslie asked quietly, she had finished reading. A nebulous idea was forming in her mind.

"This doesn't apply to you, but when senior military are involved, the President (or at the moment, Acting President) and the Secretary of Defence may attend."

"I am not pretending to know your business, but can you call a postponement to these proceedings?" Krys asked.

"You are in no position to make demands, Private?" Grey stated bluntly.

"I believe I have the right to discuss my defence with you in private," Krys told him. "There are things you need to know and I want to know if your plans to exploit the holes in the evidence agree with mine."

Grey had read the evaluation reports from Big River and was aware of Krys's high IQ. He agreed to call for a postponement.

The one-hour break was barely adequate, but the court was recessed. They were led to a secure room and certain interested parties were annoyed that a mysterious malfunction stopped them listening in to the supposedly private discussion.

"Listen carefully," Krys said to Grey. "I feel you are an honest man and will fight for the truth. I really can't tell you about me before the past ten days, but I am sure that all those charges are false. My name is Kryslie Ward, not Christine Trent, and I have never been in the military."

She went on to tell him what she had discovered at the refugee centre and what they believed they had done to her. She was able to tell him the words they would use to make her work for them. "I believe those traitors are trying to determine if I am an agent working against them. I think you need to double check all the information you have about me. In fact, if you have a doctor run a blood test to determine my blood type, it will prove I could not be Trent. I am willing to bet that things won't go that far – or if it does, the prosecution will suddenly withdraw all the charges."

"Why?" Grey was baffled.

"I think, apart from wanting to check I'm not an agent, that they want me to come to the attention of the acting president, so he might put me onto his staff."

"That's a bit of a stretch," Grey told her.

"I know, but I feel it fits."

"We will see about that," Grey decided. "I'll organise the doctor. It won't take me long."

Guards replaced her lawyer and they watched her like she was a dangerous wild creature. Krys ignored them. She was aware of a flaw in her scenario. From Tym's account, the Vice President and Secretary of Defence were part of the conspiracy. In some way, the conspiracy wanted her working for them. It made sense that if the VP freed her, she would be grateful to him and agree to work for him. But, what would happen when Tym walked in with a newly sworn in President Wallis? Let her be a mole in his office? She could hardly wait!

Kryslie was impressed by her defender, as he cast doubt on all the evidence presented by the prosecuting lawyer. When the third day arrived, and it was to be the turn of the defence, she sensed the ripple of surprise from inside the courtroom. When she was brought in, she was not surprised to see the two previously empty seats were filled. She recognised the new President. The other man, she surmised, was the Secretary of Defence. Both the newcomers were scrutinising her carefully, but Wallis recognised her and the Secretary was full of glee at how well this scheme had worked out.

By the end of the day, no one doubted that the case against Krys was fabricated. The evidence of the blood test proved it beyond doubt. The real Private Christine Trent had a completely different blood type. The sample had been analysed in the courtroom to prevent claims of evidence tampering.

The Chairman of the panel deferred to the President and he dismissed the charges and made an apology to Krys for wrongful incarceration.

The decision was a sensation. The media representatives following the President went into a frenzy of activity and tried to interview the defendant – but Krys could not be found for comment. She and her lawyer left the courtroom, once all charges were dismissed, and made their way via a rear door to a car that took them to a hotel in the centre of town.

Grey only went because Krys wanted to repay his hard work with diner and drinks. He was astounded when an invitation arrived for them to join the President's party, in a private dining area in the very same hotel. Kryslie however, had been pre-warned by her twin.

The President had left the military court amidst tight security, with everyone expecting him to return to the Whitehouse. Wallis had chosen otherwise. Tymos had suggested that he needed to talk to Kryslie.

"So, what is this information that you claim to have for me?" Wallis asked once his party was alone. He looked at Grey as he spoke.

Grey deferred to Kryslie and she detailed all the things she had mentioned to her lawyer about the activities at the refugee centre where he had been prisoner. Wallis nodded as various points were mentioned.

He had put aside his questions about her to concentrate on the more important matter.

"Thank you for bringing this to my attention," Wallis stated without further comment. He warned Lieutenant Grey that he was not to mention the matter to anyone else.

Later, after Grey had departed, when he was alone with Krys and Tymos and the security men were outside of the room, he spoke less formally.

"Some one that I trust implicitly has suggested that you would be an asset to my staff. I would like to know why."

"What do you know about me?" Kryslie asked softly.

"Pretend I know nothing," Wallis suggested. "I know what was written in the papers about you was fabrication, and whilst I recall someone like you, it was twenty years ago and in another country."

Kryslie glanced at her twin, giving him a look of enquiry.

"If he thought he recognised me, he has never mentioned it," Tymos said with a mental shrug.

"I can make sure that the people you have working for you are not traitors."

Wallis did not act as if that suggestion was absurd. "I have a trace of that talent myself."

"I know. You were at Rapid Creek," Kryslie stated, surprising him. "Surely you recognised my brother."

Wallis scrutinised her again. "It hardly seems credible – and you and he haven't changed. I thought Tymos to be a son of that other that I knew."

"If you trust Grainger's assessment," Kryslie spoke carefully, guessing who Wallis meant in terms of someone he trusted. "He knows things about us that no one else does. What was twenty years ago for you, was less than a fortnight for us. We cannot explain how, or why, but we are here to help the cause of Peace."

Wallis smiled and relaxed. He also eased the strong mind shields so that they could read what he now thought. He trusted them, and he knew they were special. They had achieved wonders at the time in the past when they had met. He was very grateful that they had come again, to help him. He did not choose to discuss the past any further. He knew now, in his very soul, that he could trust this woman as he already had learnt to trust her brother.

Changing back to an earlier topic, Wallis said, "You don't need to warn me about my Vice President. I knew his leanings when we agreed to run together. He needed my charisma and I needed the votes of those who secretly followed him. What I didn't know was how far he would go to destroy this country. However, there are things I know that he does not realise I am aware of and he will soon discover I am not a mouse. Tell me how you plan to draw the real enemy out of hiding."

Krys smiled at his accurate reading of her mind and told him her intention.

Chapter 15 - Chasing the Enemy

Kryslie became the President's aide, privy to all his plans and constantly scrutinized by his security people. The monitoring was her idea. She was certain that those who thought they controlled her would soon contact her.

The war had turned against the enemy once Wallis was in control. Vice President Jacksmith had chosen to disassociate himself from the Secretary of Defence, who had been allowed to resign, citing ill health. He was in fact under guard in the military prison. With Tymos acting as a war advisor and providing a means to shield the aircraft electronics from interference, the enemy bombers found themselves under implacable attack and turned to flee.

With the cessation of overt hostilities, the covert attacks increased. Every day, important men, politicians, scientists, leaders in many fields were found to be missing. The President was under pressure to act in a certain unacceptable manner, to get the men released.

However, all of the missing men had been traced and when the Politico-Science summit was only days away, the missing men were secreted away from their prisons under the noses of their guards. No one was seen on any of the security devices to identify the rescuers.

Soon after, the subversives at the refugee centre were arrested, and their computers confiscated. Deveraux had believed his security protocols were impenetrable, but it only took Tymos half an hour to break them. Then, all the people who had been treated by Deveraux at the refugee centre were brought in for questioning. Kryslie had memorised all the names and aliases of the mind-treated agents and the current placement of those people had been found in a file on the group's computer.

Kryslie was sure that the mind behind the scheme would be very angry by now and she expected to be contacted. She and a few strategically placed others were the only ones still free. Publically it was held that these few had passed thorough stringent security and psychiatric tests.

When contact was made, via the phone, Kryslie recognised one of the word triggers that Deveraux had created for her. She recorded the conversation and had the call traced. The contact asked her for nothing in that initial call, but told her to go to a particular place.

The contact arrived early to check the area and found nothing to indicate monitoring. Kryslie was followed by associates of the contact and they reported that she had not been tailed. Once they spoke another of the trigger words, and Kryslie seemed in a daze, they checked her for wires and listening devices and found her clear. Only then did they question her listened avidly when she spoke of a list of American agents that were working in alliance countries. They told her to get the list for them. They asked for her knowledge of certain matters and were elated with what she revealed. Their controller would be pleased with what she knew. Then they asked her to get several specific documents that only the President and Vice President should have known about. That request sealed the guilt of Jacksmith. Kryslie agreed to get what they wanted. She acted as if it was a legitimate request, never indicating that she was not under their control.

Kryslie hadn't needed to wear a listening device, not with Tymos attuned to her mind. When unanticipated questions were asked, Tymos passed on the question and Wallis's answer. He and Grainger were working with the President to get the evidence needed to convict the foreigner who was inciting the covert attacks. Only the top men in the Security services were privy to this unorthodox investigation, and they would only mobilise their subordinates when arrests were authorised.

Foreign agents, already noted and identified, followed Kryslie back to her Washington apartment. Those she had spoken to, thinking they were safe, went to their higher ups to report. However, what Wallis had dubbed 'Grainger's private army', were following these men and were photographing and identifying those they spoke to.

Wallis spoke to Grainger, much later that evening.

"Still no indication of the top man," Wallis queried.

"No," Grainger confirmed. "He is a canny one. It is my guess that he will take our bait, as soon as Krys lets on she has what he thinks he wants."

"This is the part I don't like about your plan, Tamir," Wallis admitted. "What if he takes Krys and has her killed?"

"Remember who we are talking about, Mr President," Grainger obliquely reminded him. "Krys and Tymos know what they are doing. We might not get the evidence to fix the man behind the war, but he won't escape them. They can act across borders, when we are constrained by treaties or agreements. And, with him on the run, suing for peace will be a formality."

"I hope you are right, Tamir," Wallis sighed.

Grainger learnt that Krys had been abducted when Wallis called him the next day. Tymos confirmed it and began passing on information from his sister. She hadn't seen the top man, but she was in their American headquarters and had identified more of the upper echelon of agents. The faces of these men were passed to Tymos, mind to mind, and he picked them from covertly obtained security or monitoring records.

Tymos, using Krys as an anchor, transmitted into the enemy's secret headquarters. He gained access to their computer records and downloaded them all to a palm-sized, high capacity portable hard drive. This went immediately to the presidential investigators. A raid was planned.

Tymos knew that the leader wanted Krys and planned to smuggle her out of the country. They were going to let him. As Grainger had told Wallis, this leader was unknown and therefore there was no evidence against him. The downloaded files might give them something, but they doubted it.

The man was retreating, he would soon know that his organisation was finished and all his agents compromised. He might realise that even the ones that took Krys out of the country were known.

Tymos hoped that some of Grainger's army, that comprised Tymorean missionary descendants, would apprehend these men before their leader silenced them.

The raid failed to capture anyone; the headquarters were deserted and the computer wiped clean of data. There was no sign of Krys or any lead to how she was taken away. Tymos knew, but was saying nothing and Grainger and Wallis didn't ask him. He just assured them, privately, that she was well.

Krys allowed herself to be drugged, but knew the drug would not affect her for long. She wanted the men to think her helpless. She only pretended to be unconscious and though her body was sedated, her mind was fully aware. She knew, and reported to Tymos, when her initial escort was dismissed after seeing her aboard a foreign registered freighter. New men, more obviously foreign, replaced them as her guards. Tymos reported in turn when Grainger's army found the initial guards dead, and weighed down with chains, in the water near where the freighter had been docked.

When the freighter had gone beyond American claimed waters, a helicopter landed on its deck and the still supposedly unconscious Kryslie was taken on board and flown to the nearest land claimed by the Eastern Alliance. The men who had guarded her on the ship came with her.

The helicopter was being tracked by satellite and from its route, Tymos made his own estimate of her probable final destination. A stealth fighter was made available to him and he parachuted from that down into a deserted area of one of the Alliance countries. He began to make his way closer to the main city. He was in contact with the American Intelligence agencies and they confirmed the landing place of the helicopter.

Kryslie had been transferred from the helicopter to a private jet, well before he arrived, but he was not concerned. He searched the helicopter for clues, found none, and then spent several days tracking the pilots and guards. They too, were dead and unable to tell him anything.

He told his sister what he had found; a warning that the man they were after was utterly ruthless.

When she sensed that the drug had almost gone from her system, Kryslie allowed herself to stir and seem to wake up. It was in character for someone waking from a long period of drugged sleep to be slow to get up. She opened her eyes a fraction and spent time examining the ceiling above her. She took in the detail of all she could see before slowly moving her eyes to scan another section. There were recessed downlights, perfectly placed for providing the subdued lighting in the room. She saw part of a magnificent abstract mural in pastel colours. Around the edges of the room, more downlights, currently turned off, which would provide brighter light when required.

Her impression was of a room in some luxurious mansion, until she turned slightly towards the window. The glass there appeared tinted, but when she adjusted her eyes to examine it more closely, she saw it was thick security glass with a reinforcing layer of wire mesh between glass layers. She normalised her eyes again before stirring and while rolling slightly in the bed, she checked for and found a tiny fish-eye security camera in the ceiling design.

To see more of the room, she needed to sit up. Groaning as if it was an effort, she turned and freed her legs from the blankets. That was when she realised she was now clad in an expensive silk nightdress and had nothing under it. She looked around to see if her clothes were anywhere nearby, and saw, not the business suit and skirt she had been wearing but a designer outfit hanging on an antique brass clothes rack.

On the chair beside the bed was a silk lounging robe. Feeling a slight chill, Kryslie stood, feigned unsteadiness and walked on deep pile carpet to the chair. She donned the robe and decided to explore what she expected to be her prison.

The first of the three doors she saw was locked. The second led to a bathroom, with a deep spa bath and gold plating on all the tap fittings at bath and hand basin. A curtained off corner held the other necessary fitment, and she made use of it.

Before she returned to the other room, she washed her face and hands, making use of the thick soft towels.

Some of her bemusement transmitted to her twin. She heard his mental hello, and had the sense of him asking how she was.

"Better than I am acting," she admitted. "And my prison is most luxurious - with some high-tech monitoring equipment. Even in the bathroom."

"I am not surprised. The house where you are belongs to Emir Hur Massin. Just a little country mansion outside of Tel Abbas," Tymos supplied.

Kryslie did not need to know how her brother had found her, he was her twin, and the bond they shared was strong. "I've been here five days. What has been happening?"

"Wallis and Grainger have everything under control back in America," Tymos assured her. "The enemy attack forces have melted back into obscurity - the few that escaped the counter offensive that is. Jacksmith made a very public resignation, citing a lack of confidence in the President - he was a laughing stock in the press. Wallis appointed a replacement - one of his aides from when he was Governor. He had the full support of all the relevant bodies."

"What about here? Have you learnt anything?" Kryslie insisted, delaying her return to the bedroom, by finding a new toothbrush and paste in a cabinet near the basin, and putting them to use. "Where is Tel Abbas?"

"It is the second biggest city in the second most important country in the Eastern Alliance," Tymos summarised. "Again, not surprising. Most of the agents being tracked by American Intelligence have ties to this country. It looks like the subversives originated here, and the whole war effort as well."

"I mistrust the obvious," Kryslie thought back, as a shiver of premonition crept down her spine. "Do you think they suspect I was involved in the round up of their agents?"

"They were watching you at every step," Tymos reminded her. "You spoke to no one - vocally. And for good measure, some spiteful presidential assistant claimed you were mixed up with the traitors, and you were never trusted because the intelligence people were always watching you. Jacksmith used you as his reason for distrusting Wallis - called him gullible."

Kryslie thought about that. Jacksmith was a traitor, and his claims were a last ditch attempt to discredit Wallis. "So, do these people think I am a traitor or a loyal follower of Wallis?"

"I would say, both," Tymos gave his opinion. "But they will feel they have you controlled."

"So what is their game, if they are keeping me here?"

"Caution. There is a massive hunt to find you. There are whispers that you know too many secrets. Wallis is concerned for your safety, and fears that if the enemy have you they will torture you to find out all they can."

"Charming," Kryslie said wryly. "Tortured by luxury."

"I think that would be to keep you sweet," Tymos proposed teasingly. "That whole mansion has been watched by the absolute latest surveillance equipment. A flea couldn't jump unnoticed. Moreover, it is all very deceptively innocent looking. I think they are keeping you here to see if you were followed, or if you try to get a message out now that you are awake again."

"I have been awake more often than they realise, but I usually couldn't sense anyone. Except the maids who brought in the food and had to get it into me, and some kind of doctor who examined me inside and out with some kind of portable equipment. Whatever drug they have been giving me, blocked me from sending to you - and that must be a fluke."

"I knew you were okay," Tymos assured her. "I really don't think there are many people there - and those are mainly guards. Though a man in a western style suit went in there earlier today, and I haven't seen him come out."

"Where are you?" Kryslie asked.

"Not too far. I have some equipment, courtesy of the American intelligence agents here. I have hooked into the security system at the mansion, but only the exterior cameras and external warning devices."

Kryslie heard the sound of someone moving around in the other room, and took a few moments to sense the person's thoughts. A man, confident that he could handle any woman, but believing he would have no trouble with this one.

"I think, I have a visitor," Kryslie warned her twin, mentally.

He sent back, "Make yourself look stunning, Sis. He might be the man we're after."

Kryslie concentrated harder, finding her psychic senses were working again. "No, it's the doctor again."

The man was standing, halfway between the bed and the door, and he had a briefcase sitting on the floor beside him. He gave her a slight bow, when she emerged from the bathroom and stopped.

Kryslie gave him a rapid look, and asked, "Who are you?"

"I am Doctor Michael Pritchard, Miss Ward. I have been attending you during your stay here."

He spoke American, but she detected a trace of a foreign accent.

"Why am I here?" Kryslie asked. It was an obvious question.

"I am afraid that I am not at liberty to give details, but if you are patient, all will be explained. I have been asked to examine you, to ensure you have recovered."

"What happened to me? I can't remember anything."

"We are hoping that your amnesia will soon be overcome," the doctor said, but he was lying.

"Yeah," Kryslie tried to sound like she agreed with the hope. She was not going to admit that she knew she had not had amnesia before, and wondered what drug or treatment they had used with the intention of removing her memory. It must have been why she had been unable to mind touch her twin for the past five days. With a shrug, Kryslie went and sat on the side of her bed, and let the doctor examine her.

At first, the doctor did the usual things, took her pulse, listened to her breathing, and checked her temperature. Then he spoke softly, in a low voice that she just heard, and patted her shoulder.

Kryslie felt her body jerk, as her mind recognised the keywords that the doctor back at the refugee centre had used to program her. She did not try to overcome the response of her body, just listened intently to what the doctor said.

First it was a question, "What is your name?"

"Miss Ward," she answered obediently. If they thought she had no memory, she would use the name the doctor had just called her. It seemed like the right answer.

"Where do you live?"

Kryslie remained silent, as if thinking. The doctor asked other questions, trying to get an answer, and he smiled when she could not. Then he requested her to do a number of things, unethical things, beginning with, "You will stand up and get undressed."

Kryslie knew that he was testing her and expected that if she were acting, she would not go along with his commands. She gave no sign of awareness when the doctor began to undress himself and came over to her. He took pleasure in molesting her, but he went no further than touching her. In his mind was the knowledge that he had needed to find out if she were a virgin, and if so she was to be delivered to someone in that same state.

While he redressed, he had Kryslie stand still nude - as a further test. He kept her that way, as he implanted hypnotic commands.

These began with stressing to her supposedly unresisting mind, that she had no idea of her identity, and no memory of the last two years of her life. He wanted her to believe she was anti-American - no surprise there. He gave her mind reasons for hating the Americans. These she would just 'know' later.

He used a mixture of truth and fabrication - telling her that she had been spying for the Eastern Alliance, and reached a high position with the enemy government, but had been discovered. Alliance agents had rescued her from certain torture and incarceration.

Any Americans that wanted to believe the disgraced vice-president, or the spiteful rumours that Tymos had deliberately circulated, probably did believe she was a traitor.

What actually surprised Kryslie as she listened to this fabricated version of the truth, was that they didn't try to find out what other secrets she knew. Perhaps the former vice president had told them all they wanted to know, or perhaps they really didn't believe a woman would be told anything of real importance.

After a while, the nature of the hypnotic suggestions changed to what Kryslie considered to be a distilled version of how the local women were expected to behave, and comport themselves. Never mind that she was physically and intellectually skilled - women were expected to obey their male protector. In her case, she was never to speak of her life in America.

In the back of her mind, she heard her brother's mental voice. "Don't they trust that over the top mind wipe of your memory? Any other person would be a semi-vegetable by now."

Kryslie returned a mental image of herself shrugging.

The lecture had moved onto the legal punishments for disobedient women and what she ought to expect for the things she had done - even if she didn't recall her actions.

Every word of what the doctor said to her was stored in Kryslie's extremely retentive memory. She quickly examined all possible implications and ramifications. She knew how to act, to seem to be obeying his instructions.

In the brief pause when the doctor seemed to have finished his spiel, Kryslie had a fleeting glimpse of a well-dressed figure in the doctor's mind. She recalled that glimpse and studied it like it was a snapshot, knowing that Tymos was also aware of it.

"Bingo," Tymos thought back at her.

Kryslie silently agreed, but had to attend to the doctor's final instructions.

"You will get dressed in your night clothes again, and then count silently to sixty. Then you will wake up and you will not remember my visit."

Seeming to obey, Kryslie put the silk nightgown back on and returned to the bed. She sat there for longer than the indicated time, and then shook her head as if trying to clear it. Looking around, she seemed to notice the clothes again, and stood to walk over to them. She was acting more like a sleepwalker, or one who was acting on a forgotten routine. However, she dressed with her back to the observing camera. The unseen watchers had seen enough of her when the doctor was examining her and she was supposed to be a modest, demure female. She left off the headscarf since she was alone in the room.

Her actions then were intended to imply that she had indeed forgotten who she was. She began a systematic search of the two rooms she had access to. When she found the wardrobe, full of expensive women's clothing, she stopped to study the fabrics and colours. They were all akin to the one she wore - long sleeved, ankle length and with a high neckline.

On the floor, under the dresses, were six pairs of boots. She reached for a pair that would complement the deep blue dress she was wearing. She found stockings in a drawer below one containing silk underclothes. The shoes were a perfect fit. When she finished lacing them up, she continued searching the room.

There was nothing in the room to give her any information. The two magazines on a small table were written in a foreign language, and there was nothing to provide entertainment, or communication. No TV, no computer, no audio equipment, or books. She even checked behind the two leather armchairs, and felt in the soil of the two decorative potted plants.

The two other doors she could see were both locked. One probably led to a passage, the other she guessed to be an adjoining bedroom.

Finally, she went to look out of the window, confirming at the same time that the window had reinforced glass, and was sealed shut. Outside though, was a lush green garden with exotic trees forming part of a magnificently landscaped formal garden. There were sections of lawn, some secluded, with paths winding through trees and bushes, and colourful flowerbeds.

It was a pleasant view to enjoy while she waited for her captors to make their next move.

One of the locked doors opened with an audible noise. Kryslie spun around to see a well dressed man stride into the room and come towards her. He was the man she had glimpsed in the doctor's mind, and since she was supposed to be a demure female and have no memory of the man, she chose to dart behind the nearest armchair.

She was sure this was the man she was after. His mind felt covetous, as if he, by having her in his control, had obtained a valuable possession. She sensed snippets of ideas on how he could use her against the despised United States. He had indeed incited the useless and wasteful war that had caused so much destruction, and the deaths of thousands of non-combatants. It had still not slaked his hatred.

The man stopped within conversational distance of the chair and began speaking in a soothing tone in his own language. Kryslie took the meaning of the words from the man's mind, but kept staring at him as if she didn't understand. His words sounded calm, but he was pretending to tell her off as if she was a naughty child, and warning her of consequences. It was virtually the same as what the doctor had told her, and she ignored it - wondering instead, why she was hearing a rumbling like distant thunder, in her mind.

An idea came to her that was so astounding she was momentarily stunned. She had planned to ensure the man's downfall and death, now she needed to change her plans.

"Krys?"

The man had changed to speaking American and was suddenly beside her and urging her from behind the chair. His touch returned her to the present and she tried to pull away.

"You don't remember me," the man sounded concerned, and pitying her. "I hadn't realised that your amnesia was so bad."

In a distant part of her mind, she felt her twin snort with amusement and mentally comment, "Really, now?" She sent a quick, "Shh!"

"You... know me?" Krys asked, looking at him, studying his face as if he was her lifeline.

"My dear, of course I do. You are the child of my dearest friend."

Kryslie listened to the fabricated background he was giving her. It explained her intelligence, her physical skills and why she had been in America. She allowed her body to relax as he spoke, until he stressed, "You have had a very lucky escape, and now you should put aside any childish notions of playing spy. You are a grown woman, and you must now act like one."

"I don't remember anything," Kryslie claimed with pitiful frustration. "I didn't even understand you when you first spoke." She made her body tense again, as if fearing his anger. The man collected her into a gentle embrace and used one hand to brush strands of red hair from her face.

"It is probably because you left here at a very young age, though I would have thought your father would have spoken to you in his own language. Maybe you were too exposed to the barbaric American culture."

"What do I do now?" Kryslie asked in a small voice, hoping to learn something of the man's plans.

"I will see you are married to a good man who will treat you well."

Kryslie made a calculated move and pressed herself closer to the man, and made herself tremble. Being married off to some other man, was not what the Guardians of Peace had meant when they planted the astounding idea into her head. She looked down and said nothing but sent a very primal emotion to the man's mind. She knew when his body reacted in the way she intended.

He stiffened, almost imperceptibly. He had intended to use her to discredit or damage the Americans and their allies, now he was considering more immediate amusements.

"I don't know how to be a good wife to a man I don't know," Krys said after a while. She put her arms around the man and hugged him. "I don't even remember who you are."

The man hugged her back. "My dear Krys, I am Abdul bin Halil."

He didn't say he was the leader of the small country, the neighbour to the one where she was effectively a prisoner, but she knew it from his mind and from the commands of the Guardians.

He was thinking that now was the time to lie low. He needed time to rebuild his organisation if he wanted to try again to ruin America.

Krys sensed that he was considering debauching her personally, rather than giving her to his current host. She began to insert ideas into his mind, amongst the erotic ideas he was already giving himself.

Tymos touched her mind as she was doing this to confirm that the man had given his identity and to give her what information was available about him. The leader of the Eastern Alliance was rabidly anti American, but a brilliant man in the field of politics. If anyone could unite the rest of the splintered non-aligned countries, he could.

Krys considered that in terms of world politics. If he united all the non-aligned countries that would give him even more power than he already had. It would lead to a bipartisan world. Would that make it easier to unite all the world nations – merging two groups, not dozens?

"Is it wise to give him ideas like that?" Tymos queried his sister. "He is power hungry already."

"It will keep him busy in this part of the world for some time," Krys told him. "And if he dreams of founding a dynasty, it will give me a chance to sow the seeds of peace."

Tymos realised what she meant and his mind revealed his embarrassment. "Are you sure that is the right thing to do?"

"Yes, the Guardians have spoken to me."

Tymos made no further comment. "I'll contact you later!"

Krys didn't worry about her twin's abrupt withdrawal; she needed to keep working on bin Halil. He was now trying to make her want him.

She obliged him by nestling closer to him and letting him nuzzle her hair and begin to feel her in an intimate way. He soon recalled himself and told her that he was taking her home.

Chapter 16 - Willing Prisoner

The flight in bin Halil's private jet lasted half an hour, and it landed on a sealed strip amidst a sea of sand, and near groupings of desert palms. She only saw this when she emerged from the plane with bin Halil's arm around her. As he guided her down the steps, she felt the furnace like heat of the desert. For the trip amongst strangers, she had worn the filmy veil that was designed to cover her head by wrapping around the face. On the plane, she had been able to wear it loosely, now she was glad to have it around her face for it kept the sun from her eyes and hid them when she adjusted their shape to scan the area around her.

Close by was a white stretched limo, parked under some of the palms. As they emerged, the car drove to the foot of the ramp. In the distance, amidst a larger grouping of palms was a large low structure. A road ran from the airstrip to the house. No other signs of habitation were visible.

It was clearly meant to be a remote retreat.

The car stopped and the driver emerged, trotted around the car and opened the door. A blast of cold air greeted Kryslie as bin Halil urged her to enter. As she watched him follow her into the car, she saw that the boarding stairs of the plane were lifting and the engines were revving up again. There would be no convenient plane to fly if she was thinking of escape, and walking off would be foolish.

Bin Halil did not speak to her during the short ride to the house. That meant that she was not permitted to speak either. She had many questions she wanted to ask - reasonable ones if she had in fact lost her memory. But women were not meant to speak unless invited. Still, a great deal could be learnt from quiet observation.

At the house, bin Halil once again directed her by having his arm behind her and urging her forward. Six servants, clad in loose fitting tunic tops over loose white pants that were bound at the ankles and held up by a wide waist belt, bowed as he entered. Bin Halil made no acknowledgement, just gave orders. Krys understood the foreign words, only because the meaning was clear in his mind. She was to bathe and refresh herself after her trip, as his intentions could wait until she met his fastidious preferences.

Two women, also clad in white loose fitting outfits, emerged from an adjoining room and took Kryslie by the hands. They led her along a long passage with a white marble tiled floor and bare cedar wood walls, into a lavish bathing room. It was even grander than that in the suite in Tel Abbas. The bath was big enough to fit three people, and was surely an extravagant luxury in the midst of a desert.

It soon became apparent that the women were to wash her, for when she was in the filled tub and tried to begin washing herself, the women deftly removed the soap from her.

Kryslie decided to let them do what they had been ordered to do. She wanted to ask questions, but she had yet to master the language and she already knew that bin Halil liked his women silent and obedient. Now was not the time to start stirring things up.

So she was washed, all over, including her hair, and then once dried, was anointed with fragrant oils and dressed in a filmy pale green gown that really did not hide anything. Her hair, normally just below shoulder length, was plaited into dozens of small beaded braids.

When the women were finally finished, a light tea of fruits and nuts, was waiting for her on a low table. A light sparkling white wine was cooling in an ice bucket on the table.

Kryslie sat where indicated on a soft cushion by the table, and ate at the women's urging hand signals.

They retreated to near the door, and conversed in whispers. Kryslie felt their surface thoughts, mainly curiosity about who she was and where their master had found her. They had never seen hair as red as hers.

Bin Halil did not come to her until it was nearly dusk. By then, the table of fruits had been cleared and Kryslie had been left on her own. She chose to stay seated on the cushion, in a pose of meditation, and pretend to be unaware of his entry.

What was going to occur, was without doubt. She had schemed for it, roused bin Halil to fever pitch to achieve it. It was a sign of his mental strength that he had stopped himself back in Tel Abbas, and had waited until now to have her. He was a hard and dangerous man. She needed to remember that.

He came and sat on another cushion, a larger one, suited to lounging, and watched her. He wouldn't wait too long Kryslie knew, for she was intensely aware of his arousal.

Her own body began to mirror his condition, and that helped her to achieve the state she wanted for her body. She had been applying a bio-feedback technique she'd learnt back on Tymorea. This time it was not to ease the aches and pains from strenuous physical activities, but to speed up her body's monthly cycle and prepare it for the conception of a son. The knowledge of the process had come to her from the memories she had shared with the Governors of Tymorea.

Bin Halil finally tired of watching her, and leant forward to undo the front of the sheer gown.

Kryslie met his eyes, and then looked away, as if shy. She didn't object when his hand began moving over her bare flesh, for she sensed that he was only now noticing her physical perfection. He was coveting her, recalling her physical skills, and gloating at his control over her and it was exciting him.

His touch was surprisingly gentle, and he leant even closer and began to kiss her - on the neck, and moving lower.

"Come," he ordered, beginning to rise, and urging her to her feet. He drew her towards the huge king size bed, just visible behind a part opened curtain. He stopped her short of the bed, and brushed her gown off her shoulders so that it fell to the floor. "Now, you will undress me."

It felt like some other mind took hers over. She seemed to be a different person, shameless and wanton. She had no experience to guide her now, only her own instincts. However, it seemed that bin Halil liked women like that.

She soon learnt that he was a skilled lover, for his mere touch was sending unfamiliar sensations racing through her, as he lifted her and carried her the three steps to the bed.

First, he roused her to a state of lust akin to torture, and then took pleasure in being the first to penetrate her, hard and harshly. He intended to hurt her, and he could see that he was, but while the red headed woman refused to cry out, he could indulge himself. He did not try to satisfy her then, waiting instead for her to beg him for that pleasure.

"Do you want pain, or pleasure?" he whispered in her ear, as his hands continued to rouse her.

"Please," was all Kryslie allowed herself to say.

"Please, Master," bin Halil insisted, and Kryslie echoed him. He thought he owned her, but he had played into her hands. Her body was ready, now. All he had to do was perform again....

Bin Halil rolled off her, and smiled with deep satisfaction. Debauching the American woman had proved to be so much more satisfying than coupling with the complaint women of his own country. They all wanted to bear him a son and become pampered lapdogs. This woman, one of the despised liberated American women, had to beg for his attention.

He thought, because she just lay there, that she was glad he had finished with her. She would find out that she was wrong. The night was merely beginning.

He began to kiss her again, from her neck to her knees. He felt her tremble, and thinking her afraid, grinned to himself.

Kryslie felt the sensations beginning again, and rolled to one side, for she was trying to concentrate on the fine chemical balances in her body. Had she conceived yet?

Some voice in her mind said, "No, it will not be that easy. This man has only ever sired females. You must make him work harder."

She thought of how harsh he had been, but that same sense told her, "That was his anger and his maleness speaking. You must challenge him to greater heights. You must join with him."

She had joined with him. In spite of her deliberate lack of reaction, when he had finally chosen to pleasure her, it had been a most satisfying experience. Could it get better? If she forgot her loathing of him? Could she?

It was after all, her purpose she was working for - a seed of peace. Had she put her whole being into that task? No, she hadn't. But did that voice truly mean join minds with him?

He wasn't at all telepathic, but it did seem as if she could read his surface thoughts, and some of his deeper ones more readily now. Would he sense any of hers? Would he sense she was only pretending to be obedient?

No, she realised with certainty. He was too arrogantly sure of his power. He believed he owned her. It was her turn to torment him to the pinnacle of lust.

All through that night, Kryslie kept bin Halil challenged. He would never admit that his strength was not superior to that of a mere American woman. It was not until near morning that Kryslie sensed the subtle changes in her body that indicated conception. She let herself drop into an exhausted sleep, with no sense of guilt. She had discovered that she enjoyed the sensations she had experienced, and there was no one on Earth or Tymorea to judge her actions.

Moreover, it was war, really. She had not asked to be taken here, nor for him to choose to make her his sexual plaything. And while she had joined her mind to his, she had delved deep into his psyche. She knew some of his deepest secrets now - things that he wanted no one to find out.

His unguarded thoughts had told her that he had taken many women, most of them willing to pleasure him in exchange for the possibility of having his son. They craved the prestige they would gain if they did. Yet he had only ever sired girls. The women, in many cases, had aborted the child once they knew for sure that it was female. When the tests were inconclusive, or the woman had not dared to have the forbidden procedure and the child was carried to term - the mother was paid a considerable sum of money and sent off into obscurity. Krys knew now that most of those women, and their children were dead. Proof of his failure as a man, erased.

One day, Kryslie vowed, he would pay for those deaths, but for now, he had to live and fulfil the first stage of a master plan he had conceived of founding a dynasty to rule the entire Eastern Alliance, and later the world.

Kryslie awoke alone, sprawled naked on the low bed. It was well into the day, judging from the warmth of the room and the amount of light coming in through the window. As soon as she moved, she felt the stiff soreness in her body and gave an involuntary groan. She considered ways to alleviate the stiffness and decided that a tepid bath would be the best option. She smelt of sweat and sex.

Her movements, slight though they were, brought a servant to speak to her from the other side of the bed curtain. She only understood part of what the young woman said - the words for 'refresh herself'. They had been used the previous day, and without effort, her retentive memory had stored the foreign words and the context in which they were used. She was already learning the language and was able to answer in the local version of, 'yes'.

While bathing, this time washing herself, the young woman stayed nearby providing scented oils for her to choose from, and later more of the wickedly soft and thick towels. Kryslie did not try to talk to the woman, who was really little more than a girl, very shy and knew no American words.

From her mind, Kryslie knew that her parents had sent her here in the hope that she would come to bin Halil's attention. The idea both interested and repulsed her. She probably would interest bin Halil, but for a time at least, her virtue would be safe.

Kryslie closed her eyes and allowed her body to relax completely. Automatically, she began the bio-feedback technique to relieve the residual aches and pains. After a while, she turned her attention to a deeper level and revelled in the knowledge of the new life within her. It would be her secret for a couple of months, a malicious part of her mind gloated. The calculating part began planning to keep bin Halil's attention for as long as possible.

She returned to the sleeping room, almost an hour later, dressed in a similar style to that in which she had worn from Tel Abbas. The bed had been stripped and remade and the curtains were drawn back. A tray of food awaited her on the low table. Her stomach growled as an aromatic smell reached her nostrils. She wasted no time sitting herself on a cushion by the table, and beginning to eat the rolled flat bread with the savoury filling. This was better food than she had expected bin Halil to provide for her. The sliced tropical fruits must surely be an expensive delicacy out in the desert.

The young woman emerged from the bathing room, carrying the damp towels. She would have been cleaning the chamber, making it spotless in case the master wished to use it. Without a word, she left the room, but as she went past, Kryslie smelt a hint of some of the expensive perfumes and this made her smile. The young woman might be happy to tolerate the master's attention if it meant having such things.

Kryslie finished eating, relishing time alone, and wondering if she was expected to do anything other than laze around and wait for the Master's pleasure. No doubt, if there was, she would be summoned. However, this would be a good time to investigate the room. Then, she would see if she would be allowed to stroll around the mansion, and increase her knowledge of the language.

At the window, as she looked out on an enclosed courtyard and an amazingly lush garden, she felt the faintest touch of her brother's mind.

She sent a mental hello, and to her surprise, only touched his outer mind. He replied with a reserved, "How are you?"

Though he had shielded his mind from hers, Kryslie could still sense his emotions through the deeper twin bond.

"I never thought my twin was a prude," she teased him gently. She felt his mental embarrassment as he relaxed his mind shields, and understood the cause if it. She had kept her own mind tightly shielded from her twin the previous night when she had been occupied with bin Halil, perhaps though, something had leaked through the twin bond.

She sent a mental apology for giving him discomfort, and then told him, "I have no regrets. I took advantage of his own desires, and after the first time, it was mutually enjoyable. No one back home will criticise my choice. He thinks that he owns me, body and soul, but in fact, I own him. I have what he wants, no, what he craves. When he realises that I am carrying his son, he will ensure no harm comes to me. I will have high status in his household."

"Can you be sure of the sex?" Tym asked her.

Krys sent him a mental chuckle. "The man has taken any young virginal woman he wanted and only ever had daughters. When I needed to be sure of conceiving a son, I knew what to do. It is something Governor Xyron teaches the women who go to be missionaries."

"I'm sorry, Krys, it was your choice, and I know you can look after yourself, but I didn't expect you to do this…"

She sensed the un-thought memory of, "All night."

"I hadn't intended it to last all night, and as pleasant as it was, I still want that man dead. However, if he can unite all those fiercely independent little countries, he will be working for us. He is ruthless, intelligent and ambitious enough to achieve it and really is the best choice for leader."

"How can you be sure that your child will not become like his father?"

Kryslie chuckled mentally. "I want you to bring a few of Rhyn's group to this country. They are to blend into the culture. I intend to have this child tutored by Tymoreans. We have nine months in which to get them in place and trusted by bin Halil. I think, soon after he is born, we will be moving on."

"I'll bring them and train them," Tymos promised. "What else do you need to do?"

"Choose a suitable woman amongst bin Halil's women, to foster the child. I will teach her how to maintain the master's interest. That is something our foster mother taught me, amongst all the political, martial and scientific skills."

She sensed that Tymos understood and agreed with her plan, and he summarised it with near malicious glee, "So in twenty years or so, when his son succeeds him, the son will be more receptive to western ideas, and imbued with the desire for peace."

"Exactly!" Kryslie confirmed. "So tell me, how did the Science Conference go?"

This time, Tymos sent a mental laugh. "Be prepared for bin Halil to be a little irritated. It went really well. The delegates voted overwhelmingly, to have scientific research made independent of political affiliation. The representatives from that part of the world were amongst the most fervent advocates for devoting effort to projects for peace, not war."

"Their own choice?" Kryslie marvelled. "I thought they would fear for their lives if they did that."

"They are intelligent men," Tymos told her. "And they know that their resolve will be sorely tested, when or if they return home. When it came to the choice of join the majority or be cut off from all the latest developments…they saw the benefits."

"I have one concern," Kryslie thought after a moment. "If the science council is apolitical, it would share, should share, all the discoveries with all of the nations."

"Peaceful projects," Tymos reminded her.

"Yes, but…there is nothing to stop bin Halil from coercing the scientists from his country."

"Grainger has arranged safeguards," Tymos assured her. "So let him worry about that. What is of immediate importance is the upcoming World Summit meeting. All of the worlds leaders are invited, even those who are from within the Eastern Alliance. There is only one agenda item, and that is Peace."

"Do they want to draw bin Halil out?" was Kryslie's immediate thought.

"Would he come?" Tymos thought back with all seriousness, but in the back of his mind, he held a teasing reminder of how his sister had spent the night past.

She ignored the teasing and asked, "You have not told anyone about bin Halil, have you?"

"Not yet, and as far as I can tell, there is nothing at all to link him to the war in any connection. What are you thinking?"

"That if he felt his involvement was unknown, he will absolutely insist on being there. He will probably offer to represent all the other little Kings and Emirs."

"Even if he is pounced on and questioned about what he knows?"

"I will bet that he has an answer for everything," Kryslie predicted. "He is a ruthless bastard. When is this meeting to begin?"

"In four months time, why?"

"Well, by then, I will be able to tell him I am pregnant, and I will be far enough along that they will be able to tell it is a boy. It will also give him time to lobby the other leaders with in the Alliance into letting him represent them, and if they were all reluctant to go to America, or wherever this meeting is to be…?"

Tymos instantly comprehended her idea. "Leave things with me," he assured her.

While Kryslie played the role of bin Halil's latest concubine, and kept the man busy between supper and breakfast, she kept aloof from the servants, and hid her growing mastery of the local language. During the day, she frustrated anyone who tried to give her orders, by her apparent lack of understanding. Bin Halil, was not interested in teaching her, and his mind revealed that he preferred that she could not make friends with the servants, in case she dared to try to escape.

He still did not trust her completely, although she had given him no reason to doubt his control of her.

However, after several days, Kryslie knew that bin Halil was growing increasingly distracted. He had heard of the proposed World Leader Summit, and it worried him. He tried to question Kryslie, only to be frustrated by the total amnesia, he believed he himself had caused. He had to send out some of his remaining agents to find out what they could.

He spent most of the daytime hours either on his satellite phone, or the internet, talking to the kings and emirs of the other alliance countries. At first, all but one flatly refused to give him any authority to speak for them. They saw him as an upstart with no royal ancestry. He had usurped control of his country after the unexpected death of the last ruling King.

His one firm ally, who still believed bin Halil's promises of great wealth, was keeping secret records of the weapons and planes that the other leaders had in reserve.

Kryslie caught a hint of this from his mind. The continued intimacy made it easier for her to pick up his thoughts and ideas, and pass useful snippets to her twin. Tymos pounced on that idea without revealing the possibilities it inspired. She soon guessed what he was doing. He was causing apparently random events, within the alliance countries - which, by one means or another, was either severely damaging stockpiled war supplies, or destroying them completely.

Just when bin Halil was beginning to win over the other leaders, and gloating to himself about being a step closer to controlling them all, he heard news of the sabotage that caused his deeper plans to receive a major setback.

He spent another week becoming increasingly angry and then abruptly gave orders for the jet to be ready, and for Kryslie and two servants to pack for an immediate departure. He was returning to his city mansion, where he was closer to the hub of his many business enterprises.

He quickly grew annoyed by Kryslie being ignorant of the language and of himself being the only person she understood. He didn't even question the idea of getting her a language tutor, and having the name of the perfect candidate popping into his mind. He believed that he knew of the man, and later, when he did think to question his decision, his credentials were in perfect order.

He had no idea that Kryslie could insert ideas into his mind, or pick up details of his business, or that she was doing it as she was relaxing him with a massage.

Although the relationship that bin Halil had with her gave her physical pleasure, Kryslie did not mistake it for love. She knew the man was using her, and thought he was dominating her, and his real essence was arrogant and selfish. He went for what he wanted and did not care who he walked over in the process.

Yet while he thought he was her master and that even intelligent women were no threat to him, she was subtly manipulating him. As he was yet to learn her secret, the idea of founding a dynasty of rulers was merely a dream and therefore of no immediate importance. What had taken fire in his mind was the thought of becoming the ruler of all the Alliance countries.

Even when coupling with her he was scheming. Once he had learnt about the conference, he had seen the value of being the person to speak for all the Alliance countries. He wanted to be that person, even if it meant being the focus for questions about who had incited the war.

He was confident that no one in the American led united countries had any indication that he was involved and believed his mind to be strong enough to fend off all questions. He was not so confident of all the other ruling Emirs. They might, if put under sufficient pressure, or become frightened enough, betray him in some way.

There were several men that he did not trust and the thought occurred to him that if he needed to prove his openness, he could suggest them as possible perpetrators. He would even offer to help the Americans go in and neutralise them. He would make sure the men would not talk.

Kryslie did not like the trend of his thoughts, but could only suggest other, non-lethal, ways to bring the other Emirs down. However, the idea of ruining them financially and politically while satisfying, wasn't enough for him. He wanted to own them, for if he must remove them, most had able and intelligent sons to take over the country, and he would have to defeat them too.

If her subtle suggestions were not enough, she would have to trust her twin to do what he could to prevent murder and assassination.

During the next three months, Kryslie saw less and less of bin Halil and that suited her. She had been ordered to have lessons in the local language, and obey his chief servant.

Obligingly, she attended lessons with the tutor, who was one of Rhyn's network of Tymorean descendants. The man had infiltrated into a position of importance in one of the neighbouring countries, and was helping more of his kin to blend in to the culture.

Kryslie was able to coach him in ways to attract and keep bin Halil's interest and confidence. He in turn, was increasing her actual knowledge of the language, and keeping her abreast of the activities of the missionaries acting with her brother.

Then, when free of her lessons, she spent time with bin Halil's other women. While earning their respect and liking, she was subtly spreading modern ideas amongst them and amongst the servants. She had already chosen the two women who she wanted to be the chief carers for her son, and was deftly preparing them for that role. She did not have to warn them not to seem to be to partisan towards her. They knew from girlhood that it was not wise to be friends with one who displeased the master.

Timing the announcement of her pregnancy for the day before bin Halil was to leave for the World Conference, was a deliberate act to have his mind unsettled while he was in Geneva, Switzerland.

Having the physicians confirm that it was a son brought out his deepest desires, and caused him to start second-guessing his plans. Finally, he decided that it was an omen of the rightness of his intentions.

Chapter 17 - The Seeds of Peace

Tymos, once again back in America, kept his sister apprised of the progress being made at the World Conference. He was attending the meetings, as an aide to President Wallis, but was watching the delegates. He gave shrewd advice to the President in between sessions, and was positioned where he could watch bin Halil during the talks. He did not reveal the main focus of his attention to the President, but did pass on his observations to his sister. He summed them up as, "He's the only person here who has not had enough of war, and he knows it. However, he has no choice but to play along. After all those little accidents involving his war supplies, he is going to need time to rebuild."

To which Kryslie replied, "He'll feel safe enough for a time, and be sneering at the rest of the world for being mice."

After two weeks of talks and discussions, a treaty was drawn up and signed by all the Nations attending. The treaty was primarily an agreement that no nation would wage war against another.

However, there were several other equally important sections. Of these, the one that Tamir Grainger had fought for, was the formation of World Science Council as an independent, totally neutral body for the advancement of science for peaceful purposes. It would also act as a watchdog, to act against the use of science to create weapons of war, or for purposes against the common good. Its charter mandated a commitment to equal opportunities for scientists of all nations.

A neutral body, called the World Council, was created to oversee the treaty. It was to be made up of high-level representatives from each of the signatory nations. A subordinate body of the Council would be an investigative committee, with the authority to impose sanctions and punishments on individuals and countries that acted in contravention to the treaty.

Tymos, working with Wallis and Grainger, provided the careful wording for the World Committee Charter and that for the Investigative Committee. It kept him busy for over a month. However, by that time, the ruling bodies of all the signatory nations, except those for which bin Halil was speaker, had also ratified the Peace treaty.

Bin Halil was in no rush to return to his country, and this made Tymos thoughtful. He had several of the Tymorean descendents watching his activities, but he seemed to be acting in an irreproachable manner.

President Wallis invited the Alliance representative for private talks, aimed at having the Alliance countries join what was coming to be called the United World Nations. However, with genuine sounding regret, bin Halil declined to commit to that, on the basis that he was not authorised to speak on that aspect of the talks.

During this private session, Wallis seemed to find bin Halil a reasonable man, urbane, courteous, intelligent, and so raised the questions that his government wanted answered. The question of who was behind the war?

The act was perfect. Bin Halil claimed to regret the actions of his neighbours, but denied irrefutable knowledge of the instigators. He had, he said, fought to keep his country neutral. He was considered an upstart because he had taken over his country when the old childless Emir had died.

Tymos was listening and watching the talks from a nearby room, making use of the security audio-visuals. He pondered the wisdom of telling Wallis that the man was a snake and a polished liar.

Finally, he decided to keep silent. Bin Halil would unite all the Alliance countries into a union to equal the United World Nations, and that would keep him busy in his part of the world for many years. Time for Krys's son to grow to maturity. He had been too careful to draw any attention to himself during the war. All his actions had been done through others, all clues to his agents would lead foreign spies to countries other than his own. By the time he began subversive activities again, the Investigative Committee would be well established.

"I will return home and hold talks with the Emirs," bin Halil lied smoothly. "I will talk to them in a way that will encourage them to think of peace. I hope to bring their agreement to you, though I must be wary of those you fear may wish to bring war again."

Wallis was drawn into bin Halil's trap. He offered the help of the new Investigative Committee, once the representatives were selected from each country, to locate those responsible for the war.

Tymos listened, and kept his face expressionless, as bin Halil named a dozen men as those he 'feared' were responsible for the war. These men may indeed be guilty, or they may simply have become liabilities - but when they later came to be scrutinized, Tymos was sure that irrefutable proof would be found. Anyone who had helped bin Halil during the past war, was likely to be given to the Committee for punishment for war crimes, or likely disappear into fatal obscurity.

When the nominated emissaries from each nation were officially appointed and sworn to the World Council, Tymos knew it was time to rejoin his sister. He made his farewells to Grainger during the celebrations that followed.

"It's time for me to go, old friend," Tymos admitted with regret. "I look forward to our next meeting."

"I will be ready for you," the scientist promised. "Though I suppose that you still do not know when that will be? Another twenty years, like it has been between each of your visitations."

Tymos shrugged and smiled faintly. "It will be as the Guardians of Peace will it. I suspect, that once again, we will not have aged much when that time comes."

"In twenty years, you might be mistaken for the next generation," Grainger shook his head with awe. "I could wish to have that ability to stretch the time that I have. There is so much that I want to do."

Tymos spoke to distract the older man from his sense of mortality.

"I will give Kryslie your regards."

"She is well?" Grainger asked, eyebrows raised. Tymos had never told him what she was doing, and he only hoped that he might now.

"You must have guessed where she is," Tymos maintained his trace of a smile. "However, she is indeed in excellent health and playing an important role in promoting peace."

"It cannot be easy for a woman to do much there," Grainger said with concern.

Tymos's smile widened to a grin. "The people there have no conception of a woman like Kryslie. She is working in their blind spot."

"Then I must not hold you here, go in Peace my friend."

Grainger watched as Tymos took out his transmitter. "I could have an aircraft put at your disposal."

"This way is untraceable," Tymos grinned. "I have people to brief on my way to Kryslie. I'll just make use of one of the empty rooms."

When he was alone, Tymos transmitted the first stage of his journey to rejoin his sister.

Since he did not need to enter bin Halil's country through its physical borders, Tymos was able to meet with the eight Tymorean missionary descendents that Rhyn had reassigned there. His first priority was to adjust the colour of his noticeable red hair to black, and darken his skin tone to match that of the local population. Kryslie, with her startling hair colour stood out enough. Another like her would spook bin Halil.

Then, after discussion with the missionaries, particularly the one who was tutoring his sister, Tymos decided to insinuate himself into the hospital as a male nurse. This was based on a conversation the tutor had overheard, that implied that bin Halil had decided to have his son born in the most modern of the hospitals in his country, where there was the best of medical help available if needed. Tymos's choice was not without risk, for in that patriarchal and traditional country, nursing was a woman's role. However, it was only a matter of a few hours after receiving his beautifully forged credentials, that they were fully provable in the relevant databases. One of the older Tymoreans, was listed as a reference, and she was ready to add her recommendation.

He applied directly to the hospital and his credentials were accepted, warily. They seemed reluctant to agree to his working there, but with persuasion, Tymos pointed out that his strength would be an asset when lifting patients and moving heavy equipment at times when orderlies were normally excluded. The hiring officer seemed to consider the applicant as some kind of simpleton, for why else would a male choose such a subordinate role, if he could train to be a doctor.

A subtle mental nudge made the man agree to give him a trial, had him included on the weekly roster and soon after, to forget about him. Tymos began working that same day, having to overcome the same initial prejudice with the other staff, but soon proving his willingness to do whatever he was asked.

He was assigned to the wards containing male patients who needed the most care. There he helped with the menial tasks of attending to their personal needs, washing them and bed making. Meanwhile the senior female staff studied his work. They soon realised what an asset he was, as he seemed to have a very gentle touch and the patients settled very quickly after his attention.

Within a week, the staff had sensed an indefinable something about him that seemed to be making the seriously ill patients recover. By the following week, when Kryslie and her retinue, came for her next routine check up, he had been fully accepted and no one was surprised when he was assigned to the rooms where Kryslie was to be examined.

He had not expected bin Halil to be with her, but he didn't dither in the man's presence as some of the nurses did. He went about his duties as if this group was as common as any other. That was until Kryslie, who had given no outward sign of knowing he was there, chose to object to the presence of a 'male nurse'. That she was acting like a pampered high-class woman, was a deliberate move. It bought him under bin Halil's scrutiny, and the man was in turn reacting true to his traditional upbringing.

"Have that man removed," was bin Halil's immediate reaction.

The two guards waiting by the door, moved to come over, but Tymos had glanced at his superior, and obeyed her nod that he should leave. He did not look at bin Halil as he went, and did not try to wrench free of the grip of the guards. He had Kryslie guiding his behaviour, and she had caught the subtle signal bin Halil gave the guards for them to hold the male nurse until he could question him.

While he waited outside, Kryslie thought at him that the other staff were being quizzed about him, and all were extolling his skill, willingness and polite demeanour. One even dared to admit to how he seemed to help the sickest of patients. Not one of them called him slow or stupid.

After a while, bin Halil emerged, and studied the oddity that the man represented.

"Why do you choose a woman's task. Are you too stupid to become a doctor?"

Tymos bowed correctly to bin Halil, and spoke politely. "Sir, I have had no opportunity to train for such an important role. However, I am told I have a skill for healing, and sometimes my strength is a benefit. I do not believe the work to be demeaning; I am helping sick people get well."

Without appearing arrogant or subservient, Tymos was projecting a sense of confidence in himself, and the strength of his conviction.

Bin Halil studied him for a while longer before saying, "I want to talk to you again. Wait for me to summon you."

Tymos bowed again, but before he had straightened, bin Halil and his guards had returned into the examination room.

Later, the two guards returned and ordered him to, "Come with us."

They did not hold onto him this time and Tymos took that as a good sign. Their destination was a room that had been usurped by bin Halil. It was probably the office of a senior physician, and it showed signs of a hurried evacuation with several medical texts opened on the table and a page half filled with neatly written notes.

"I have had you checked out, Salamin ," that was the name Tymos was using, "and it appears your story is true. I am going to allow you to attend my consort, when she is secluded here for the birth of my son. I want only the best care for her, and I want you to act as my eyes at other times. Will you do that for me?"

"Sir, I will indeed give the lady the best care, but what do you fear if I must also watch her?"

"I am not expecting trouble, but I am an important man and I have enemies. I simply do not wish the mother of my son to be inconvenienced, or endangered by anyone. I do not wish my son endangered. Should anything untoward occur, once my son is born, the child will have priority. I have many women, but this coming child is my only male issue."

Tymos considered the statement for a moment and bowed. "I understand, Sir."

"Phew!" Tymos sent mentally to Kryslie once he was well away from bin Halil, and taking time for some iced water from the staff canteen. "I passed his scrutiny and I have to make sure no one hurts his son. For now, that means doesn't hurt you."

He felt his sister's amusement. "You will be being watched now, to make sure you don't have any unsuitable friends, acquaintances, or habits."

"That is no trouble."

"And if he thinks he can get you to stop me doing anything unsuitable, he can think again."

"Again, a non-issue. I know you won't do anything of the kind. However, one thing was plain…"

"Let me guess," Kryslie interrupted. "Once his son is born, I am no longer important."

"In a word, yes," Tymos agreed.

"Yeah, well, that's not unexpected," Kryslie decided. "I have never been anything more than a pawn in his plans."

She was being driven back to bin Halil's mansion in an air conditioned limousine and pretending to doze so that no one would notice her attention was distracted. "It won't matter what he thinks to use me for," she went on, thinking at her twin. "Because I believe we will be moving on soon after this child is born. Which is as well, I do not want to be a part of any plan of his. I have given him the son he secretly craved, and that is enough."

Tymos agreed with her. "Do you think that he still wants to use you against the Americans?"

"Not in the same way," Kryslie considered. "It has become more complicated. He has tried to keep it quiet that I lived in America for a time, but word has leaked out. And, because I am pregnant with his son, I have become something of a celebrity."

"That would make it difficult for him to up and kill you," Tymos proposed.

"Bro, if he decides that he wants me dead, he will have an impeccable public reason. However, having me at the hospital for the birth, means he won't try to have me die then. Do you know if word of me being here has leaked back to America?"

"No," Tymos thought back definitely. "What are you thinking?"

"Nothing important, as I said, we will probably be leaving before he can organise anything. In fact, I need to get away from that hospital before they even think me recovered sufficiently to move."

"Krys, will you be well enough…"

"Bro, I will have to be. Listen, we can't both disappear at the same time. You need to sneak in some proper clothing, and be seen to leave as normal after your shift. Make yourself noticed. Then, when I am finally allowed to rest, you sneak back."

"Yes, you are right. And I can give you whatever energy and healing you need," Tymos assured her. "And I will do something else too. Our friends can begin to lay the groundwork for reasons to explain your disappearance."

He felt Kryslie's mental laugh. "Not to explain, but to suggest a possible cause. No, make multiple possible causes, many conflicting alternatives to keep everyone guessing. Make it seem like I went voluntarily, or I was abducted, or killed by Americans for being a traitor, or killed by locals because I am an American. I don't care if they play into bin Halil's plans or not. Once I have gone, he will have everyone think the worst of me anyway."

"He shouldn't, since he was the one who made you what he thinks you are," Tymos countered.

"True, but even though he has been enjoying his perceived dominance over me, and I have been a properly obedient female, flattered by his attention, fearful of losing his good opinion, and all that - he still distrusts me. Moreover, he still hates me. Now whether or not he plans to use me after the birth, my disappearance is going to anger him. He might be glad to be rid of me, but he will want to be the cause of it."

"Let him be - we won't be around."

"Not for a while," Kryslie agreed, but she began to feel a shiver of disquiet.

"What is wrong?" Tymos asked, sensing the change in her mood.

"Nothing that I can do anything about. I just had the feeling that when we leave here, I won't have seen the last of bin Halil."

Tymos didn't belittle her concern. Instead he asked, "Have you a date for when you go into seclusion?"

"This Friday. It is traditional to start preparing for the birth a month before the due date. I insisted on having Sheena with me. She is loyal to me, dislikes bin Halil, and acts simple to put him off. He countered by insisting that Alexi goes with me too, thinking that she was more loyal to him than to me. What bin Halil doesn't know, is that Alexi is a very intelligent woman, who appreciates the benefits of being his favourite and was a very attentive learner. I taught her how to keep his attention, and that she and I should seem politely antagonistic towards each other. She is the one I have chosen to be the foster mother for the child."

"Are you sure that there will be no threat to Sheena when you vanish?" Tymos considered.

"I don't need to tell any of bin Halil's women the inadvisability of defending me when I go. It is an instinct in all of them that when the master starts being displeased with one of them, that the others give that one a wide berth."

Once Kryslie was installed in the private suite in the hospital, Tymos had plenty of time to study the two women with her. He was impressed by both of them.

Kryslie was pretending to be concerned by the impending birth, as if fearing something would go wrong. Sheena was a source of down to Earth common sense, and insisted that Kryslie get what exercise she could while waiting out the final days. Alexi may have sounded more high-handed and condescending, but Tymos had no doubt of her concern for his sister.

The two guards that stood duty inside the suite, or rather the twelve men who rotated the duty, were all friendly towards Kryslie. But then, four of them were Tymorean missionary descendents.

During bin Halil's daily visits, Alexi was a different person. Outwardly concerned for the mother-to-be, but speaking disparagingly to bin Halil under her breath. When Tymos had contrived to be in the suite on some duty or other, at the same time as the visit, he could see and sense how she was using Kryslie's subtle teaching.

Kryslie warned her twin when she felt the first twinges of labour starting. Tymos risked transmitting himself from his lodgings to the hospital. He was in the suite when she chose to announce the cramping pains she felt. She added mentally to her brother, "I have been told, quite often, that first babies take their time. This child might take hours to finally come out."

It seemed she was right, even though Tymos unstintingly shared his power to help ease the intensity of the cramps and to give her strength. Together, they tried to reach the mind of the child to reassure him that all would be well once he emerged.

Tymos hid one concern in the most private shielded part of his mind. He had never heard his sister refer to the child she had conceived as her son, only as 'the child'. He feared that she intended to reject the boy, or want nothing to do with him. He had forgotten how closeness made their minds more open to each other.

"Tym, I cannot afford to become attached." Her emotions were under fragile control, and he sensed them now. "I am going to have to leave him. I won't have time to know him…"

Tymos squeezed her hand gently in understanding. It was going to tear her heart apart. He should have known that she would not hate the child because of the man who sired him.

"I am here for you, Krys," Tymos assured her mentally.

"I know that bro, and I cannot say how much and how deeply, your being here means to me."

Tymos, sharing his power with Kryslie and helping with the birth, had never experienced anything like it. He felt every contraction, every agonising moment, and wondered how ordinary women survived it. He swore to himself that he would never cause any woman he came to care for to have to go through this. However, at the moment of the birth, he shared on a deep level, the burst of intense emotion, pride, achievement, love and relief and an overwhelming joy. It transcended any other experience.

He held the boy as he emerged, seeing the slicked down dark hair and the olive skin - he sensed the child's mind, so bright, so clear, even at moments old. Then with a shock, he felt the child's potential - his inheritance of Tymorean power. It should not be...the child was only half Tymorean...

Regretfully, Tymos ensured that only the potential intelligence would manifest. The power must remain forever dormant.

Even as Kryslie's body finished the birth process, she was aware of what Tymos had sensed. Her child was not just any child of mixed heritage. She was a Great One, the only female of that rank in Tymorean history, and it seemed that made a difference.

After an eternity, while Tymos shared his healing energy with her and she ached to hold her son, the stirrings of an inescapable force began to manifest. Resolutely, she resisted, while she insisted on holding her son. And then she was, the nurses giving him to her first, and not to his father. She filled all her senses with him, hearing his lusty cry, smelling the perfume of the cleansing water, feeling his soft skin and the fierce grip on her finger, and watching his face to memorise every feature.

Kryslie touched her son's mind again. This child was truly her son. He would be more like her in essence than like his father. Bin Halil might claim him, might try to hide the truth about his mother from him, might try to make him hate her, but he was her son.

"I love you, little son. I cannot stay and watch you grow, but I will always love you and when I can return, you will be grown. But I will always be there for you and I hope you will know me then."

Alexi took the baby from her, and their eyes met. Something in them gave Kryslie a shiver of apprehension, she stared and Alexi whispered, "I will treat him as my own, I promise."

Kryslie watched the look on bin Halil's face as he held his son. Something fierce, possessive. His mind was filled with the vision of the child growing up to be like himself.

Sheena, interrupted the moment, by bringing her a fresh hospital gown to wear. She was unusually subdued, and when Kryslie asked a question, merely by raising an eyebrow, Sheena glanced at bin Halil and muttered, "I do not believe what he is saying about you."

Kryslie waited until bin Halil had left the room, following the crib with her son to the nursery. Tymos was attending the child too, so she had no worry for the boy.

"What is he saying," she asked Sheena in a whisper.

"That he has discovered you are really a traitor," she hissed. "You are not! And you would never harm your child."

"No," Kryslie assured her. "Though it seems like my usefulness to him has indeed ended. I didn't come here to spy on him, or undermine him. He brought me here, did something to make me forget being American. Some of my memory is returning, and I am sure he has ill intentions for me. Please, whatever happens, I want you to help protect my son. Will you do that?"

"Of course! Do you doubt me?"

"No, never, but if he should repudiate me, and send me away, don't risk yourself. It would be best if you were angry at my …duplicity. If bin Halil thinks you are too friendly with me, he may send you away too."

"I wouldn't care…I had no choice but to be with him. I dislike him."

"I know, but I need you to look after my son. I don't want him to be like his father."

"For you, I will stay. For the baby."

"Thank you."

Finally, Kryslie was left alone to rest. The nurses assured her that her son was comfortable in the nursery. They believed it. They also assumed that she had decided not to feed him herself, for they also explained that they had given him a bottle and he was sleeping.

Kryslie didn't sleep. From her twin, she learnt that her son was to be transferred back to bin Halil's mansion later that night. A wet nurse was waiting, and Alexi and Sheena would go with the child.

"What of me?" Kryslie asked him.

"I can't read him like you can," Tymos said with concern. "I think you need to leave, and soon. I left clothes in the towel cupboard in the bathroom, and a transmitter. Do you have the strength to use it?"

"Yes," Kryslie assured him. "Where will I go?"

A vivid image came into her mind. "My apartment in town. It is only about a mile west of here. I will come there as soon as I can. Tell me when you arrive, and I will raise an alarm. Then I will join you."

"What about the guards?" Kryslie reminded him. "I can't disable both in a hurry right now."

Tymos thought quickly, he had seen the guards leave, but others must have replaced them. "Are they from the regular group?"

He sensed Kryslie examining the guards through slitted eyes. "No. I have never seen these two before."

"I'm coming."

Tymos materialised close to the wall, with the gathered up privacy curtain screening him from view. In the darkened room, he was like a wraith and the two guards, intent on watching the seemingly sleeping woman never saw him coming. They had less than a second to see the fist that knocked them unconscious. "Do you need help getting dressed?" he asked mentally.

"I can manage," Kryslie assured him, already sitting up and swinging her legs from the bed. "You get back. Be seen."

Tymos didn't question her further, he went.

As Kryslie dressed, ignoring the discomfort in her body and the weariness, she was aware that Tymos was going with her son back to bin Halil's mansion. After dressing, she took the transmitter. A green light should have indicated when it was charged ready to use. She was sensing the two guards waking up in the other room, and knew she needed to hurry. The units powered up from her own personal Tymorean power. She must be too weak to transmit right then. She needed to calm her mind to think. Immediately, knowledge came to her - not from the memories of the Governors of Tymorea, but from the Guardians themselves. She could draw on the energy emitted from electric lights, as if she was a photoelectric cell. She moved to the light switch and turned it on, and then imagined herself as a plant absorbing light. Finally, the green light showed on her transmitter and she recalled the image her brother had given her. Moments later, she was there, and safe.

Tymos breathed more easily when his sister arrived at his apartment. He was in the process of helping Alexi from the limousine when she had the wrapped bundle of the baby in her arms. He heard bin Halil's personal phone ring. His eyes went to the man and he saw bin Halil stiffen and heard him cursing in his own language and issuing commands that made it obvious that Kryslie's absence had been noticed.

Realising that Tymos was within earshot, he kept his commands to 'find her'. He turned then and ordered the women into the house, and tersely told Tymos, "You may go now."

Although it was what he wanted to do, Tymos only went far enough to be out of sight, before pausing to listen. His hearing was keen enough to hear bin Halil change his commands to, "Find her and bring her to my other house."

It seemed that Kryslie had left just in time. Now he needed to join her, for he could feel the forces of time pulling on his own body.

Tymos transmitted to his apartment, and went at once to his sister. She was looking pale, as she sat on one of his cheap wooden chairs. He helped her stand, sent his own energy into her; they did not know what situation they would arrive in next. He gave a last glance around his apartment; there was nothing there to tell anything about him or give anyone a clue to where he went.

They both relaxed, giving in to the inescapable forces. Once again, they seemed to be plucked from the physical world, and time rushed past.

Chapter 18 - Final Coming

The grass grew over an even surface, where once there had been only the skeletons and cellars of ruined buildings. Around the memorial park, new dwellings had been built to replace the old, though some of the original buildings remained, miraculously untouched or determinedly restored.

The war was only now fading from the memories of the people who had survived, but a new generation of children were laughing on the playground.

Two red headed adults paused to look around the park, seeming to see what lay beneath the grass. Death had given way to life, and hopelessness to the promise of the future. There was no overt threat here, no danger to be wary of. However, the rushing through time had brought them here - they still had the Guardians' work to do.

They remembered the Tymorean descendents they had met in their previous coming. If there was a new threat to be met, that group would know.

Tymos glanced at his sister, concerned by how pale she looked. She shook her head telling him she was fine, or would be with rest.

"Rhyn?" he thought strongly, as he pictured the face of the coordinator of the descendents.

He felt a burst of surprise, and the realisation, "You have returned! Where are you?"

"Close, we think. Where are you?"

"I am in the old house where you came after the war," Rhyn explained, thinking the answer, knowing that Prince Tymos would read it there. "I have restored it. The original owners died, but no one questioned my being here. I am around the edge of the park."

"We will be with you soon," Tymos promised.

Kryslie nodded to the east. "That way."

With the sun shining from a cloudless sky, they did not hurry. Kryslie felt the warmth restoring her energy, but the children's voices reminded her of the child she had just deserted, mere minutes before. In this time, he would not be a little child anymore. How many years had passed?

Tymos spotted the house that was enveloped by a faint mauve aura, and nudged his sister to get her attention. He felt her mind return to the present.

"I wonder if he has heard from the others," she spoke aloud. "Surely we must be at our proper time now."

She put on a burst of speed, so she was heading for the house at a fast walk. She timed her crossing of the road to fall neatly between the moving shapes of two modern cars.

They stopped outside of the force field protected house, and studied the protection.

Neither chose to ring the bell, instead, Tymos sent a questioning thought inside. "Rhyn? May we come in?"

"Come in! Certainly," was the surprised reply as the mind recognised the source of the thought. "Surely the field would not stop you."

It wouldn't stop them, but they needed to act like the local people. Transmitting inside from the doorstep and suddenly vanishing would be extraordinary.

The door swung open by itself and the young people entered. Neither had ever been in the restored house before but they walked unerringly through several immaculately neat rooms until they came to a room with a large painting that seemed to glow faintly mauve.

Adjusting their eyes to see through the picture hologram, they saw the room beyond. It was full of computers and screens. They walked into the picture.

An old man was seated at one control panel and he turned as they entered, swiftly standing so he could bow in respect for the rank of his visitors.

"Prince Tymos, Princess Kryslie," Rhyn welcomed them. "Your return now, was unexpected."

"Then we are not late?" Kryslie asked.

"Late!" Rhyn exclaimed. "Indeed not. If your estimate was correct, the Earth mission of which you are part will not be arriving for another five years. I still have had no contact with home base."

Kryslie glanced at Tymos in surprise. They both then realised that there must be a reason for them to come early. They had been lulled by the peaceful scene outside.

"We need to prepare for the coming of the missionaries," Tymos decided, thoughtfully. "That must be it. Rhyn, do you know the whereabouts of Tamir Grainger?"

The aging man paused a long time before answering. "Tamir has been dead these past two years."

He saw the look of distress and grief pass across the faces of his royal guests. Then it was gone, hidden inside, as the problem of finding his father's research became their focus.

"He was such a brilliant man, and a very good friend to all of us. He must have known he would not see you again and that grieved him. He told me of the promise he had made to you, and asked me to help. I was to tell you that he had left a puzzle for you in the Hall of Science at the Washington Campus of the WSRA University. He also told me that when you returned, each of you would need a background and references. I have them here."

Rhyn moved slowly towards a blank section a wall panel that glowed faintly mauve. He depressed a switch off to one side. The glow disappeared and a deed box was revealed behind a panel of Perspex. He gestured to Tymos, who removed the clear plastic and removed the box, and then took it across to a cleared bench in the centre of the room.

"I have respected your wishes and not mentioned you in any of my reports," Rhyn assured them. "I did not understand your reasons then, but Tamir Grainger explained you were 'in transit' and your return to this world was difficult."

Tymos smiled at that simple statement of a complicated fact.

"We have completed our transition," Tymos spoke, suddenly sure that was the truth. "What we need now is to learn of world events since we were last here. I need access to your records and to contact each of the remaining missionaries."

"And how long it has been since we were last here," Kryslie asked.

"I am at your service," Rhyn bowed again. "The war has been over for nearly twenty years. All of us have kept working and reporting. The data is stored on the computer." He told his guests how to access everything they needed.

"May we use your home as a base?" Kryslie asked with polite deference.

"I would be honoured, Princess Kryslie," Rhyn agreed. He withdrew back to his interrupted task and let his houseguests access the computer.

If he was surprised at the speed at which they flicked through file after file, and assimilated the information in the last twenty years of records, he made no comment. He could recall tales from his grandparents of the great power of Tymorean Great Ones – people the like of which he had never expected to meet. Tymos and Kryslie, he believed, had to be such people.

"Why did your great grand parents return without their children?" Kryslie asked, startling Rhyn from his mind's wanderings.

"Their children were born here and considered it home and they were old enough to look out for themselves," Rhyn hastened to explain further. "They, my great grandparents, knew they must obey the order to return, but felt their work was important. Those who had married other Tymoreans, trained their children to work with them, and taught them Tymorean lore and history and ethics. The children agreed to carry on the work and only married within their group to keep the bloodlines pure. We still try to help the cause of peace..."

"We are very grateful for their efforts," Kryslie assured him, gently trying to ascertain the cause of Rhyn's mental hesitancy. "We will ensure that their efforts are recognised and when our mission base is established we will introduce them to their Tymorean kin."

"It will be strange to meet one's great grandparents," Rhyn mused, the idea blossoming in his mind. "The few of us that remain have feared that the new missionaries will scorn our efforts. May I tell them to expect you?"

"Of course," Kryslie agreed instantly. "We have met some of them already, and we are looking forward to meeting the others. They were of great assistance to us in the past and have continued to be so. In fact, you could ask them to propose possible sites for our base and advise you of their ideas."

Kryslie did not even hint that she and Tymos had already seen the report from him on that very subject. He had yet to write it, but knowing Rhyn's efficiency, he would write it soon."

They finally turned their attention to the deed box. It had a faint glow about it, but Tymos instinctively knew how to manipulate the box to remove it. It was like a simple puzzle. Turn box on its side, then its top, then the other side and back on its base. Then repeat the handling, by placing it on its front, top, back and base.

The glow vanished and Tymos lifted the lid. A letter lay on top of two folders of documents, each labelled in the intricate script of Tamir Grainger. From Rhyn's reports, they had learnt that Tamir Grainger had succeeded in separating science from the power-seeking politicians and helped lay the foundation for a lasting peace. He had created the World Science Research Authority as a neutral, world-spanning organisation.

The letter was written in the script of the formal Tymorean language that Grainger must have learnt from his missionary father, Tamir Janzoet. He began with the correct formal greeting to Prince Tymos and Princess Kryslie of the Royal house of Tymorea.

The letter read, "I have seen in a vision that I will die before I can keep my promise to you. I have entrusted my father's works to the Hall of Science at the university that I founded. The means of obtaining them should be obvious to you when you go there – as indeed you must.

"When you came twenty years ago, only Kryslie came to the attention of the Science Council due to her outstanding scores in the refugee evaluation tests. As she later became a member of President Wallis's staff, there is a certain amount about her in classified files. However, there is little available now except for a few photographs taken when she was travelling with the President. Her disappearance never became a matter of public record.

"When the WSRA took over the Science Council, I gained access to her file and filled in many missing details. Therefore, I was able to claim that she married a brilliant scientist of my acquaintance and gave birth to twins – boy and girl. Details of your early life have been created for your perusal. These include notarised birth certificates, early school records and documents appointing me your guardian after the death of your parents."

A second page accompanied the first, but it was obviously written at a later time for the writing was shaky.

"I have seen your final coming. You will arrive before the rest of the Tymorean mission. You must come to the university as soon as possible and take charge of my father's work. Unless the Tymorean Earth Mission has this data, they will be detected by the people of this world. I remain your faithful servant, Tamir Grainger Janzoet."

A young woman walked into the room and stopped in surprise at seeing two strangers. Rhyn noticed her apprehension and began to introduce his guests.

"Hillary, dear, I'd like you to meet..."

"Tym," Tymos interrupted, before Rhyn could give his royal title.

"Krys," Kryslie added. She smiled at the woman who seemed to be about her own age.

"But you're..." the woman blushed a brilliant crimson. Her mind was a confusion of thoughts, foremost was her recognition of their Royal status and it was conflicting with the knowledge that she had learnt from her parents.

"Guilty," Tymos agree with a lopsided grin. His tone and words cause Hillary to look back up at him.

"I didn't mean..."

"We know. We are odd cases. Yes, we are the Tymorean High King's eldest children. Yes, we were born on Earth nearly a century ago, but we are not that old! While we were on Tymorea being trained and doing things we had to do, a lot of time passed in a kind of stasis."

"But we still can't contact them," Hillary protested.

Tymos quickly explained the situation on the world that Hillary only knew of from stories.

While Hillary was trying to assimilate the idea of a whole world where time had stopped, Tymos quickly explained how the Guardians had brought them back to Earth before their kin were to arrive.

Hillary looked dazed.

Kryslie said, jokingly, "Sounds simple when you say it fast, doesn't it? Something smells nice."

"Oh!" Hillary blushed again. "I brought Rhyn his dinner. I didn't know he had guests. I have more. I usually bring a few days' meals at a time, so he can warm one up each day. I can fix more..."

"That would be wonderful. I feel as if the last time I ate was twenty years ago," Kryslie kept her face straight as she said that.

Hillary laughed at the absurdity of her comment. They had not mentioned to her that they had been skipping through time.

By the end of the evening, Hillary was perfectly at ease with her two new Tymorean friends and no was no longer fearful of the coming of more Tymoreans.

"We will need to examine that missile site," Kryslie said to her brother when they were alone that night. Hillary had left, and Rhyn was already asleep.

"We will do that first," Tymos agreed. "From the science reports, I can see why Tamir was so insistent that we get his father's data quickly. The knowledge of force fields has increased to an alarming extent and the detectors they are using to study radiation are not very different from force field detectors. However, we do have some time – we know when the mission will arrive. We simply have to ensure that the final defences are ready to operate before they arrive and can be activated immediately."

"Very glib, brother," Kryslie remarked thoughtfully. "But even though we both know a lot about the types of force fields and their effects, we never did get to learn all about how to make the generators from nothing."

"We can learn from the Earth scientists," Tymos proposed. "However, we need to have detailed geological surveys of the area – or rather of all the areas that Rhyn will have in his report. The topography will need to be considered too."

Kryslie yawned suddenly. "We can start tomorrow. Right now, all I want to do is make use of one of Rhyn's guest rooms."

Tymos found himself agreeing. He sensed that his sister was very tired, even though he was still feeling alert. His mind betrayed a touch of concern.

Kryslie knew why she was tired, but kept her mind shielded from her twin. Even though she was trying to consider what she needed to do in this time, her mind was on the time they had just left.

In spite of her brother's healing energies, her body knew that yesterday she had held her newborn child, and her hormones were those of a new mother. It was hard to convince her body that her child would now be a man of nearly twenty. She doubted if even her twin could really understand how she felt.

Rhyn did not question the movements of his guests, but he knew that the Royal Prince and Princess had been visiting each of the missionaries that reported to him. He noted, too, that the reports showed a marked improvement as if the writers were now revitalised and proud of their roles.

Details of all proposed sites for the Tymorean base were given to Tymos, who, with Kryslie, checked each and reported their findings to Rhyn to record. They had, however visited the radiation site even before it was suggested, but only reported to Rhyn on the aspects that were in the report Homebase had received.

Because they already knew that site was the chosen site, they examined it thoroughly. For the purposes of camouflage, they obtained radiation suits.

Rhyn had contacts within the WSRA, provided by Tamir Grainger. In truth, neither Tymos nor Kryslie needed them because their power was strong enough to protect them from even this extreme level of radiation.

The radiation was the result of an experimental missile crash and as a result, the area was fenced off at a radius of fifty miles from the impact point. Suits such as they had borrowed, were the best available and they were only rated to protect to a level to enable humans to penetrate ten miles from the edge. The limit was marked by a small research shack, called Emmanuel's Hut.

They split up and looked at different sections of the blackened and radiating zone.

"There is an extensive underground cave system near the crash site," Kryslie reported to her brother. "We could make use of them. It would probably be better to have most of the base underground."

"Could we open up the cave system without weakening the rock structure?" Tym asked.

"Yes," Kryslie confirmed. "But we would need to get equipment from somewhere."

"That will be a big job," Tymos mused. "Though I expect that Rhyn can help us source what we will need."

They knew that they did not need to worry about the cost - for Rhyn had told them of the trust account set up by the original missionaries and carefully invested and added to over the succeeding decades. It contained a staggeringly large amount, more than enough for whatever they needed to do.

Of his own findings, Tymos said, "The hills around the crash site are neatly placed for creating a radio telescope."

Both were mentally creating a list of what needed to be done to prepare the site for occupation, having in mind the memory of the intended base design.

"Once the excavating is done, we will have a place to work on the shield generators," Tymos proposed. "Or at least after we can get power into the cavern."

"And do it all while going to school!" Kryslie pointed out wryly. "I will write a letter to the university tonight and ask for an interview to sit the exams. I will get Rhyn to send it by express delivery. That way, they won't be able to trace an electronic letter to his place."

Tymos and Kryslie walked the boundaries of the area that was to become their base. It was an arbitrary circle still deep within the blackened and radioactive blast area. At evenly spaced intervals, they were planting devices with a multifunction purpose, each modified from commercially available products.

Primarily, they were passive detectors of heat and motion, but were also radiation meters and would become in the future, part of a communications array. A second device placed in tandem with the first would later become part of one of the protecting force screens for the base.

"OH!" Tym suddenly exclaimed. He was ahead of Krys. The sense of shock and an image in his mind had her hurrying to catch up to him, and she saw what he had found.

Not simply the single burnt skeleton that Krys had seen in his mind, but the remains of a once lusty tribe of gypsies.

The missile that had caused the devastation had landed as the tribe was sitting around their campfire. The stark remains of the wood and metal of their caravans was still discernable.

"We will have to tell Rhyn," Kryslie said in a soft voice. "He can arrange for what needs to be done."

"I wonder if this is the remains of the Mont de Ray tribe?" Tym asked thoughtfully. "So long ago, when we told Tamir Janzoet to hide amongst the gypsies – I had a premonition of this."

"We could not have prevented it," Krys told him, bringing to mind everything she had read in the reports about the incident. "It was a pivotal incident in bringing about peace between the two alliances, and in bringing the world's scientists together to pursue peaceful technology."

Tymos nodded his agreement, and began to walk again along the perimeter track. Neither he nor Kryslie spoke much after that and when the day's task was completed they transmitted back to Rhyn's house to report their find.

"Those missiles were the worst kind available during the war. The WSRA took control of them to prevent them ever being used. They planned to convert them to technology suitable for space exploration," Rhyn commented to hide his sadness. He seemed to have forgotten that Tym had read all his reports. "This one they used to launch the communications relay satellite. It developed a fault in the guidance system." He thought, but didn't say that "wildcat" scientists from the non-aligned countries, resentful of the WSRA taking control, had deliberately sabotaged it. Even the Tymorean missionaries had been unable to prove if the allegation was true or not. "It returned to Earth and exploded on impact. You saw the result and unless science can find a way to remove the radiation, it will be thousands of years before that area is safe."

"There were some fortuitous elements in its landing point," Tymos commented. His words were pitched as an idle observation, but he was intending to influence Rhyn's mind, very subtly. "The ring of hills around the site of impact does enclose most of the deadliest emanations. The ground is slagged right at the centre, but only for a five-mile radius. The radiation suits we borrowed from one of the monitoring huts are only rated for venturing about ten miles in from the outer barrier. The distance between the hills is about twenty five miles."

Rhyn was instantly interested. This was more detail than the other Tymoreans had been able to obtain about the site. His people had to rely on local equipment, and his missionaries, even with their trace of Tymorean power could not penetrate much further than the humans.

Tymos told Rhyn all that they had observed, except for the caverns, knowing that when he read the report in the future, back on Tymorea, he would see the possibilities that he did not elaborate on now.

The entrance examinations for the WSRA universities were instigated to separate prospective students into levels of intelligence and overall potential. All twelve campuses were orientated to the study of science and all had a prestigious reputation. The Washington campus, however, only took the elite of the candidates. The entry requirements for Washington were more stringent, requiring references from other academic sources as well as personal references and an Honours level pass in the exams.

The exams themselves tested intelligence as well as existing knowledge. Anyone who achieved a pass in the exams, even if not offered one of the places in the twelve universities, was guaranteed a place at their choice of 'lesser academic institutions'.

Kryslie, on behalf of her brother as well, wrote to the Washington University Vice Chancellor, expressing their wish to sit the entrance exam and asked for an interview to discuss the request.

The letter was at first treated with amused contempt, by the Vice Chancellor's assistant.

"Arrogant presumption," was the muttered comment of Sharon Wright. She knew that the invitations to those chosen to sit the exams had been sent out months ago. The exams were due to start that very week.

Her face quickly lost its amused look when she turned to the accompanying academic references. They were notarised by none other than the late Professor Grainger – founder of the University.

She took the letter into her boss.

Vice Chancellor Don Gilchrist read the letter and the references and his expression and unnatural fidgeting, betrayed excitement.

"At last!" he exclaimed. He instructed Sharon to, "Contact them right away – make them an appointment for as soon as they can get here. Have Stan Burroughs notified to be available at that time. And If I have any appointments that clash – reschedule them."

Sharon blinked in amazement, but simply agreed in a quiet voice. Gilchrist caught her look and smiled.

"Grainger told me about his two young protégés. I expected to meet them well before this. From all he said, they are quite exceptional."

To someone who had helped sort out the thousands of applications, the academic references had not seemed out of the ordinary. She controlled her urge to shrug and decided to wait and see what she thought when she met the two people.

At eight thirty the following morning, Sharon Wright looked up from her work and found two red heads quietly entering her office. They were both dressed smartly in two-piece suits. There was no doubt in her mind that the two were twins and when the woman spoke, the softly accented and beautifully modulated voice confirmed that she was one of Grainger's protégés.

"Hello Sharon. I am Krys Ward and this is my brother Tym," Kryslie spoke.

Sharon couldn't help smiling. She had expected arrogance from these two, but Krys had been most polite and accommodating on the phone the previous day. Now they were both proving to have none of the 'I'm better than you' attitude she had encountered from many potential students.

Someone, she decided, had trained them in courtesy and had not let their high intelligence be an excuse to be rude. The force of their personality was unmistakable, but at the same time like a refreshing breeze.

"The Vice Chancellor will be along shortly," she told them. "He is looking forward to meeting you. Do you mind taking a seat for a few moments?"

As she returned to scanning her job list for the day, she observed that the two red heads sat quietly, without fidgeting, or staring around the room, or reading the magazines or even trying to watch her work.

In fact, there was no trace of nervousness about them. It was as if the result of the interview was a foregone conclusion in their favour. Well … maybe there was a little arrogance there.

Tymos and Kryslie heard a muted buzz just before the door to the inner office opened. Sharon stood up and introduced the two guests to her boss.

"Good Morning, Sir," Tym said, nodding to the Vice Chancellor. "It was very good of you to see us so quickly. We appreciate that your time is valuable."

"Indeed," Gilchrist agreed. "However, I was keen to finally meet Professor Grainger's protégés. I had hoped to see you at the funeral, but that is irrelevant now. We will talk in a small room down the passage, since there are a number of others who expressed a wish to meet you."

Gilchrist led the way, and Tymos and Kryslie followed him into an informal meeting room where three others were waiting. The Vice Chancellor introduced them to the waiting people and was pleased that neither Tymos nor Kryslie seemed nervous to be the focus of the three important people.

One of the men, wearing a business suit, stood up and introduced himself. "Stan Burroughs," he said reaching out to shake hands with each of the newcomers in turn. His grip was returned with equal pressure. "I am the liaison between the university and the WSRA."

"Doctor Ken Andrews," the second man introduced, "I am the chairman of the selection panel for entry into the university." He had a casual zip up jacket over his white shirt.

"Dana Trent," the third person, a well-presented woman in a designer suit, introduced herself. "I am the Government's Science and technology advisor. I was also Professor Grainger's Chief Assistant until shortly before his death."

The relatively scant information each member of the interview panel had about the applicants was in the front of their minds. Tymos and Kryslie needed only to brush those minds with their telepathy to read what was there and sense that they all wanted to know more.

When everyone was seated, Gilchrist began. "In your letter to us, you stated you intention to sit the entrance examinations for the university. I am aware you had a very unconventional education. On what basis do you consider that you will be able to pass the exam?"

Gilchrist deliberately injected a note of scepticism into the question. He was implying that he did not believe their intelligence. He was pleased to note the lack of defensiveness or outrage in their reaction.

Tym Ward smiled almost ruefully. "When Professor Grainger became our mentor, he encouraged us to become interested in science. He recognised that we were bored by the snail's pace of the usual school system. He instigated a more radical education for us. He set challenges for us and when we thought we knew everything about a subject, he would bring in an expert to quiz us."

"And deflate our egos back to an acceptable level," Kryslie admitted with a deprecating grin.

Krys had used the memories of the four officials in the room to disarm them. Grainger had implied to these people that his protégés had been 'difficult'. Each felt they knew exactly what that implied. They were all impressed by the lack of such behaviour now.

"He made sure that we had a thorough grounding in non-science subjects too," Krys continued. "And he encouraged us to be placed in this university. A few years ago, we told him we thought we were ready to pass the exams."

Tym took over the narrative again. "He looked at us over those half moon glasses of his and said, yes we probably could but we were too young."

The comment about the glasses convinced them all that these two had known Grainger well. Only his closest friends knew of his preference for the antiquated reading glasses in his final years. None of his official portraits showed him with them.

Tym continued spinning their story, basing it on the notes Grainger had left for them.

"He said he had written a report about us for the university and implied that you wouldn't accept us until now. In fact, he challenged us to prove that we could support ourselves without relying on other people."

"We discovered," Kryslie explained, "that there were some things that you can't learn from books and other things that simply being smart can't solve. We had to learn to deal with all sorts of people, and to handle money. We never really had to do that before. And all sorts of other things. But now we are ready to be students here."

The casual assumption of being able to pass the exams at honours level did not pass unnoticed.

Ken Andrews chose to question them. "Tamir Grainger told us very little about your background, only that he had known your parents, briefly. What can you tell us about yourselves?"

Tymos shrugged.

"We don't remember our parents. All our lives, until recently, we were cared for by foster parents. We never got on well with any of them until Professor Grainger became our mentor."

Tym paused as if remembering things and decided to skip mentioning them. "He had discovered that our mother was someone he knew, also called Krys Ward. She was a special advisor to President Wallis. He had lost track of her and was surprised to discover us. You would have copies of our birth certificates, with our father's name on it. So you know as much about him as we do."

"How old are you?" Stan Burroughs asked thoughtfully.

"We are twenty years old," Kryslie told him, meeting his eyes.

"Then you would have been born soon after the war. What did become of your mother?"

Dana Trent leant forward as if very interested in the answer.

"Prof tried to find out," Tymos said without a smile. "I don't think he ever did. We found a news clipping from a sensation seeking paper that implied she had been abducted or defected to some foreign power. We looked at other papers from that time but nothing was mentioned. Not even an obit."

Krys decided enough questions had been asked. "Can I ask what relevance these questions about someone we don't even know, have with our application?"

Gilchrist relaxed back into his chair. "There was no question of refusing your application, and I have no doubt you will both do well. We make a point to interview all the candidates that are potentially eligible for a place here. When we are finished, have a word to my assistant and she will give you the times for the exams."

"Your mother had a brother," Dana Trent said unexpectedly. "He can't be found either."

Burroughs and Andrews stared intently at her. Tymos and Kryslie did too, sensing that Trent was suspicious of them and on the verge of an intuitive leap.

"I am surprised that I never met you," Trent went on, still unaware of her bombshell. "I was very close to the Professor; he was like a father to me. Anyway, when I tidied up his affairs after his death, I found a file about your mother. It was from when she was found after a bombing raid and went to an evaluation centre with amnesia. I tried to confirm the details with the State Department, but they claim information about her is classified. But the Professor had added details about a brother."

The woman was on the verge of making a connection so Kryslie chose to distract her.

"I would have liked to have known you," Krys told Dana earnestly. "But then again, back a few years we were brats. He was the one who finally found a couple to foster us who could handle our nonsense and keep us physically and mentally challenged."

Kryslie broadcast an image of a couple of highly intelligent spoilt delinquents. She saw Dana shudder and sensed mentally, that the woman was glad she had not met them sooner.

Doctor Andrews was now thinking excitedly of the possibility that if the mysterious mother of these two applicants had a brother, that there might me more like them around. It distracted him sufficiently to stop him from asking any more personal questions.

Stan Burroughs shared that thought but was more determined to keep an eye on these two. He intended to ensure they worked for the WSRA in the future – as soon as they finished their degree.

Gilchrist ended the interview by wishing them well in the exams.

The hardest part of the examinations was playing down their intelligence to something below the highest known human IQ. Tymos and Kryslie found the knowledge questions on the individual data tablets to be very easy, having learnt so much from their Tymorean teachers and the minds of the three Tymorean Governors as well as being naturally intelligent themselves.

They easily achieved the requisite level to attend the Washington University and became just two new faces amongst the thirty new students going through the formalities of enrolment and orientation.

The latter took a week and involved lectures and informal gatherings during which they met the brilliant men and women they would be studying under. They also met their fellow students of higher years, learnt their way around the huge campus and prepared for their new routine.

Initially the new students attended lectures and received assignments, such as at any other university. The difference was that what those other universities might teach over three years was expected to be achieved much sooner. The students were encouraged to learn for themselves using pre-recorded lectures, films, library resources and World Wide Web sites. When they had proved their competence in each unit, they could move on at their own speed.

In addition, they were immediately involved in high-level research, which encouraged them to learn any aspects of a discipline for which they lacked knowledge. The students thrived on the routine, often resenting the enforced physical activities that took them out of the classrooms and labs but ensured their physical and mental well-being. However, they gained knowledge of far greater depth than obtainable elsewhere and in a wide range of scientific disciplines. They learnt not only the theory but also the hands on knowledge of how to build the equipment to take theory into practice.

Tym and Krys worked as a team, approaching two different subjects from basics to advanced frontiers of knowledge – by reading reference books, journal articles, and working with pioneers in the field. What one learnt, the other knew too.

During their time in the laboratories completing research assignments, their initial successes at the assigned tasks often led to the senior researcher giving them more difficult duties and often listened to their suggestions for improving the efficiency of experiments. Their ideas often resulted in unexpected and exciting results.

To try to prevent knowledge being used for war or destructive purposes, the students studied the ethics and social impact of their disciplines. It forced them to be aware of the implications of what they were doing – both the benefits and the drawbacks.

Each student had their own special areas of interest, but by the end of their years at the university would have thorough knowledge of how their favoured discipline related to all other fields.

The Hall of Science at the University of Washington was famous for its displays. Visitors came from all over the world just to see them. This museum, if you could rank it as such, occupied a building of its own. It had five levels each with the floor space equal to a football field.

The displays covered so much of Earth's history in the sciences that even a week's visit didn't give a visitor more than a surface appreciation of the depth of knowledge involved.

The students at the university were encouraged to become familiar with all the exhibits in all the sections, as a lesson in the failures and successes and mysteries of science.

The Grainger Exhibit was seen as a personal challenge to every student. It was a single display in a large room, created by the founder of the university, Tamir Grainger. He was remembered as a man of unsurpassed brilliance, and his portrait was on the wall, facing his legacy to the university.

At first glance, the display appeared to consist of a crystal conglomerate on a waist high pedestal. In front of the stand was a low table with a rolled up scroll - looking ready to be unrolled and read.

With the brilliant fluorescent lights shining on the display, a new visitor could be forgiven for thinking they could walk over and touch the crystals.

However, when such a visitor approached to a distance of two metres from the crystals, the presence of an impenetrable force field was quickly obvious. Not only did it prevent any closer inspection of the crystals, it triggered the fluoro lights to flick off and duller incandescent down lights to shine on the crystals. Only at this time was the true beauty of the crystals apparent. Light appeared to emanate from within the. It scintillated through the visible spectrum as the energy absorbed by the crystals with the fluoro light on was radiated at a gradually changing wavelength.

Outside the barrier of the force field, enclosed in a glass box on a second table, was a piece of parchment. The elegant handwriting was that of Tamir Grainger.

"CRYSTALS: These crystals are extra terrestrial in origin and were excavated from a meteorite that crashed on the moon. When excited by light of a certain wavelength they emit radiation of an unusual nature. The force field that surrounds the crystals emanates from the crystals.

My challenge to all future scientists is to unravel the secrets of the crystals and put their properties to use for the good of mankind."

Tym and Krys had, like their fellow students, spent part of their time observing or measuring the complex scintillations of the crystals. They had, like everyone else, apparently failed to learn their secrets. However, it was an act. As soon as they had first seen the crystals, they had recognised them as being native to Tymorea. For Grainger to have had them, he must have inherited them from his missionary father, Tamir Janzoet.

Although they had only seen pictures of the mineral before this, they knew a great deal about it from their studies on Tymorea, and more from the knowledge shared with them by Professor Governor Xyron. At any time they chose, they could penetrate the force field and recover from within the exhibit, the information Tamir Grainger had left for them.

The reason that they had not yet done so was that they were not ready to use that information. When they finished excavating the chamber under the radiation site, and designing and building the shield generator – then they would retrieve Grainger's data.

In the mean time, they appreciated the deceptively complex security around the exhibit.

Chapter 19 - Tamir Janzoet's Legacy

They visited Rhyn regularly during the years of their university career, as well as spending many hours at night enlarging the underground chambers at the radiation site. Their absence was never noted because the students at Washington University were not restricted to that campus, but were able to study under any of the scientists at any of the campuses, or any that worked for the WSRA. In addition, both Tym and Krys were so often seen together, that if people saw one of them, they knew the other wasn't far away.

Everyone had discovered their apparently insatiable eagerness for knowledge, so if either of them could not be found in one place, they usually had been somewhere else on the campus.

In truth, with their personal transmitters, they simply needed Rhyn to activate the long-range beam to terminate in the grounds of the university, tap into it, and transmit to his house - half a continent away. It enabled them to keep in touch with developments outside the scientific field – particularly in the area of world politics. From there, they could also transmit to and from the caverns.

After their first visit to the other Tymorean missionaries, Tymos and Kryslie stayed away from them and spoke only to Rhyn. The Tymorean co-ordinator ensured that they were not mentioned in any report, even though they still did not have contact with home base.

During their visits, Rhyn had spoken of his friendship with Tamir Grainger who had in turn, insisted that no mention be made that he was Tamir Janzoet's son. Nor had he ever personally contacted any other of his father's kin. He was adamant that only Tymos and Kryslie were to receive his father's work.

They were never certain if Rhyn understood that they had skipped through time or if he thought that the un-ageing Great Ones had simply been elsewhere and chosen not to be in contact. He was, however, convinced of the importance of Grainger's records in respect to the soon to arrive Tymorean mission.

On a visit early in their fourth year at the university, Rhyn was uncharacteristically agitated, and he quizzed them about getting Grainger's works.

It was clear to both Tymos and Kryslie that the old man had had a premonition of the future. When they tried to see the vision in his mind, it had already faded.

"We can get to them any time," Tymos assured Rhyn gently. "What is it that concerns you?"

Rhyn was uncomfortable, believing that he was imagining things because he was old. He had never been trained to understand such visions.

"The shields must be ready as soon as they come," was all he said. "Are they ready?"

"Not yet," Tymos admitted. "We are still building the generator. We will be able to take it where it is needed when they arrive."

"I don't know where the base will be," Rhyn said, worried. "I won't be able to tell them. Homebase doesn't know about us. When my ancestors returned they were not going to mention us. When the mission comes, they won't know to contact us. It was our duty to keep trying to reach them. We were taught how so that we could give them the history of this world. They will need that. You told me to suggest places for a base. How will they get that information? How will they know where to find you?"

To Tymos and Kryslie, it was apparent that Rhyn's premonition had been of his death, and that he had seen he would die before the Tymorean mission arrived. He had seen that the scientists of Earth would have the means to detect the base unless Grainger's works were used.

The old man was almost rigid with dismay.

He feared that all he and his forebears had done to ensure the success of the Tymorean Mission would come to nothing.

Kryslie took his hand in hers and spoke gently to him, encouraging him to relax by sending soothing energy to his mind and body.

"Respected Elder," she said using the Tymorean term of respect. "What you saw is but a vision of what might be. It is a means by which the Guardians of Peace communicate with us. Let me assure you that we will have the shields working before the base is built and installed where they will be needed."

"But you don't know where..."

"Hush," Kryslie quietened him. "We are aware that you don't know where the base will be, but we do. Remember our insistence that no mention be made of us in your reports?"

Rhyn nodded.

"It is because when we left Tymorea it was with the rest of the Earth Mission. We were sent back in time by the Guardians and have, since then, skipped through time until now. It seemed to us that there were points in Earth's history that we needed to experience. The important point is that before we left, we had access to all the information you and your predecessors had gathered. It means that the advance missionaries received your signal, and your reports were sent on. Those reports did not mention us, and we have not, until now, discussed what we know will happen in the future. We did not want to create a paradox. All you must do is continue as you have. All will be well."

"I won't be here when they come," Rhyn said finally.

Tymos took the old man's other hand as he squatted beside Rhyn's chair.

"If anything happens to you – I will personally take over your duties. I will ensure that Homebase receives your reports. I will instigate the homing beacon for them to find us. I will also continue to co-ordinate the others and their reports. When the mission arrives, you and your generation of missionaries and all those that have gone before you will have the recognition you all deserve. The base will be safe."

Rhyn relaxed at last, nodding acceptance of the assurances.

"If you have any other visions, please share them with us," Kryslie urged.

"We will have to step up our schedule," Tymos commented to Kryslie as they worked together on a physics assignment. They had spent more time with Rhyn than they intended and needed to return and go directly to their practical session. "I'm going to see that I am assigned to work with the scientific engineers group. I should be able to manufacture the parts we need for the generator. I have the drawings we did and the specifications."

"Then I will get myself assigned to work with Doctor Emmanuel, he is the one most likely to build something that will detect the other shields that will be around the base," Kryslie decided. "At least the excavation is almost complete. That will give us more time. When do you think we should go for Grainger's information?"

"As soon as we can," Tymos decided. He was beginning to have a sense of urgency. "I should check his father's work in case I have to make modifications to the generator. That group of foreign scientists should be gone by Friday. What say we aim for Friday night?"

In fact, Kryslie did not have to approach Doctor Emmanuel. He sent an assistant to find her. The renowned physicist had wanted both siblings to help him with his latest experiment, but he settled for one. In his mind, there was the sense of something that set those two students above the other brilliant students at the university. It was partly their ability to listen quietly, understand fully and work efficiently and without fuss. They seemed to know exactly how and when to improvise for best effect. They also seemed to have the knack of being able to see to the heart of a problem and suggest solutions.

Kryslie had not worked under Emmanuel for two years, but she quickly evaluated the progress he had made since then.

The study of force fields and shields along with their characteristics and generation was still in its basic stages, but Kryslie could predict a rapid expansion of knowledge. In fact, scientists had been dabbling with the theory for almost a century. A large volume of knowledge had been destroyed when Tamir Grainger had blown up one of the former World Science Council high security research centres. Then, the thrust of the knowledge had been to use the phenomena for destructive purposes as the world had been on the brink of war. Now it was being rediscovered for use for exploring space and for other peaceful reasons.

Emmanuel had explained the aims of his current research. He was trying to develop a force screen that would block out radiation, for example to protect a vessel travelling in space. He had begun with his successful screen for blocking solid objects and was now modifying its properties.

As an adjunct to that project, he was developing a device to measure the effectiveness of the screen, which in effect was a force screen detector. He had not begun to think of it that way as yet. He considered it a modified radiation detector.

Kryslie, however, was aware of its potential and that he intended to test his new screens at the site of the radioactive missile blast. There was no danger yet, but in the future, he might discover more than he bargained for.

Kryslie was intending to monitor his activities, even though the initial tests would be small-scale lab tests.

Tymos and Kryslie visited the Grainger exhibit shortly before it closed to the public on the Friday afternoon. They were surprised to find Emmanuel still there and staring thoughtfully at the exhibit. He had been hosting a discussion on force theory with the foreign scientists who had just left for a pre-departure banquet in their honour.

Emmanuel did not seem to be aware of the quiet presence of the two students. His mind was exploring a tangent suggested by one of the departing scientists.

Tymos thought at his sister, "I will check the security. You keep him occupied or get him to leave."

A minute nod was her only reply.

"Sir?" Krys spoke softly.

Emmanuel turned around, somehow not surprised by her presence.

"My Japanese colleague suggested to me that my new device might also be adapted to detect the presence of force fields," he told her neutrally. "The only existing force field that I know of is here."

"We hardly need a detector for that, Sir," Kryslie said with quiet logic.

Emanuel smiled at the wry humour.

"No, we don't. What we need is something that can tell us the properties of this one."

"It is impervious to physical penetration," Krys stated.

"It also lets light out, but does it let light in?" Emanuel commented. "And how the hell is the field generated? Light excites the crystals and it emits the radiation that produces the force field. The crystals are converting light energy into something else."

Kryslie stood motionless, letting Emmanuel think and not contributing any suggestions. The scientist turned slightly and noticed Tymos, was also unmoving.

"Sometimes, you two remind me of Tamir Grainger. The way he had of waiting for you to make that intuitive leap – to discover something he already knew. What do you know about those crystals? Did Grainger tell you anything?"

"We were not with him when he set up the exhibit," Kryslie said with a casual shrug. "It was not his choice to tell us anything about it."

"No, indeed," Emmanuel appeared to be remembering. "Grainger was brilliant. He knew more about force fields than I have yet to discover. He gave his students the basic ideas, the basic theory, but held back on anything more. He has left notes that we haven't even begun to understand. He once said that if we could solve this puzzle, we would be opening the door to a greater knowledge."

Emmanuel snapped back to the present.

"Young man, what have you been doing with that object?"

Tymos gave a wry grin and casually flipped a palm-sized device into view.

"Thinking along the same lines as you, Sir," he admitted as if caught out. "I was trying to detect any other electrical input to this area besides lights."

"And..." Emmanuel prompted.

"Nothing in the walls and the floor, only in the roof," Tymos admitted.

"The walls are two foot thick permacrete, with an inner layer of insulation. The floor is three foot thick, again with an inner layer of insulation," Emmanuel revealed. He had already checked out the room. "The only power in the ceiling goes to the lights. The ceiling is also three foot thick. The conduits run above the permacrete and then directly down to each light."

"It is not the only radiation in the room," Tymos decided to admit. "The security system has infra red detectors located in the angle between roof and walls and narrow UV beams criss-crossing the area."

Emmanuel made a decision.

"I am going to order this exhibit sealed," he said, watching for but seeing no reaction from the students. "No one will be allowed to enter without my express permission. Tomorrow at 0800, meet me at my lab. Both of you."

Kryslie feigned excitement. "Yes! We'll be there."

Tymos nodded, unable to read the man's intentions beyond the desire to study the exhibit.

Emmanuel shooed his students out ahead of him and allowed the door to lock behind him.

"Go and join the hi-jinks going on over at the student union," Emmanuel suggested. "Clear your mind of science for tonight."

The scientist strode off down a passage towards the stairs leading down to the lower floor. The security office was at ground level.

Tymos and Kryslie trotted the other way, heading for the stairs closest to the student union building. They waited until they were outside to discuss their findings.

"The lights are hardwired directly from the power grid," Tymos said softly. "It only goes through a surge protector. They are on all the time, except when the proximity detector switches them off. That is done via a computer link, not an on/off switch. In the event of a power failure, there is a backup generator dedicated to that circuit. It probably takes less than half a minute to cut in."

"What about the IR and UV beams?" Kryslie probed.

"Powered the same way," Tymos confirmed. "But they are only effective outside the force screen."

"So we need to cause a major power blackout," Kryslie decided. She kept walking, but her mind went elsewhere.

Tymos walked beside her, waiting for her to return her attention to the present and watching out for dangers around them.

"I think we can cause a storm," Kryslie said quietly. "It has been a warm day. If lightning puts out the power, security won't be too alarmed. After all, the walls in that exhibit room are like a strong room. We will just need to be in and out before the generator cuts in."

"Let's do it," Tymos agreed.

Darkness had fallen and with the revelry in full swing, no one noticed that Tymos and Kryslie had left the Founder's Day party. There was no curfew, nor security patrols on the campus, so the twins walked sure footedly through the darkness to the corner of the grounds near the electricity substation that serviced the campus. The building was huge because of the enormous power demand it needed to supply.

They were now clad in dark clinging clothes, so that when they sat on the ground near the outer fence, they were hardly visible. If they had been seen, it simply looked as if they were meditating. In fact, they were sensing the power in the Earth and drawing it into themselves. This is something they could do on Tymorea, but they also had a connection to the Earth, as it was their birthplace.

The power flowed through them directed by their minds to force moist hot air to rise and coalesce into clouds. The clouds became thicker, but did not drop their moisture. A breeze began to build, bringing in more hot moist air. The process became self-sustaining and lightning began to flicker between the clouds. Delicately, Tymos created a zone of different electrical potential around the power input line.

Accompanied by a deafening thunderclap, lightning struck the substation building. Without waiting to be sure of the damage, Tymos and Kryslie transmitted to the exhibition chamber.

The room would have been completely dark except for the faint light being emitted by the crystals. By adjusting their eyes for the dimness, it was enough for them to use to see. They arrived outside the force field, took a moment to analyse the field that existed without the light. It was still impermeable to solid objects, but without the artificial light, it was no longer impermeable to their transmitters. They transmitted in, ran behind the pedestal supporting the crystals, and grabbed a box from within the base of the pillar. A second box, set in plain view, they left alone.

Without stopping to examine their 'treasure' they transmitted back through the force screen, then as the lights came on, they transmitted back to Tymos's room.

The lights were still out in the student quarters, but Tymos moved without hesitation about his room, taking the box and placing it in a prepared hiding place. Then both he and Kryslie changed out of their dark clothes and placed them in the same place as the box. Tymos sealed the hole with a screen of Tymorean power, effectively hiding and protecting it from human observation. They both redressed in their party clothes and joined the students milling about in the dark, lightning lit student cafe.

Tymos and Kryslie were unaware that they had underestimated the suspicions of the security guards. Having just been told to seal the Grainger exhibit, the guards decided that the sudden power outage - caused by a very localised, unpredicted thunderstorm which caused lightning to strike the exact place that could black out that part of the campus – had to be sabotage.

Two guards raced up the five flights of stairs to check the Grainger Exhibit. The other four duty guards stayed watching the security monitors, counting down to when the generator would come on line.

In the instant that the screens covering the exhibit came back to life, they saw two dark figures vanish. The IR monitor showed fading thermal images of two figures. Several of the UV beams beeped red on the monitor, and then flashed green. Whoever or whatever had been there, had not entered or left by the doors, since the alarm on the lock had not activated.

They attributed that anomaly to the generator coming on.

Kryslie ventured down to get breakfast as soon the cafe opened next morning. Even at six o'clock, the place was busy. The buzz of conversation was mainly about the previous evening's power outage. That event had effectively stopped the party, though a few people had obviously gone off to start their own more private get togethers instead.

A slight Japanese girl slid into the seat beside Kryslie.

"Krys, have you seen Jimmy?" Alice Ishamura asked. James Fujawa, also a fourth year student was her fiancé.

Krys looked at Alice and felt a shiver of premonition. "Not since early last night – at the party. Why?"

"He went off somewhere with his brother. They had been meeting with their Uncle, the one who was in that group of visitors that left yesterday. Jimmy said he would not be long. When the party broke up, I went back to my room. I expected him to look for me there. When he didn't, I checked his room this morning. His bed hadn't been slept in."

"He may have stayed with his brother or uncle overnight," Krys suggested. "If he doesn't turn up by tonight, maybe you had better contact the student co-ordinator. If I see Jimmy, I will tell him to call you."

Alice had gone when Tymos slid in next to her.

"I have heard a buzz that there was a break in at the Grainger Exhibit last night," he said very softly. "Two students are being held for questioning and the police have arrested a man for sabotaging the generator."

"Who is the man they caught?" Krys looked to be keeping her attention on the people walking around the cafe.

"No idea, but he is Japanese. They are waiting for an interpreter."

"Jimmy Fujawa is missing." Krys told her brother.

Tymos assembled the facts in his mind. "His uncle was here, and isn't his father into weather control research?"

"Yes, and I never considered the possibility that the hot air wasn't natural. All I saw was the potential to create a storm," Kryslie admitted. "And it was something that the uncle said that got Emanuel to close the exhibit. Do you think that the uncle was trying to steal the crystals to study them - perhaps to beat Emmanuel to a solution?"

"We will need more data," Tymos decided. "Have you finished? We need to find out what is going on and if it is Jimmy in trouble, what he is supposed to have done."

It was unspoken between them that if their own actions had resulted in trouble for the others – they would own up.

The mystery of the whereabouts of Jimmy Fujawa and his elder brother Terry Fujawa was solved when Tymos and Kryslie walked into Emmanuel's lab fifteen minutes later. Several campus security men were watching the pair in Emmanuel's office and investigators were talking to the physicist out in the lab.

"I have checked the exhibit," Emmanuel was saying. "Nothing has been touched. There is no indication, except on the security tapes that anyone even entered the room."

"How valuable are the crystals?" one of the two investigators asked. He was thinking ordinary attempted theft.

"I couldn't put a price on them," Emmanuel admitted. "From a scientific viewpoint, they are unique. They exhibit properties that I and scientists all over the world wish to understand."

"So, why did you close the exhibit?" the other investigator asked. They were still trying to figure a motive for the incident.

"I wish to make observations – without the interference of guests and observers," Emmanuel claimed. "I have a week before the next scheduled group of foreign scientists arrive to make their own observations. I am also the appointed curator of that exhibit."

Kryslie sidled around the lab to a point near Emmanuel's office and pretended to study a model of Emmanuel's new device. In effect, she was probing the minds of the Fujawa brothers. She liked Jimmy. He was very intelligent, honest and straightforward. He and his brother came from a scientific family and they had never hidden their deeply ingrained loyalty to their kinfolk. Krys would have said he was incapable of doing anything criminal. After a time she sent a thought to Tymos, who was still listening from an inconspicuous position to the conversation between scientist and investigators.

"Tym, they were intending to break into the room and grab the crystals," Krys told her brother. "Their uncle was convinced that once it was completely dark in there the force field would be gone. Their father was working to create a storm, only we interfered and things happened faster than anticipated. When the power went out, they had to hurry their schedule and the uncle who was fixing the generator was careless - he shocked himself. The boys were to go and grab the crystals and take them to the eldest brother Jacob. However they were caught as they were about to enter the room."

"They haven't really done anything wrong," Tymos thought back. "Except obey their elders as they were taught. I don't think they deserve to be kicked out of the uni for that. Especially when we actually went in and it was our figures that were caught on the security film."

"You know how strict the university is about obeying rules – especially about keeping out of areas declared off-limits," Krys reminded him. "I will be speaking up if they choose to do anything more than issue them with a warning."

"And if they kick us out – it will not stop us working on our real mission," Tymos agreed.

Emmanuel spotted Tymos, and then glanced around and saw Kryslie.

"I expect you know about last night's happenings?" he asked Tymos directly.

"Some," Tymos admitted cautiously.

"You have seen who I have in my office?"

Tymos nodded again.

"You would know young Jimmy fairly well – what is your evaluation of his actions in trying to enter the Grainger Exhibit when it was closed to all?"

Emmanuel watched Tymos closely but saw no change in his expression. To Tymos, the scientist's mind betrayed nothing more than interest in the answer to his question.

"I cannot speak for Jimmy's esteemed relatives, but Jimmy himself is more interested in working on weather control than force fields. I can see no reason why he would break into the exhibit for himself, but he might with pressure from his family."

"Yes, that was my evaluation too. However, he did and the matter must go before the Chancellor. Their uncle, Elgin Fujawa, and I have some history between us. He would like nothing more than to solve the puzzle first or prevent me from doing so. He would stoop to use his family to further that aim. So why were you and your sister suddenly more interested in that Exhibit yesterday?"

"It wasn't sudden," Tymos said flatly. "We have always had a great interest."

"Yesterday you were prepared with a scanner that showed you all the security measures. Last night – events happened..."

Tymos said nothing, but continued to meet Emmanuel's gaze without reacting.

"Were you involved with the Fujawa brothers?" Emmanuel demanded of Tymos.

"No," Tym said flatly. "Nor with the man the investigators say they have."

"Did you go into the exhibition chamber after I closed it last night?" Emmanuel demanded suddenly.

Tymos said nothing. Emmanuel turned to look at Kryslie. He met her gaze but she too said nothing.

Emmanuel came to his own conclusions, but his mind did not elaborate.

"Both of you remain in the lab," he said coldly. "You will come with me when the Vice Chancellor summons us. I will have an answer to my question. You can, individually evaluate the results of the field density meter tests. You can give me your evaluations later."

Emmanuel strode from the room. Neither Tymos nor Kryslie spoke aloud or glanced at each other, they simply began the task set.

Tymos and Kryslie sat next to Emmanuel and listened to all the reports of the night's events and the investigator's report on the man that was caught.

The Vice Chancellor questioned the Fujawa brothers, who denied entering the locked room, admitting only that they were about to. The security film was shown, but the timing was out by about a minute.

When Tymos read in the Vice Chancellor's mind the intention to expel the two students, he finally spoke up. His admission caused all the academics on the panel to re-think the evidence.

"Terry and James were not the figures on the security film, Sir," Tymos said, standing up. "My sister and I entered during the interval of the power going off and the generator going on. We only went in for a few seconds and left before the guards arrived. We were not aware of any other attempts to enter the chamber. It was simply that we were there when the power went off and the security lock was unpowered. It was a unique opportunity to observe the crystals without lights."

"Did you approach the crystals," Emmanuel asked as the question assumed importance in his mind.

"The force field was still present." Tymos's statement did not answer the question, but it redirected everyone's attention.

The Vice Chancellor, Don Gilchrist turned a stern, disappointed look at the two students he secretly acknowledged were the best that had yet passed into the university.

In the back of his mind, he noted that they did not seem any older than when they had first walked into his office. In addition, their attitude had not changed either. They still did what they set their minds to do, even if it wasn't done the accepted way.

"Many of the students have protested the strict rules of behaviour that exist on this campus," Gilchrist said slowly, his attention on the four students in the room. "Our charter is to produce scientists of only the highest ethical standard. Mr Fujawa and Mr Fujawa, I appreciate your obedience to your family, and you are fortunate that your actions proceeded no further than your intention to contravene our rules. You are both to consider yourselves warned. Another incident of this nature will result in you being asked to leave the University. As it is, I am revoking your travel privileges. The rest of your study will be undertaken on this campus only. Until I notify you differently, you are restricted to the campus grounds and must adhere to your published schedule. In your free time, you may study in the library or your quarters. It will be a serious matter if you cannot be located if required. This may not be the end of this matter. Do you both understand?"

The brothers nodded and gave a bow of respect to the Vice Chancellor. They were relieved to be allowed to continue their studies and very thankful to be allowed to leave the room. They flashed a look of gratitude at Tymos.

Gilchrist waited for the Fujawa brothers to be gone before he expressed his disappointment in the two top students of the university, who were an example for the younger students as well as some older ones.

"However, the example of opportunistically breaking rules is not an example we wish shared with other students. I am sure you both understand."

He received a flat, "Yes, Sir," from both Tymos and Kryslie.

Gilchrist placed the same restrictions on them as on the Fujawa brothers, as well as restricting them to the campus grounds. After ensuring that they understood their position, he kept them standing while he looked thoughtfully at them. He dismissed the rest of the disciplinary panel and waited until the twins and Dr Emmanuel were the only ones remaining in the room with him.

"You are not as blasé about your mentor's exhibit as you have tried to make out, are you?" Gilchrist accused them. "You have been treated no differently from any other students but the low down is, almost everybody expects the two of you to unravel Grainger's mystery. Have your illicit activities given you any new insights?"

"Perhaps," Kryslie hedged. "The crystals still glowed in the dark."

"Perhaps?" Gilchrist insisted.

"The only comment we got from Professor Grainger relating to his exhibit was that the secret should be obvious if we had the wisdom to see it," Kryslie told the Vice Chancellor.

"And I suppose his mentioned his favourite motto – true wisdom is when you can see in the dark," Gilchrist asked them.

"We have...heard that," Kryslie commented, but it had not been from Grainger. It had come from the Elders of Tymorea. "We never took 'see' to be in the visual sense."

"Well, perhaps you will be willing to discuss your insights with Emmanuel?" Gilchrist suggested. "You are both assigned to him for the next week. I admit I have a wish for a team from this university to solve that mystery."

After that comment, he did dismiss the Ward twins, although he doubted that they were at all penitent.

Chapter 20 - Grainger's Legacy

It was Emanuel's observation that the more intelligent a student was, the less they liked to do dull, routine, repetitive work. Therefore, he deliberately set Tymos and Kryslie to analysing year's worth of observations, looking for correlations between the available light in the exhibition chamber and the emanations of the crystals. He didn't expect any revelations, but he did intend to remind them that science at Washington University was a team effort.

As he assembled a trolley with his precious new machine and all the equipment he expected to need, he watched the Ward twins attack the data with the concentration he expected of them. Neither voiced a complaint about the task, even between themselves.

For their part, Tymos and Kryslie already knew a great deal about the crystals. It meant that they could visually scan read the data and ignore most of it. They concentrated on the relatively few data sets where there was direct correlation between the available ambient light and the crystal emanations. Most were data sets they had measures over the years. Included in these were measurements taken over the night period when the exhibit was normally closed and the UV beams were active.

Between them, they assembled the data in tables and as graphs that showed, firstly, the wavelengths of light available, and the wavelengths emanating from the crystals. A constant time lag and wavelength shift could be deduced.

The effect was confirmed during the night experiment. Every time a UV beam was aimed at the crystal, the same time lag elapsed and light was emitted at the shifted wavelength, causing a peak on the graph.

The time period of the UV flashes was the same as that of the graph peaks. Moreover, not all the emanations were in the frequencies of visible light.

Kryslie printed out the important data and placed it in a file folder, then continued to scan useless record sheets. She carried the folder when Emmanuel told them to leave the task and accompany him to the Grainger exhibit. Tymos had, in his pocket, the palm sized device that he had used in the room the previous day. He offered to push the heavy trolley.

Security men stood outside the chamber, but they let Emmanuel and his aides in. Tymos and Kryslie helped Emmanuel to connect his machine to an outside power supply, and direct it at the crystals. The miniature screen glowed to reflect the radiation hitting a small portable screen. Once, operating, Emmanuel had Tymos standing on steps to hold the screen at varying heights, so that he could record the results.

Kryslie watched the screen and saw the first indication that the force field was actually spherical in shape. She pointed it out to Emmanuel who was ecstatic.

However, the intensity of emitted radiation seemed to be constant all over the sphere. Emmanuel stood still and thought intensely.

He barked a question at Tymos. "What would you try now, Mr Ward?"

Tymos was not tricked into answering without thinking. He and Kryslie had already considered how much help to give their 'teacher'.

Kryslie answered instead of Tymos. It caused Emmanuel to spin around and give her his full attention. "You need to study the effects of a much narrower range of radiation."

"The visible electromagnetic spectrum being too wide?"

In answer, Kryslie presented him with a graph, showing the intensity of various wavelengths of the fluorescent light and other radiation versus the crystal emanations, where the peak was off set to a different wavelength.

Emmanuel scanned the graph with great interest. He noted the time lag as he scanned the nighttime graph. He also looked at the graphs where the irradiating light was only the incandescent down lights.

"Describe what you saw when you came here in the dark," Emmanuel insisted.

"The crystals were still emitting light and the force field was intact," Tymos described the changing colours of the emissions.

"Were they becoming less bright?" Emmanuel quizzed.

"We were not in here long enough to tell," Tymos claimed.

The scientist returned to an earlier idea. "How would you suggest narrowing the wavelength of irradiating light?" Emmanuel asked his students.

"Filters," Kryslie said promptly.

"The down lights are always on," Emmanuel reminded her.

"Turn them off," Tymos said, straight faced and logical.

Emmanuel was reminded of the previous night's events, and his suspicions of the two students increased. "And the two of you 'just happened' to be nearby when the lightning hit the substation," he remarked with quiet intensity. "The first and only time the power here has ever been interrupted."

Neither Tymos nor Kryslie reacted, even with a shrug. They simply returned Emmanuel's stare. Finally, his waiting for a reply seemed to force a response.

"As far as I know, this campus does not have any weather control apparatus," Kryslie avoided the implication of fore knowledge and planning the lightning. "I will admit I am sensitive to storms building. Who, however, could predict where lightning would strike?"

"Who indeed?" Emmanuel said drolly. "I suppose you both know the security code for the lock?"

He took the lack of a reply as an affirmative.

Deep in his mind, where even Kryslie didn't probe, he was becoming convinced that these two knew more than they were saying and that they would not come out and explain everything to him. It was also becoming obvious that they had unspoken reasons for helping him and probably a hidden agenda of their own. They had shown they would choose silence over lies.

Frustrating as the thought was, what little advice they chose to give him was more conducive to progress than none. His research had reached a sticking point. What they said was definitely worth considering.

"I will talk to the electricians about the lights," he agreed finally. "Anything else?"

Two identical shrugs were his only reply.

"While I am organising the extra equipment and the electrician, what will you be doing?"

"I wanted to study the Westphalen Engineering Exhibit," Tymos said at once.

"That exhibit is directly beneath this one," Emmanuel challenged, sensing something odd.

Tymos gave a deprecating grin. "Just so it won't be hard to find me if you need me."

Kryslie sensed that Emmanuel would accept the activity, but had doubts about the reason for Tymos's interest.

"Doctor, do you need any help? I could hunt up those filters that were part of the Open Day display three years ago," Kryslie offered. "If they are not in the basement of this building I will ask around."

"Look, but if you can't find them, come back and see me first," Emmanuel insisted. He was mindful of the condition that their whereabouts were to be known at all times.

"Will do!" Kryslie agreed. Once they were out of the exhibit chamber, she walked off with her brother.

"I wonder how long it will be before he remembers that the Westphalen Exhibit is being dismantled for renovation," Kryslie said softly. They were walking down the back stairs.

"He is in the throes of a scientific breakthrough," Tymos countered. "I think I will have enough time to see what I need to see, whilst he is upgrading his experimental program."

"Tamir Grainger certainly put a lot of thought into that display. There is more than one aspect of force fields being demonstrated there, not to mention the nature of the crystals. It wasn't until I realised that the sphere around the crystals was bisected by the floor that I thought how he must have set up the display."

Kryslie was impressed by Grainger's ingenuity.

"Me too," Tymos admitted wryly. "And we are supposed to be the great and wise thinkers. The floor is coated with a substance that stops the force field. It doesn't actually penetrate into the concrete. That pedestal is hollow, and a slight adult could squeeze in there. If there isn't some kind of conduit leading to the pedestal, I'll go back to Tymorea and ask to be taught with the babies."

"Isn't science so deceptively simple once you understand it?" Kryslie laughed quietly. "Even in the dark the force field is still there – so Tamir had to have a physical means to get out of the force bubble once he had set it up. The isotope that is powering the force field is still in there. The field blocks solid objects both ways. He knew we could transmit through it in the dark, but he can't activate a transmitter. He is only half Tymorean. The logic is positively blinding, but I doubt that the Royal nursemaids need to fear your presence."

Kryslie left her brother when he entered the display sponsored by Westphalen Engineering. She continued down to where she expected to find the coloured filters and some other equipment that would help Emmanuel examine the crystals.

Tymos stood at the door and took in the activity within the room. Workers were already starting to remove wall panels to expose power conduits, pipes and the building framework.

The Dean of the Engineering Faculty was directing some first year students who were carefully dismantling delicate equipment. He readily welcomed a pair of hands that he knew would not need close supervision.

Tymos chose the exhibit closest to the part of the room directly beneath the pedestal in the chamber above. The false roof hid what he hoped to find, and he mentally nudged a worker to begin dismantling the roof near him.

The Dean gave his workers a short break, but Tymos opted to continue and a short time later, he had the opportunity he wanted. He climbed the ladder and visually scanned the raw concrete above the false roof.

He saw no sign of a crack in the surface beneath the pedestal. He pulled out his palm-sized scanner and ran it over the concrete. On three sides of the spot he had mentally marked 'x', the scanner told him there was three feet of concrete with a softer layer in the middle – just as Emmanuel had stated.

On the fourth side, there was only three inches of concrete, a wide gap, and a second layer of concrete above the soft insulation layer. Moving the scanner around, told Tymos there was a tunnel in the concrete from below the pedestal towards the wall where the door was. Now he only needed to find the access point to the tunnel.

Scrambling down from the ladder, he climbed another that was below a hanging panel near the door. The tunnel continued past that point, ran over the passage and into the back stairwell.

He shared a mental laugh with his sister who was then back in Emmanuel's lab testing the filters.

Kryslie thought back a warning. Emmanuel was reviewing the recorded data and had noticed the force field wasn't circular, because of the floor.

Even as she informed her brother, Emmanuel stood up and rummaged through the equipment Kryslie brought up from storage. He found the device that would scan walls and permitted himself a knowing smile.

"Bro, I think he might be heading your way," she warned with a mental grin. "He has a scanner but it is not very efficient."

Tymos was on the floor and packing equipment when Emmanuel walked into the room and gave him brief nod of recognition. Without inviting help, the scientist began to scan the roof.

As he finished packing the equipment from a display, Tymos watched from the side of his eye. The scientist walked to and fro, but it seemed his scanner could not detect the tunnel in the concrete. Finally, he came and stood by Tymos. "You have already checked for an access tunnel, haven't you?" Emmanuel accused. "Are you still here because you haven't found it?"

Tymos shook his head, taped the box shut, and labelled it. He sensed Emmanuel getting angry with him. "I will show you," Tymos offered softly without any sense of trying to get the better of the older man.

He turned and walked from the room, getting a wave of thanks from the Dean, who would later be happy to agree to Tymos working in his department.

In the rear stairwell, he stopped on the landing and nodded at the ventilation grille.

"There is a tunnel in the permacrete between this floor and the one above. It runs from under the pedestal to here."

Emmanuel nodded. "Have you ventured in?"

"No," Tymos readily admitted.

"After last night's activity, your restraint amazes me," Emmanuel said pointedly. "I will assume that you really do intend to follow the rules and remain studying here. I had my doubts."

Tymos did not let the cutting remarks ruffle him.

"You went to lengths to remind us that science here was a team effort," Tymos remarked quietly. "In this matter you are the team leader."

"So I am," Emmanuel agreed. "When exactly were you going to tell me of your discovery?"

"When I went back up," Tymos claimed.

"And when are you and your sister going to come out and share all you know with me?"

Tymos didn't answer, and he knew that Emmanuel knew it to be an evasion.

"I don't know of any person on this campus who wouldn't jump at the glory of making a major discovery – is that what you are trying to do?"

"No," Tymos admitted, surprising the scientist. He looked up and saw Kryslie coming silently down the stairs. Emmanuel saw her too.

"We will tell you what we know when you ask the right questions," Kryslie promised. "As for the glory, you are welcome to it. You deserve it. The last thing we need right now is any more official notice."

"Then let us proceed back up to the exhibit," Emmanuel instructed. "We will use the filters, and wait for the electricians to install isolation switches. And then, we will explore the tunnel. You two, will assemble for my inspection, all the equipment you think we will need tomorrow. And I want a written rationale for what you propose."

"Yes, Sir," Tymos agreed, realising that Emmanuel had figured out their tactics.

"I would also like to examine that scanner, Mr Ward. It must be an improvement on currently available technology."

"I still want to improve it further," Tymos remarked, permitting the scientist to look at it as they returned up the stairs."

Emmanuel stood back and watched Krys and Tym Ward carry out the experiments they had devised. The previous day's results had been interesting and had confirmed the need to control the ambient light. They were repeating the filter experiments without the down lights and UV lights.

Then Tym measured the emanations from the glowing crystals. They were constant, as if there was an energy source still present.

"Sir, there are three different wavelengths being received," Tymos reported. "One in the visible spectrum, one in the far UV and one that may be an intrinsic attribute of the force field itself."

"What do you predict to be the wavelength of the exciting radiation?" Emmanuel asked neutrally.

"All the other wavelengths are shifted down," Kryslie noted. "The original radiation would have to be in the region of gamma rays."

"So, now we know the reason for the insulation in the walls floor and roof," Emmanuel noted dryly. "We also know that no trace of heavy radiation has been detected outside of the force field. What do you two plan to do next?"

Emmanuel watched his students, trying to learn from their reactions, but they both had those under near perfect control.

"Discover what is still powering the crystals," Tymos said carefully. "I don't believe that the force field penetrates the floor. If you were to traverse the tunnel, you should come up with in the force bubble."

"Why a bubble, not a sphere?" Emmanuel quizzed. "What scientific data leads you to that conclusion?"

"Logic," Kryslie told him. "If the field occupied all of the space inside the bubble, it would have been difficult for Professor Grainger to have left after initiating the field."

The scientist's smile indicated that he had already reached that conclusion. "One of you put on that conveniently present radiation suit and get in there. Take a shielded box to put the crystals in. The other can continue to monitor the emanations."

The students did not need to discuss who did what. Nor did Tymos protest and offer Emmanuel the opportunity to traverse the tunnel, because he knew the man disliked narrow, dark, enclosed places. Kryslie went with him to the ventilation shaft grille in the stairwell. They met no one for the stairway had been blocked at the floor below the Westphalen level.

Tymos couldn't quite reach the screws that he needed to remove, but Kryslie supported his weight easily. When the cover was free, he pulled himself into the tunnel and began to commando crawl. He recalled being drilled in such actions when being educated on Tymorea.

Kryslie ran back to the upper level and took over the recording of the emanations. The room was only lit by the scintillations of the crystals, but she didn't need more light than that.

As soon as Tymos wormed his way out of the pillar, he looked for, found and insulated a small pellet of a radioactive substance.

Kryslie measured the reduction of the emanations and the weakening of the force field.

Emmanuel switched on the down lights – the scintillations resumed, but the force field did not. He strode across to Tymos, who pointed to a box behind the pedestal.

"I want to repeat this morning's experiments with the light, in the absence of the force field," Emmanuel said, attempting to open the box. "Is there a small crystal that I can take to analyse the structure?"

Tymos examined the conglomerate in the box where he had placed it, as Emmanuel continued to struggle with the lead coated box from behind the pedestal.

The sudden flinging open of the door startled everyone in the room. Three dark clad figures with only their eyes showing sprang into the exhibit chamber brandishing weapons that were unfamiliar even to Tymos and Kryslie.

Emmanuel froze; his mind full of anger at the intrusion just as he was on the verge of his greatest triumph.

Tymos didn't seem to move but he closed the opening in the pedestal and hid the lead box with the isotope. Kryslie stared back at the eyes of the man who held a weapon aimed at her. He did not seem to notice her hand movement as she removed a data disc from the recorder and inserted a blank one; nor did any of the intruders notice her reach for a switch.

The intruders did not talk, but indicated by signs what they wanted.

Emmanuel hugged the box closer to him as one of the intruders approached. His weapon was pointed at the scientist's face; a finger was on the activation switch. The man's free hand reached for the box.

A second man reached for the crystals. Tymos removed a glove and touched the crystals at the same instant as the man. A flash of light brightened the room as that intruder slumped to the floor.

The leader of the intruders hit Emmanuel in the face with his weapon and tried to wrest the box from him. Tymos reached for the attacker and with casual ease, gripped both the arm with the weapon and the one trying for the box. Emmanuel stumbled back. The third man fired at Tymos, who was swinging the second man into the line of fire. The searing beam of white-hot energy charred Tymos's suit, and killed the unwitting shield. The third man swung his weapon back onto Kryslie and called out a warning to Tymos in accented English.

"I will kill this woman. Bring me the crystals."

"They will zap you like they did your friend," Tymos warned. "You will need insulated gloves."

"Bring them here!"

Tymos shrugged and seemed to be complying. Kryslie was inching away from the monitoring equipment, as the man watched Tymos. He was attempting to use his other hand to remove the data disc from the machine. He caught sight of Kryslie's movement and fired at her, but when he glanced there, she was not where the beam was directed.

Emmanuel, trying to deal with the pain of a broken nose, thought he was hallucinating. Krys Ward had been inches away from the gun, but when it fired, she was behind the intruder and beginning an attack of her own.

When the security guards that had been summoned by Kryslie arrived, she and her brother each held a struggling intruder with contemptuous ease. They had torn off the black face coverings, to reveal men who appeared Japanese. It took two guards to continue to subdue each surviving intruder. Tymos removed the hood of the radiation suit and told the guards what had occurred.

Kryslie squatted by the now seated Emmanuel and appeared to be gently swabbing blood from the older man's bleeding and broken nose.

Emmanuel was shaking with reaction, but he did not protest Krys's attention for it seemed the pain in his face was diminishing.

A short time later, Don Gilchrist arrived with a first aid team. Tymos repeated his report.

"I want everything of value from this exhibit placed in the safe in my office until we ensure this matter is over."

He took in everything in the room, the damage from the intruder's weapons, the dead intruder, the scorch marks on Tymos's suit and on the wall and then the injury to Emmanuel.

Four more guards had arrived with him, and at Emmanuel's nod, Tymos passed over the lead covered box, the lead insulated isotope and reached over to pick up the crystals. This time there was no flash as he touched them. Kryslie removed the full data disc from her pocket. The security guards departed at once.

Gilchrist watched the first aid team treating the scientist and then turned to the two students.

"Take all the equipment back to the lab and then report to the medical centre," he instructed.

"We're fine, Sir," Kryslie said quietly, but looking at Gilchrist, she knew now was not a good time to dispute his instructions. She couldn't even sense his reasons. "Yes, Sir," she said after a moment.

Doctor Emmanuel, with white plaster now adorning his blackening nose, stopped by the two tables where his students were being examined.

"My thanks for your quick thinking and calm actions," he told them sincerely. "I hope you are not affected by causing that man's death."

Tymos gave a slight shrug. The dead intruder would have had no qualms about killing all of them and was in fact intending to do just that before he left. Tymos had no regrets about the death of such a man. However, the investigators might still give him a difficult time. "I did not kill him," Tymos said. "And I think they were intending to kill us."

Emmanuel gave him a considering look, and retreated from the medical centre.

Tymos was still considering why Gilchrist had insisted on the thorough medical check. Kryslie thought back at her brother, "I re-activated the security cameras to get the guards to come. They would have seen the crystals zap the first man." She knew Tymos had sent a surge of power through the crystals. "And they probably saw how quickly I moved when I was about to be fired on."

"I am glad the Elders back home can't see us now," Tymos thought ruefully. "We haven't done a very good job of hiding our power."

"Let's wait and see what they do and deal with it when it happens," Krys thought resigned. "I really don't want them expecting more from us than we want to give."

They were escorted from the medical centre by two of the security guards and taken to the Vice Chancellor's office.

As they entered the outer office, they both flashed a smile at Sharon Wright. They knew her from their first visit and the subsequent occasions when they needed to give her things.

She returned the smile, remembering that these two had that effect on her. Somehow, she could not reconcile their courteousness with the terse report about their rule breaking two nights ago. She had not believed it when she had to type it and add it to their files.

The smile reassured her that they were not expecting trouble from the investigators in her boss's office.

The smiles had reverted to suitably earnest expressions by the time they entered Gilchrist's domain.

The Vice Chancellor introduced the investigators, explaining they were from the World Council's Investigative Committee. They were involved because the WSRA universities, like the WSRA itself, were considered politically neutral and any 'warlike' actions happening there come under their aegis.

Gilchrist then sat back and let the investigators ask questions. His mind was betraying nothing, but he was listening intently and studying the body language of the two students.

Tymos and Kryslie spoke in turn, each giving their perspective of what had happened and what they had done. They kept their reports terse and factual, emphasising that they had not wanted Dr Emmanuel's discoveries stolen.

The investigators wanted to know about the crystals, since Emmanuel had mentioned the flash that had stunned one of the intruders.

"I didn't want the man to take them, but he must have touched them an instant before I did. For which I am glad," Tymos said.

The answer seemed to satisfy the investigator, as it agreed with what they had already heard from Emmanuel.

Kryslie was asked to confirm that she had switched the security camera back on, and was praised for her quick thinking. She was asked how she had managed to switch the discs in the recording machine.

"I managed to do it while his attention was on the others behind me," Kryslie claimed. "I was watching his eyes. The gun was pointing at me, but his attention was not there. Oh, he would have seen me if I moved from that spot, but he could not see my hand."

When the investigators admitted to seeing the security film and being impressed by her lack of panic in their actions, Krys had an inkling of what was coming next.

"We are not in the habit of letting others arbitrarily control our actions," Kryslie admitted, and from the smirk on the investigator's faces, she knew they had heard of their escapade of the other night.

"How did you get from in front of that gun to behind the attacker?" one investigator asked, he was just getting to the point of his comments. He had seen the rapid change of position and didn't believe it possible.

Krys permitted herself a slight grin. "That old trick!" She snorted with casual distain, and then looked at Gilchrist. "Do you mind if I show them? I'll need a little bit of room."

Gilchrist waved for her to go ahead, and Kryslie cleared a space between the wall and the chairs. She told one investigator to pretend to be the intruder.

She performed a self-defence manoeuvre that she had been taught on Tymorea, but slowed it down considerably. It still looked fast, but her audience could follow the action.

"A little slow, compared to the security film," Gilchrist remarked.

"I didn't have a horrible looking weapon pointed at me this time," she said tartly.

She received a murmur of amusement.

"Where did you learn that?" the investigator wanted to know.

"We had a personal trainer some years back," Kryslie told him.

"Can you do that again? Slower?"

Krys complied, but decided not to do it slowly, just at the speed that a normally fit human could achieve. Any slower than that required a great deal more control than doing it fast.

Tymos decided to take the attention off his sister. "Sir, have you identified the three men?"

He spoke to the investigator.

"Yes," was the short answer. "What is the nature of your interest?"

Tymos knew he had to word his answer carefully. "I was concerned about my friend, Jimmy Fujawa. Two nights ago his relatives tried something and I hoped Jimmy wasn't involved again."

"The Fujawa brothers helped us identify the intruders," the investigator decided to admit. "We are satisfied that they were not involved in this attack."

Tymos nodded his thanks for the information.

There were only a few more questions before Tymos and Kryslie were told they could leave. The security guards saw them out of the administration building.

"Why did you remind everyone of our indiscretion?" Kryslie asked her brother as they walked to the accommodation block. "I had already determined they had heard about it."

"I did want to know who was behind the intrusion," Tymos admitted. "But if they keep remembering - it might chill Stan Burroughs's burning desire to have us working for the WSRA as soon as we graduate."

"We intend to work there though."

"I know, but it would be better if we did not arrive with trumpets blaring. It is not conducive to being inconspicuous."

"Nor is an honours pass from this university," Krys suggested.

"No..." Tymos agreed.

"What made you think about that?" Krys asked.

"I caught a flash of thought from Gilchrist - that we did not look any older than we did four years ago. It made me consider what the Elders said about previous Great Ones and how we thought we might have a very long lifespan. We might not age, or we might age very slowly. It would be harder to hide that fact if we are too well known."

Tymos sensed his sister considering what he said and then her agreement.

"Let's look at Grainger's data before we get into more trouble," Kryslie suggested.

Dr Emmanuel rejoined Gilchrist after the investigators had left. The Vice Chancellor was satisfied with the outcome of the interview. The investigators were not going to make an issue of the death of the intruder — being convinced it was the fault of one of the prisoners whilst Tymos was defending himself. The investigators felt that the people behind the intrusion would not try again.

However, the Vice Chancellor had sensed something off key about the Ward twins that he couldn't put his finger on.

"You were listening, Clem. Do you think they were telling the truth?" Gilchrist asked his friend.

"It was the truth, just maybe not all of it," Emmanuel decided. "I think I have got them pegged. They don't lie, but if I ask them something they don't want to answer, they just stay silent, or sometimes aim to distract by stating something else that is true. What's bothering you?"

"There is something about them..."

"I agree," Emmanuel admitted. "I am sure they know a lot more than they let on. They remind me of Grainger. Kryslie finally said that if I asked the right questions they would tell me the answers I want."

"Hmph!" Gilchrist exploded. "Only the ones they want to answer!"

"I set them looking through reams of data, but within an hour they had worked out graphs that showed correlations that dozens of students and the most advanced stats programs never saw. I assume they suffered no ill effects from the incident." Emmanuel was willing to ignore the strange behaviour of the twins, since they had helped his research so much.

"It seems not. I insisted on a thorough physical, but the doctor says they are exceptional physical specimens, with very fast reflexes and a high fitness level. The only oddity was a slight abnormality around the eyes. They both have it so it might be a genetic trait," Gilchrist reported.

"They don't seem to want to court publicity," Emmanuel remarked. "Which is surprising. I would have said that every student at this university dreams of the acclaim they would have for making a great scientific discovery. Tymos has a hand scanner that is a thousand times more sensitive than any I have ever used, and merely said he wants to improve it further."

"Maybe we can't expect anything different from Grainger's protégés," Gilchrist sighed. "However, I will be taking greater interest in their activities from now on."

Tamir Janzoet, the Tymorean father of Tamir Grainger, had written his notes in the formal Tymorean script. Tymos studied the neat and precise diagrams as Kryslie read firstly his reports and then his abstract outlining the thrust of his research. Finally, they both studied his experiments and the specifications of the force fields.

"This last one is a scrambler field," Tymos told Kryslie, and she came to study it. "It is intended to be outer most. It randomises anything trying to probe for force fields."

"That first one is what we were trying to do before we left. It uses the radioactive emissions to power it and transmutes the radiation to light – like those crystals were doing. The emission can be channelled to power a second shield and have the light emission removed..."

The twins studied the information until the morning. By then they knew what they had to do to apply it.

Tymos managed to scrounge an hour each day to work within the Engineering Department crafting the precision parts needed. The Dean of Engineering assumed it was for a project in one of the other faculties, so he only reported that Tymos was learning to construct equipment.

Even though Tymos and Kryslie were stretching the hours in each day, they never seemed tired. One or the other was always easy to find should a check be made, and could summon the other who would transmit back quickly.

Kryslie visited Rhyn at night, whilst Tymos kept a presence. At other times, Tymos was away finishing the excavation of the cavern and installing the generator for the vital protective screen. During those periods, Kryslie was conspicuous and being charming to the guards who appeared whenever she went anywhere in the open.

Chapter 21 - Slipping Away

The end of their five years of study was rapidly approaching. The final year students had finished their projects, written up their work for publication and most had high paying jobs lined up for after graduation. Stan Burroughs, the WSRA liaison, had already approached the Ward twins and offered them positions well up in the WSRA hierarchy. He had received a polite promise to consider the offer carefully and was wondering who else was after their services.

Just under a week before the graduation ceremonies, Tymos received a message via his email box

It had simply said, "Call home, urgently."

Tymos had known that it could only mean one thing and he had summoned his twin with a terse mental call. She had simply excused herself from a casual conversation with a friend, moved out of sight, and transmitted to her brother's room.

For the past five years, they had been just like the other highly intelligent students - but the time was coming when their real mission would escalate in importance.

"Hillary wants us," Tymos had told his twin.

"Well, we have done all we need to here. I will go and see what she wants." Kryslie pulled a device from her pocket. It mimicked the latest mobile communications devices, but was more than it looked and it had not been designed by human scientists.

She activated a signal on a frequency unknown to humans. "Hillary, activate the long range beam in ten seconds."

Without saying goodbye, Kryslie transmitted from her brother's room to a secluded area of the university gardens. The glowing mauve of the terminus was just opening. She transmitted along it.

One look at Hillary, the brown haired woman who had tended Rhyn for over five years, coupled with what her emphatic senses were telling her - was all she needed to understand the call. She used her communicator and spoke to her brother. "Rhyn is dying. Can you pack everything? I will re-activate the beam in an hour."

There was very little that he needed to pack. Both of them had only a small wardrobe of utilitarian clothing and one fancy outfit. Personal belongings were few and they did not need to take electronic texts. After stuffing his own things into a small backpack, he transmitted to his sister's room.

He tidied up the few loose ends, arranged for their electronic book readers to be returned to the library, emptied their university email boxes, and placed the room keys in an envelope, which he left at the security desk. For the brief moments that he was there, the security camera was inactive.

As he walked out into the darkness, with two backpacks, he drew on his power and blended into the shadows. Exactly an hour after Kryslie had left, the long-range beam was reactivated. He saw the mauve glow of the terminus and stepped into it.

Hillary took the two backpacks when he materialised. Tymos paused only long enough to say, "If anyone calls asking for us, you haven't seen us," before hurrying to join his sister.

Kryslie had one of the old man's hands in her own, which were glowing faintly with mauve light. Tymos sat on the other side of him and put his hand on the aged, dry skin on Rhyn's forehead.

With that touch, Tymos knew that the old man was on the pinnacle between life and death.

He glanced at his sister, who thought at him, "I am holding him here, but he was already in a coma when I arrived. Hillary said he was asking for us."

While Kryslie was able to start wounds and illnesses healing, he was able to speed heal. But he could not heal the tired, body that was already shutting down, but maybe he could hold back death long enough to hear the words that Rhyn had needed to say. He sent a flow of energy into the old man.

After a few moments, the wrinkled eyes opened. They had gone from brown to black and although they could see nothing, the old man sensed who was with him.

"Prince Tymos, Princess Kryslie." The voice was like the whisper of a leaf being blown over dust.

"We are here," Kryslie assured gently. She increased the pressure of her grip, very slightly, as she willed her own healing energies into the frail body.

Rhyn's voice became a little stronger as he said, "I have seen them coming. The advance missionaries."

Memories of a frightening vision began to stir in his mind. Tymos concentrated on them as Kryslie urged, "Tell us what you have seen."

"The desert. They will come there," the voice dropped to a horrified whisper. Kryslie leaned closer, to listen. "But the army is there, doing tests. The dome that glows will be found."

Rhyn was not a scientist; he knew nothing of force fields and protective screens. Yet the old man knew the mauve glowing dome was Tymorean - for he was speaking words given to him by the Guardians of Peace.

In the mind images, there were other glowing areas; blue-green in colour. One by one, these glows disappeared after blinding white flashes. Then white flashed around the mauve glow, and when the light faded, people began to trot away - only to be caught, interrogated, killed.

"Warn them…"

Rhyn's eyes closed once more, and his breathing became laboured. His agitation, caused by the scene in his mind of Tymoreans dying, sent a spasm of pain through him.

Tymos shared it, eased it, as Kryslie spoke to the old man's mind. "We know now that we must keep them safe - that is why the Guardians gave you this vision. They have given you a great honour."

As soon as Tymos was aware of it, Kryslie also sensed the energies in the old body stop swirling. The heart stopped beating and the lungs pushed out a soft sigh of air.

Tymos kept his hand where it was for a moment longer as he uttered the words of an old Tymorean benediction.

"May the Guardians of Peace free your spirit, and make you one with them forever in Dirakee."

Kryslie released Rhyn's hand and murmured, "I will talk to Hillary."

Tymos nodded. "I will do what is needed here."

Hillary looked up from the vegetables that she was trying to prepare for cooking. One hand held a peeler, the other a carrot, but she had been looking down as if staring deep into the bench top. When she saw Kryslie, tears began to leak from her eyes and fell unchecked and she didn't protest when a gentle arm reached out to embrace her. Instead, she turned into the offered comfort.

"He knew he was dying," Hillary managed to say, although her voice was unsteady. "He was asking for you and he was so agitated. He was saying that they would be killed - the advance missionaries. That they would finally come here, and be killed."

Kryslie was aware of Tymos coming out of Rhyn's sleeping room, and going to where the clean sheets and towels were kept.

"We won't let them die," Kryslie said, drawing Hillary's eyes to meet her own. "His vision was a warning of what might happen."

"But - he was convinced it was real…"

"Yes, that is the way it seems - when the Guardians of Peace grant their faithful servants one final moment of enlightenment."

"But he was so agitated. Why did they do that to him?"

Kryslie urged Hillary to a chair at the still un-set table. She crouched next to her. "He was not in pain for long, and as to why, he knew his time was near. He was the nearest Elder to those they needed to warn. The Elders who live on Tymorea know to expect such blessings and welcome one last chance to do the Guardians' work."

She let Hilary cry softly for a while, aware that Tymos was cleaning and bathing Rhyn's body, and sparing her that sad duty.

"He was old, and this was his time - you have taken good care of him and you ensured that we came in time. You should not feel as if you have failed him."

"I have to tend to him…"

"Tymos is doing that. What else must we do?"

Hillary straightened, as she focussed on her duty. "I know what to do. He made sure his affairs were in order. He wanted to be cremated. He said he wanted his ashes to be taken to the world where his great grand parents had been born. That maybe, since you and Tymos had come, it would be possible."

"It will be done," Kryslie promised.

"I had better call the doctor, and the other people." Hillary started to stand up.

"Not just yet," Kryslie gently pulled her back down onto the chair. "What arrangements did he make about …" she gestured to where the edge of a huge picture was visible through a door. There was a mauve glow about it.

Hillary glanced at the holographic picture that hid the room where Rhyn's computers and communications equipment were hidden from casual human eyes.

"Surely they can stay here? Rhyn willed the house to me," She turned her red-rimmed eyes to Kryslie. "I didn't know everything he did, just how to record messages and reports, but I learn fast."

Tymos came into the kitchen, moving very quietly. "I will take over as coordinator, and for that your help will be very welcome - but we will need to re-locate the equipment. Do you know of a suitable place?"

"My father, Raymon Diese, owns several properties. I can call him and ask him if he can make one available. But why not stay here?"

Tymos gave her an odd smile. "We have kind of done a vanishing act from the university. They have this address as home. If they were to catch up with us, here, we'd have more explaining to do than we are prepared to permit. So if you will call your father, I will go and start preparing the equipment for the move."

Kryslie stayed with Hillary while she moved to the telephone, dialled a number and left a message for her father.

"A kind of vanishing act," Hillary commented with a shake of her head. Now that she had things to do, she was showing her strength of character. "Why did you do that?"

"Last year we had to admit to an infringement of university rules. We were warned that if we ignored or broke any more, we would have to leave the uni. We could not explain why we acted as we had, and at the time, we had not begun to build the generator that the Earthbase will need once it is constructed. As a result, our inter campus travel permission was revoked and we had to adhere to a prearranged schedule so they could find us whenever they needed to. Well, even though there is only a week left of our time there, and we had finished our studies, we still left without permission."

"You could have gone back..." Hillary suggested. With the long-range beam, it took only seconds to go across the country.

"Studying at the university was the means to an end, and unlike every other student there, we were not aiming to walk into high paid jobs. If that had been our intention, we could have taken up any one of two dozen offers - including senior research positions at the WSRA itself."

"But why not at least graduate and take up one of those positions. Don't you still need to keep track of the progress of scientific research? Like you have been doing."

"There will be another way," Krys assured her. "But we don't want to go to work at WSRA with the full fanfare and become too well known. We will wait several years and apply to work with them via the ground level entry. We will be less conspicuous that way."

"It's your choice," Hillary shrugged. "What would be your qualification if you graduated?"

"We majored in the astro-sciences," Kryslie told her. "So Doctor of Astro-science. It is more prestigious than a PhD."

Hillary finally understood why they didn't want to be well known. Too much would be expected of them and for a time, Tymos would be co-ordinating the Tymorean missionaries.

Epilogue

Vice Chancellor Gilchrist was notified when neither Krys Ward nor Tym Ward showed up at the formal end of year dinner and no message had been sent to explain why. He had his assistant go over to their quarters and insist they attend.

Sharon returned and whispered her report to him as he sat at the head table. Gilchrist felt very concerned. He immediately thought back to the previous year when the two students, now the year's joint valedictorians, had prevented harm to the eminent physicist, Clement Emmanuel, and ensured that the precious data that was at the centre of the famed Grainger exhibit, was not stolen. He had thought that incident closed, once Emmanuel had published his findings.

Perhaps it wasn't.

Or was this something to do with the other agenda that he had felt those students had? They were Grainger's protégé's, and there had been pressure on them to solve the puzzle that Grainger, the founder of the university, had left behind. However, there had seemed to be something else in their single-minded determination to get Grainger's notes. They had tried to get them by disregarding university rules. But when that had failed, they had accepted the consequences and abided the subsequent restrictions.

Gilchrist left the official dinner, giving only a terse apology, and went to the accommodation building and requested master keys from the security desk. With the duty security officer following, he strode to the elevator and took it up to the fourth level.

He went to the room assigned to Tymos, knocked first, and then used the master key. He stepped in the door and switched on the light. The room was exceptionally neat. The bed was made, the desk was clear. No clutter showed anywhere. A box of e-books occupied one corner. The security officer checked the desk as Gilchrist checked the wardrobe.

"Empty," the guard summarised.

"Let us check Miss Ward's room," Gilchrist suggested, after finding no clothes hanging or folded.

They went up to the fifth floor and found the same conditions.

"What do you want me to do, Sir?" the guard asked.

"Ask your superior to question the staff, very quietly. I want to know when they left and any if anyone knows why they left."

"At once, Sir," the guard left and Gilchrist returned to the dinner in a very thoughtful mood.

Early next morning, Gilchrist had the report from the guard detail. Tym Ward had been seen the night of the scavenger hunt, but no one knew he had left and no one had seen either of the Ward's since then. He rose and went out to his assistant.

"Sharon, can you dig out the home address for Tym and Krys Ward. I want a call put through to see if they are there. If you get anyone on the phone, I want to speak to them."

Five minutes later, she reported that the phone number was no longer connected, and the phone company had no forwarding information.

"Is there a problem, Sir?" Sharon dared to ask.

"The Ward's have left the campus, packed all their things and returned their keys." That was all he said. He stopped short of venting his displeasure.

"They left no message?" Sharon asked. "I would have expected them to let the faculty know if something urgent had made them leave. Will they miss graduation?"

"That is what I need to know," Gilchrist told her. "Do what you can to locate them."

"What about the police?" Sharon suggested.

"There is no indication of foul play, and contravening university rules is not a police matter," Gilchrist reminded her.

"There is less than a week left, Sir," Sharon protested, recalling the restriction the Ward's had been under.

"If they had the courtesy to advise us the reason for their abrupt departure, I would have arranged to have their degree's sent to them," Gilchrist said in a stern voice. "What am I expected to think – when they slip off in the night? Keep trying to find them. Since there is no answer on the phone, we don't even have a forwarding address for them."

"And if I find them?" Sharon asked.

"If you find them, they had better have a damn good reason to explain their actions. I won't authorise any formal recognition for their work here until they give one."

"So they won't graduate?" Sharon realised.

Gilchrist gave an uncompromising, "No."

****

This is the end of
The Tymorean Trust Book Three

THE RETURN TO EARTH

The story will continue in
The Tymorean Trust Book Four

EARTH MISSION

NOVELS

The Tymorean Trust Book One - POWER RISING

The Tymorean Trust - When peace rules Tymorea - Peace reigns in the universe.
Chosen to be the Advocates of the mystical and incorporeal Guardians of Peace, twins Tymos and Kryslie must first learn to control and use the power rising in them - or it will destroy them.
On Tymorea, only the ruling Triumvirate Governors are powerful enough to guide the strong-willed alien-bred twins until they have mastered their power.

The Tymorean Trust Book Two - GREAT ONES

The peace of the Guardian Planet, Tymorea, is in deadly peril. War there will create ripples of unrest and destruction throughout the settled universe. Tymos and Kryslie, still adolescents, have barely mastered their power and Llaimos is still less than a year old, but they are the three chosen to be Advocates of the mystical Guardians of Peace, to safeguard the Tymorean Trust

THE WILD ONE

Sixteen year old Jai Cassidy thought she was finally free of her family until she is discovered by her other relatives...the ones that aren't human. Jai uses her natural perversity and cunning to escape their control, but catapults herself into the middle of a deadly feud between two alien races.

SHORT STORIES:

<u>GRAFFITI GIRL</u>
Valerie has become known as "The Graffiti Girl" but she is more than just a
street artist. She sees and paints life her way.

In Valkyrie, the second story, Valerie, blinded by an explosion,
must learn to paint and see again.

GHOST WRITER
Edwina is a ghost with a mission - to find out why she died.
Only to do so, she must first help another girl.